STORY AND ART BY
NORIYUKI KONISHI

ORIGINAL CONCEPT AND SUPERVISED BY LEVEL-5 INC.

YO-KAI WATCH™
Volume 20
VIZ Media Edition

Story and Art by Noriyuki Konishi
Original Concept and Supervised by LEVEL-5 Inc.

Translation/Tetsuichiro Miyaki
English Adaptation/Aubrey Sitterson
Lettering/John Hunt
Design/Kam Li
Editor/Megan Bates

YO-KAI WATCH Vol. 20
by Noriyuki KONISHI
© 2013 Noriyuki KONISHI
©LEVEL-5 Inc.
Original Concept and Supervised by LEVEL-5 Inc.
All rights reserved.
Original Japanese edition published by SHOGAKUKAN.
English translation rights in the United States of America,
Canada, the United Kingdom, Ireland, Australia and New Zealand
arranged with SHOGAKUKAN.

Printed in the U.S.A.

Published by VIZ Media, LLC
P.O. Box 77010
San Francisco, CA 94107

10 9 8 7 6 5 4 3 2 1
First printing, January 2023

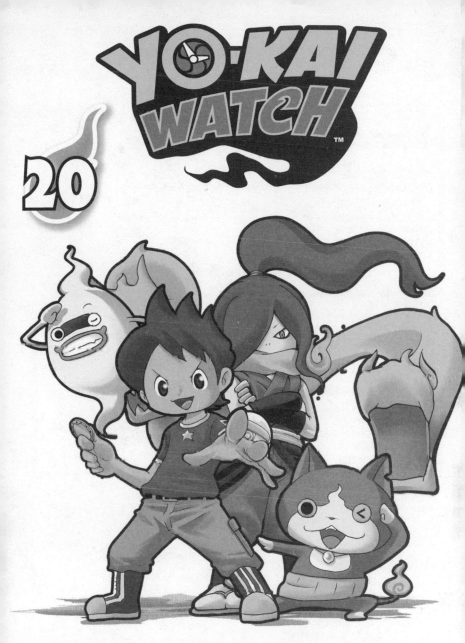

STORY AND ART BY
NORIYUKI KONISHI

ORIGINAL CONCEPT AND SUPERVISED BY LEVEL-5 INC.

CHARACTER INTRODUCTION

NATE ADAMS

AN ORDINARY ELEMENTARY SCHOOL STUDENT. WHISPER GAVE HIM THE YO-KAI WATCH AND HE'S USED IT TO MAKE A BUNCH OF YO-KAI FRIENDS!

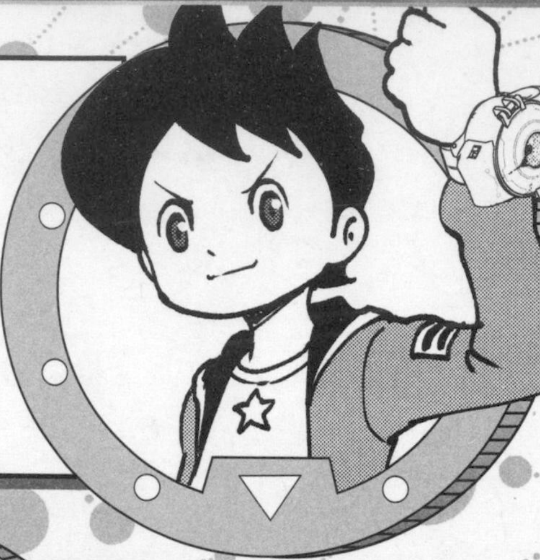

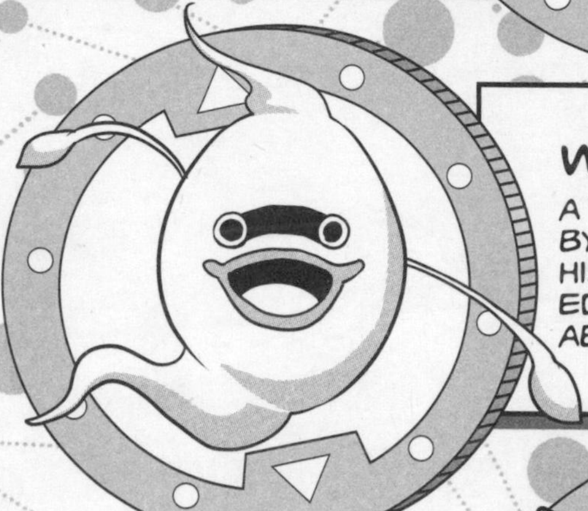

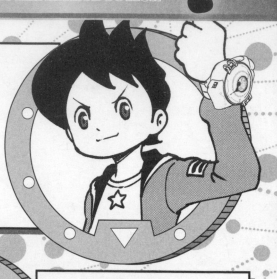

WHISPER

A YO-KAI BUTLER FREED BY NATE, WHISPER USES HIS EXTENSIVE KNOWL-EDGE TO TEACH HIM ALL ABOUT YO-KAI!

JIBANYAN

A CAT WHO BECAME A YO-KAI WHEN HE PASSED AWAY. HE IS FRIENDLY, CAREFREE, AND THE FIRST YO-KAI THAT NATE BEFRIENDED. HE'S BEEN TRYING TO FIGHT TRUCKS, BUT HE ALWAYS LOSES.

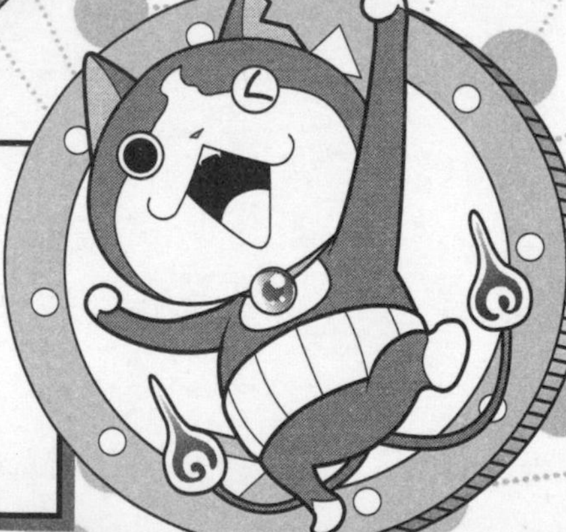

KATIE FORESTER
THE MOST POPULAR GIRL IN NATE'S CLASS.

BARNABY BERNSTEIN
NATE'S CLASSMATE. NICKNAME: BEAR. CAN BE MISCHIEVOUS.

EDWARD ARCHER
NATE'S CLASSMATE. NICKNAME: EDDIE. HE ALWAYS WEARS HEADPHONES.

TABLE OF CONTENTS

CHAPTER 207
RESET

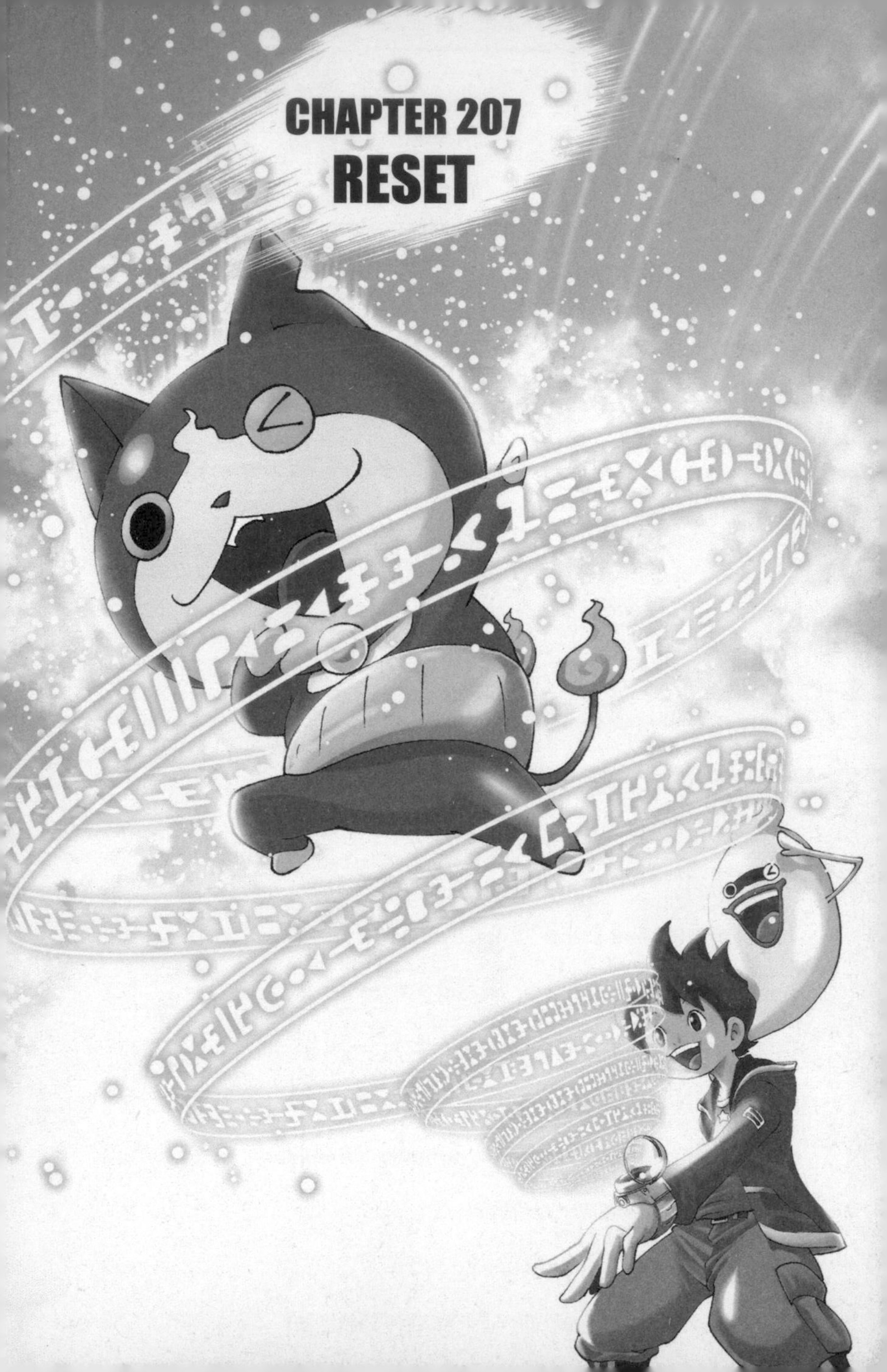

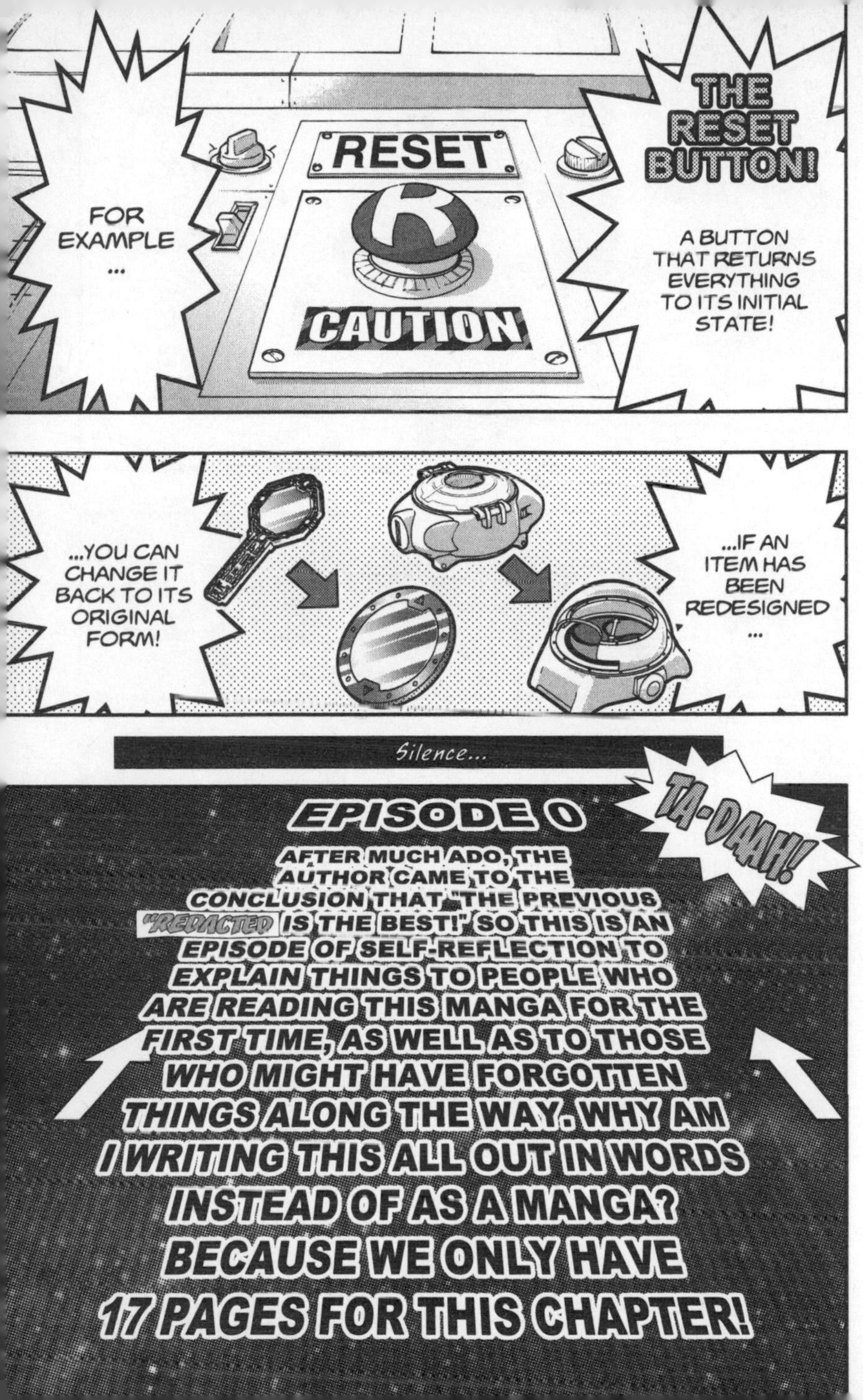
THE RESET BUTTON!
A BUTTON THAT RETURNS EVERYTHING TO ITS INITIAL STATE!
RESET
CAUTION
FOR EXAMPLE ...
...IF AN ITEM HAS BEEN REDESIGNED ...
...YOU CAN CHANGE IT BACK TO ITS ORIGINAL FORM!
Silence...
TA-DAAH!
EPISODE 0
AFTER MUCH ADO, THE AUTHOR CAME TO THE CONCLUSION THAT "THE PREVIOUS "REDACTED IS THE BEST!" SO THIS IS AN EPISODE OF SELF-REFLECTION TO EXPLAIN THINGS TO PEOPLE WHO ARE READING THIS MANGA FOR THE FIRST TIME, AS WELL AS TO THOSE WHO MIGHT HAVE FORGOTTEN THINGS ALONG THE WAY. WHY AM I WRITING THIS ALL OUT IN WORDS INSTEAD OF AS A MANGA? BECAUSE WE ONLY HAVE 17 PAGES FOR THIS CHAPTER!

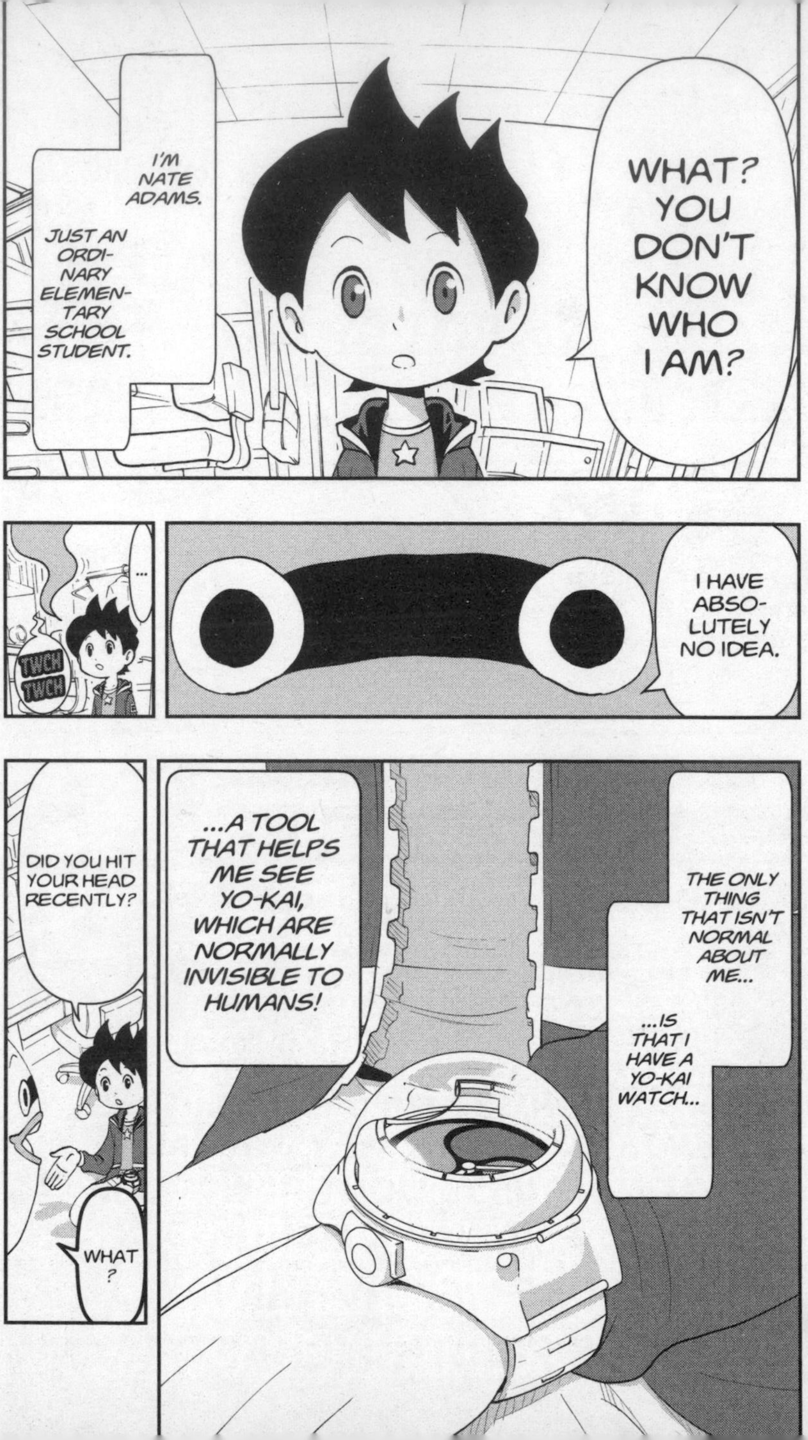
WHAT? YOU DON'T KNOW WHO I AM?
I'M NATE ADAMS.
JUST AN ORDINARY ELEMENTARY SCHOOL STUDENT.
I HAVE ABSOLUTELY NO IDEA.
...
TWCH TWCH
THE ONLY THING THAT ISN'T NORMAL ABOUT ME...
...IS THAT I HAVE A YO-KAI WATCH...
...A TOOL THAT HELPS ME SEE YO-KAI, WHICH ARE NORMALLY INVISIBLE TO HUMANS!
DID YOU HIT YOUR HEAD RECENTLY?
WHAT?

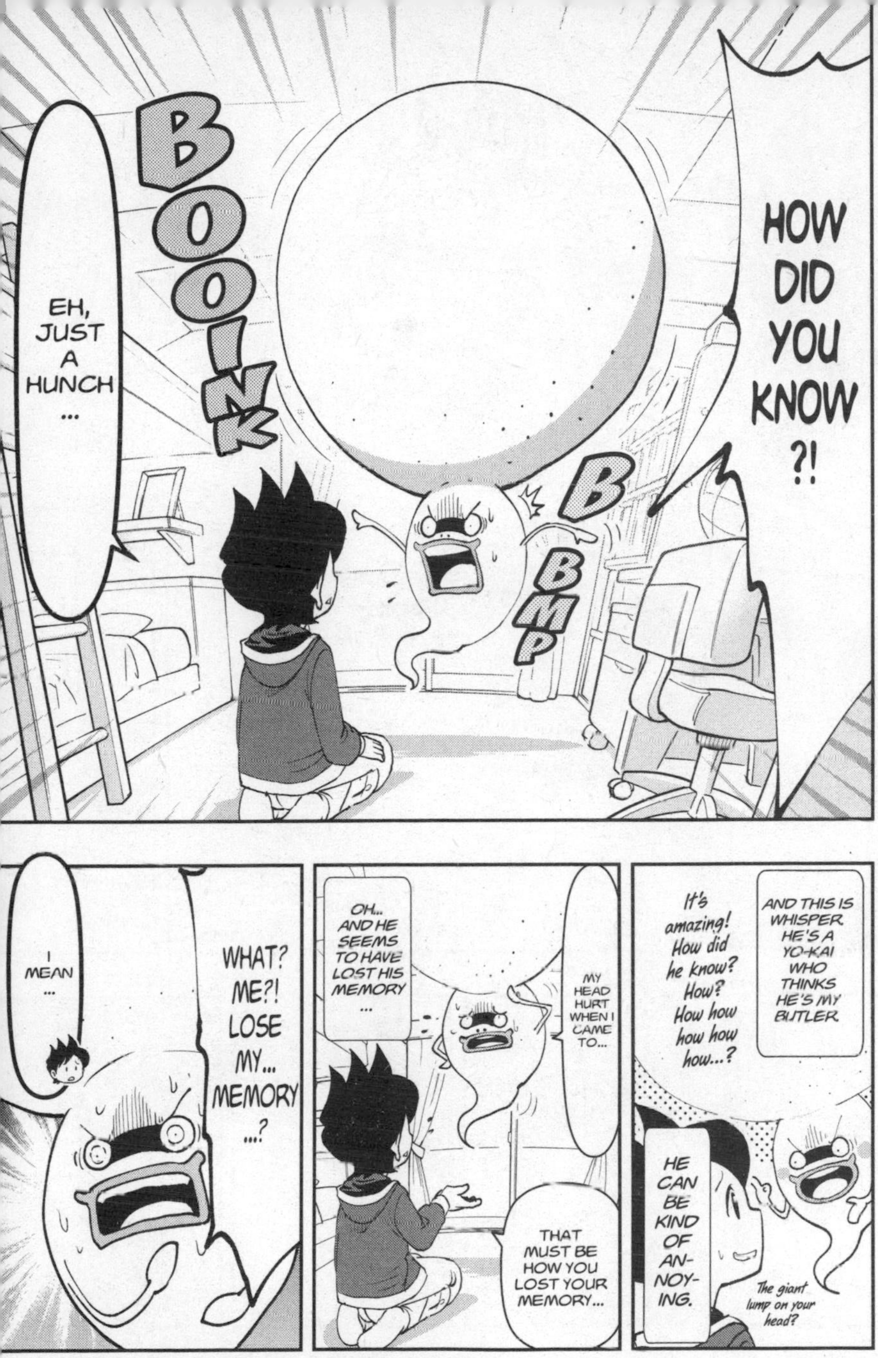
HOW DID YOU KNOW?!
BBMP
BOOINK
EH, JUST A HUNCH...
AND THIS IS WHISPER. HE'S A YO-KAI WHO THINKS HE'S MY BUTLER.
It's amazing! How did he know? How? How how how how how...?
HE CAN BE KIND OF AN-NOY-ING.
The giant lump on your head?
MY HEAD HURT WHEN I CAME TO...
OH... AND HE SEEMS TO HAVE LOST HIS MEMORY...
THAT MUST BE HOW YOU LOST YOUR MEMORY...
WHAT? ME?! LOSE MY... MEMORY...?
I MEAN...

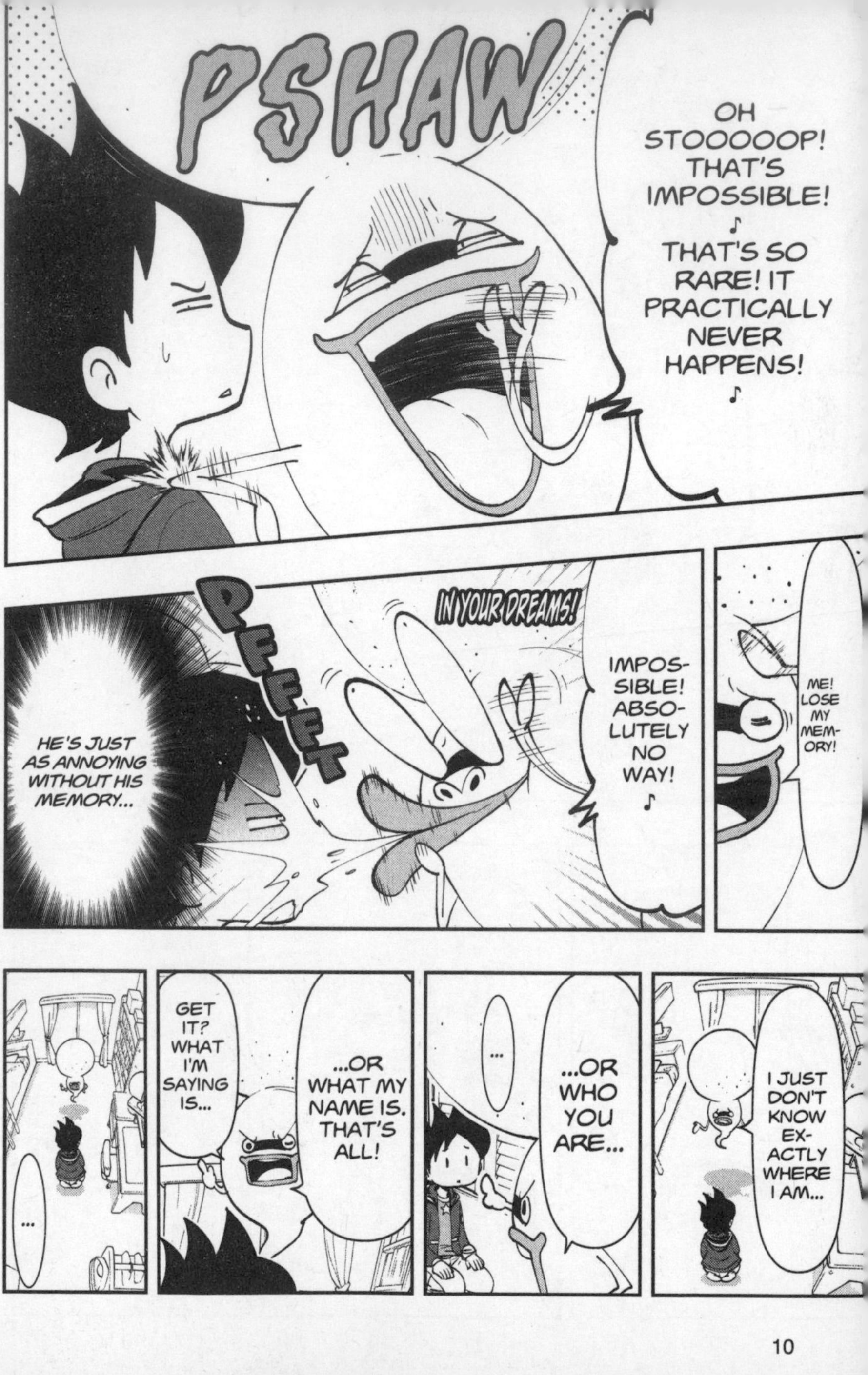
PSHAW
OH STOOOOOP! THAT'S IMPOSSIBLE! ♪ THAT'S SO RARE! IT PRACTICALLY NEVER HAPPENS! ♪
ME! LOSE MY MEM-ORY!
IN YOUR DREAMS!
IMPOS-SIBLE! ABSO-LUTELY NO WAY! ♪
PFFFFT
HE'S JUST AS ANNOYING WITHOUT HIS MEMORY...
I JUST DON'T KNOW EX-ACTLY WHERE I AM...
...OR WHO YOU ARE...
...
...OR WHAT MY NAME IS. THAT'S ALL!
GET IT? WHAT I'M SAYING IS...
...

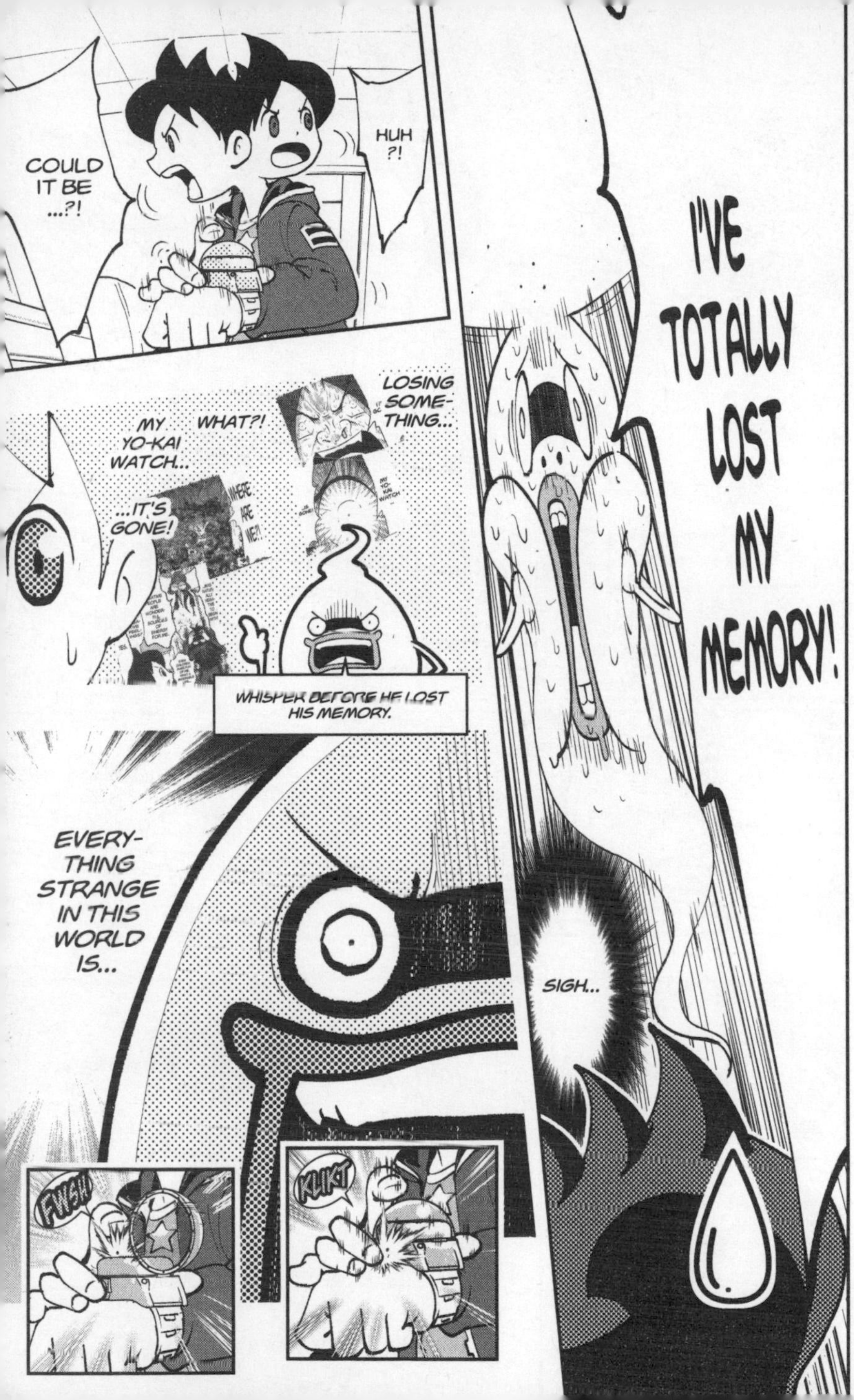
I'VE TOTALLY LOST MY MEMORY!
SIGH...
HUH ?!
COULD IT BE ...?!
LOSING SOME-THING...
WHAT?!
MY YO-KAI WATCH...
WHERE ARE WE?!
...IT'S GONE!
WHISPER BEFORE HE LOST HIS MEMORY.
EVERY-THING STRANGE IN THIS WORLD IS...
KLIKT
FWSH

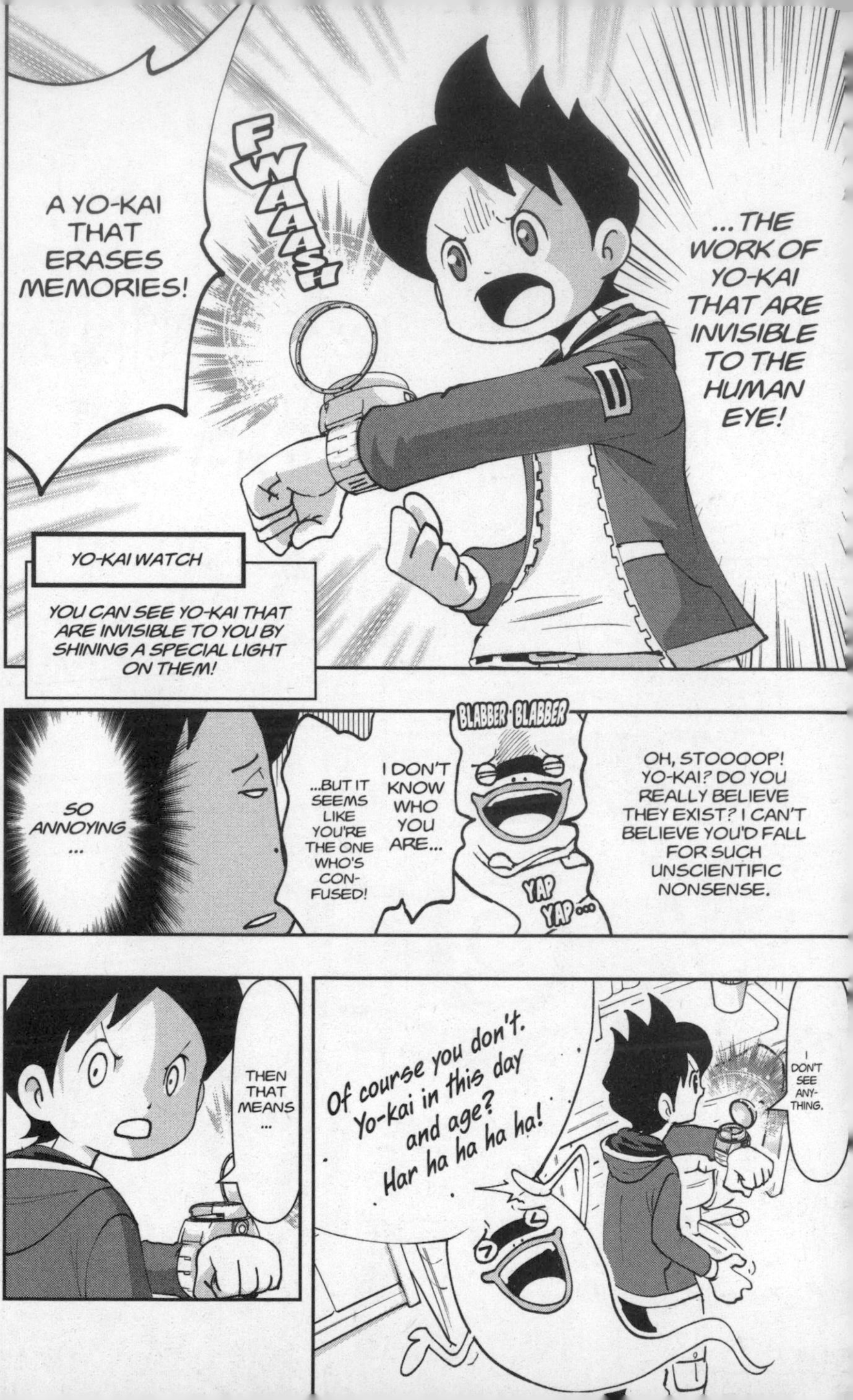
...THE WORK OF YO-KAI THAT ARE INVISIBLE TO THE HUMAN EYE!
FWAAASH
A YO-KAI THAT ERASES MEMORIES!
YO-KAI WATCH
YOU CAN SEE YO-KAI THAT ARE INVISIBLE TO YOU BY SHINING A SPECIAL LIGHT ON THEM!
OH, STOOOOP! YO-KAI? DO YOU REALLY BELIEVE THEY EXIST? I CAN'T BELIEVE YOU'D FALL FOR SUCH UNSCIENTIFIC NONSENSE.
BLABBER BLABBER
YAP YAP...
I DON'T KNOW WHO YOU ARE...
...BUT IT SEEMS LIKE YOU'RE THE ONE WHO'S CON-FUSED!
SO ANNOYING...
I DON'T SEE ANY-THING.
Of course you don't. Yo-kai in this day and age? Har ha ha ha ha!
THEN THAT MEANS...

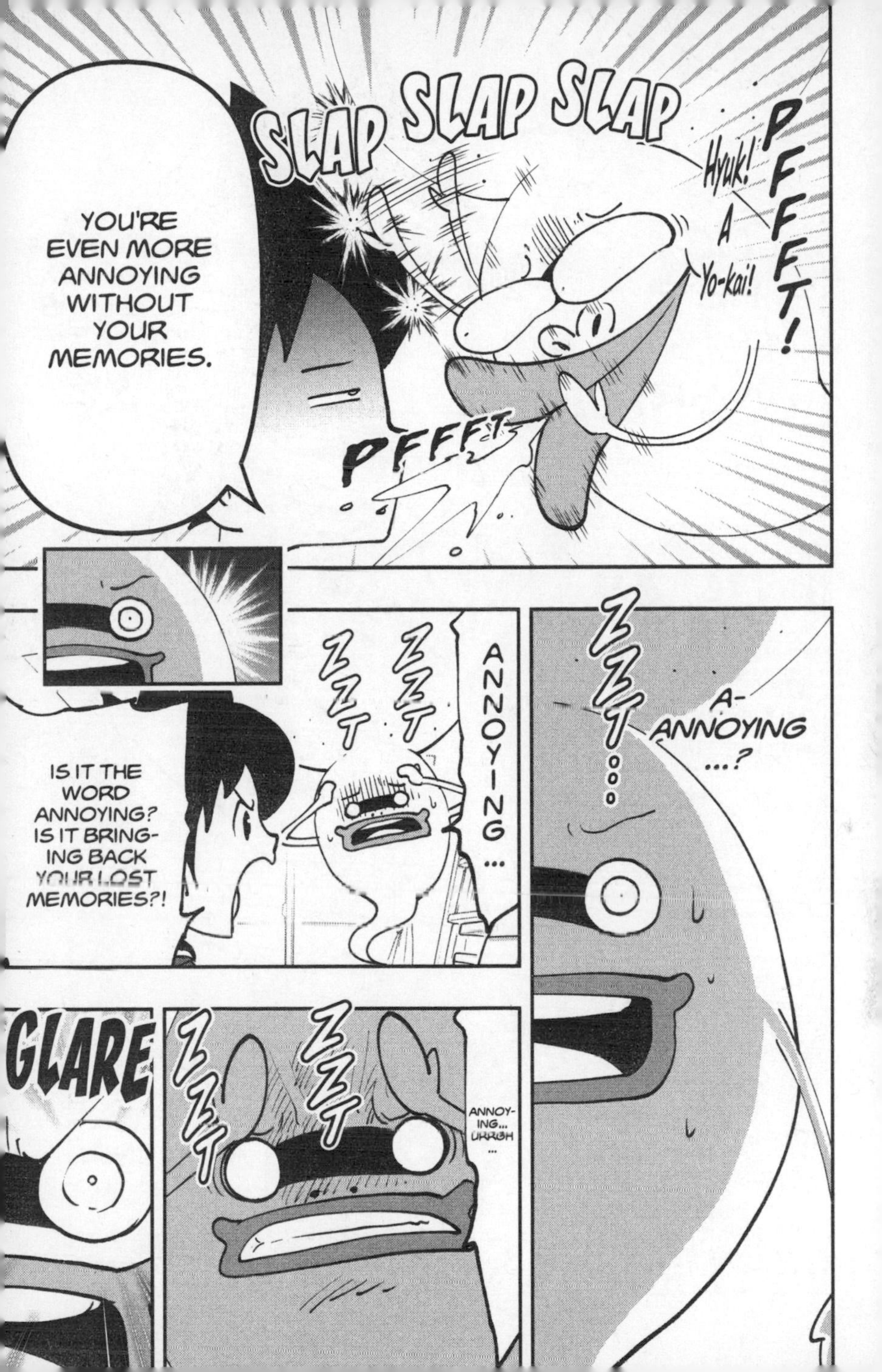
PFFFT!
Hyuk! A Yo-kai!
SLAP SLAP SLAP
YOU'RE EVEN MORE ANNOYING WITHOUT YOUR MEMORIES.
PFFFT
A-ANNOYING ...?
ZZZT...
ANNOYING...
ZZZT
ZZZT
IS IT THE WORD ANNOYING? IS IT BRINGING BACK YOUR LOST MEMORIES?!
ANNOY-ING... URRGH ...
ZZZT
ZZZT
GLARE

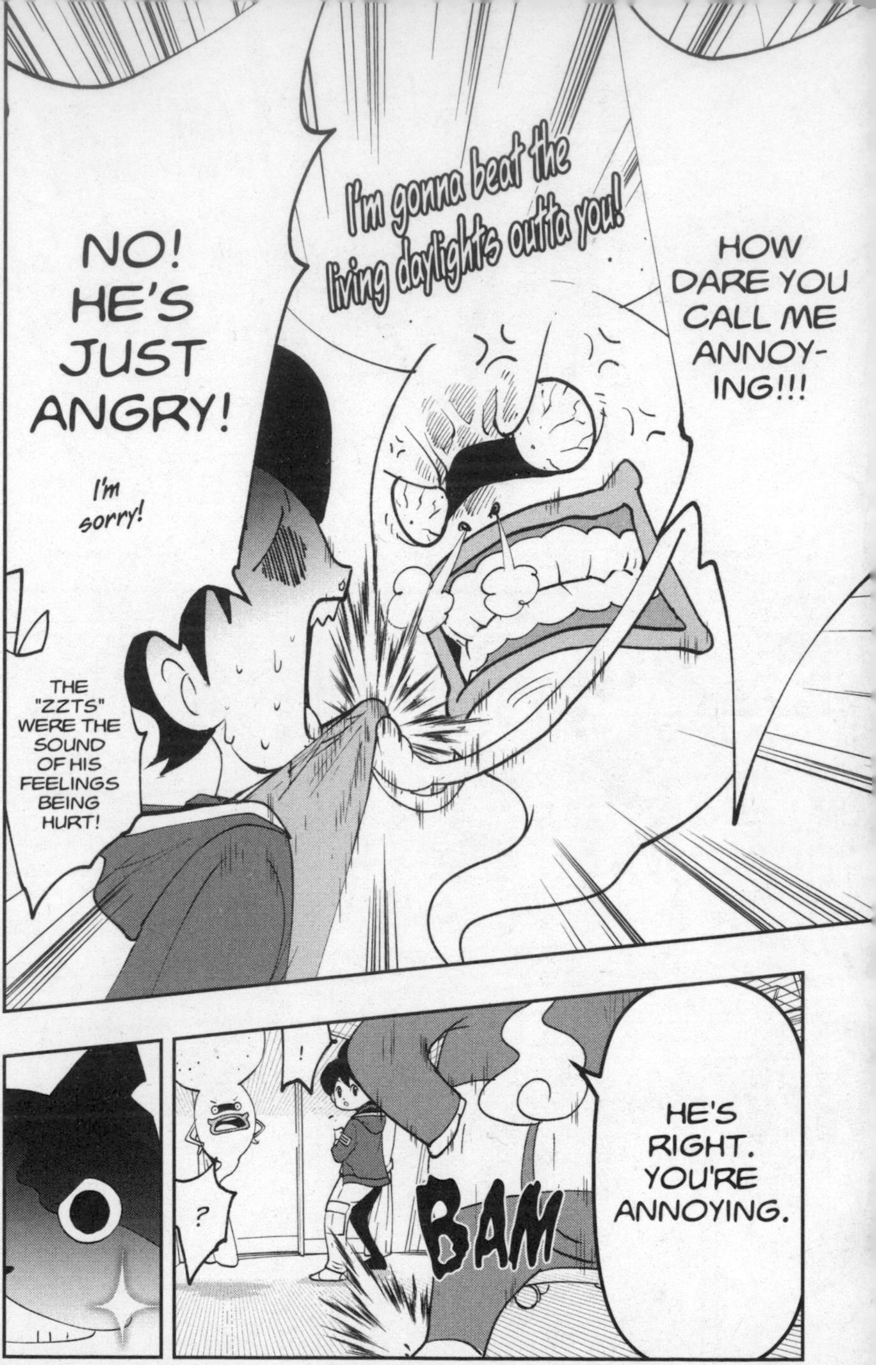
HOW DARE YOU CALL ME ANNOYING!!!
I'm gonna beat the living daylights outta you!
NO! HE'S JUST ANGRY!
I'm sorry!
THE "ZZTS" WERE THE SOUND OF HIS FEELINGS BEING HURT!
HE'S RIGHT. YOU'RE ANNOYING.
BAM
!
?

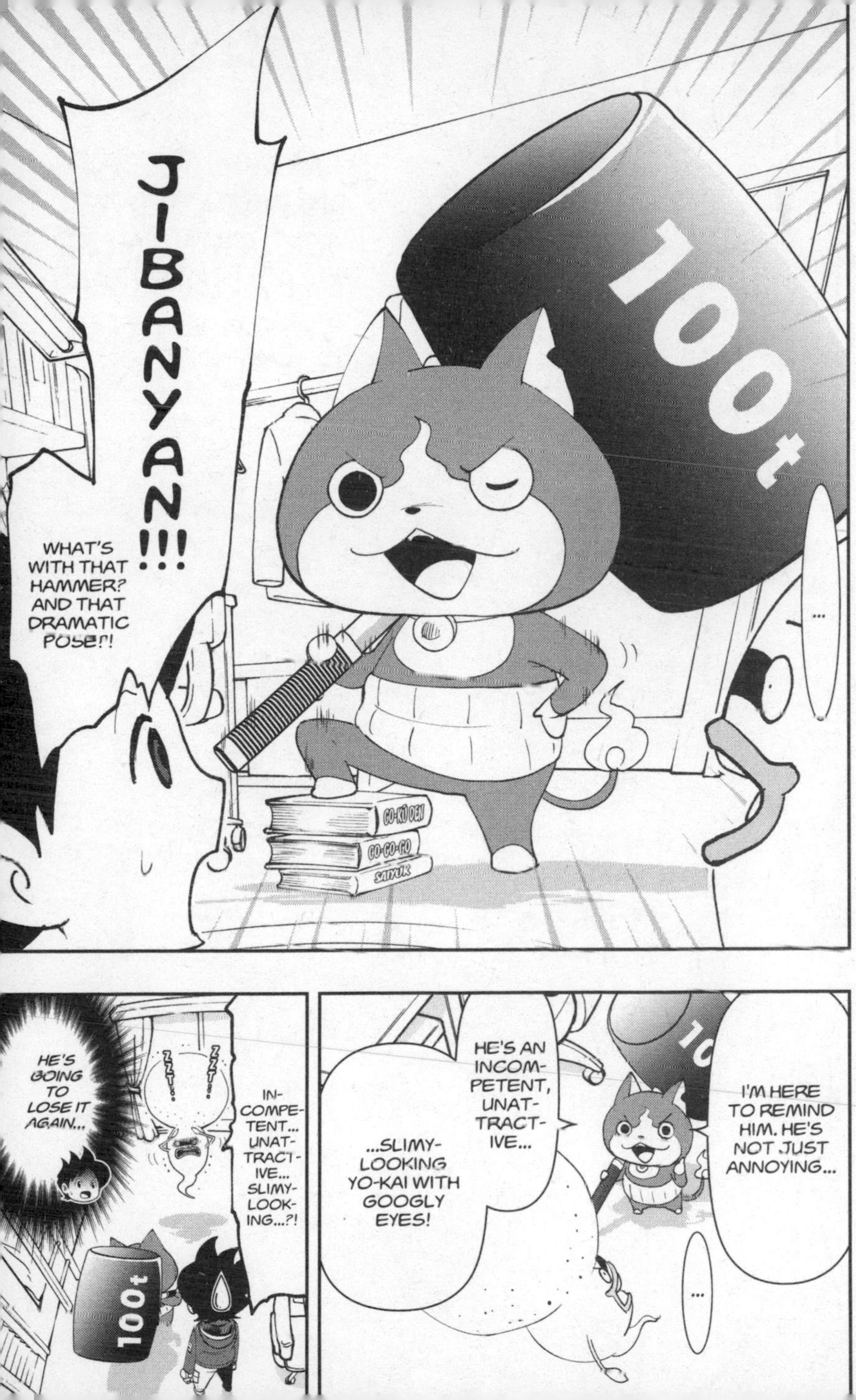
...
100t
JIBANYAN!!!
WHAT'S WITH THAT HAMMER? AND THAT DRAMATIC POSE?!
GO-KŪ DEH
GO-GO-GO
SAIYUK
I'M HERE TO REMIND HIM. HE'S NOT JUST ANNOYING...
HE'S AN INCOMPETENT, UNATTRACTIVE...
...SLIMY-LOOKING YO-KAI WITH GOOGLY EYES!
...
IN-COMPETENT... UNATTRACTIVE... SLIMY-LOOKING...?!
ZZZT!
ZZZT!
HE'S GOING TO LOSE IT AGAIN...
100t

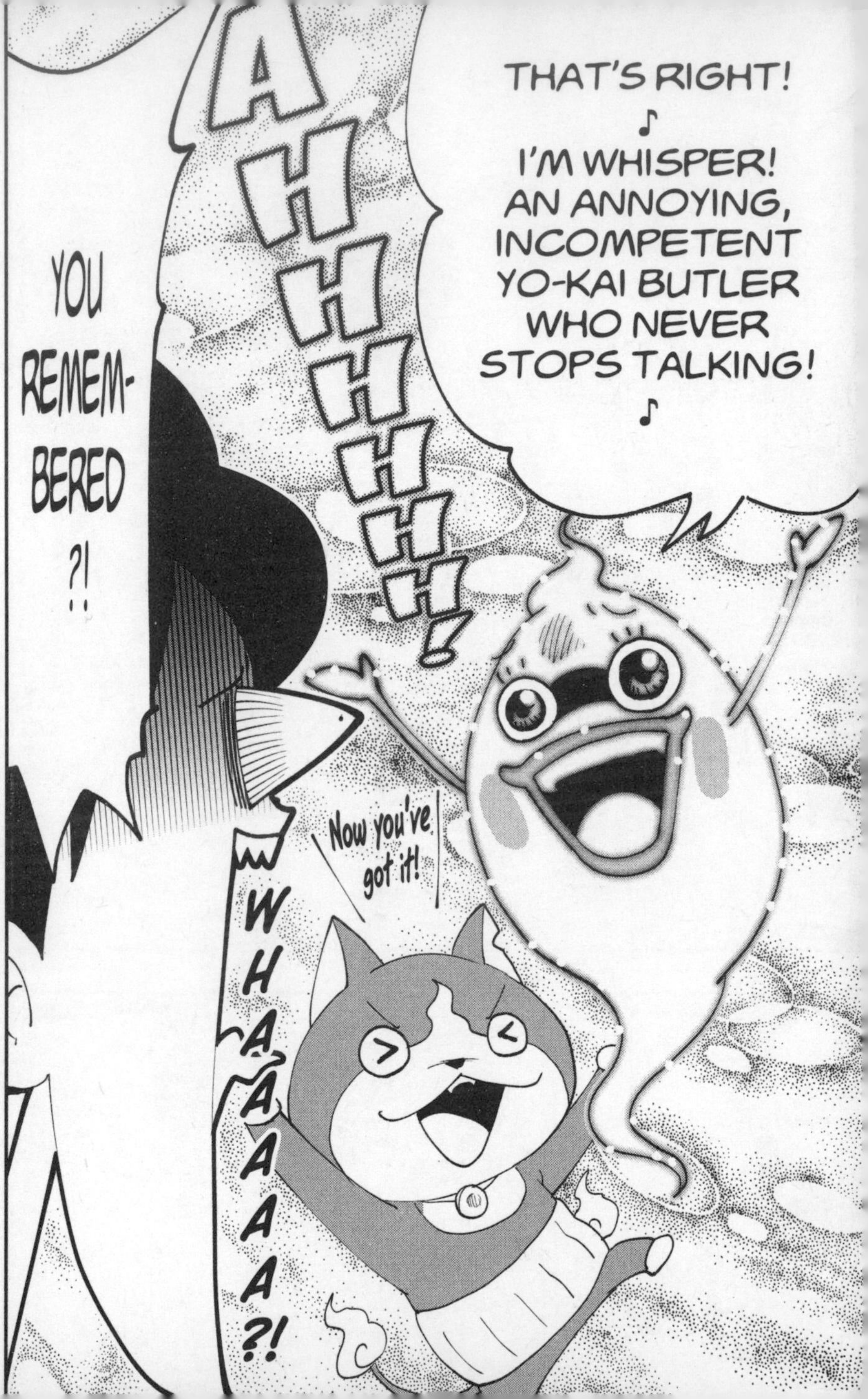
THAT'S RIGHT! ♪ I'M WHISPER! AN ANNOYING, INCOMPETENT YO-KAI BUTLER WHO NEVER STOPS TALKING! ♪
AHHHHHHH!
Now you've got it!
WHAAAAAAA?!
YOU REMEMBERED?!

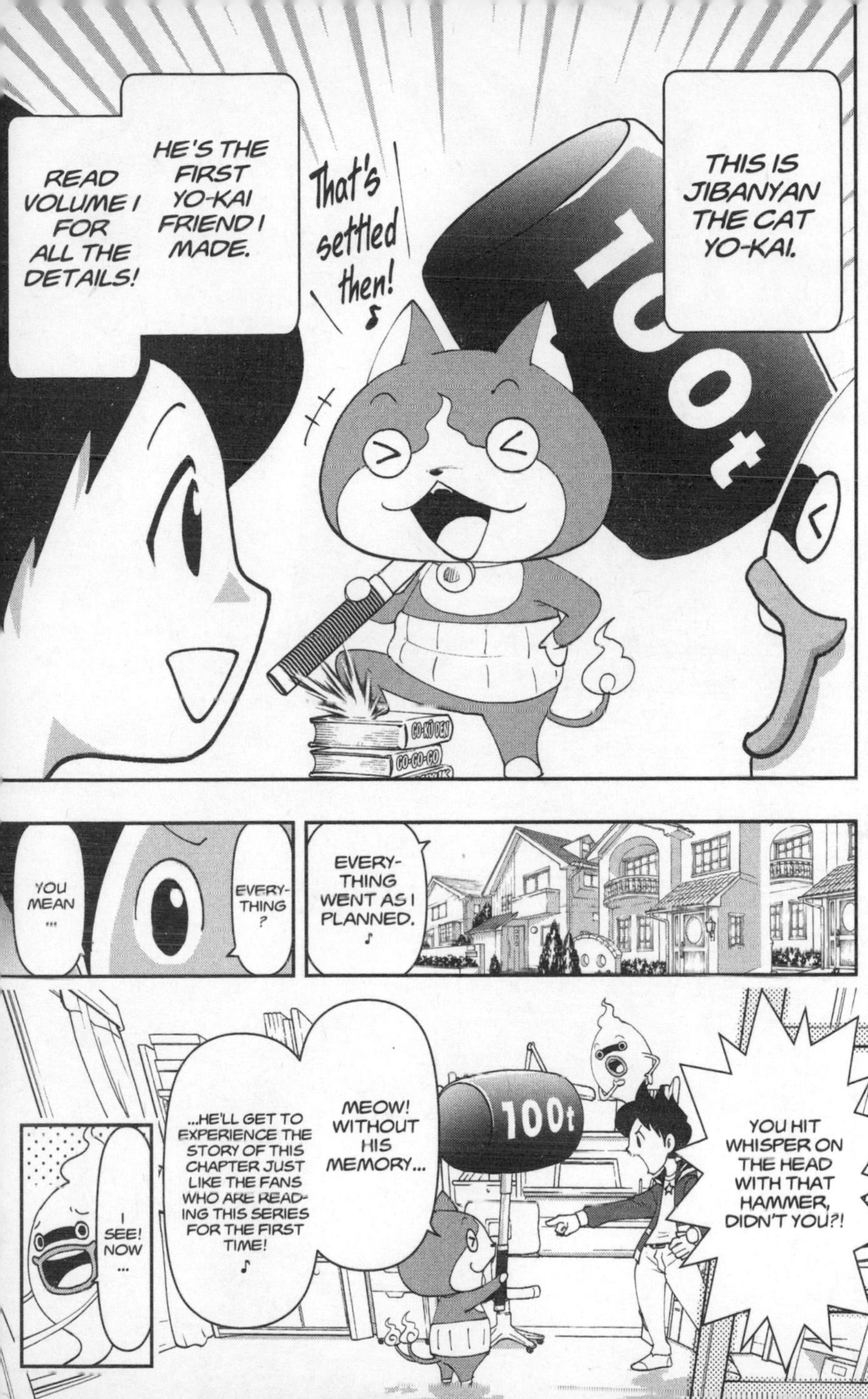
THIS IS JIBANYAN THE CAT YO-KAI.
100t
That's settled then! ♪
HE'S THE FIRST YO-KAI FRIEND I MADE.
READ VOLUME 1 FOR ALL THE DETAILS!
CO-KŌ-DEN
CO-CO-CO
EVERY-THING WENT AS I PLANNED. ♪
EVERY-THING?
YOU MEAN...
YOU HIT WHISPER ON THE HEAD WITH THAT HAMMER, DIDN'T YOU?!
100t
MEOW! WITHOUT HIS MEMORY...
...HE'LL GET TO EXPERIENCE THE STORY OF THIS CHAPTER JUST LIKE THE FANS WHO ARE READ-ING THIS SERIES FOR THE FIRST TIME! ♪
I SEE! NOW...

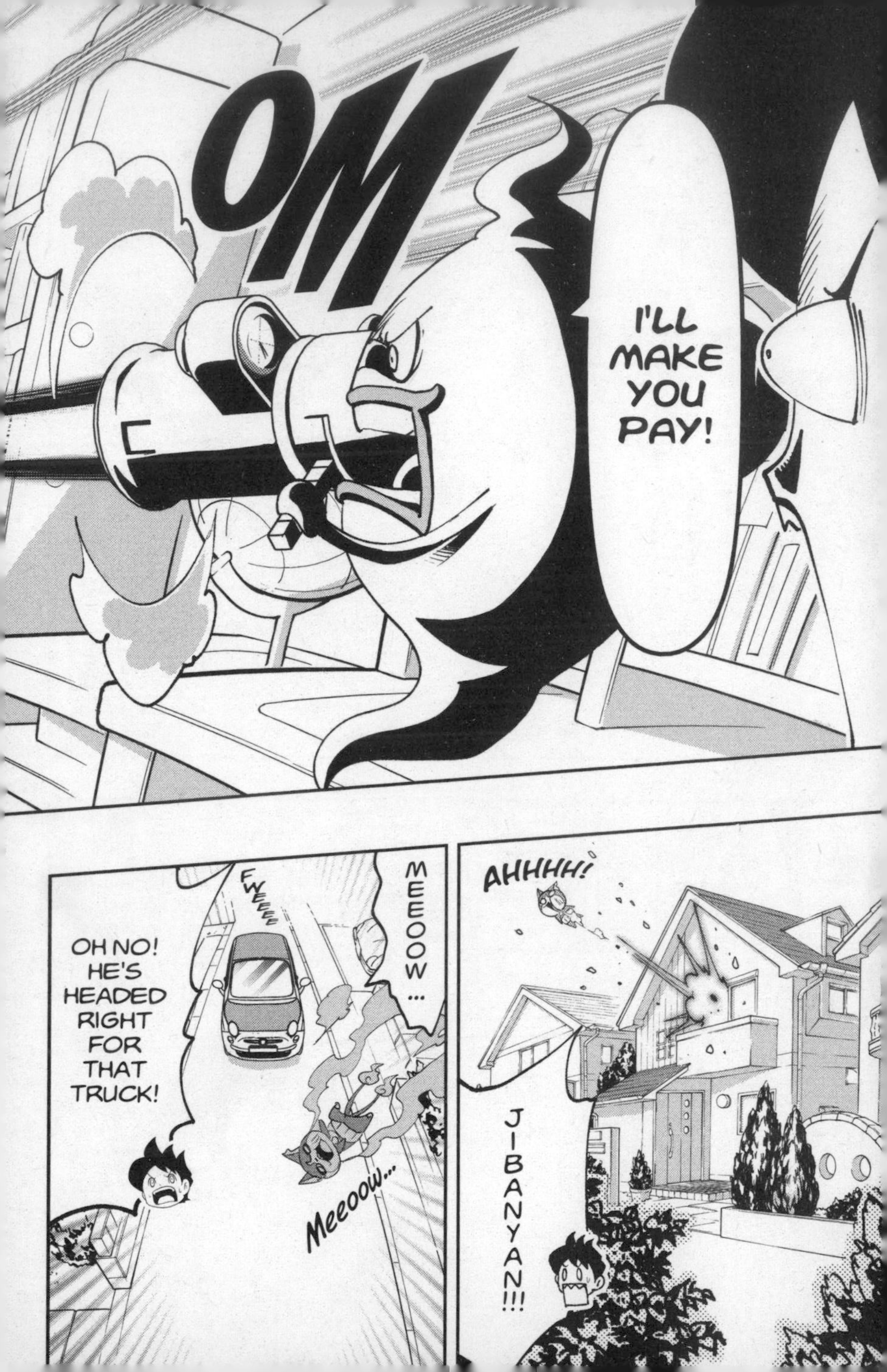
OM
I'LL MAKE YOU PAY!
AHHHH!
JIBANYAN!!!
MEEEOOW...
FWEEEE
OH NO! HE'S HEADED RIGHT FOR THAT TRUCK!
Meeoow...

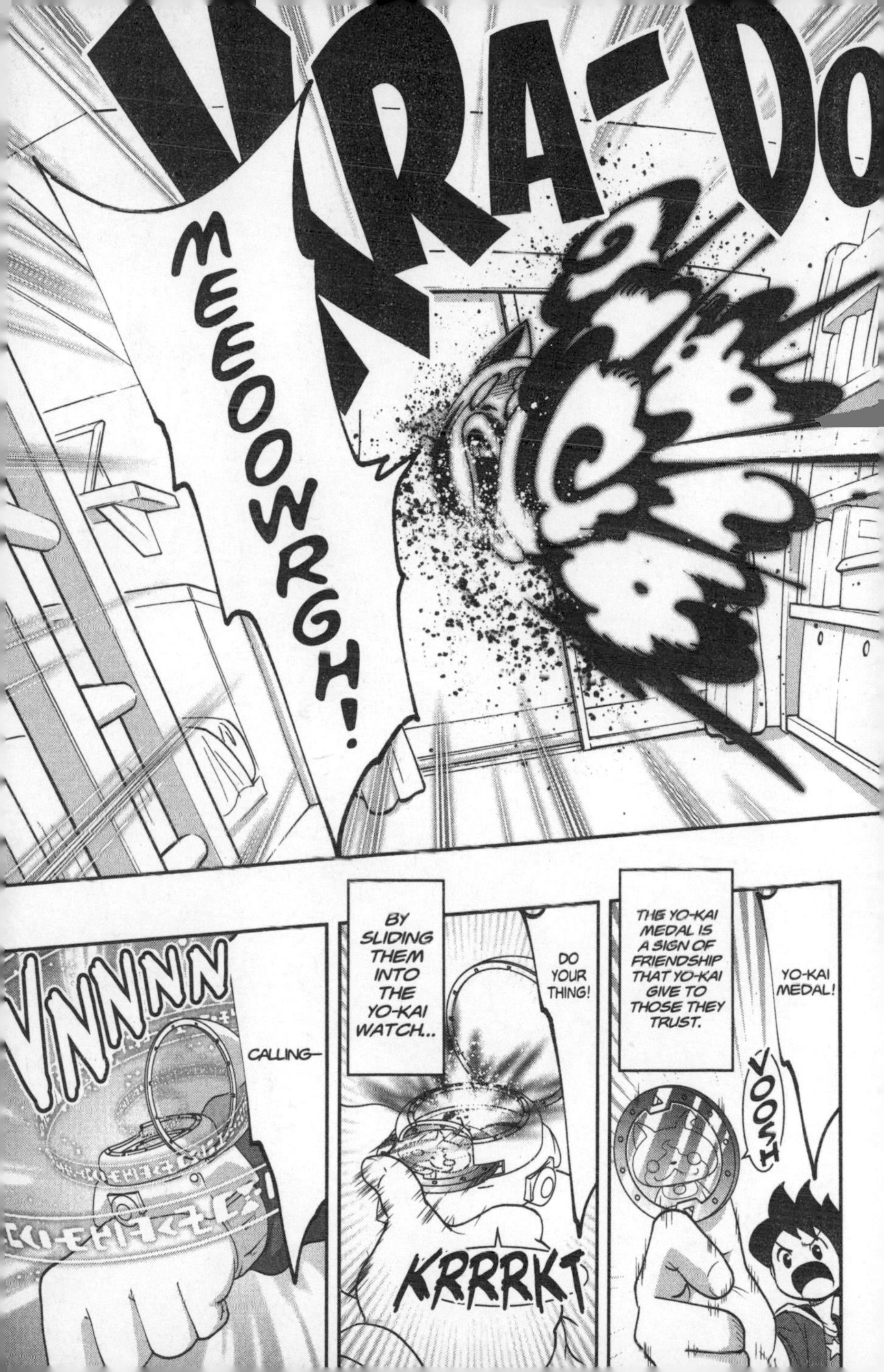
KRA-DO
MEEOOWRGH!
YO-KAI MEDAL!
THE YO-KAI MEDAL IS A SIGN OF FRIENDSHIP THAT YO-KAI GIVE TO THOSE THEY TRUST.
VOOSH!
DO YOUR THING!
BY SLIDING THEM INTO THE YO-KAI WATCH...
KRRRKT
CALLING—
VNNNNN

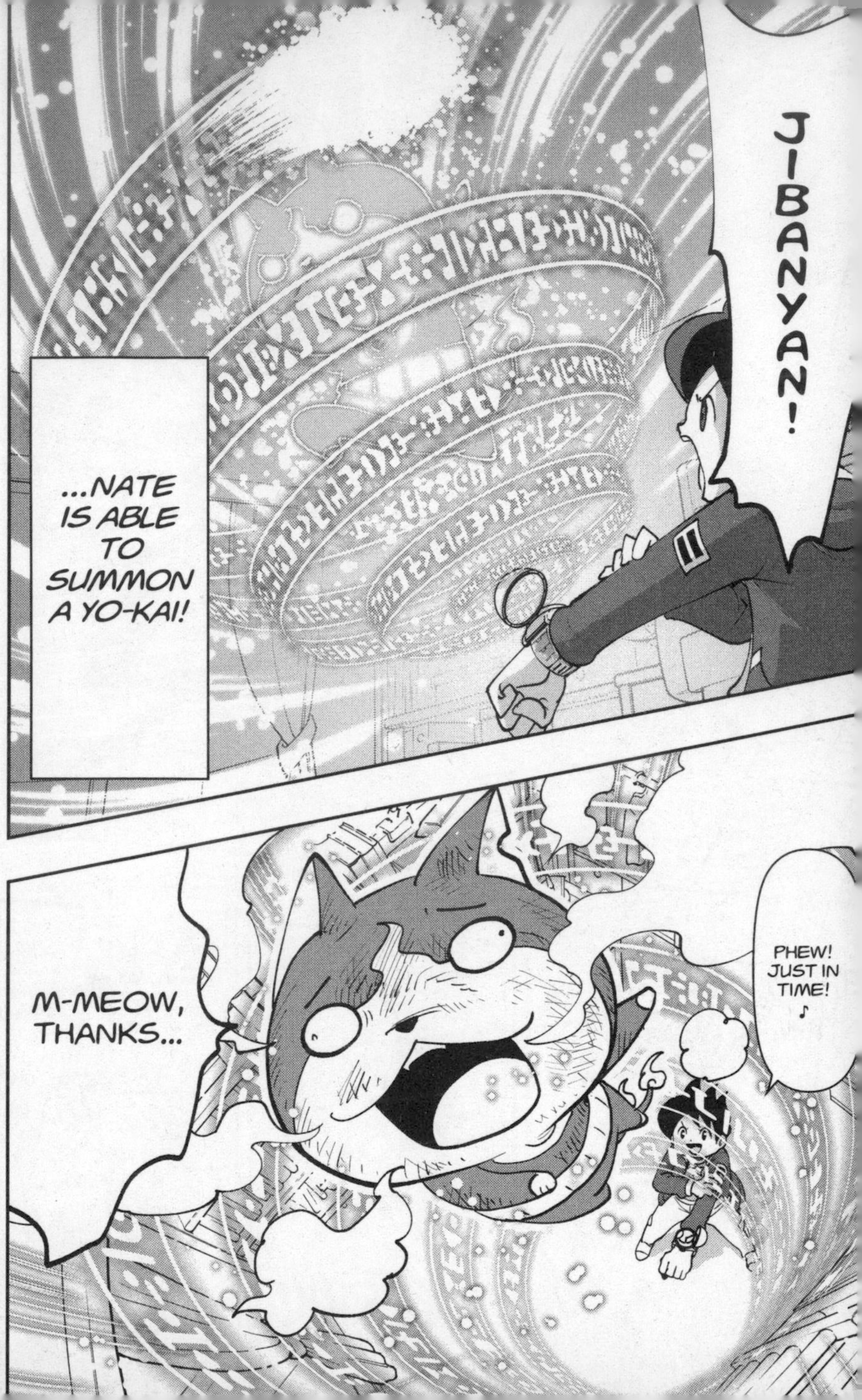
JIBANYAN!
...NATE IS ABLE TO SUMMON A YO-KAI!
PHEW! JUST IN TIME! ♪
M-MEOW, THANKS...

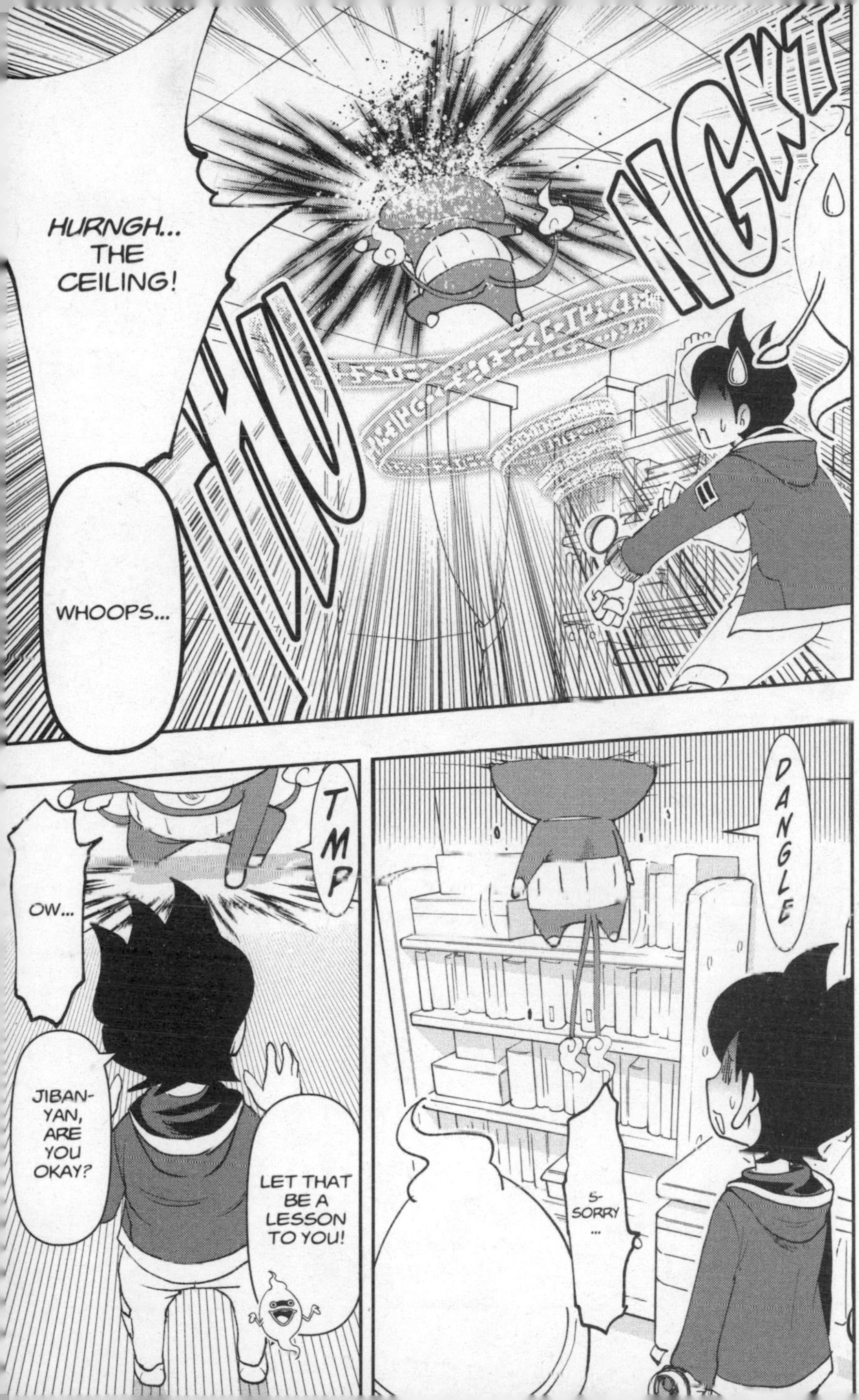
THUNGK!
HURNGH... THE CEILING!
WHOOPS...
DANGLE
S-SORRY...
TMP
OW...
JIBAN-YAN, ARE YOU OKAY?
LET THAT BE A LESSON TO YOU!

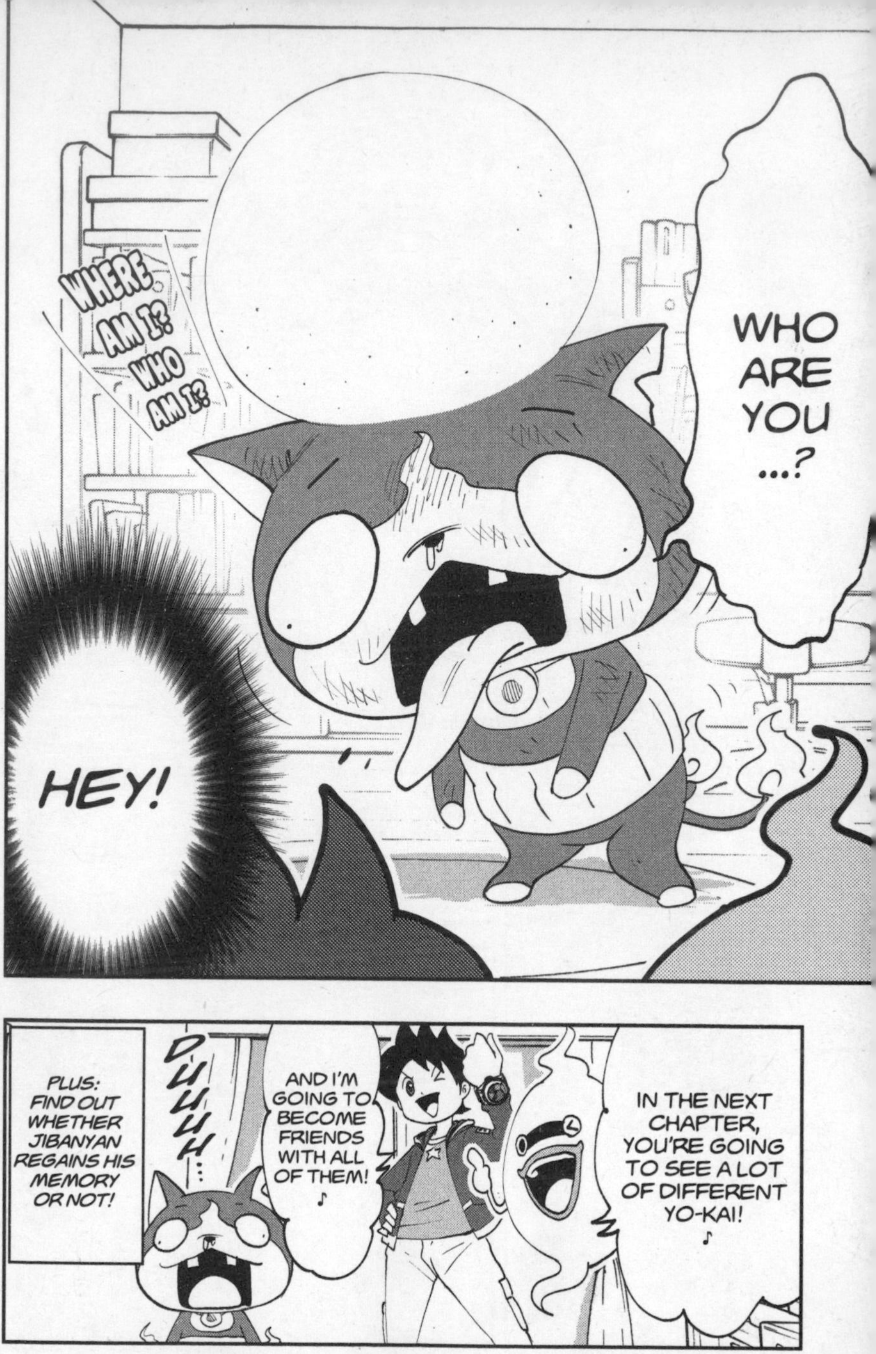
WHO ARE YOU ...?
WHERE AM I? WHO AM I?
HEY!
IN THE NEXT CHAPTER, YOU'RE GOING TO SEE A LOT OF DIFFERENT YO-KAI! ♪
AND I'M GOING TO BECOME FRIENDS WITH ALL OF THEM! ♪
DUUUH...
PLUS: FIND OUT WHETHER JIBANYAN REGAINS HIS MEMORY OR NOT!

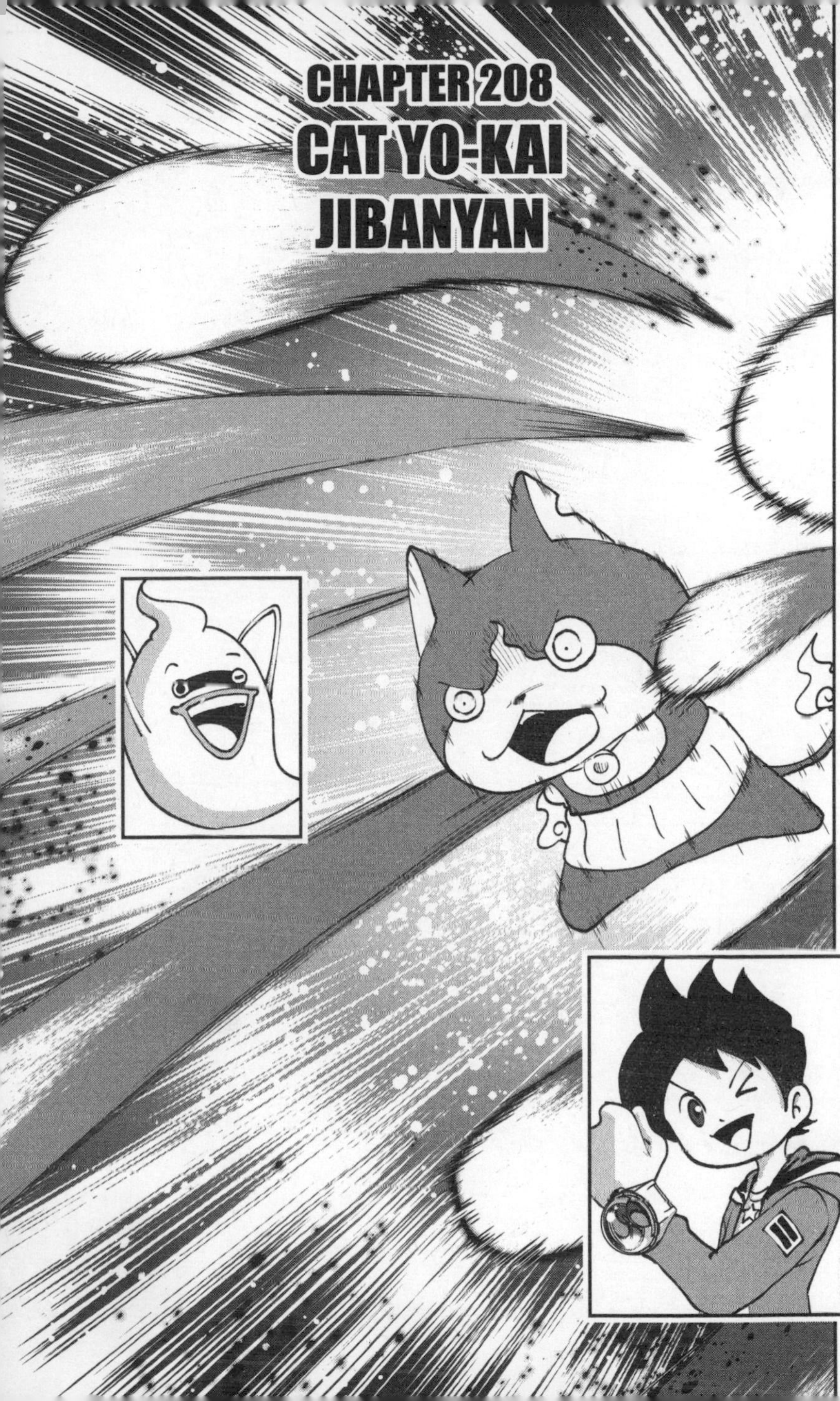
CHAPTER 208
CAT YO-KAI
JIBANYAN

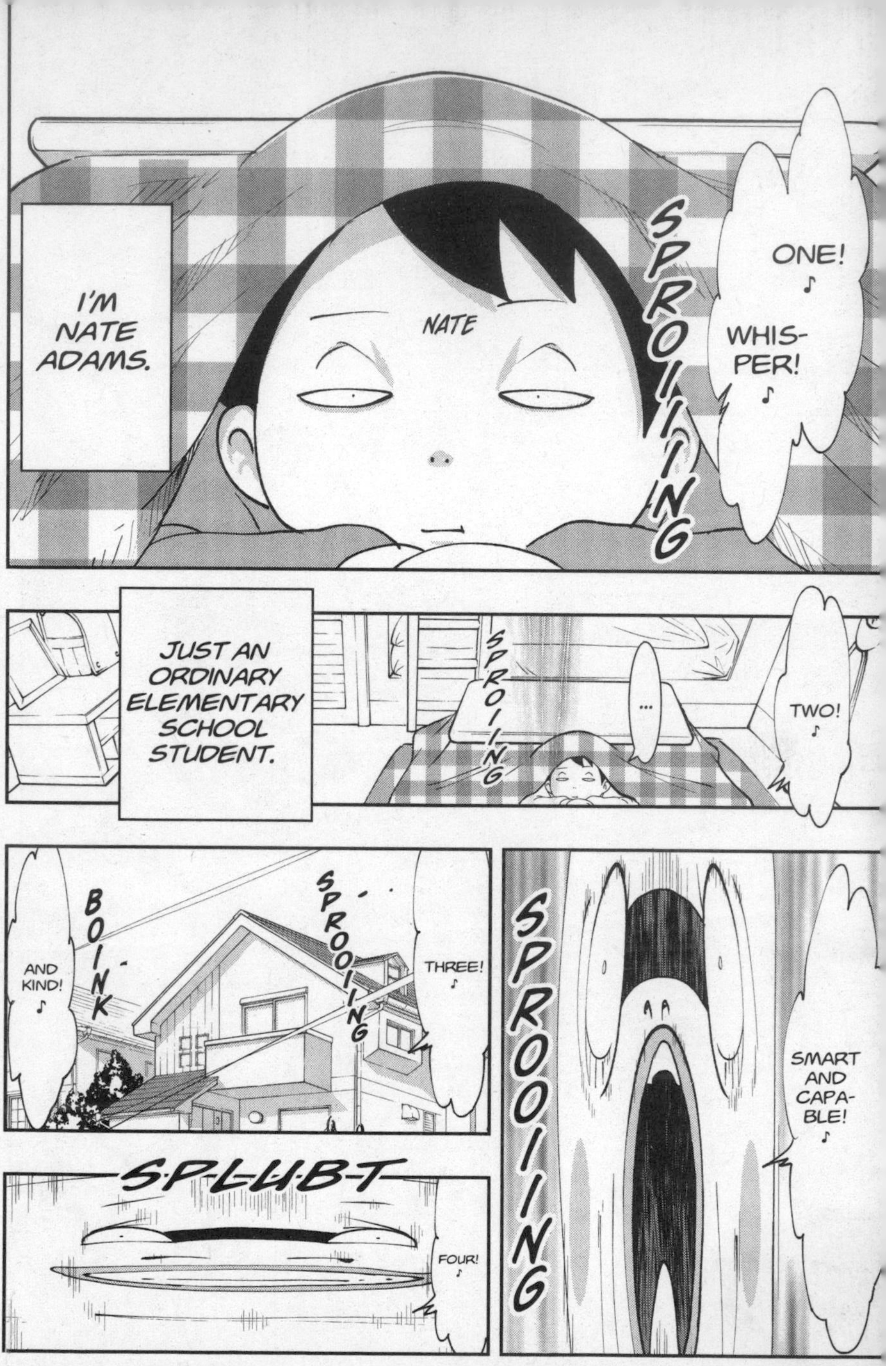
ONE! ♪
WHISPER! ♪
SPROIIIING
NATE
I'M NATE ADAMS.
TWO! ♪
...
SPROOIIING
JUST AN ORDINARY ELEMENTARY SCHOOL STUDENT.
SMART AND CAPABLE! ♪
SPROOOIIING
THREE! ♪
SPROOIIING
AND KIND! ♪
BOINK
FOUR! ♪
S-P-L-U-B-T

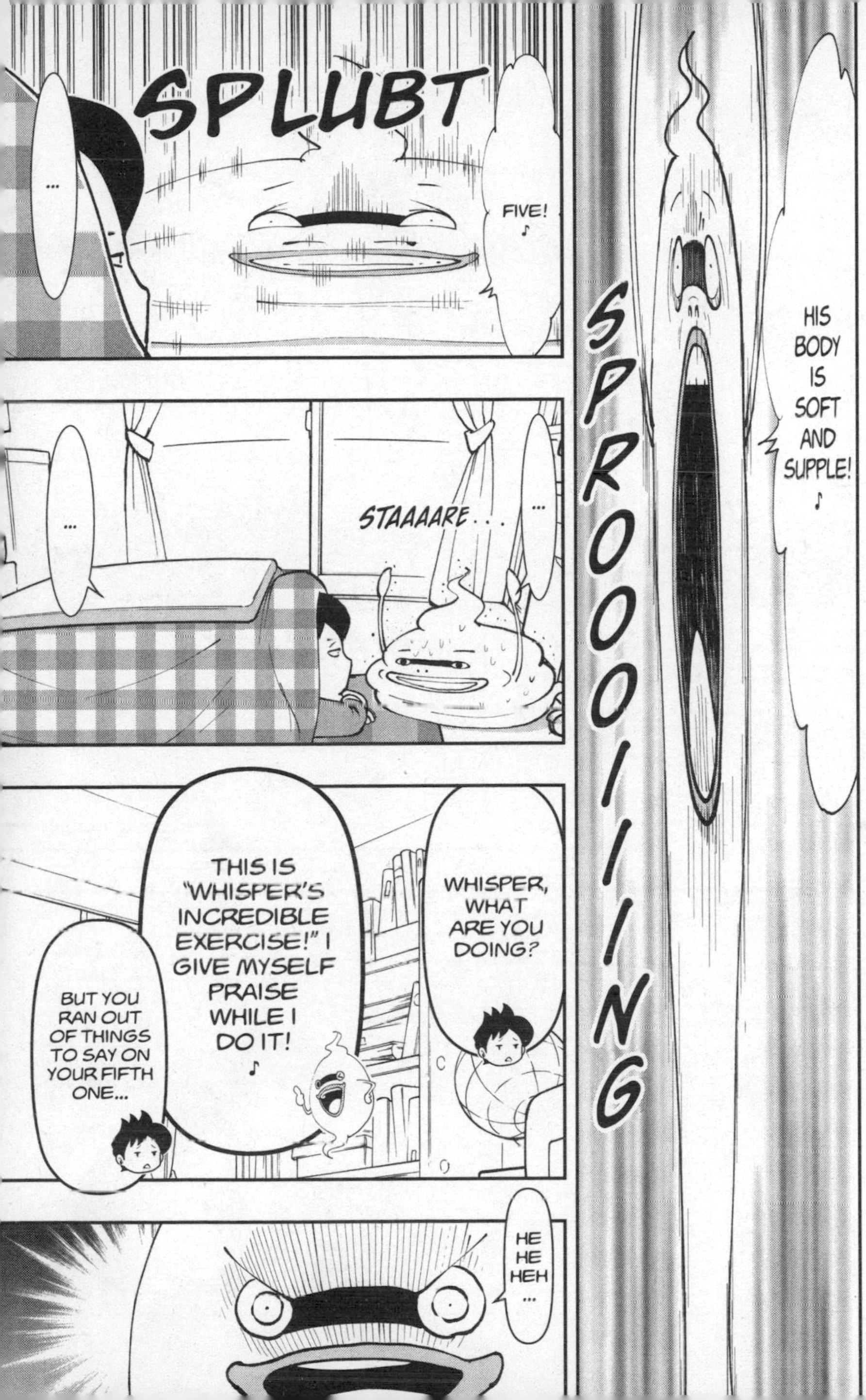
SPROOOIIING
HIS BODY IS SOFT AND SUPPLE! ♪
FIVE! ♪
SPLUBT
...
...
STAAAARE...
...
WHISPER, WHAT ARE YOU DOING?
THIS IS "WHISPER'S INCREDIBLE EXERCISE!" I GIVE MYSELF PRAISE WHILE I DO IT! ♪
BUT YOU RAN OUT OF THINGS TO SAY ON YOUR FIFTH ONE...
HE HE HEH ...

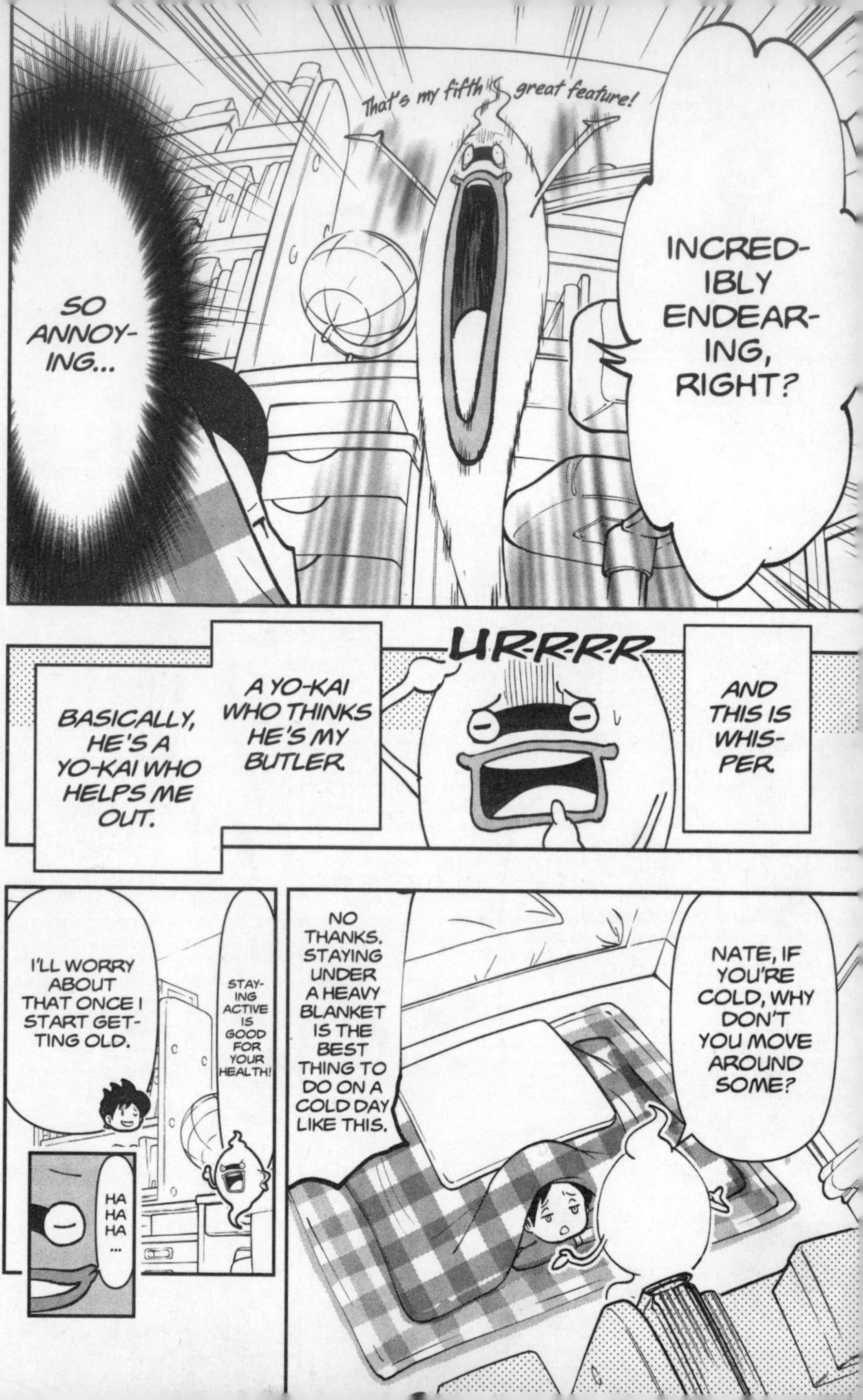
INCREDIBLY ENDEARING, RIGHT?
That's my fifth great feature!
SO ANNOYING...
AND THIS IS WHISPER.
URRRR
A YO-KAI WHO THINKS HE'S MY BUTLER.
BASICALLY, HE'S A YO-KAI WHO HELPS ME OUT.
NATE, IF YOU'RE COLD, WHY DON'T YOU MOVE AROUND SOME?
NO THANKS. STAYING UNDER A HEAVY BLANKET IS THE BEST THING TO DO ON A COLD DAY LIKE THIS.
STAYING ACTIVE IS GOOD FOR YOUR HEALTH!
I'LL WORRY ABOUT THAT ONCE I START GETTING OLD.
HA HA HA ...

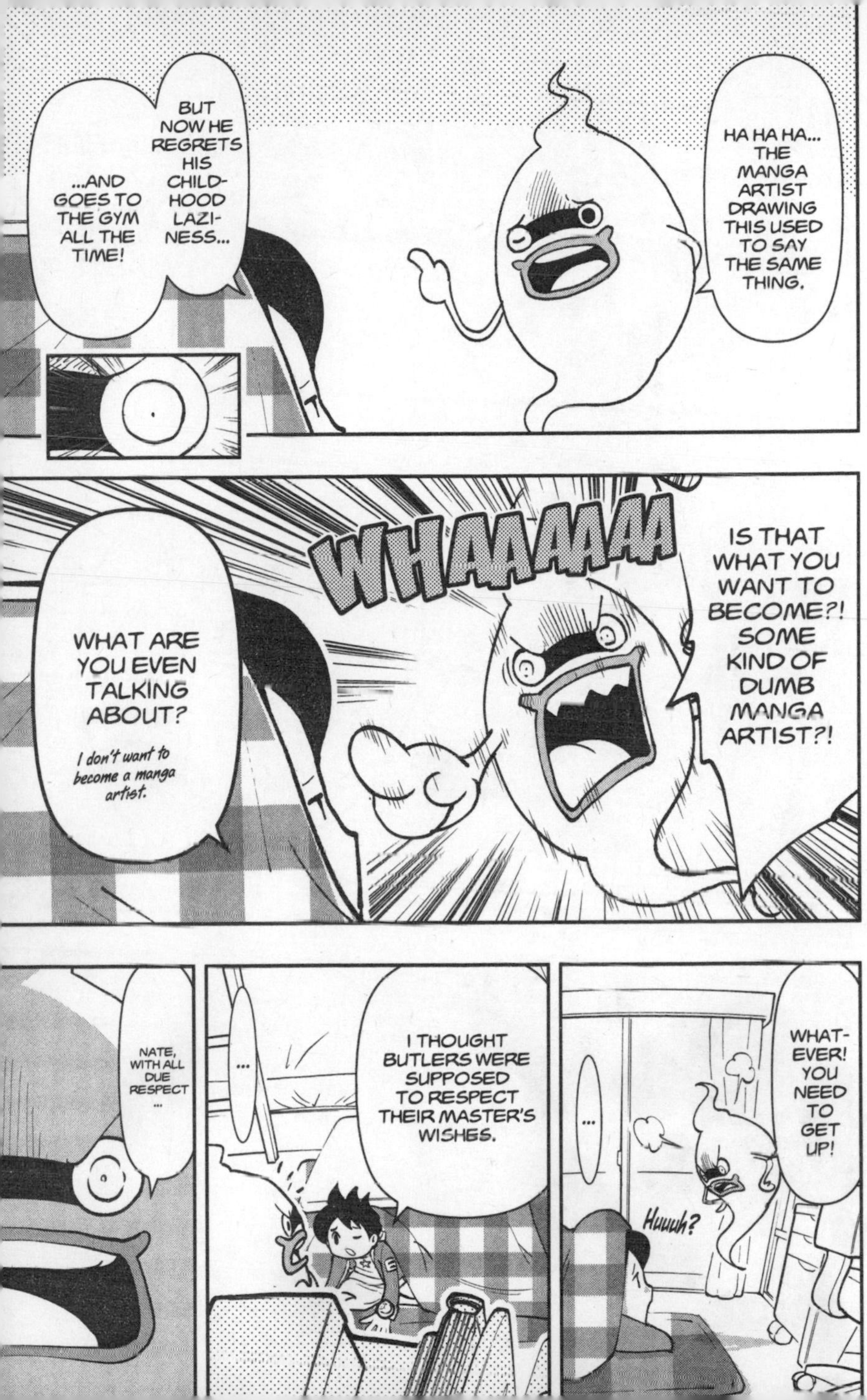
HA HA HA... THE MANGA ARTIST DRAWING THIS USED TO SAY THE SAME THING.
BUT NOW HE REGRETS HIS CHILD-HOOD LAZI-NESS...
...AND GOES TO THE GYM ALL THE TIME!
WHAAAAAA
IS THAT WHAT YOU WANT TO BECOME?! SOME KIND OF DUMB MANGA ARTIST?!
WHAT ARE YOU EVEN TALKING ABOUT?
I don't want to become a manga artist.
WHAT-EVER! YOU NEED TO GET UP!
...
Huuuh?
I THOUGHT BUTLERS WERE SUPPOSED TO RESPECT THEIR MASTER'S WISHES.
...
NATE, WITH ALL DUE RESPECT ...

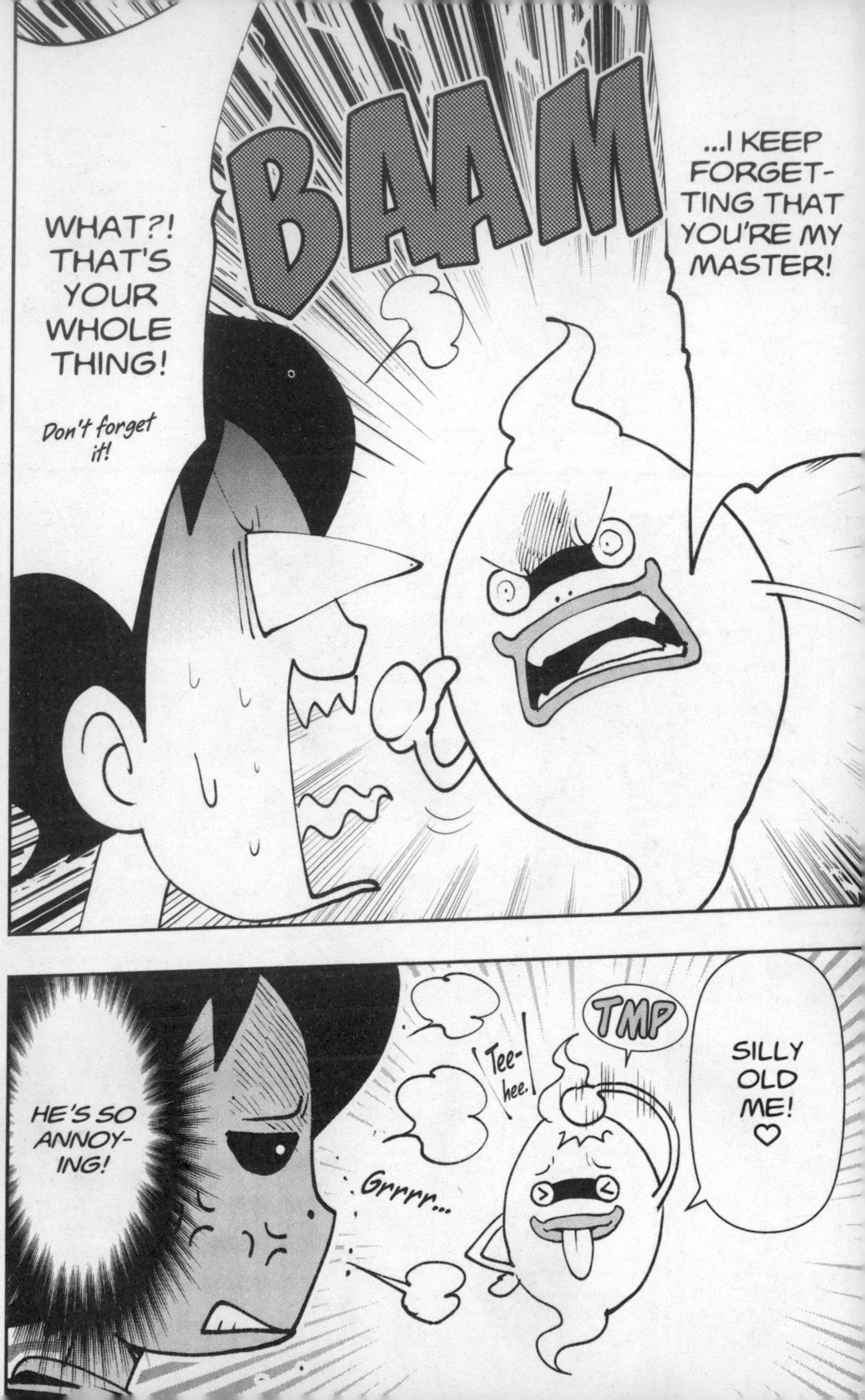
...I KEEP FORGETTING THAT YOU'RE MY MASTER!
BAAM
WHAT?! THAT'S YOUR WHOLE THING!
Don't forget it!
SILLY OLD ME! ♡
TMP
Tee-hee.
Grrrr...
HE'S SO ANNOYING!

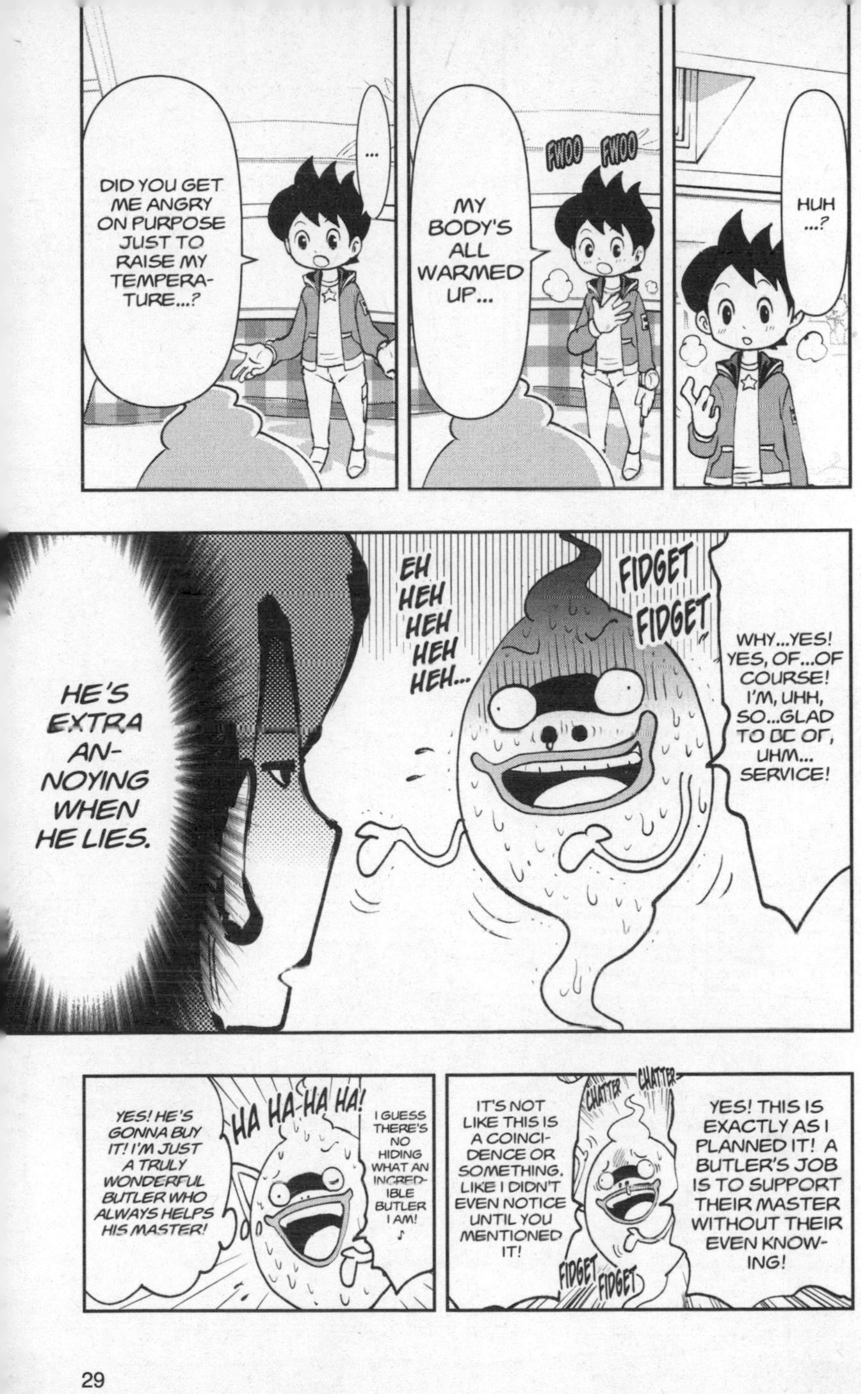
HUH ...?
FWOO FWOO
MY BODY'S ALL WARMED UP...
...
DID YOU GET ME ANGRY ON PURPOSE JUST TO RAISE MY TEMPERATURE...?
WHY...YES! YES, OF...OF COURSE! I'M, UHH, SO...GLAD TO BE OF, UHM... SERVICE!
FIDGET FIDGET
EH HEH HEH HEH HEH...
HE'S EXTRA ANNOYING WHEN HE LIES.
YES! THIS IS EXACTLY AS I PLANNED IT! A BUTLER'S JOB IS TO SUPPORT THEIR MASTER WITHOUT THEIR EVEN KNOWING!
CHATTER CHATTER
IT'S NOT LIKE THIS IS A COINCIDENCE OR SOMETHING. LIKE I DIDN'T EVEN NOTICE UNTIL YOU MENTIONED IT!
FIDGET FIDGET
I GUESS THERE'S NO HIDING WHAT AN INCREDIBLE BUTLER I AM! ♪
HA HA HA HA!
YES! HE'S GONNA BUY IT! I'M JUST A TRULY WONDERFUL BUTLER WHO ALWAYS HELPS HIS MASTER!

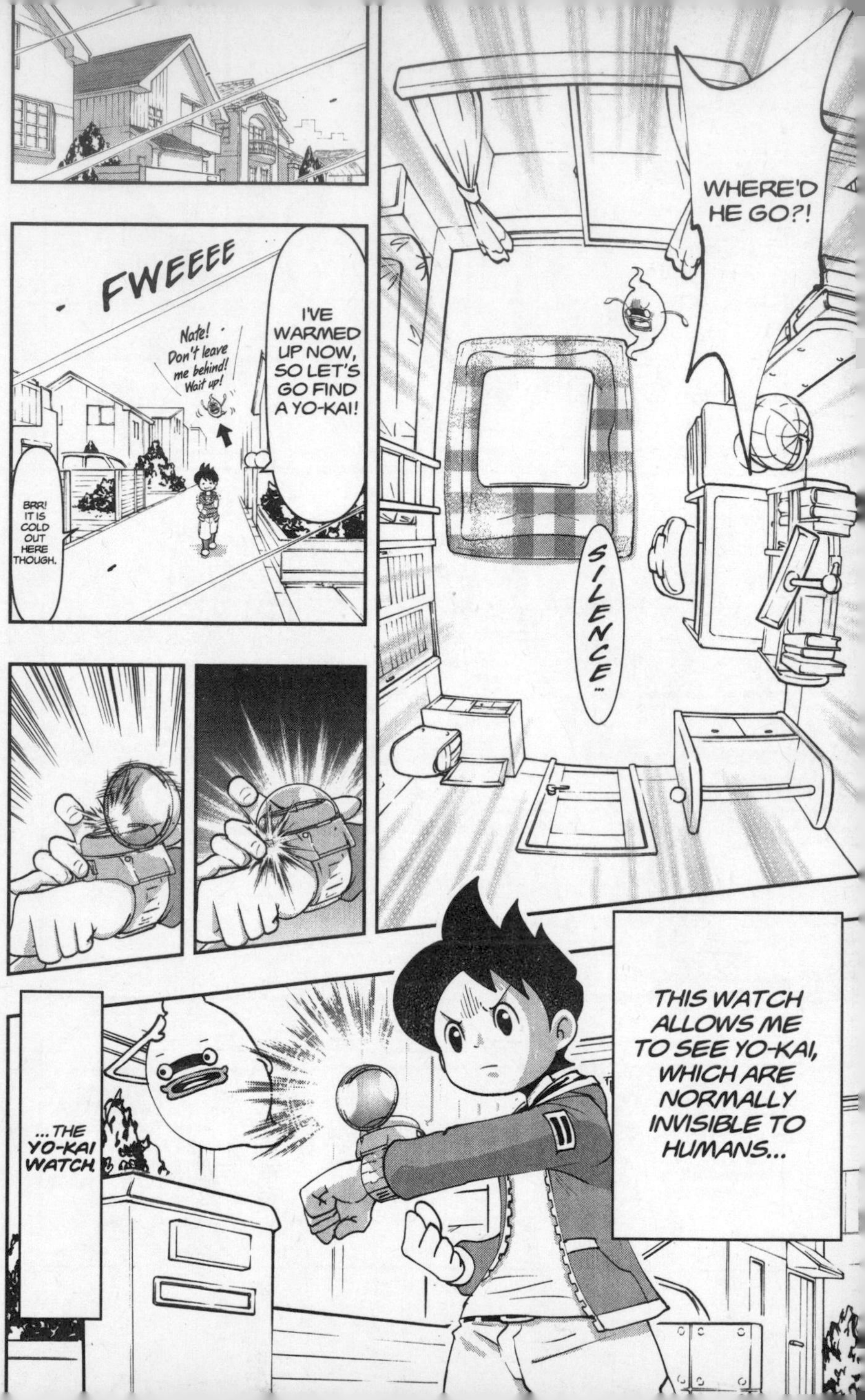
WHERE'D HE GO?!
SILENCE...
I'VE WARMED UP NOW, SO LET'S GO FIND A YO-KAI!
FWEEEE
Nate! Don't leave me behind! Wait up!
BRR! IT IS COLD OUT HERE THOUGH.
THIS WATCH ALLOWS ME TO SEE YO-KAI, WHICH ARE NORMALLY INVISIBLE TO HUMANS...
...THE YO-KAI WATCH.

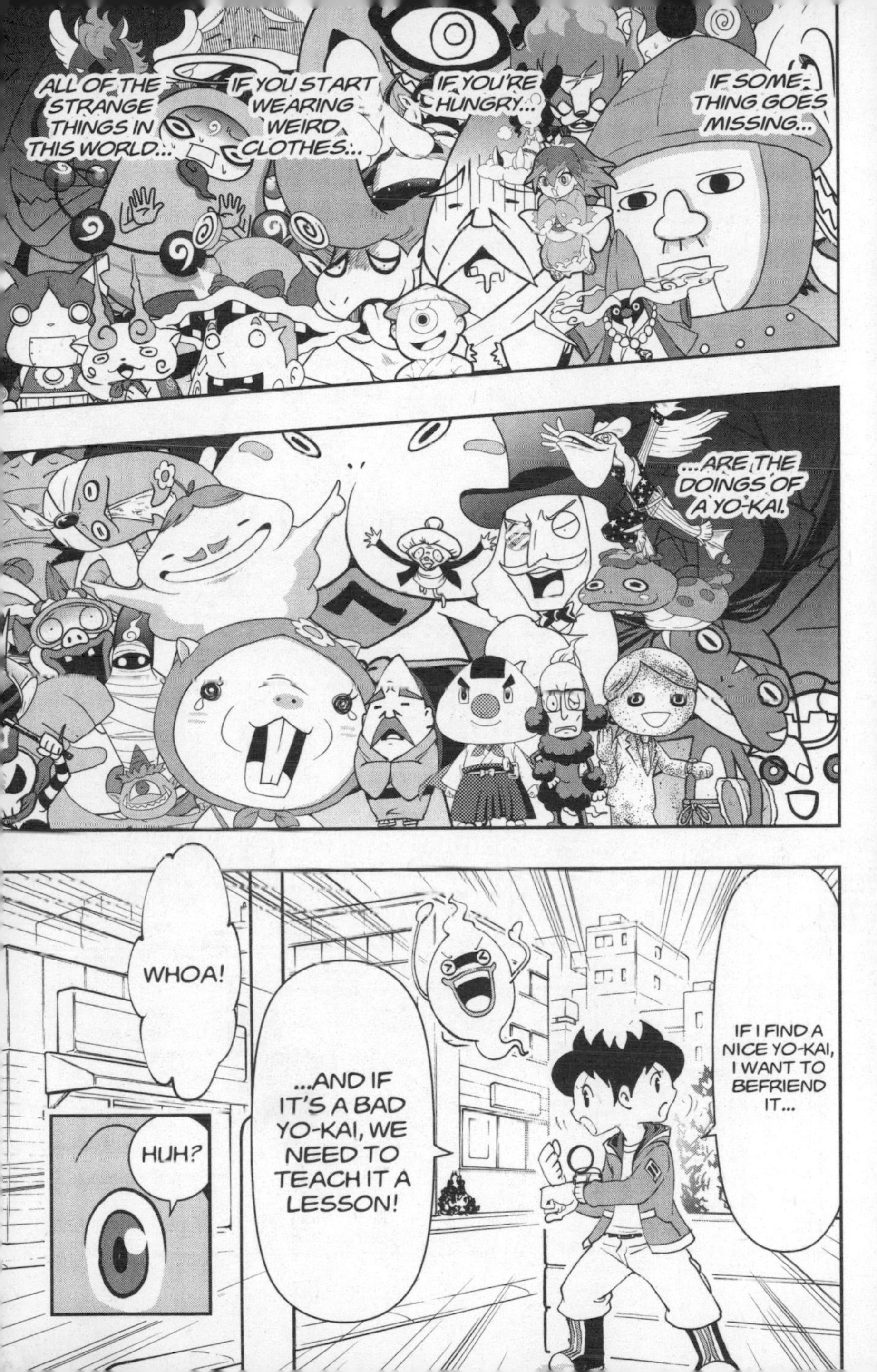
IF SOME-THING GOES MISSING...
IF YOU'RE HUNGRY...
IF YOU START WEARING WEIRD CLOTHES...
ALL OF THE STRANGE THINGS IN THIS WORLD...
...ARE THE DOINGS OF A YO-KAI.
IF I FIND A NICE YO-KAI, I WANT TO BEFRIEND IT...
...AND IF IT'S A BAD YO-KAI, WE NEED TO TEACH IT A LESSON!
WHOA!
HUH?

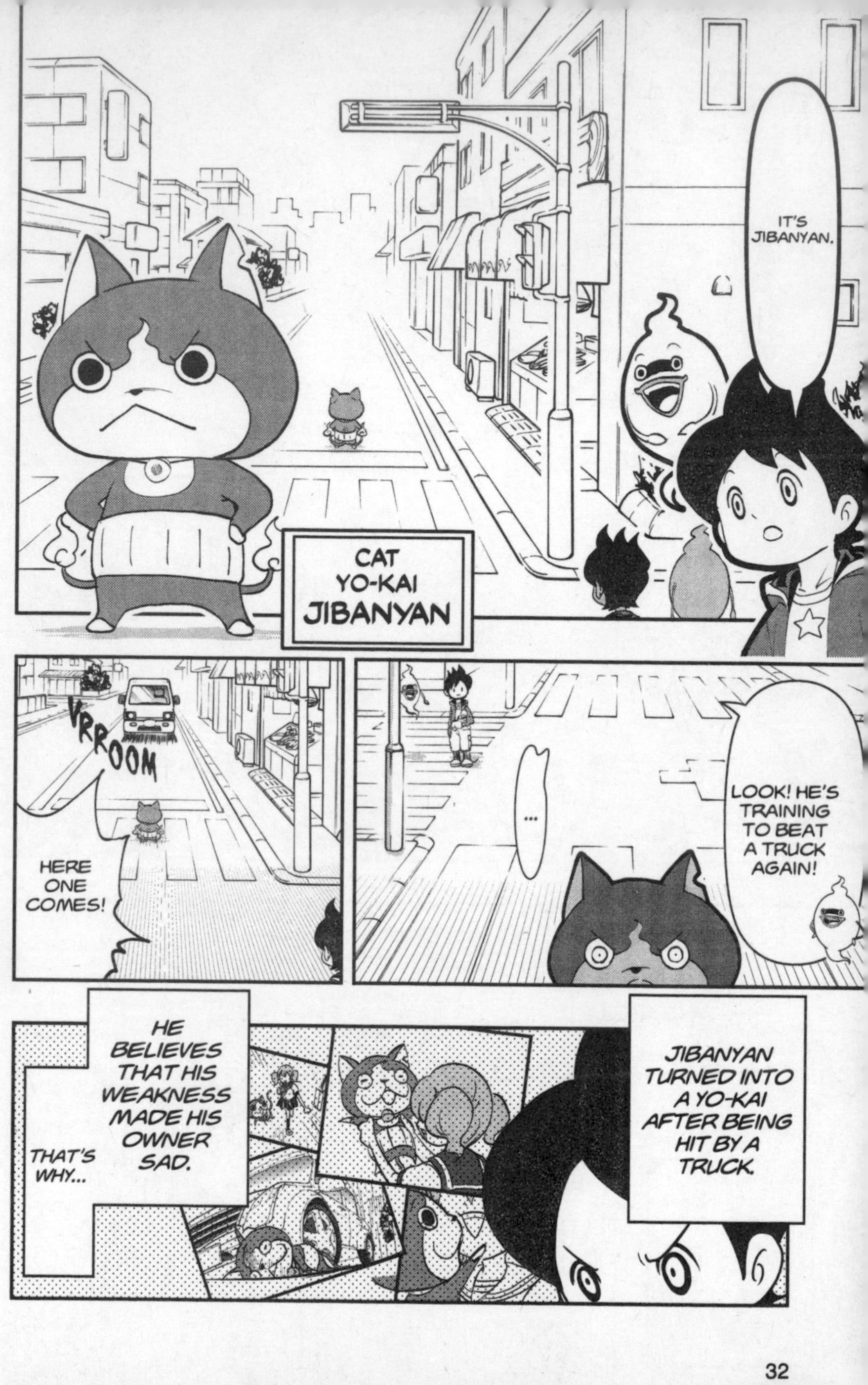
IT'S JIBANYAN.
CAT YO-KAI JIBANYAN
LOOK! HE'S TRAINING TO BEAT A TRUCK AGAIN!
...
VRROOM
HERE ONE COMES!
JIBANYAN TURNED INTO A YO-KAI AFTER BEING HIT BY A TRUCK.
HE BELIEVES THAT HIS WEAKNESS MADE HIS OWNER SAD.
THAT'S WHY...

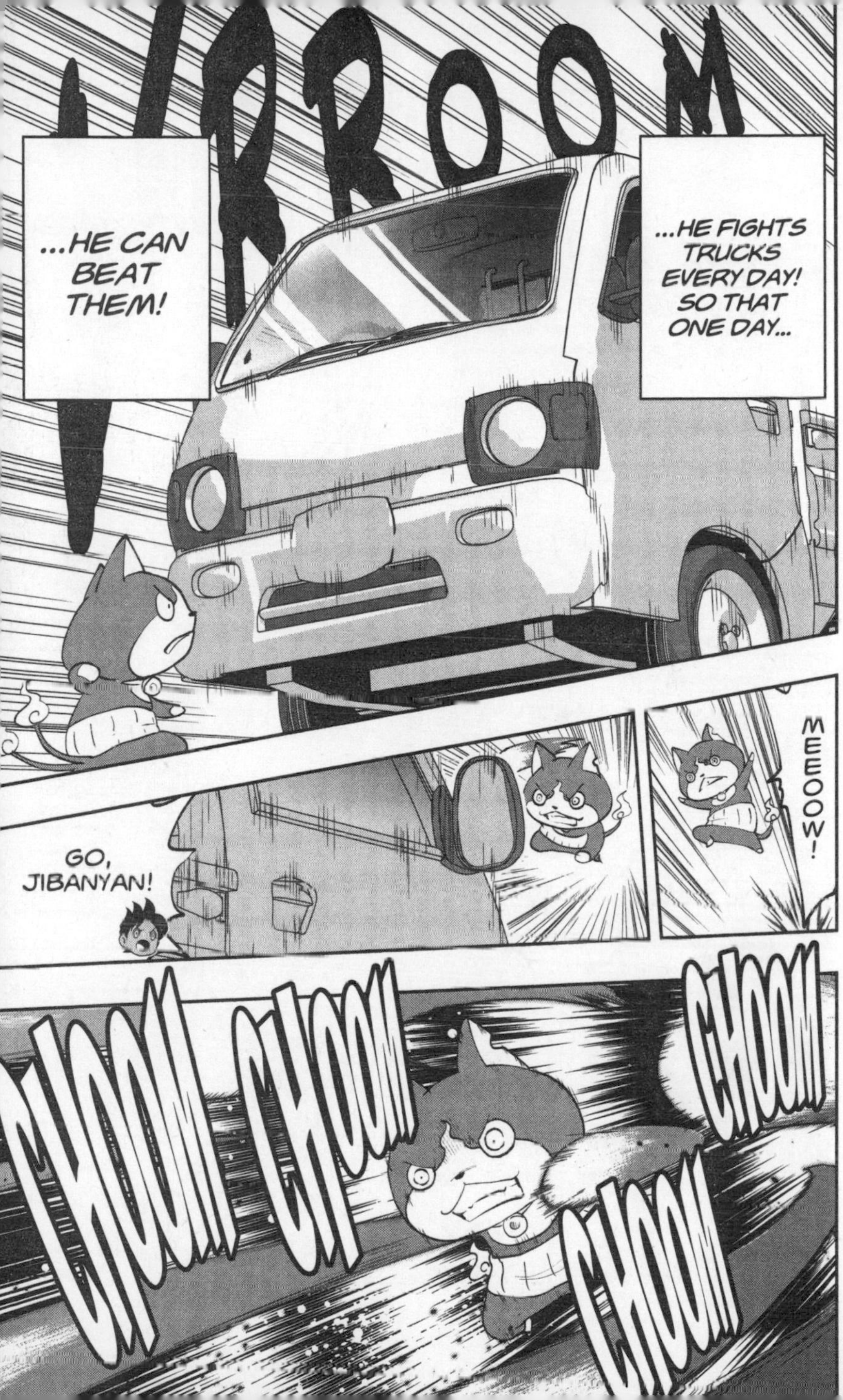
VRROOM
...HE FIGHTS TRUCKS EVERY DAY! SO THAT ONE DAY...
...HE CAN BEAT THEM!
MEEEOOW!
GO, JIBANYAN!
CHOOM
CHOOM
CHOOM
CHOOM

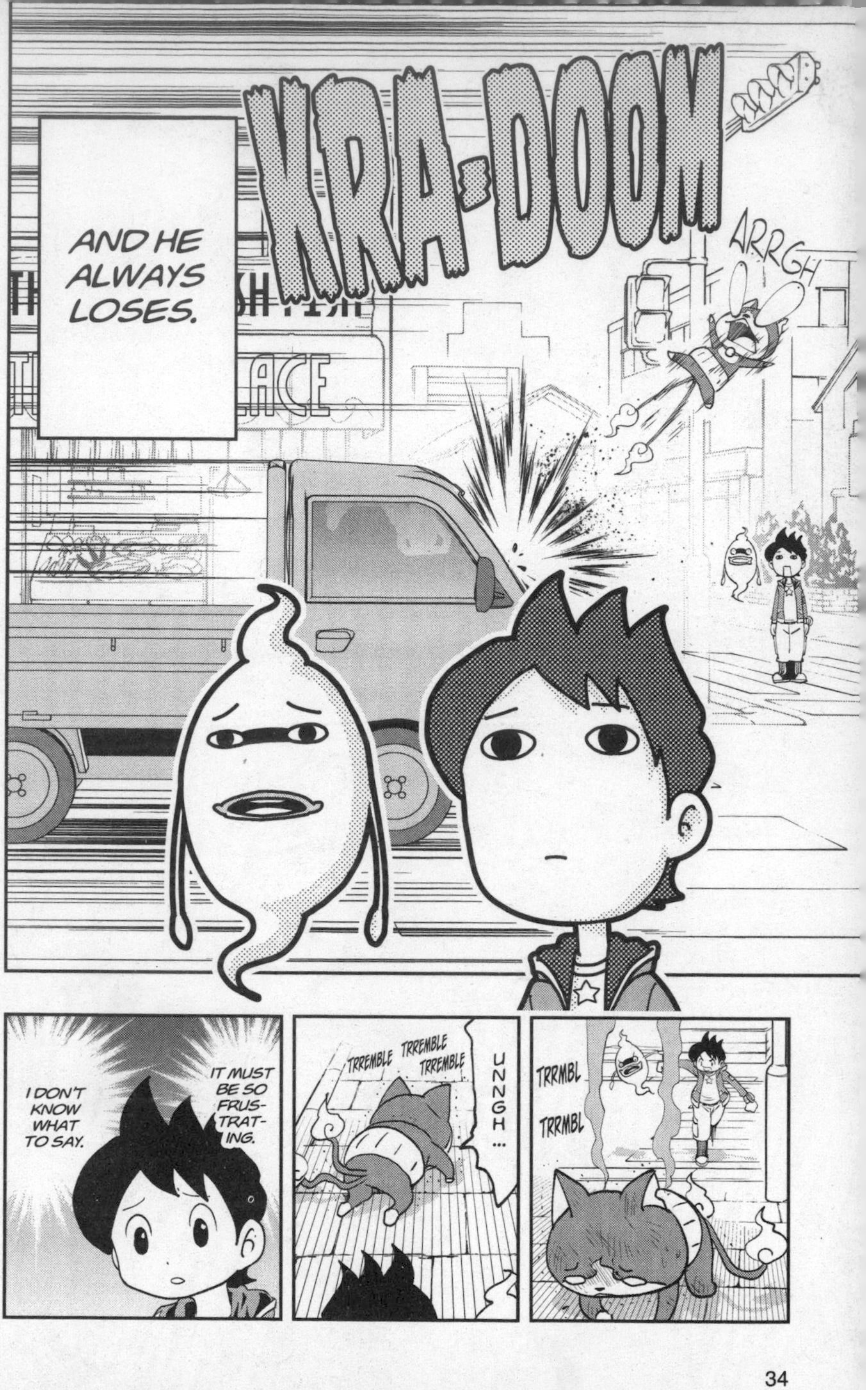
KRA-DOOM
ARRGH
AND HE ALWAYS LOSES.
TRRMBL TRRMBL
UNNGH...
TRREMBLE TRREMBLE TRREMBLE
IT MUST BE SO FRUS-TRAT-ING.
I DON'T KNOW WHAT TO SAY.

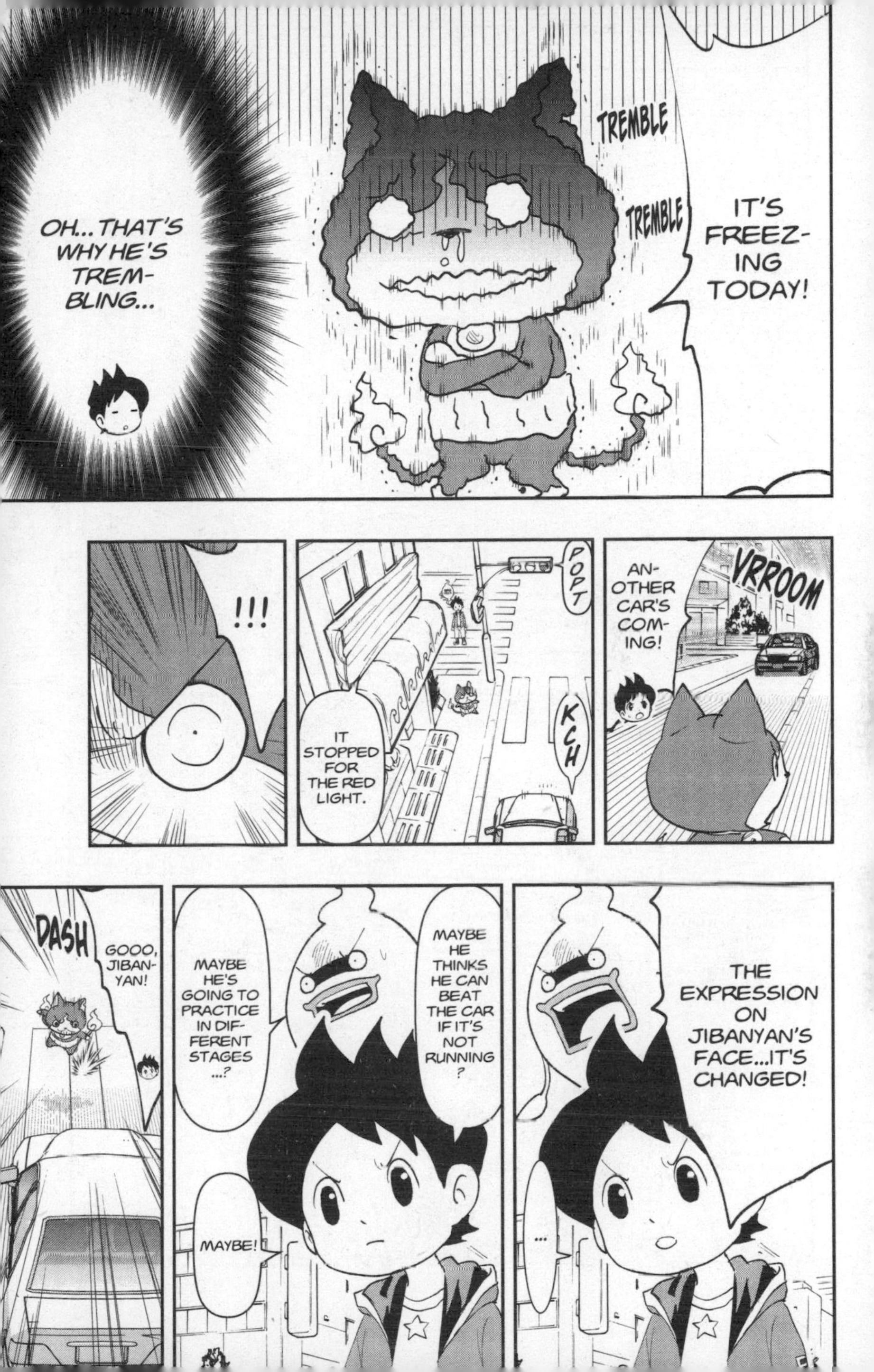
IT'S FREEZING TODAY!
TREMBLE
TREMBLE
OH...THAT'S WHY HE'S TREMBLING...
ANOTHER CAR'S COMING!
VRROOM
POPT
KCH
IT STOPPED FOR THE RED LIGHT.
!!!
THE EXPRESSION ON JIBANYAN'S FACE...IT'S CHANGED!
...
MAYBE HE THINKS HE CAN BEAT THE CAR IF IT'S NOT RUNNING?
MAYBE HE'S GOING TO PRACTICE IN DIFFERENT STAGES...?
MAYBE!
DASH
GOOO, JIBANYAN!

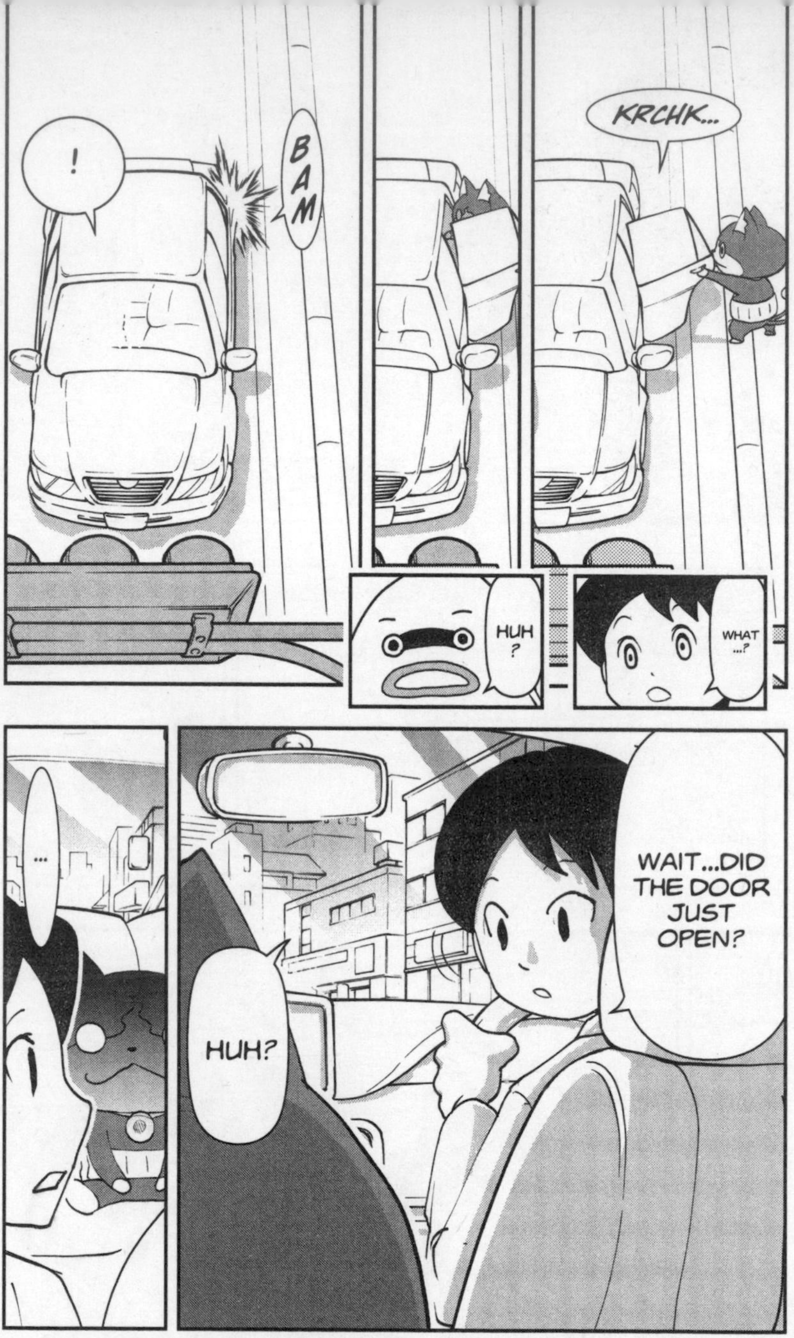
KRCHK...
BAM
!
WHAT...?
HUH?
WAIT...DID THE DOOR JUST OPEN?
HUH?
...

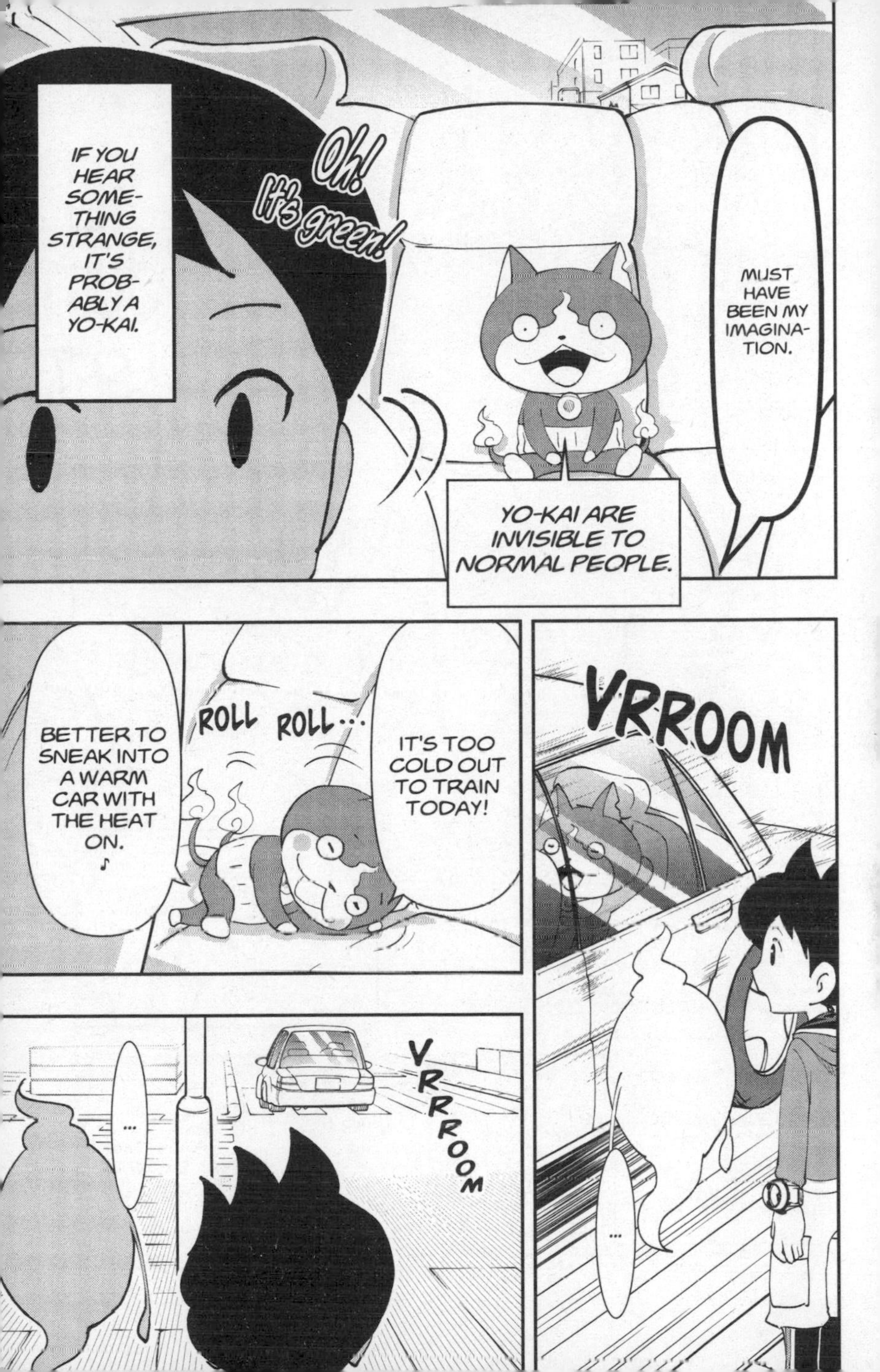
Oh! It's green!
MUST HAVE BEEN MY IMAGINATION.
IF YOU HEAR SOMETHING STRANGE, IT'S PROBABLY A YO-KAI.
YO-KAI ARE INVISIBLE TO NORMAL PEOPLE.
VRROOM
...
IT'S TOO COLD OUT TO TRAIN TODAY!
ROLL ROLL...
BETTER TO SNEAK INTO A WARM CAR WITH THE HEAT ON. ♪
VRRROOM
...

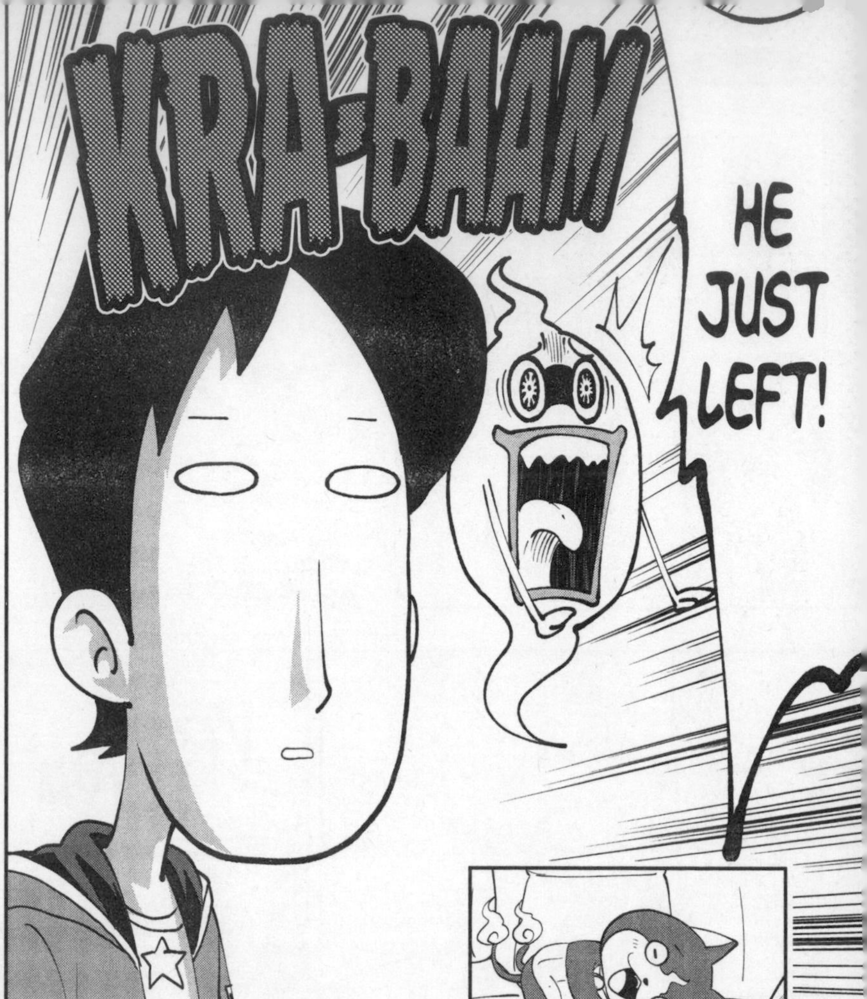
KRA-BAAM
HE JUST LEFT!

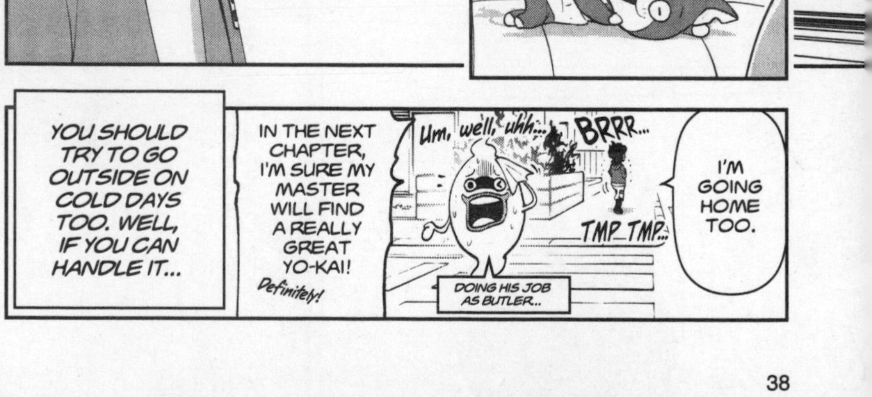
I'M GOING HOME TOO.
Um, well, uhh...
BRRR...
TMP TMP...
DOING HIS JOB AS BUTLER..
IN THE NEXT CHAPTER, I'M SURE MY MASTER WILL FIND A REALLY GREAT YO-KAI!
Definitely!
YOU SHOULD TRY TO GO OUTSIDE ON COLD DAYS TOO. WELL, IF YOU CAN HANDLE IT...

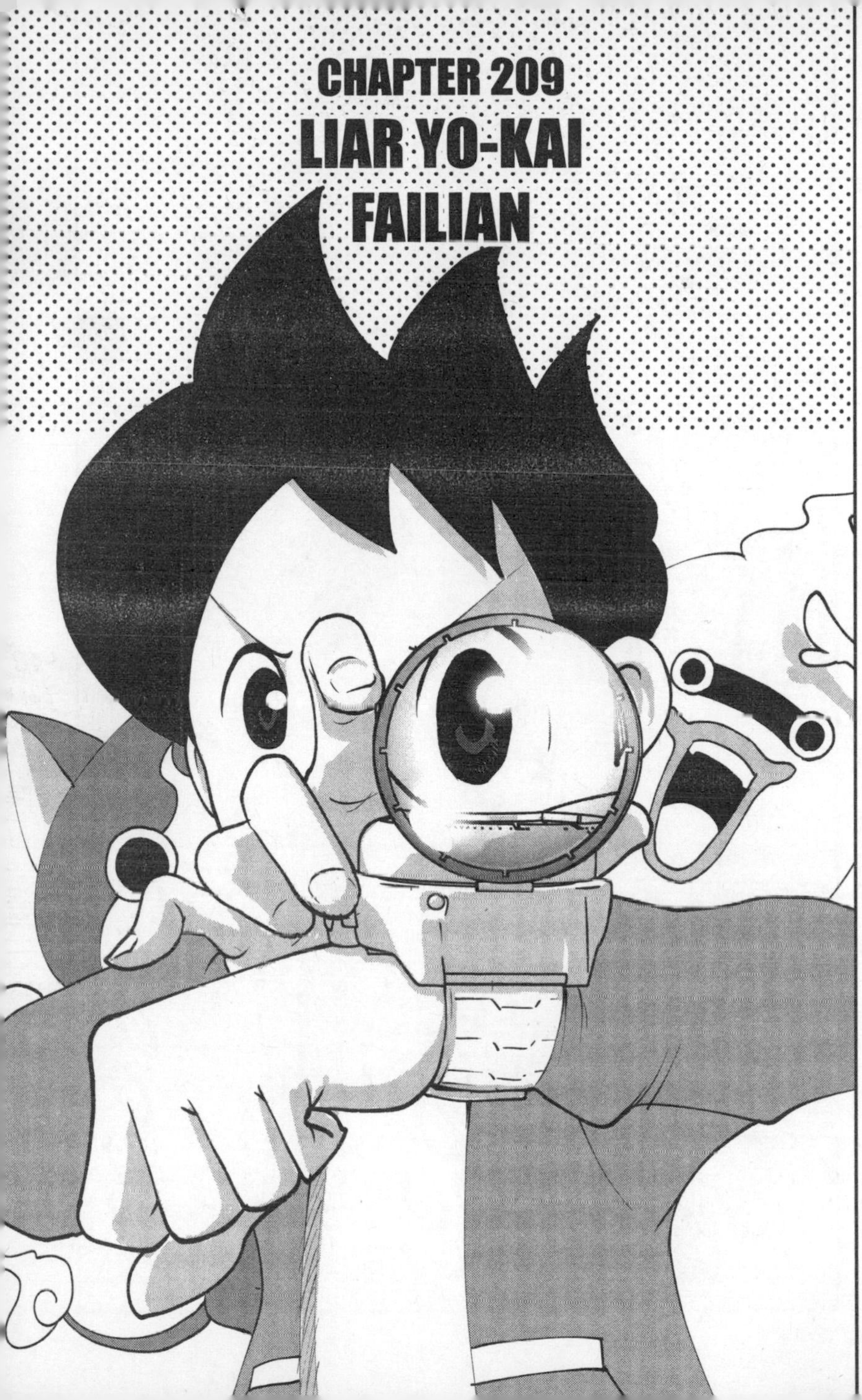
CHAPTER 209
LIAR YO-KAI
FAILIAN

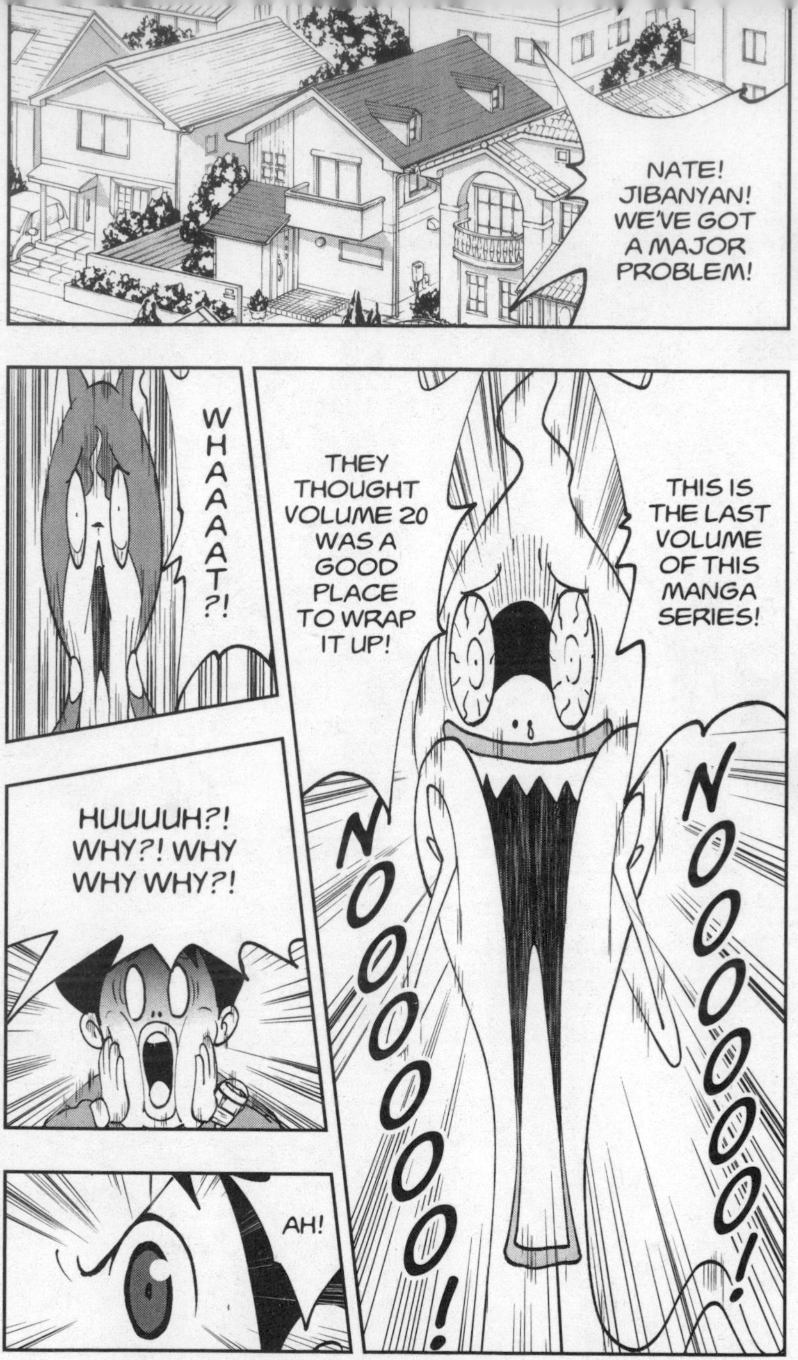
NATE! JIBANYAN! WE'VE GOT A MAJOR PROBLEM!
THIS IS THE LAST VOLUME OF THIS MANGA SERIES!
THEY THOUGHT VOLUME 20 WAS A GOOD PLACE TO WRAP IT UP!
NOOOOOO!
NOOOOOO!
WHAAAAAT?!
HUUUUH?! WHY?! WHY WHY WHY?!
AH!

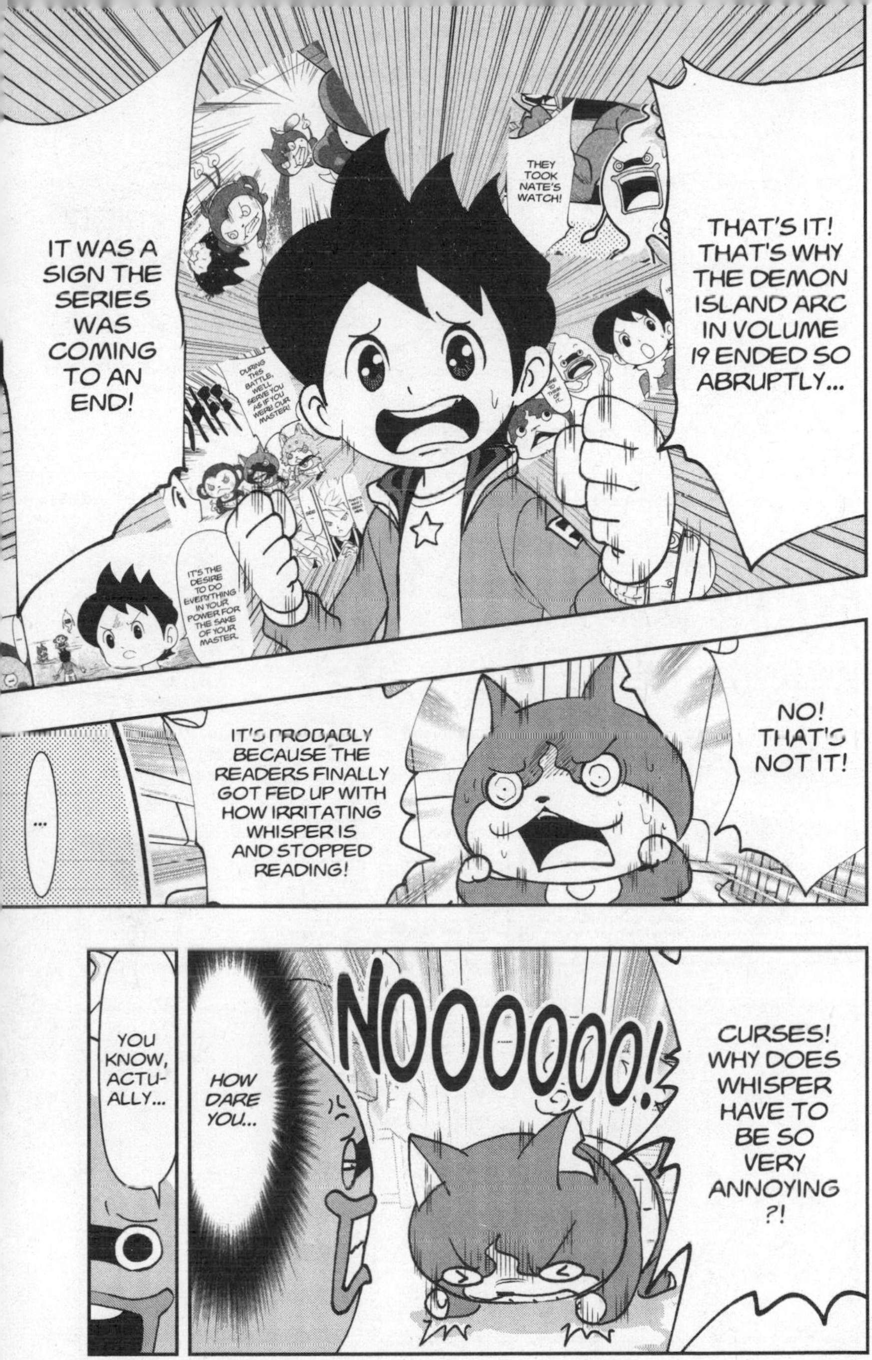
THAT'S IT! THAT'S WHY THE DEMON ISLAND ARC IN VOLUME 19 ENDED SO ABRUPTLY...
THEY TOOK NATE'S WATCH!
IT WAS A SIGN THE SERIES WAS COMING TO AN END!
DURING THIS BATTLE, WE'LL SERVE YOU AS IF YOU WERE OUR MASTER!
IT'S THE DESIRE TO DO EVERYTHING IN YOUR POWER FOR THE SAKE OF YOUR MASTER.
NO! THAT'S NOT IT!
IT'S PROBABLY BECAUSE THE READERS FINALLY GOT FED UP WITH HOW IRRITATING WHISPER IS AND STOPPED READING!
...
CURSES! WHY DOES WHISPER HAVE TO BE SO VERY ANNOYING ?!
NOOOOOO!
HOW DARE YOU...
YOU KNOW, ACTUALLY...

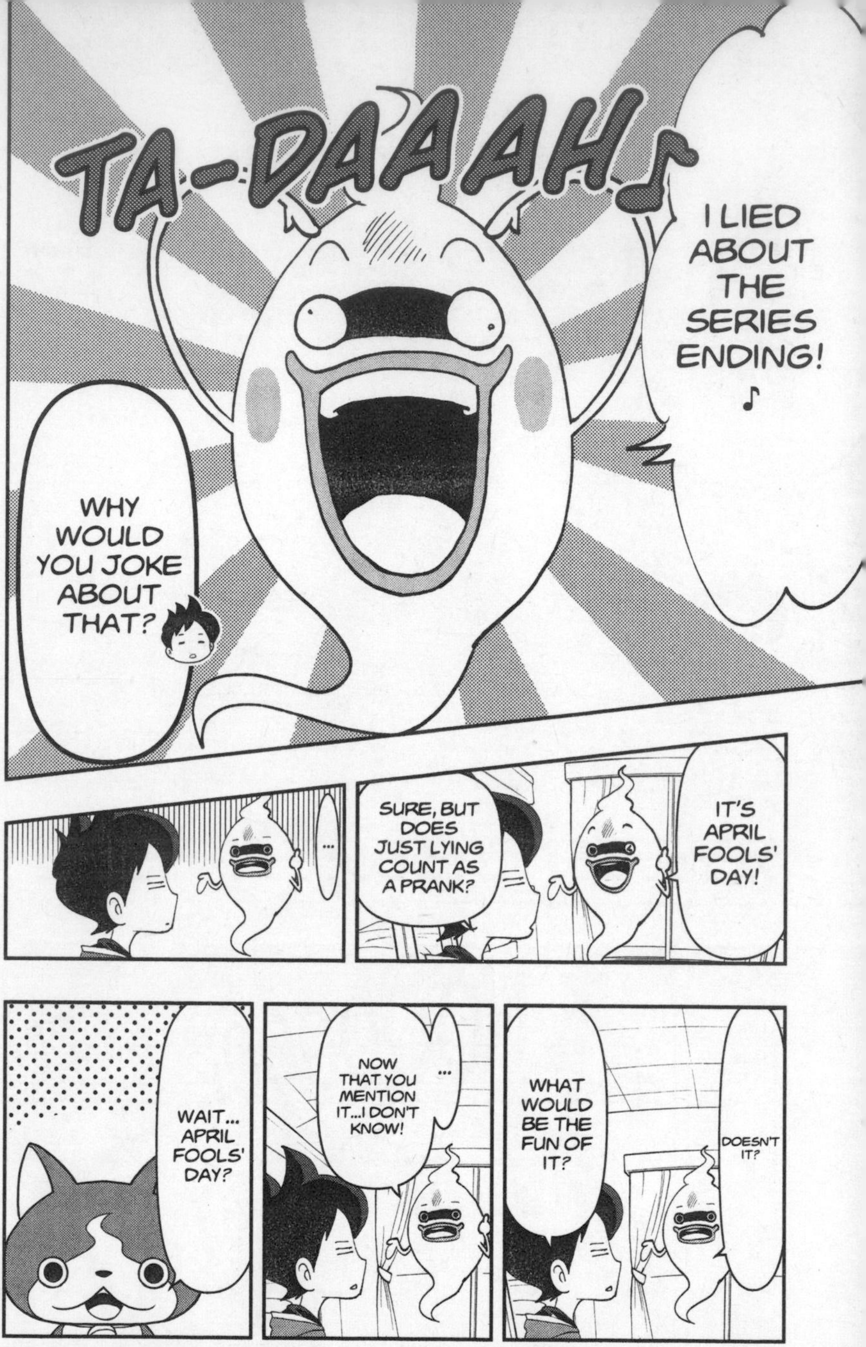
TA-DAAAH♪
I LIED ABOUT THE SERIES ENDING! ♪
WHY WOULD YOU JOKE ABOUT THAT?
IT'S APRIL FOOLS' DAY!
SURE, BUT DOES JUST LYING COUNT AS A PRANK?
...
DOESN'T IT?
WHAT WOULD BE THE FUN OF IT?
...
NOW THAT YOU MENTION IT...I DON'T KNOW!
WAIT... APRIL FOOLS' DAY?

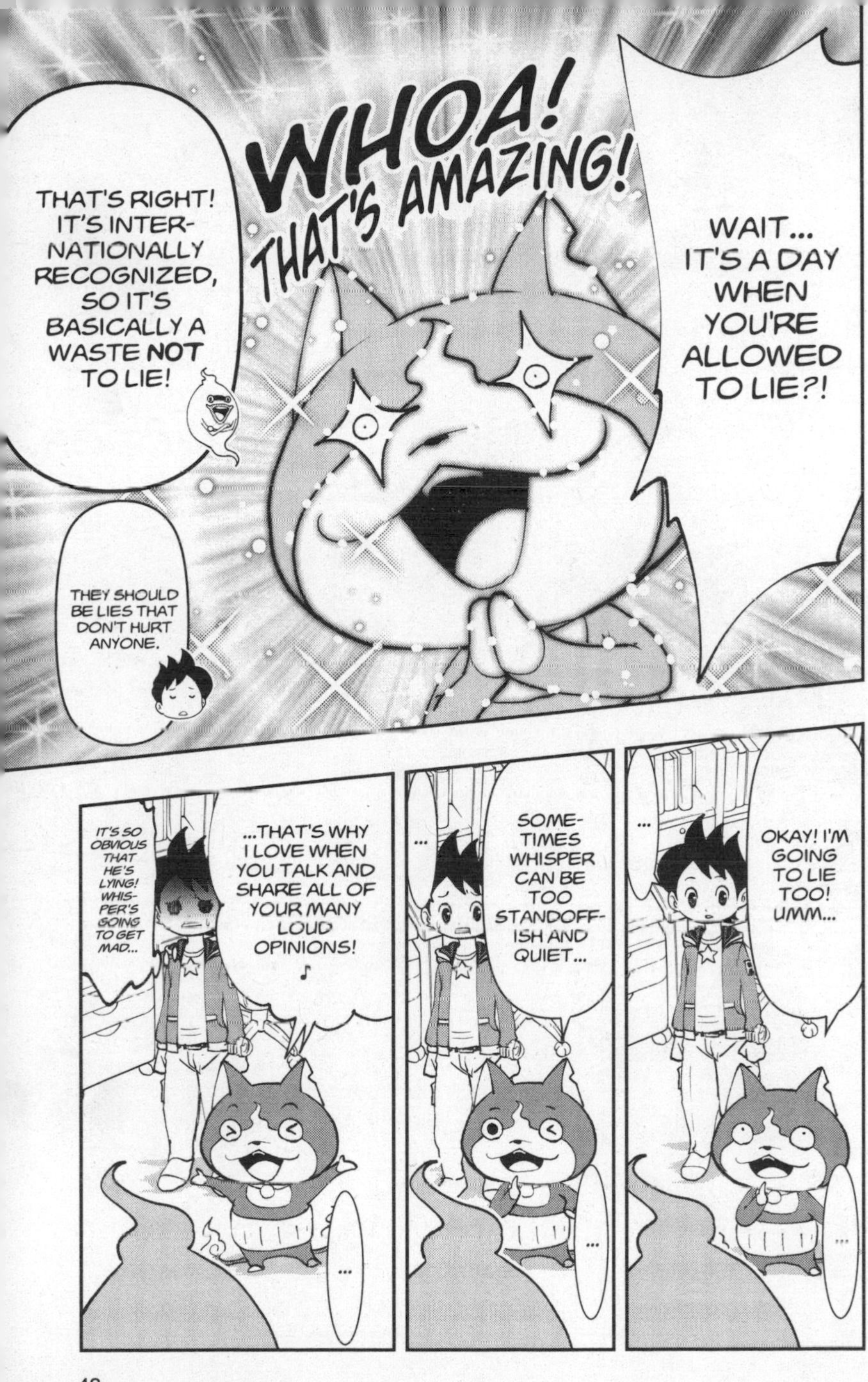
WAIT... IT'S A DAY WHEN YOU'RE ALLOWED TO LIE?!
WHOA! THAT'S AMAZING!
THAT'S RIGHT! IT'S INTER-NATIONALLY RECOGNIZED, SO IT'S BASICALLY A WASTE **NOT** TO LIE!
THEY SHOULD BE LIES THAT DON'T HURT ANYONE.
OKAY! I'M GOING TO LIE TOO! UMM...
...
...
SOME-TIMES WHISPER CAN BE TOO STANDOFF-ISH AND QUIET...
...
...
...THAT'S WHY I LOVE WHEN YOU TALK AND SHARE ALL OF YOUR MANY LOUD OPINIONS! ♪
IT'S SO OBVIOUS THAT HE'S LYING! WHIS-PER'S GOING TO GET MAD...
...

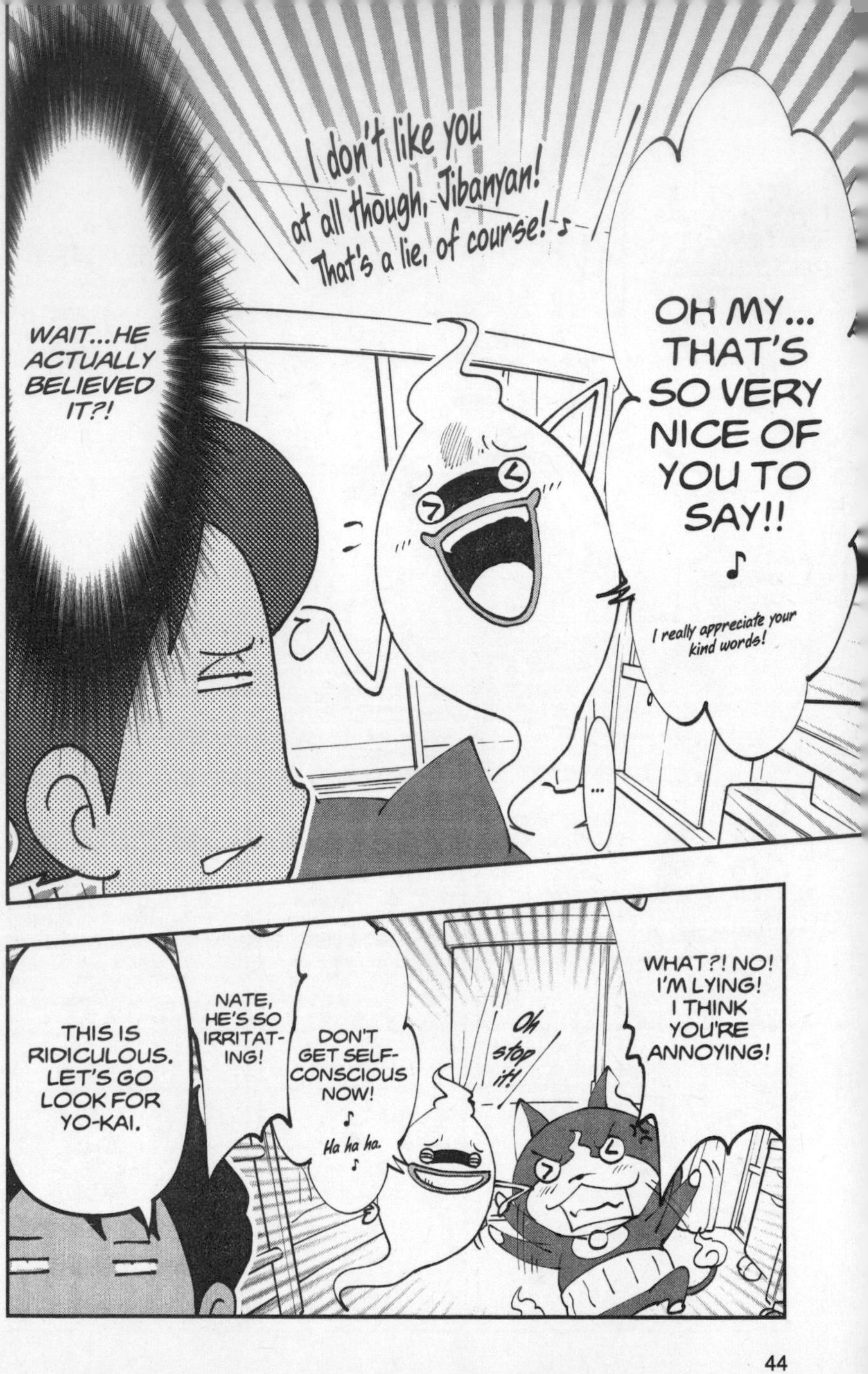

OH MY... THAT'S SO VERY NICE OF YOU TO SAY!! ♪
I really appreciate your kind words!
I don't like you at all though, Jibanyan! That's a lie, of course! ♪
...
WAIT...HE ACTUALLY BELIEVED IT?!
WHAT?! NO! I'M LYING! I THINK YOU'RE ANNOYING!
Oh stop it!
DON'T GET SELF-CONSCIOUS NOW! ♪
Ha ha ha. ♪
NATE, HE'S SO IRRITAT-ING!
THIS IS RIDICULOUS. LET'S GO LOOK FOR YO-KAI.

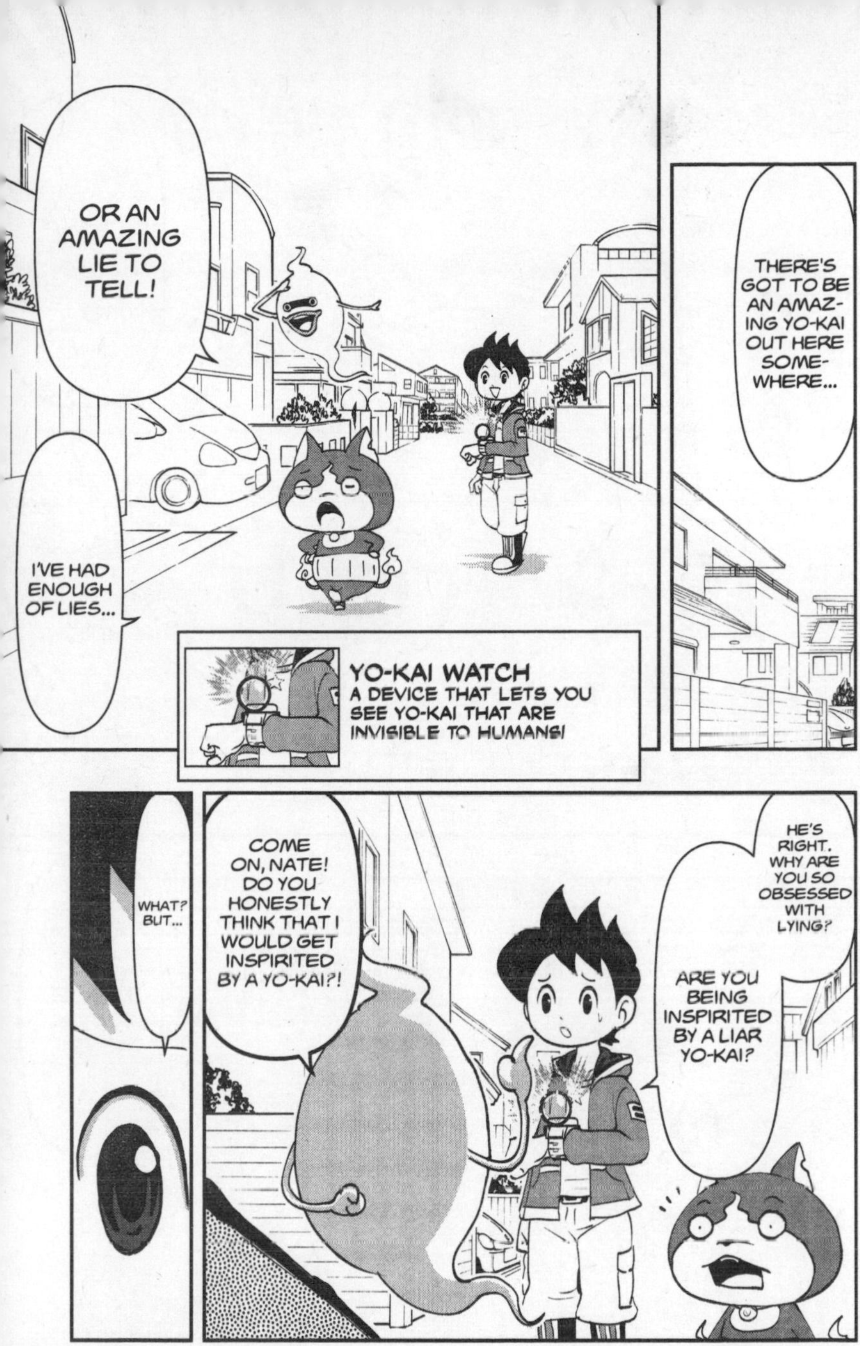
THERE'S GOT TO BE AN AMAZ- ING YO-KAI OUT HERE SOME- WHERE...
OR AN AMAZING LIE TO TELL!
I'VE HAD ENOUGH OF LIES...
YO-KAI WATCH
A DEVICE THAT LETS YOU SEE YO-KAI THAT ARE INVISIBLE TO HUMANS!
HE'S RIGHT. WHY ARE YOU SO OBSESSED WITH LYING?
ARE YOU BEING INSPIRITED BY A LIAR YO-KAI?
COME ON, NATE! DO YOU HONESTLY THINK THAT I WOULD GET INSPIRITED BY A YO-KAI?!
WHAT? BUT...

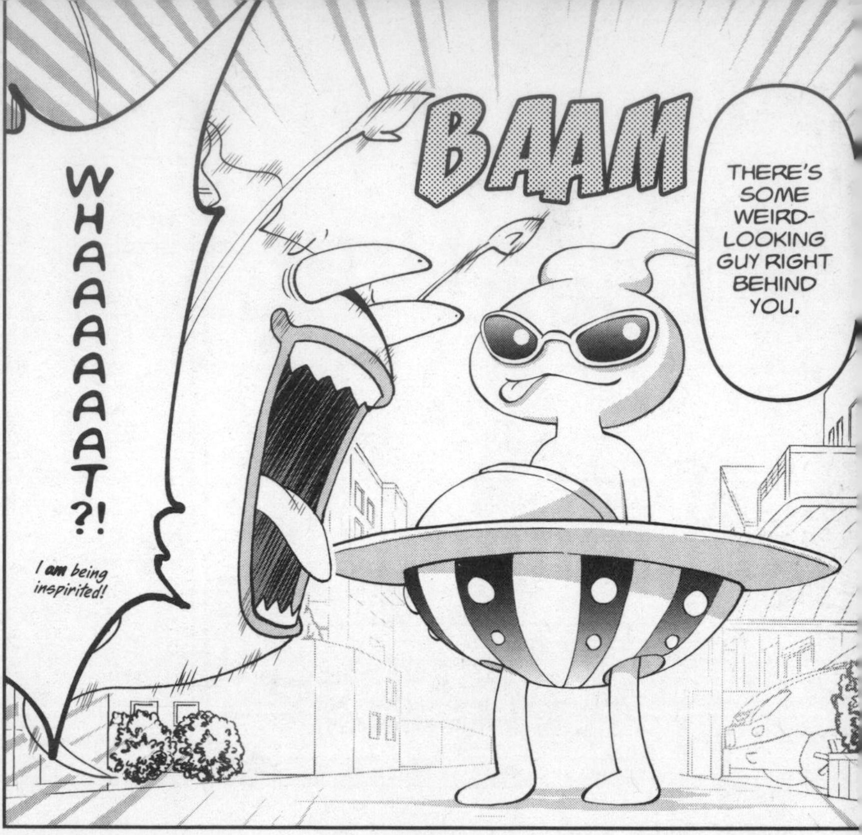
THERE'S SOME WEIRD-LOOKING GUY RIGHT BEHIND YOU.
BAAM
WHAAAAAAAT?!
*I **am** being inspirited!*

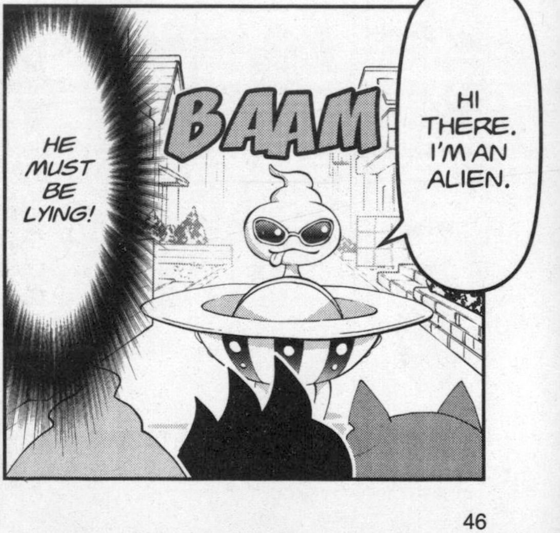
HI THERE. I'M AN ALIEN.
BAAM
HE MUST BE LYING!

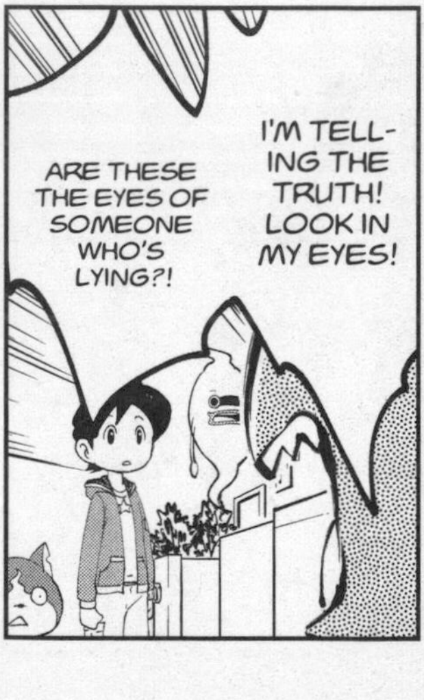
I'M TELL-ING THE TRUTH! LOOK IN MY EYES!
ARE THESE THE EYES OF SOMEONE WHO'S LYING?!

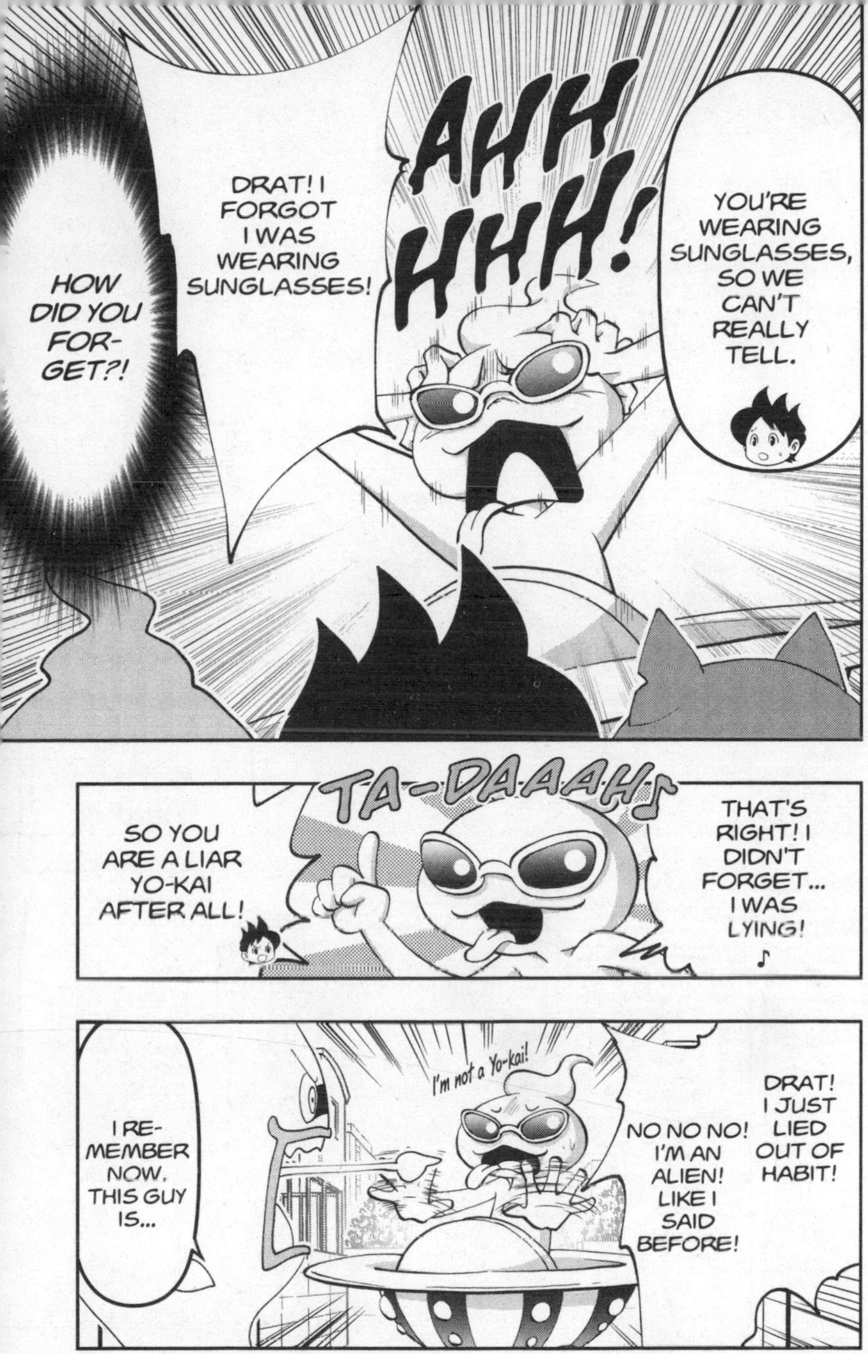
YOU'RE WEARING SUNGLASSES, SO WE CAN'T REALLY TELL.
AHHHHH!
DRAT! I FORGOT I WAS WEARING SUNGLASSES!
HOW DID YOU FOR-GET?!
THAT'S RIGHT! I DIDN'T FORGET... I WAS LYING! ♪
TA-DAAAH♪
SO YOU ARE A LIAR YO-KAI AFTER ALL!
DRAT! I JUST LIED OUT OF HABIT!
NO NO NO! I'M AN ALIEN! LIKE I SAID BEFORE!
I'm not a Yo-kai!
I RE-MEMBER NOW. THIS GUY IS...

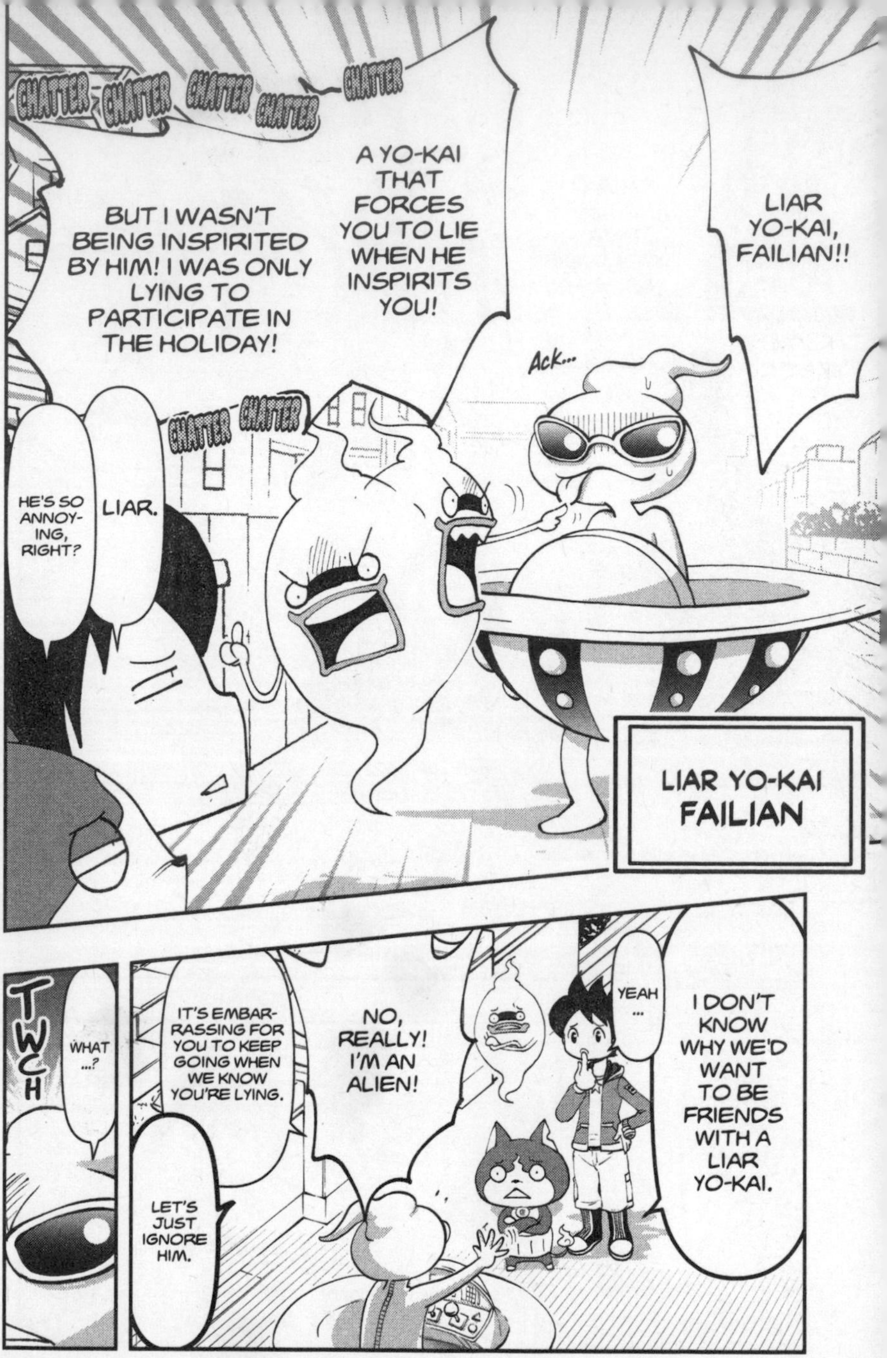
CHATTER CHATTER CHATTER CHATTER CHATTER
LIAR YO-KAI, FAILIAN!!
A YO-KAI THAT FORCES YOU TO LIE WHEN HE INSPIRITS YOU!
BUT I WASN'T BEING INSPIRITED BY HIM! I WAS ONLY LYING TO PARTICIPATE IN THE HOLIDAY!
Ack...
CHATTER CHATTER
LIAR YO-KAI FAILIAN
LIAR.
HE'S SO ANNOY-ING, RIGHT?
I DON'T KNOW WHY WE'D WANT TO BE FRIENDS WITH A LIAR YO-KAI.
YEAH ...
NO, REALLY! I'M AN ALIEN!
IT'S EMBAR-RASSING FOR YOU TO KEEP GOING WHEN WE KNOW YOU'RE LYING.
LET'S JUST IGNORE HIM.
TWCH
WHAT ...?

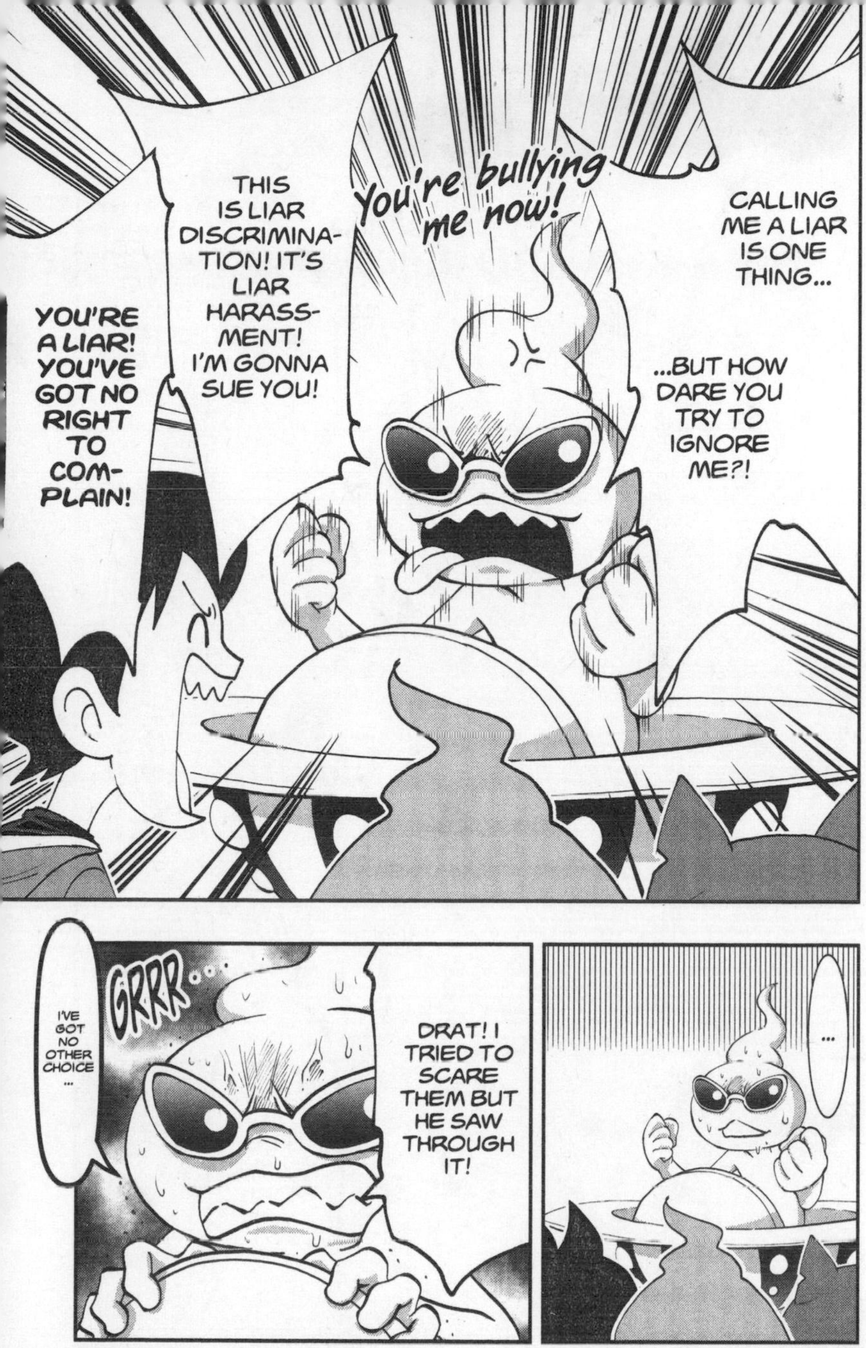
CALLING ME A LIAR IS ONE THING...
...BUT HOW DARE YOU TRY TO IGNORE ME?!
You're bullying me now!
THIS IS LIAR DISCRIMINATION! IT'S LIAR HARASSMENT! I'M GONNA SUE YOU!
YOU'RE A LIAR! YOU'VE GOT NO RIGHT TO COMPLAIN!
...
DRAT! I TRIED TO SCARE THEM BUT HE SAW THROUGH IT!
GRRR...
I'VE GOT NO OTHER CHOICE...

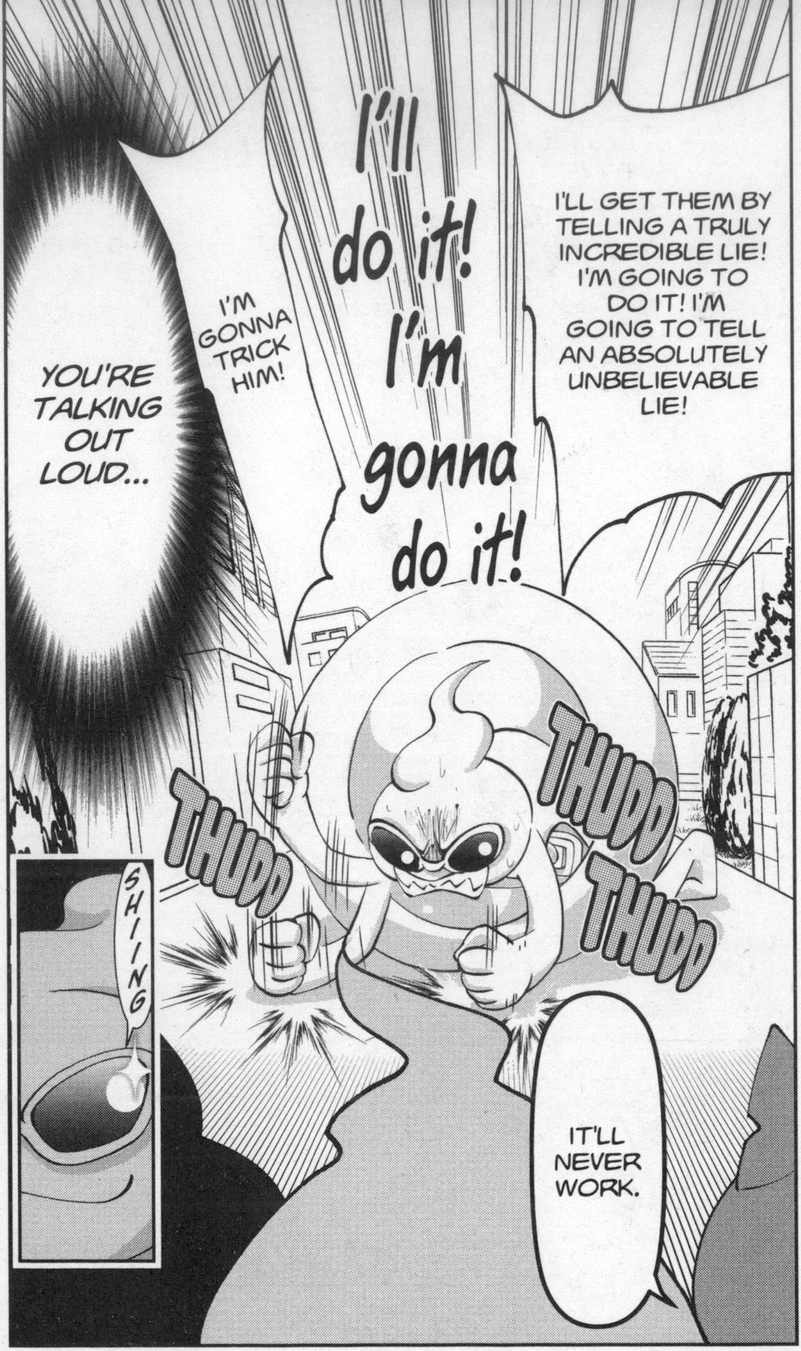
I'LL GET THEM BY TELLING A TRULY INCREDIBLE LIE! I'M GOING TO DO IT! I'M GOING TO TELL AN ABSOLUTELY UNBELIEVABLE LIE!
I'll do it! I'm gonna do it!
I'M GONNA TRICK HIM!
YOU'RE TALKING OUT LOUD...
THUDD THUDD
THUDD
IT'LL NEVER WORK.
SHIING

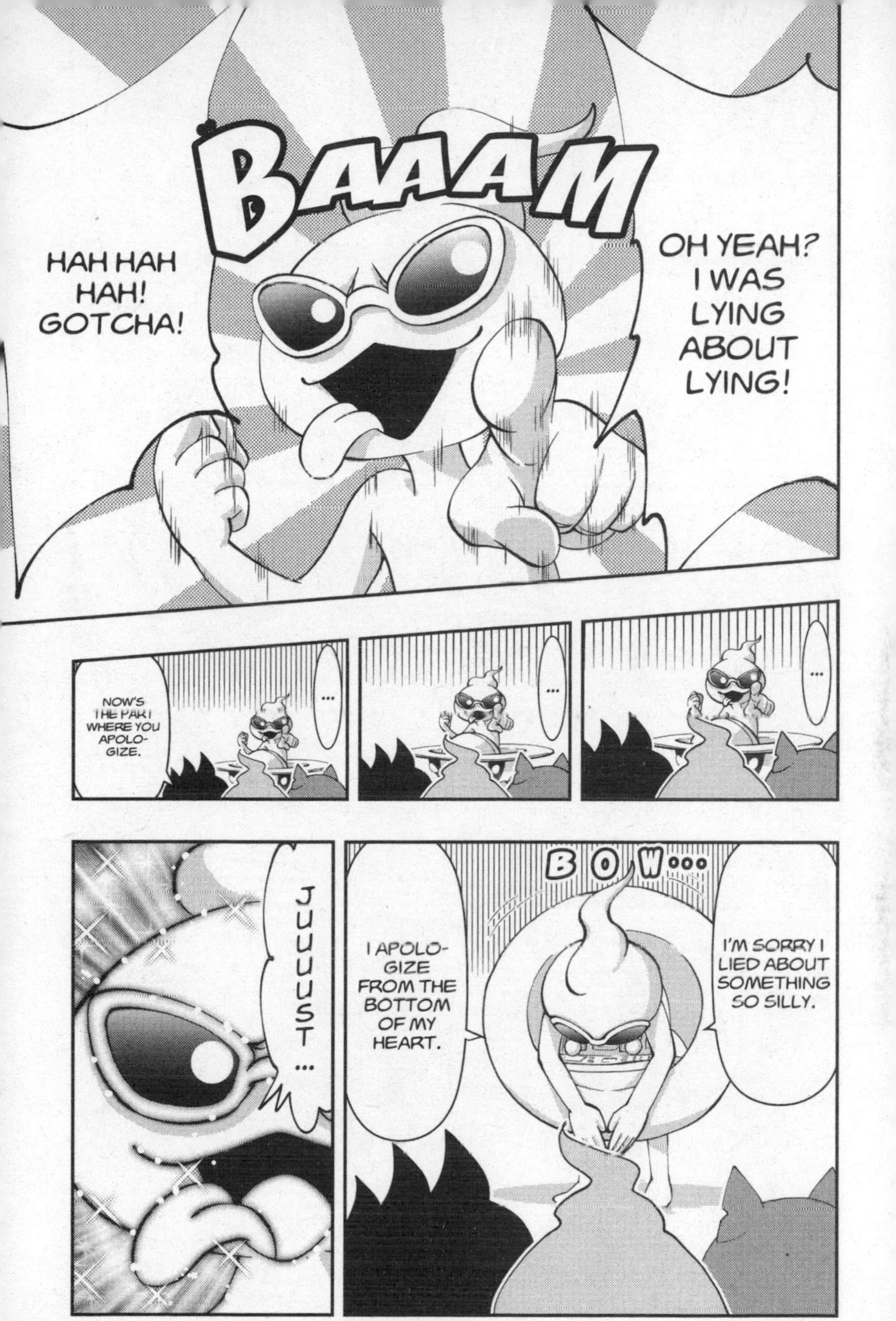
BAAAM
OH YEAH? I WAS LYING ABOUT LYING!
HAH HAH HAH! GOTCHA!
...
...
...
NOW'S THE PART WHERE YOU APOLO-GIZE.
BOW...
I'M SORRY I LIED ABOUT SOMETHING SO SILLY.
I APOLO-GIZE FROM THE BOTTOM OF MY HEART.
JUUUUST ...

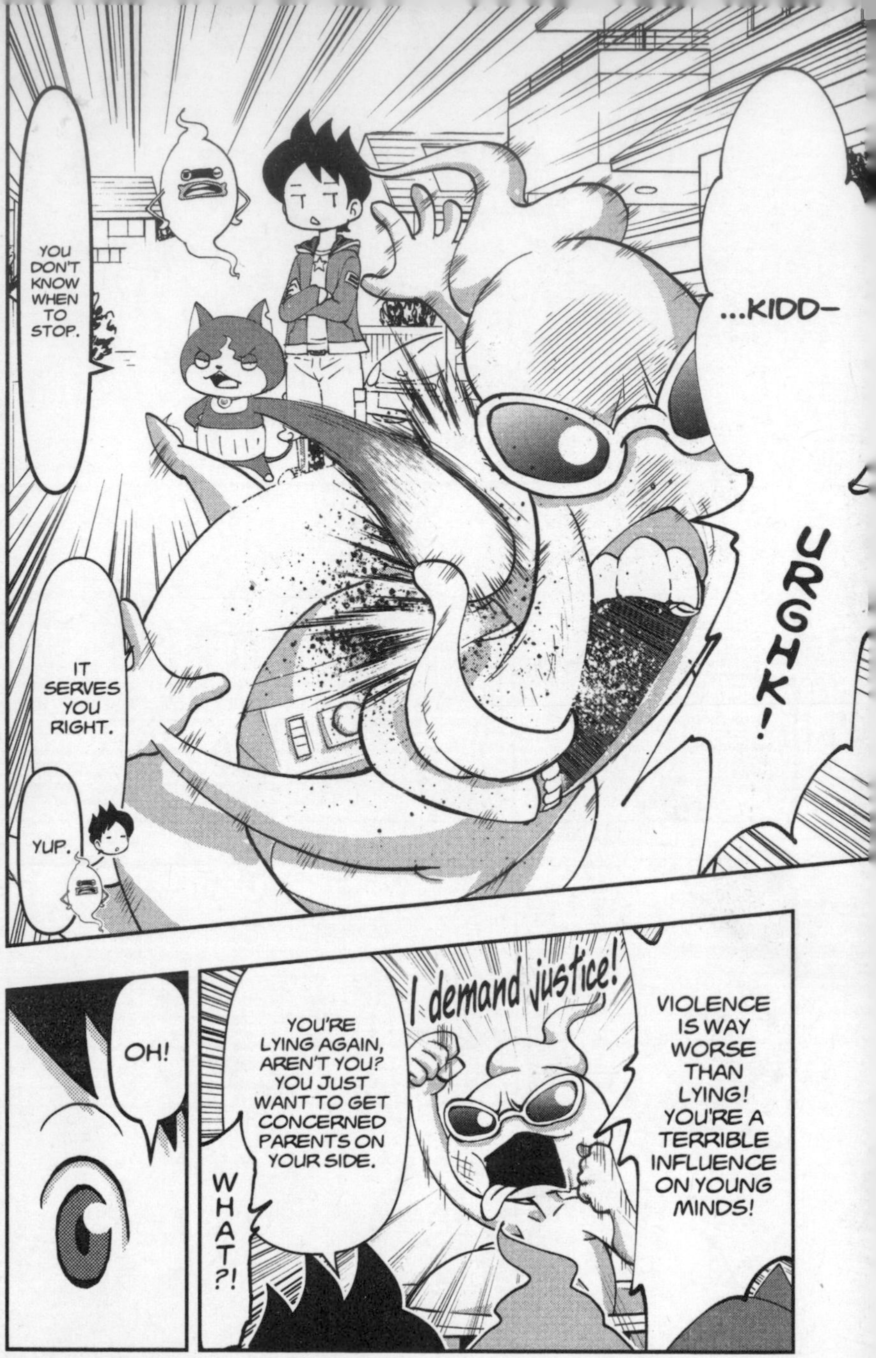

...KIDD-
URGHK!
YOU DON'T KNOW WHEN TO STOP.
IT SERVES YOU RIGHT.
YUP.
VIOLENCE IS WAY WORSE THAN LYING! YOU'RE A TERRIBLE INFLUENCE ON YOUNG MINDS!
I demand justice!
YOU'RE LYING AGAIN, AREN'T YOU? YOU JUST WANT TO GET CONCERNED PARENTS ON YOUR SIDE.
WHAT?!
OH!

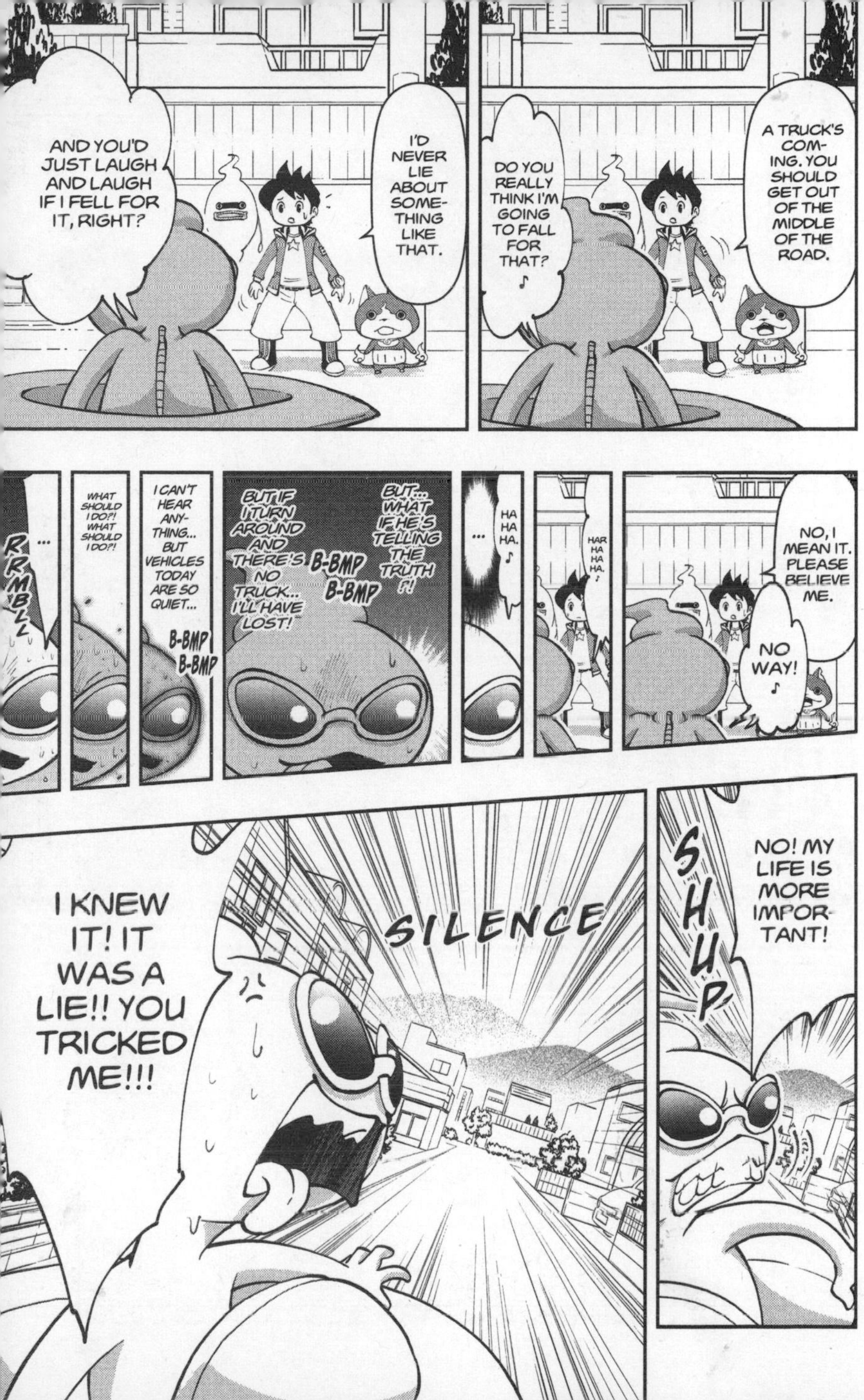
A TRUCK'S COMING. YOU SHOULD GET OUT OF THE MIDDLE OF THE ROAD.
DO YOU REALLY THINK I'M GOING TO FALL FOR THAT? ♪
I'D NEVER LIE ABOUT SOMETHING LIKE THAT.
AND YOU'D JUST LAUGH AND LAUGH IF I FELL FOR IT, RIGHT?
NO, I MEAN IT. PLEASE BELIEVE ME.
NO WAY! ♪
HAR HA HA HA. ♪
HA HA HA. ♪
...
BUT... WHAT IF HE'S TELLING THE TRUTH?!
B-BMP B-BMP
BUT IF I TURN AROUND AND THERE'S NO TRUCK... I'LL HAVE LOST!
I CAN'T HEAR ANYTHING... BUT VEHICLES TODAY ARE SO QUIET...
B-BMP B-BMP
WHAT SHOULD I DO?! WHAT SHOULD I DO?!
...
RRMBLL
NO! MY LIFE IS MORE IMPORTANT!
SHUP
SILENCE
I KNEW IT! IT WAS A LIE!! YOU TRICKED ME!!!

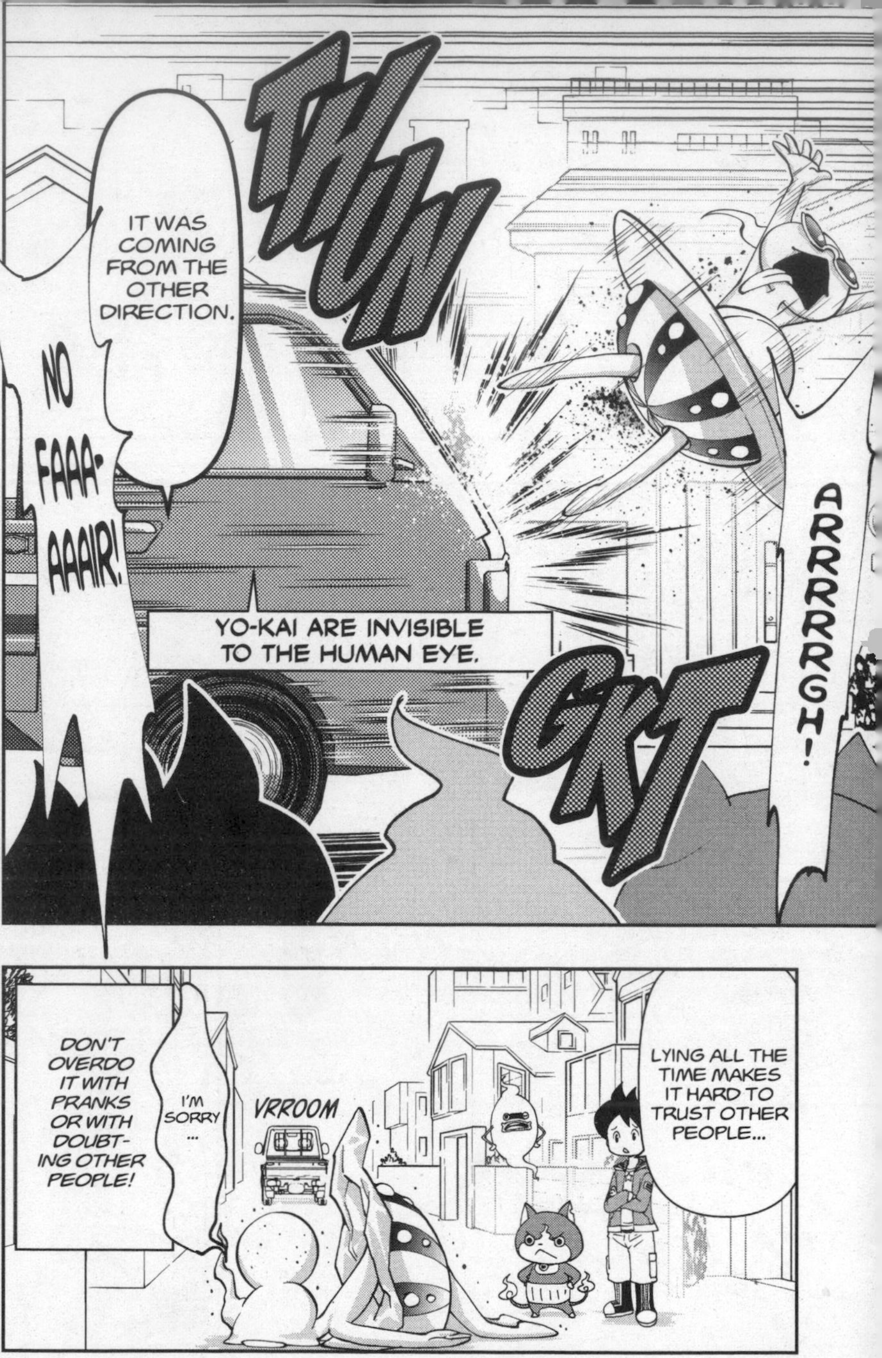
ARRRRRGH!
CKT
THUN
YO-KAI ARE INVISIBLE TO THE HUMAN EYE.
IT WAS COMING FROM THE OTHER DIRECTION.
NO FAAA-AAAIR!
LYING ALL THE TIME MAKES IT HARD TO TRUST OTHER PEOPLE...
VRROOM
I'M SORRY...
DON'T OVERDO IT WITH PRANKS OR WITH DOUBT-ING OTHER PEOPLE!

CHAPTER 210
SLEEPY YO-KAI SLUMBERHOG

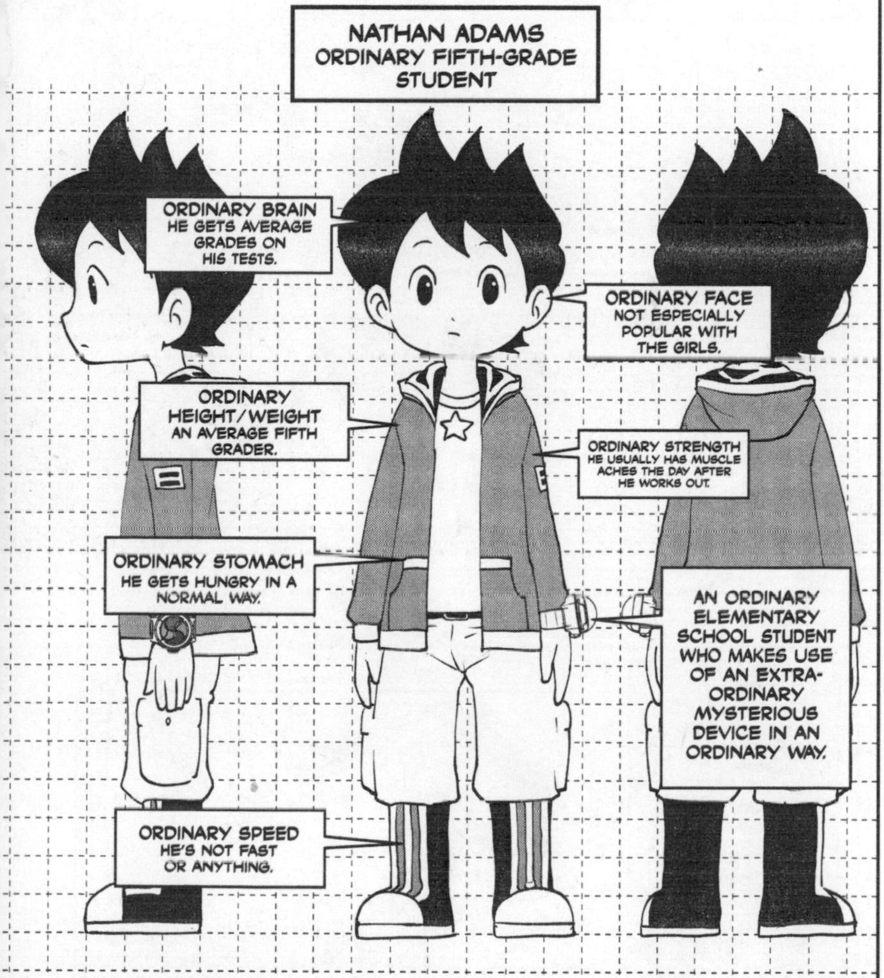
NATHAN ADAMS ORDINARY FIFTH-GRADE STUDENT
ORDINARY BRAIN HE GETS AVERAGE GRADES ON HIS TESTS.
ORDINARY FACE NOT ESPECIALLY POPULAR WITH THE GIRLS.
ORDINARY HEIGHT/WEIGHT AN AVERAGE FIFTH GRADER.
ORDINARY STRENGTH HE USUALLY HAS MUSCLE ACHES THE DAY AFTER HE WORKS OUT.
ORDINARY STOMACH HE GETS HUNGRY IN A NORMAL WAY.
AN ORDINARY ELEMENTARY SCHOOL STUDENT WHO MAKES USE OF AN EXTRA-ORDINARY MYSTERIOUS DEVICE IN AN ORDINARY WAY.
ORDINARY SPEED HE'S NOT FAST OR ANYTHING.

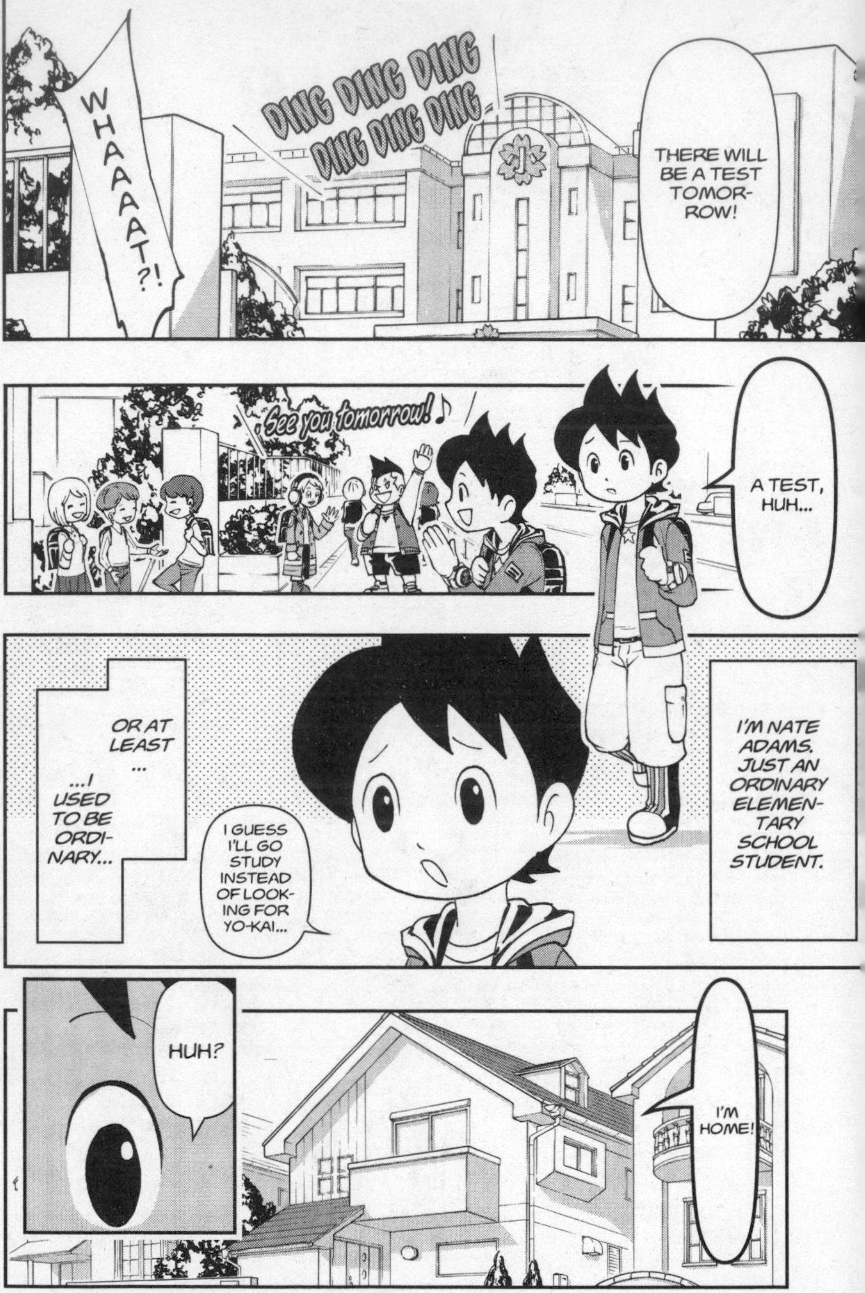
THERE WILL BE A TEST TOMORROW!
DING DING DING DING DING DING
WHAAAAT?!
A TEST, HUH...
See you tomorrow!♪
I'M NATE ADAMS. JUST AN ORDINARY ELEMENTARY SCHOOL STUDENT.
I GUESS I'LL GO STUDY INSTEAD OF LOOKING FOR YO-KAI...
OR AT LEAST ... ...I USED TO BE ORDINARY...
I'M HOME!
HUH?

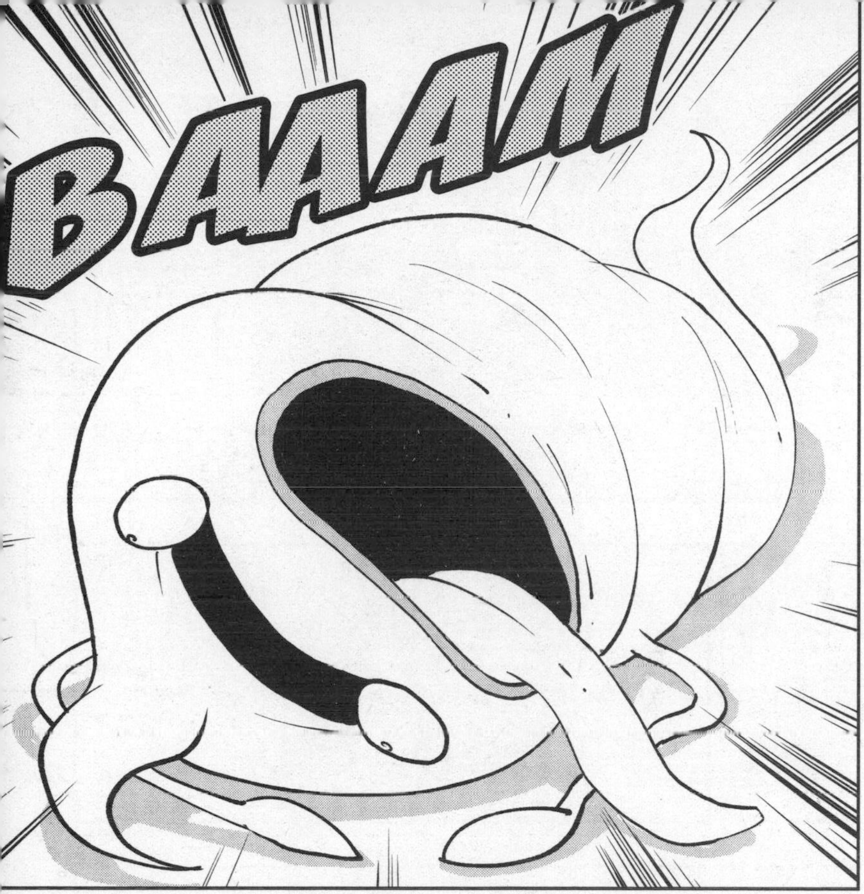
BAAAM

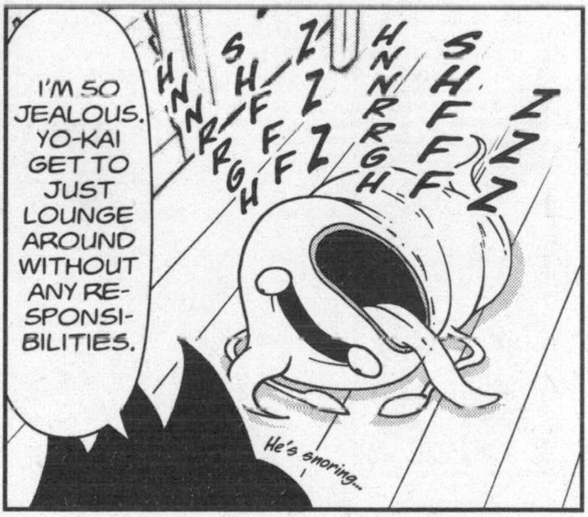
HNNRRGH
SHFFF
ZZZ
HNNRRGH
SHFFF
ZZZ
I'M SO JEALOUS. YO-KAI GET TO JUST LOUNGE AROUND WITHOUT ANY RESPONSIBILITIES.
He's snoring...

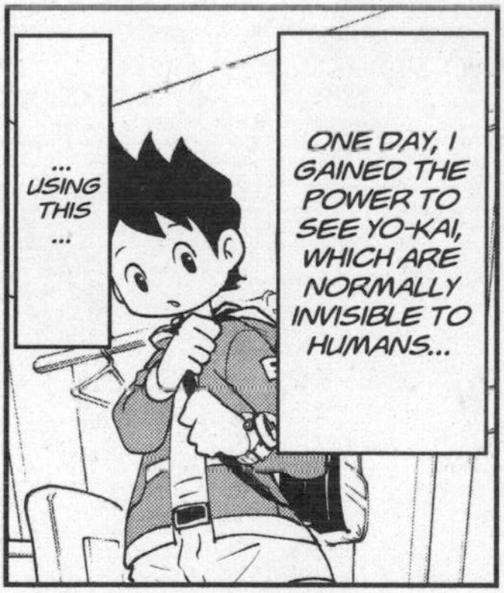
ONE DAY, I GAINED THE POWER TO SEE YO-KAI, WHICH ARE NORMALLY INVISIBLE TO HUMANS...
... USING THIS ...

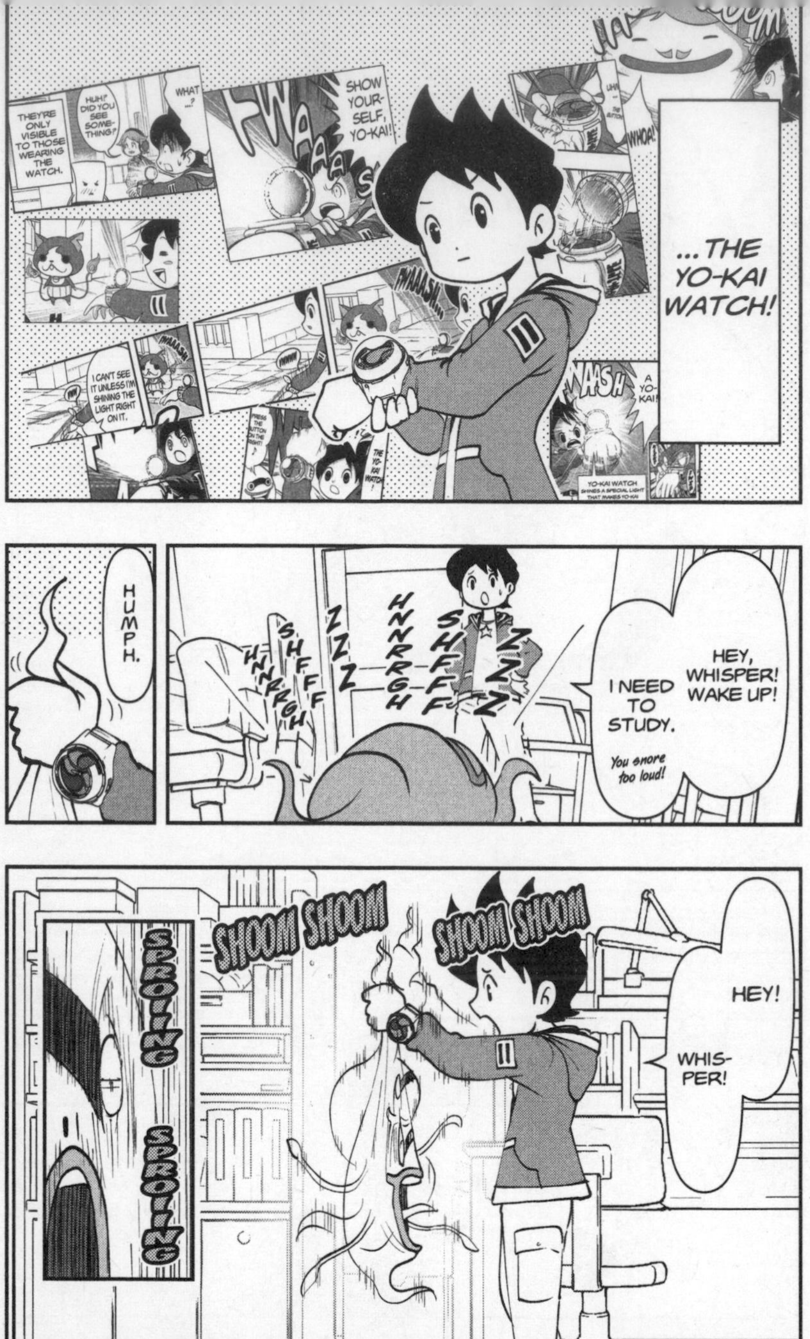
...THE YO-KAI WATCH!
WHOA!
A YO-KAI!
YO-KAI WATCH SHINES A SPECIAL LIGHT THAT MAKES YO-KAI
SHOW YOUR-SELF, YO-KAI!!
WHAT ...?
HUH? DID YOU SEE SOME-THING?
THEY'RE ONLY VISIBLE TO THOSE WEARING THE WATCH.
I CAN'T SEE IT UNLESS I'M SHINING THE LIGHT RIGHT ON IT.
THE YO-KAI WATCH!
HEY, WHISPER! WAKE UP!
I NEED TO STUDY.
You snore too loud!
HNNRRGH SHFFF ZZZ
HNNRRGH SHFFF ZZZ
HUMPH.
HEY!
WHIS-PER!
SHOOM SHOOM
SHOOM SHOOM
SPROING
SPROING

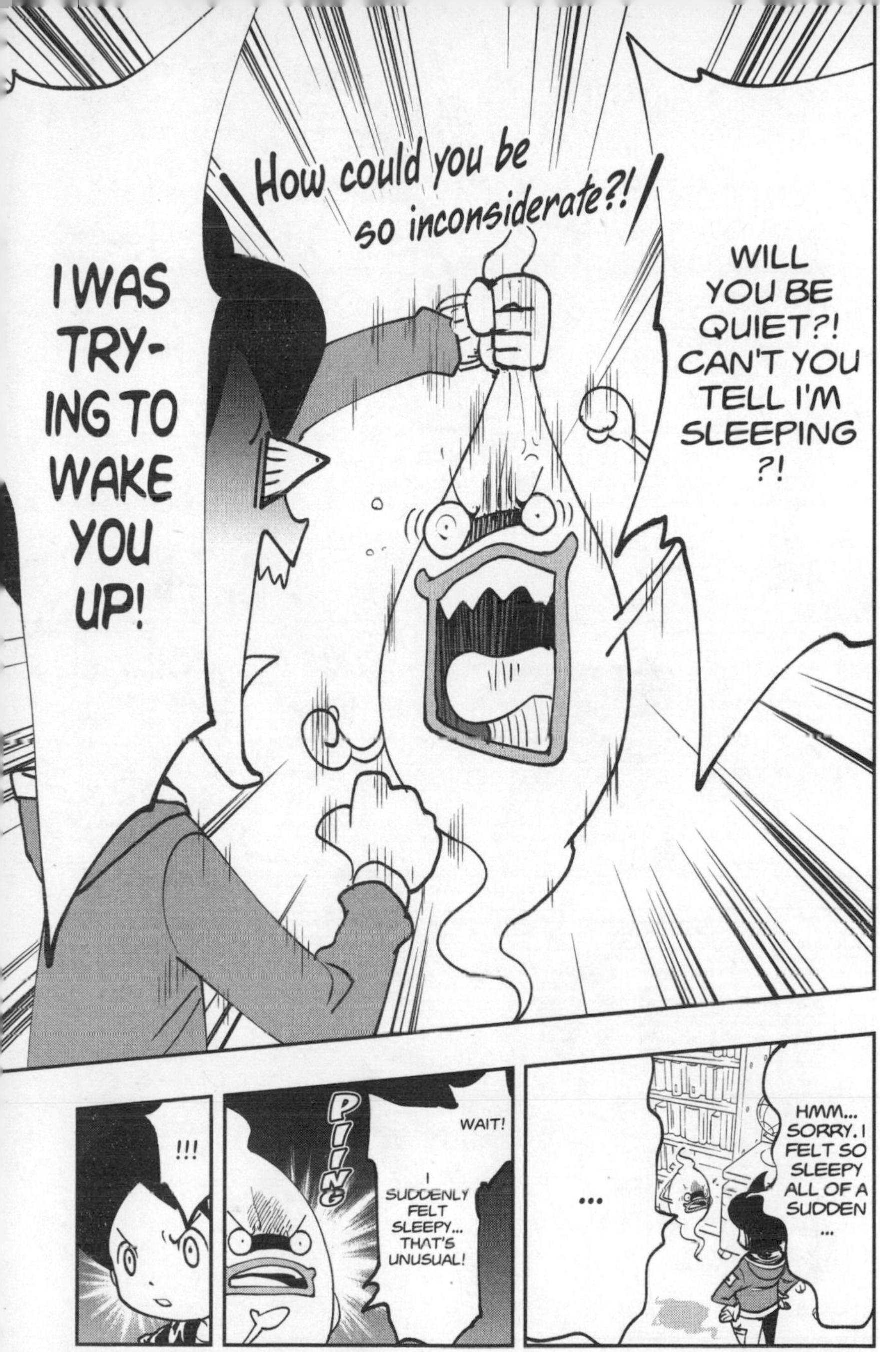
WILL YOU BE QUIET?! CAN'T YOU TELL I'M SLEEPING ?!
How could you be so inconsiderate?!
I WAS TRY-ING TO WAKE YOU UP!
HMM... SORRY. I FELT SO SLEEPY ALL OF A SUDDEN ...
...
WAIT!
PIING
I SUDDENLY FELT SLEEPY... THAT'S UNUSUAL!
!!!

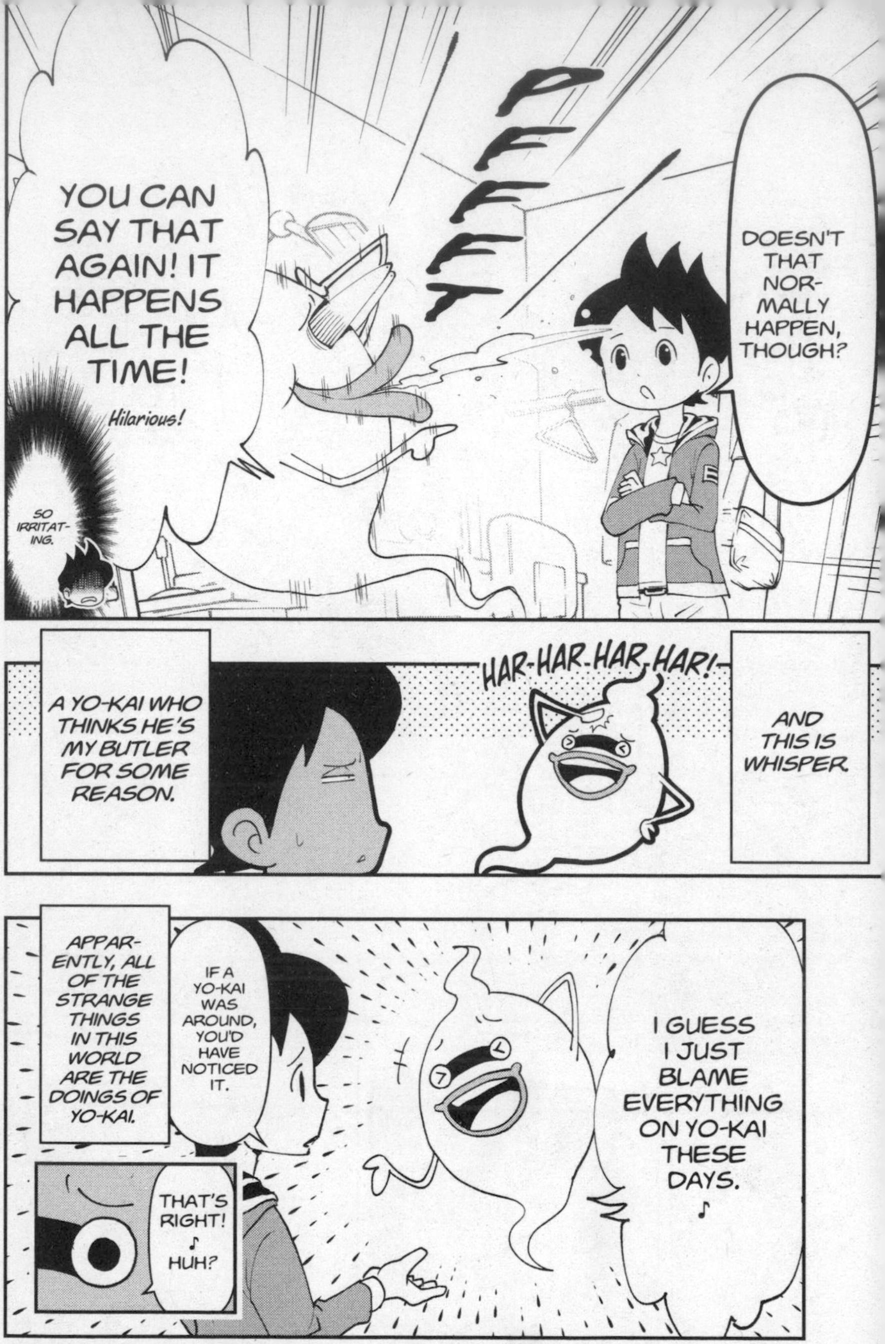
DOESN'T THAT NORMALLY HAPPEN, THOUGH?
PFFFT
YOU CAN SAY THAT AGAIN! IT HAPPENS ALL THE TIME!
Hilarious!
SO IRRITATING.
AND THIS IS WHISPER.
HAR-HAR-HAR-HAR!
A YO-KAI WHO THINKS HE'S MY BUTLER FOR SOME REASON.
I GUESS I JUST BLAME EVERYTHING ON YO-KAI THESE DAYS. ♪
IF A YO-KAI WAS AROUND, YOU'D HAVE NOTICED IT.
APPARENTLY, ALL OF THE STRANGE THINGS IN THIS WORLD ARE THE DOINGS OF YO-KAI.
THAT'S RIGHT! ♪ HUH?

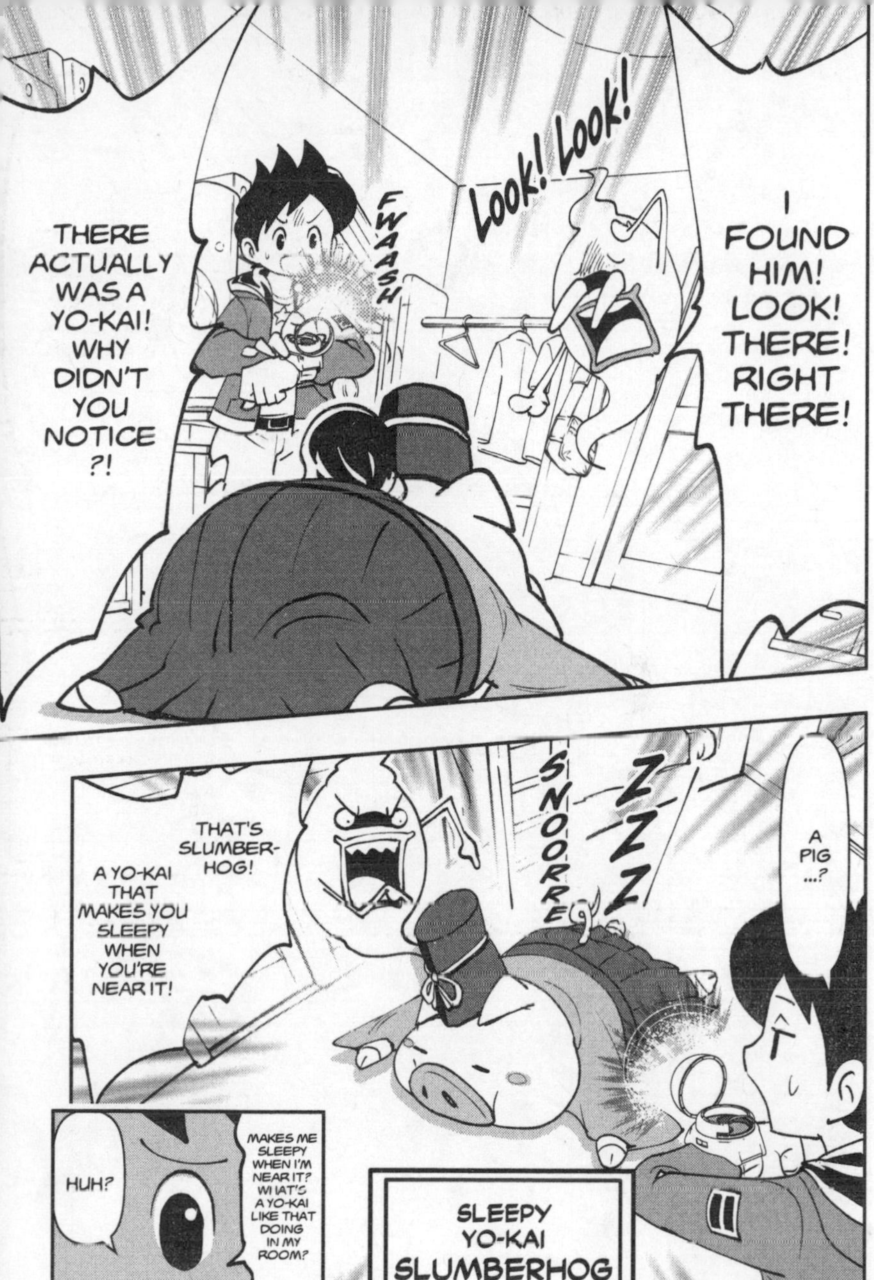
I FOUND HIM! LOOK! THERE! RIGHT THERE!
LOOK! LOOK!
FWAASH
THERE ACTUALLY WAS A YO-KAI! WHY DIDN'T YOU NOTICE ?!
A PIG ...?
SNOORRE
ZZZ
THAT'S SLUMBER-HOG!
A YO-KAI THAT MAKES YOU SLEEPY WHEN YOU'RE NEAR IT!
SLEEPY YO-KAI SLUMBERHOG
MAKES ME SLEEPY WHEN I'M NEAR IT? WHAT'S A YO-KAI LIKE THAT DOING IN MY ROOM?
HUH?

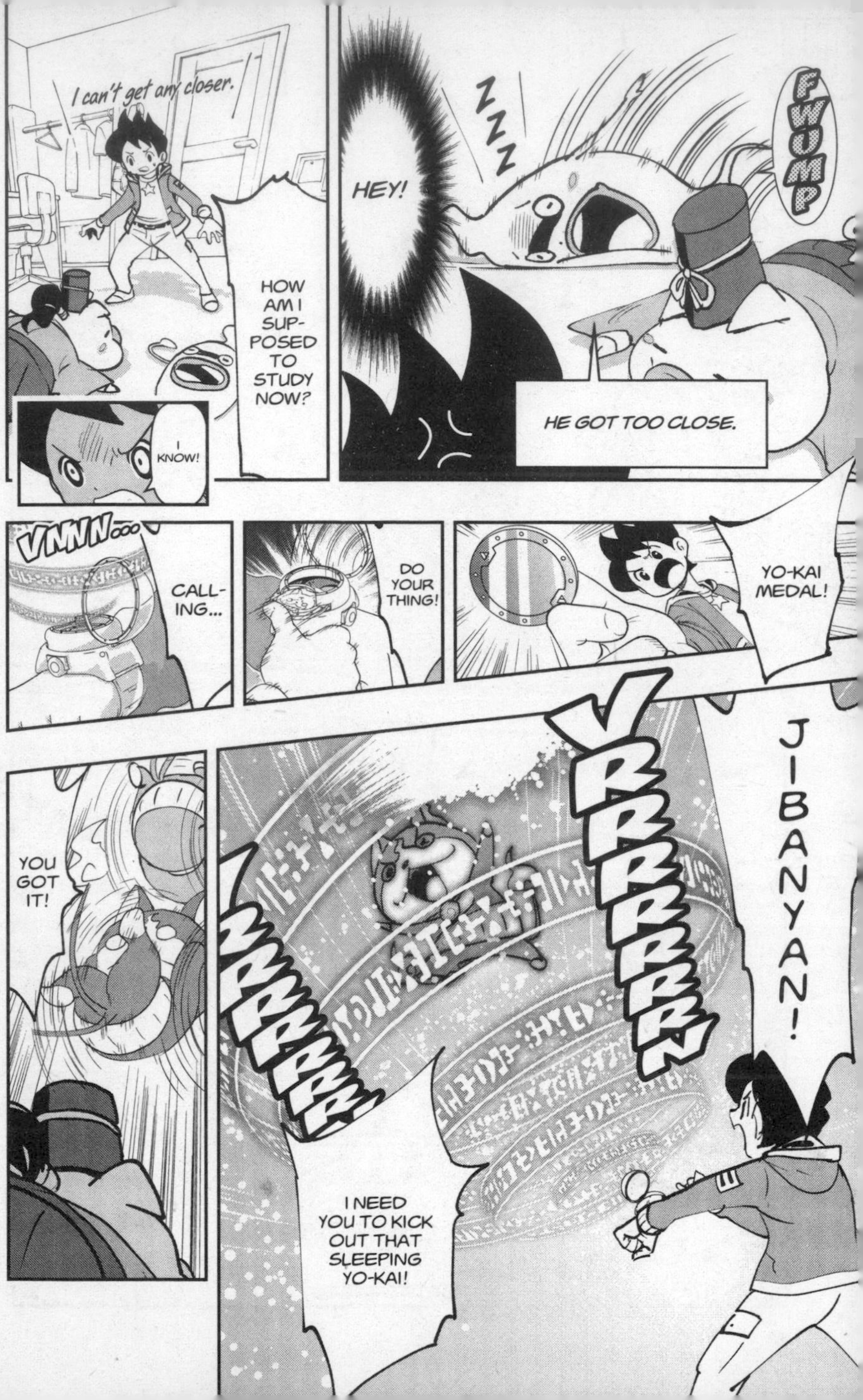
FWUMP
ZZZ
HEY!
HE GOT TOO CLOSE.
I can't get any closer.
HOW AM I SUP-POSED TO STUDY NOW?
I KNOW!
YO-KAI MEDAL!
DO YOUR THING!
VNNN...
CALLING...
JIBANYAN!
VRRRRRRN
I NEED YOU TO KICK OUT THAT SLEEPING YO-KAI!
YOU GOT IT!

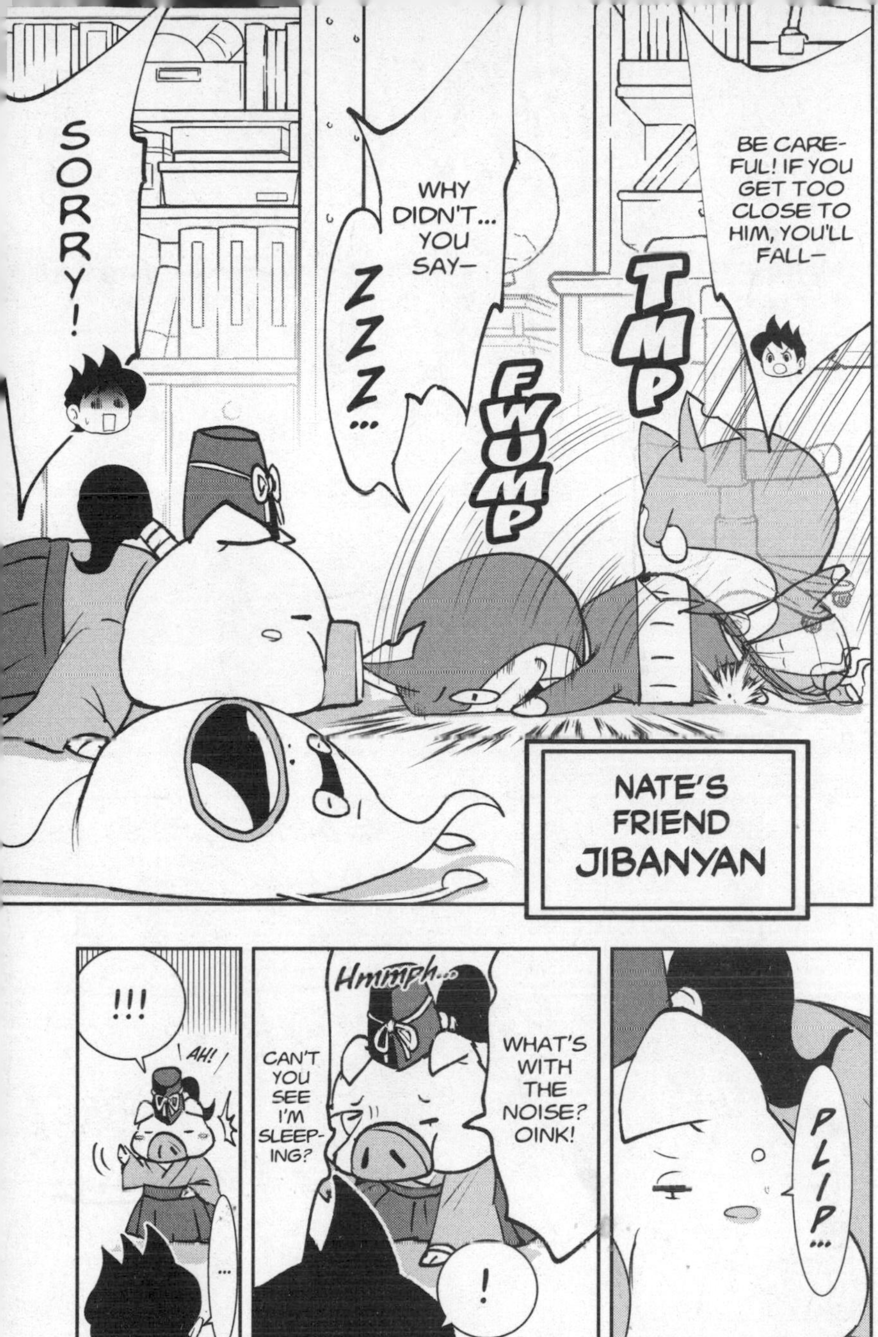
BE CAREFUL! IF YOU GET TOO CLOSE TO HIM, YOU'LL FALL—
TMP
WHY DIDN'T... YOU SAY—
FWUMP
ZZZ...
SORRY!
NATE'S FRIEND JIBANYAN
PLIP...
Hmmph...
WHAT'S WITH THE NOISE? OINK!
CAN'T YOU SEE I'M SLEEPING?
!
!!!
AH!
...

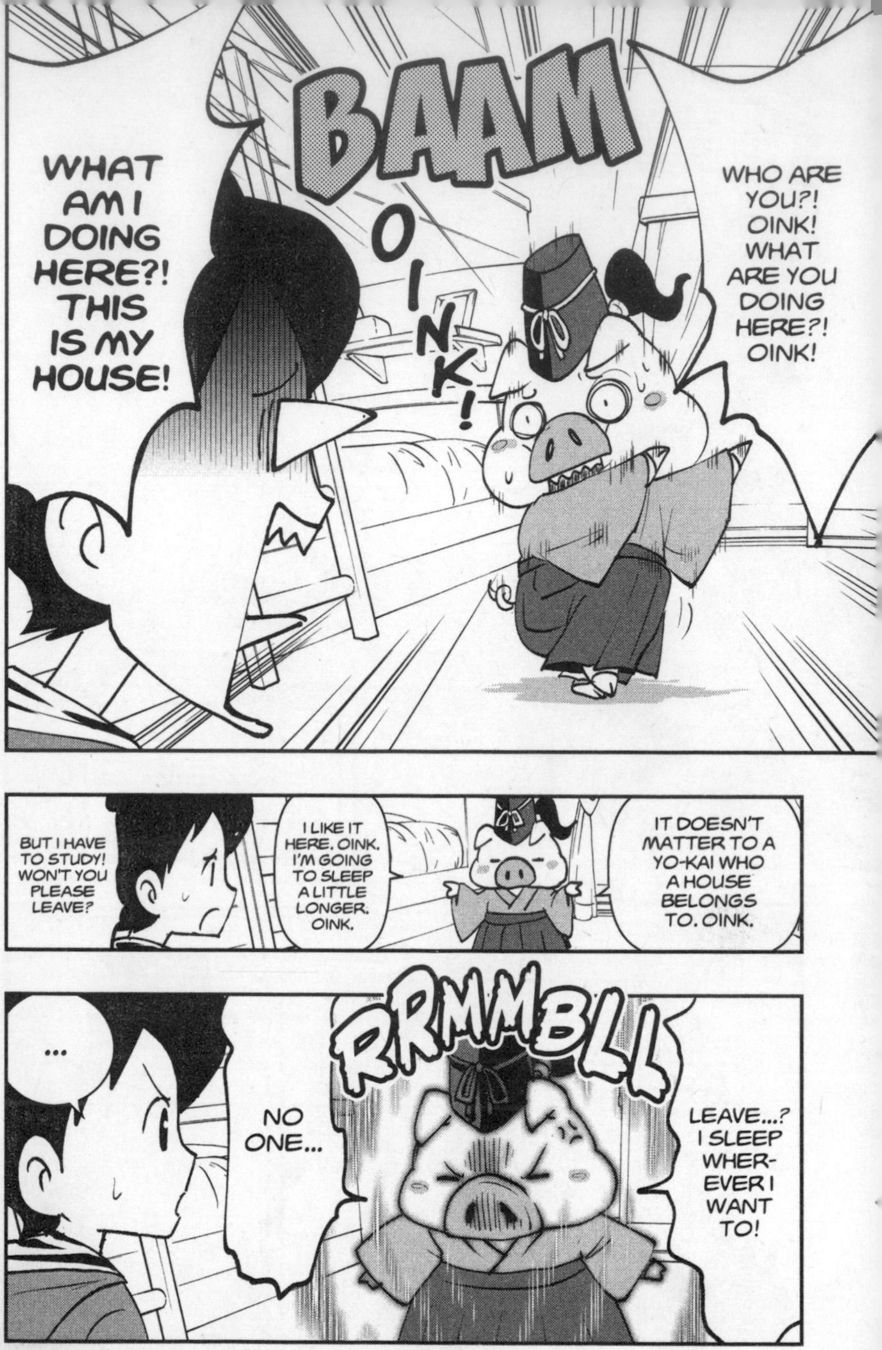
WHO ARE YOU?! OINK! WHAT ARE YOU DOING HERE?! OINK!
BAAM
OINK!
WHAT AM I DOING HERE?! THIS IS MY HOUSE!
IT DOESN'T MATTER TO A YO-KAI WHO A HOUSE BELONGS TO. OINK.
I LIKE IT HERE. OINK. I'M GOING TO SLEEP A LITTLE LONGER. OINK.
BUT I HAVE TO STUDY! WON'T YOU PLEASE LEAVE?
LEAVE...? I SLEEP WHER-EVER I WANT TO!
RRMMBLL
NO ONE...
...

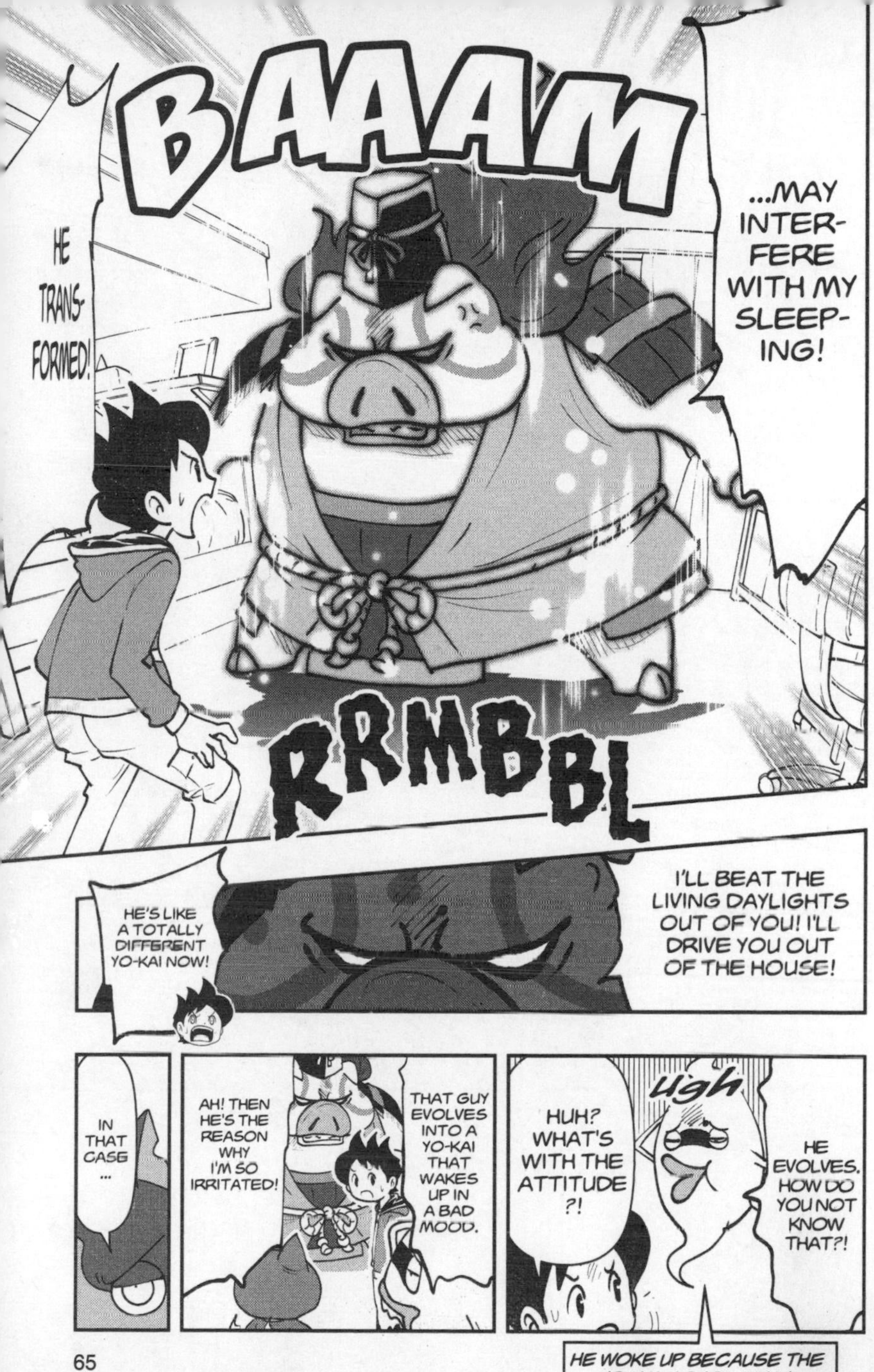
...MAY INTERFERE WITH MY SLEEPING!
BAAAM
HE TRANSFORMED!
RRMBBL
I'LL BEAT THE LIVING DAYLIGHTS OUT OF YOU! I'LL DRIVE YOU OUT OF THE HOUSE!
HE'S LIKE A TOTALLY DIFFERENT YO-KAI NOW!
ugh
HE EVOLVES. HOW DO YOU NOT KNOW THAT?!
HUH? WHAT'S WITH THE ATTITUDE?!
HE WOKE UP BECAUSE THE YO-KAI MOVED AWAY.
THAT GUY EVOLVES INTO A YO-KAI THAT WAKES UP IN A BAD MOOD.
AH! THEN HE'S THE REASON WHY I'M SO IRRITATED!
IN THAT CASE ...

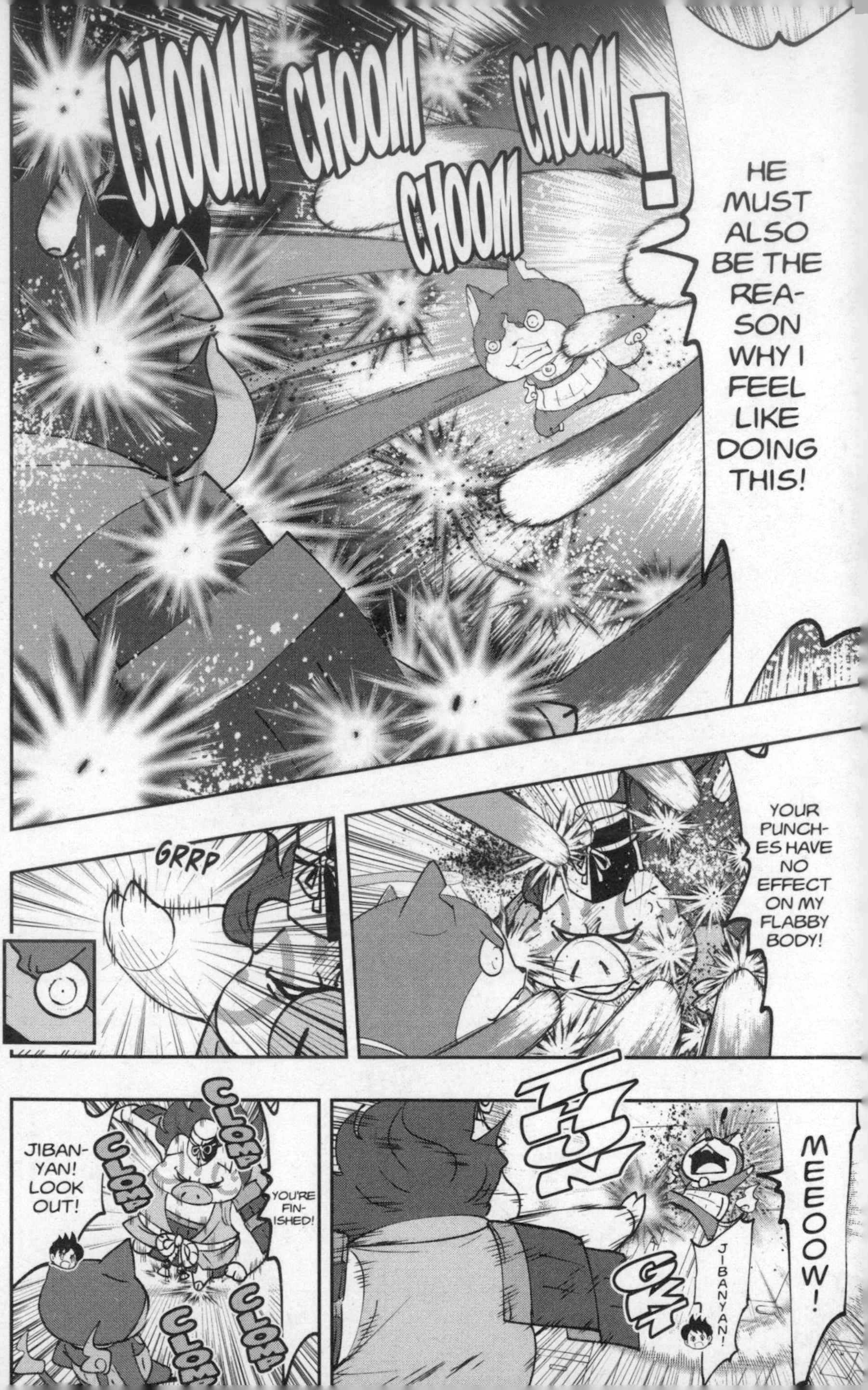
CHOOM CHOOM CHOOM CHOOM!
HE MUST ALSO BE THE REASON WHY I FEEL LIKE DOING THIS!
YOUR PUNCHES HAVE NO EFFECT ON MY FLABBY BODY!
GRRP
MEEEOOW!
JIBANYAN!
JIBANYAN! LOOK OUT!
YOU'RE FINISHED!

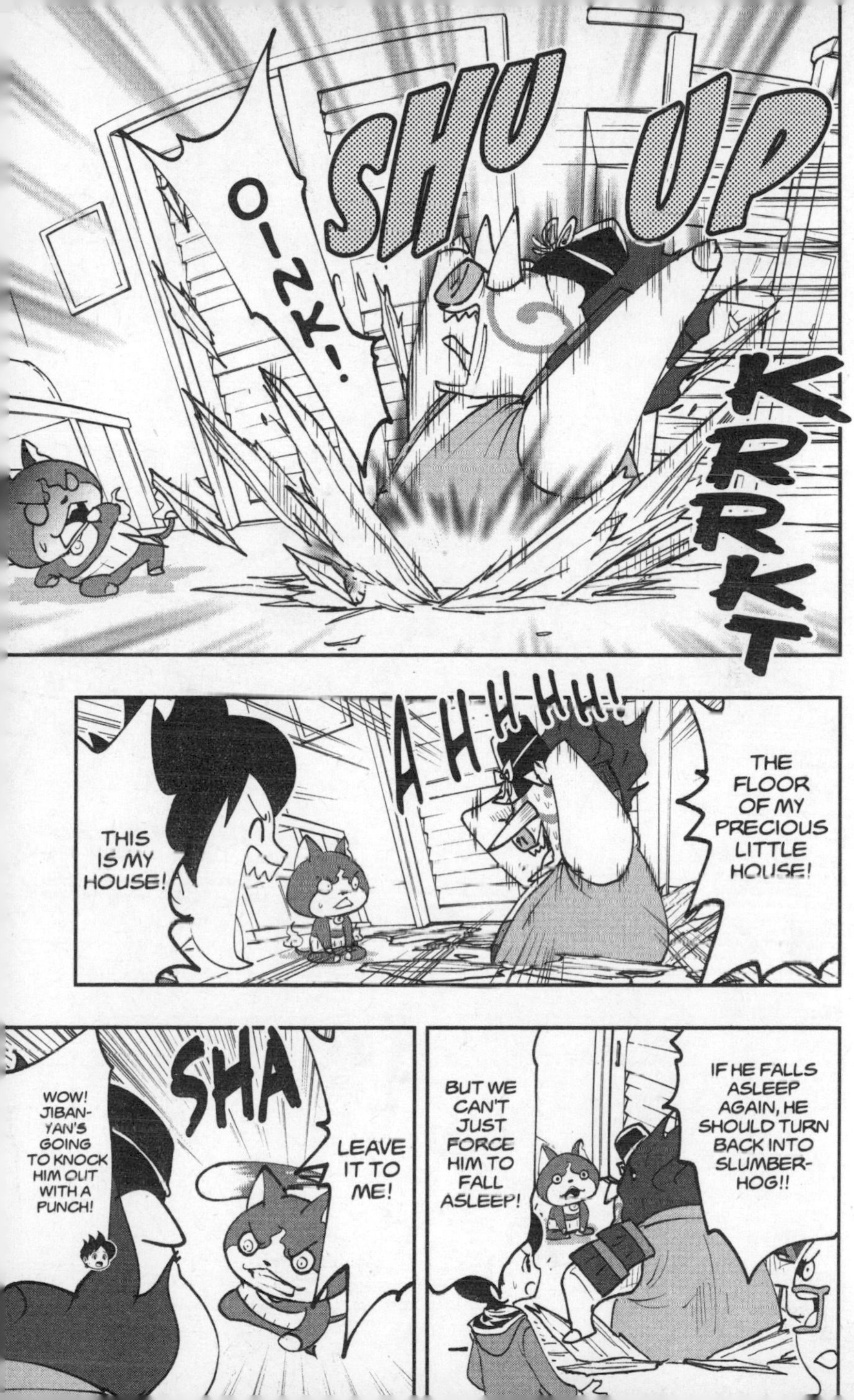
SHU UP
OINK!
KRRKT
THE FLOOR OF MY PRECIOUS LITTLE HOUSE!
AHHHHH!
THIS IS MY HOUSE!
IF HE FALLS ASLEEP AGAIN, HE SHOULD TURN BACK INTO SLUMBER-HOG!!
BUT WE CAN'T JUST FORCE HIM TO FALL ASLEEP!
SHA
LEAVE IT TO ME!
WOW! JIBAN-YAN'S GOING TO KNOCK HIM OUT WITH A PUNCH!

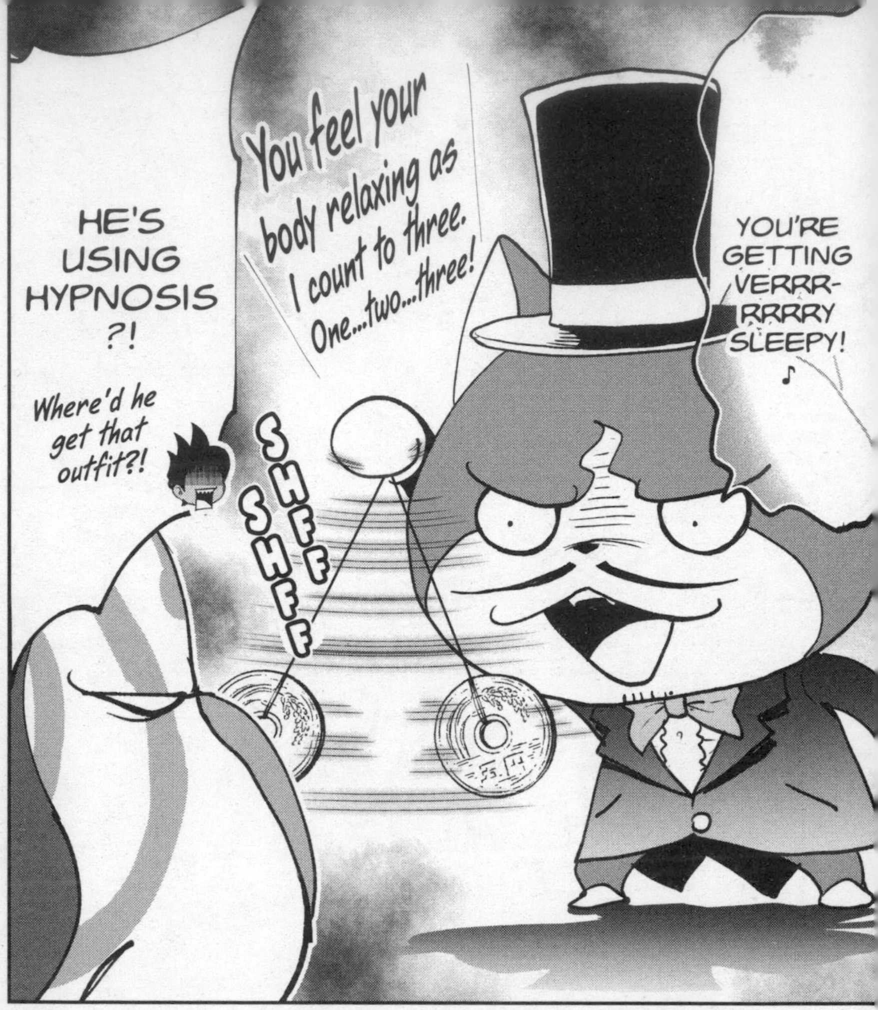
YOU'RE GETTING VERRR-RRRRY SLEEPY! ♪
You feel your body relaxing as I count to three. One...two...three!
SHFF SHFF
HE'S USING HYPNOSIS ?!
Where'd he get that outfit?!

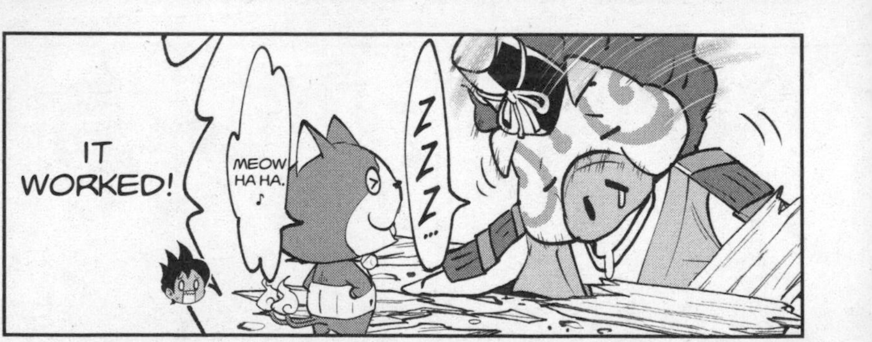
ZZZ...
MEOW HA HA. ♪
IT WORKED!

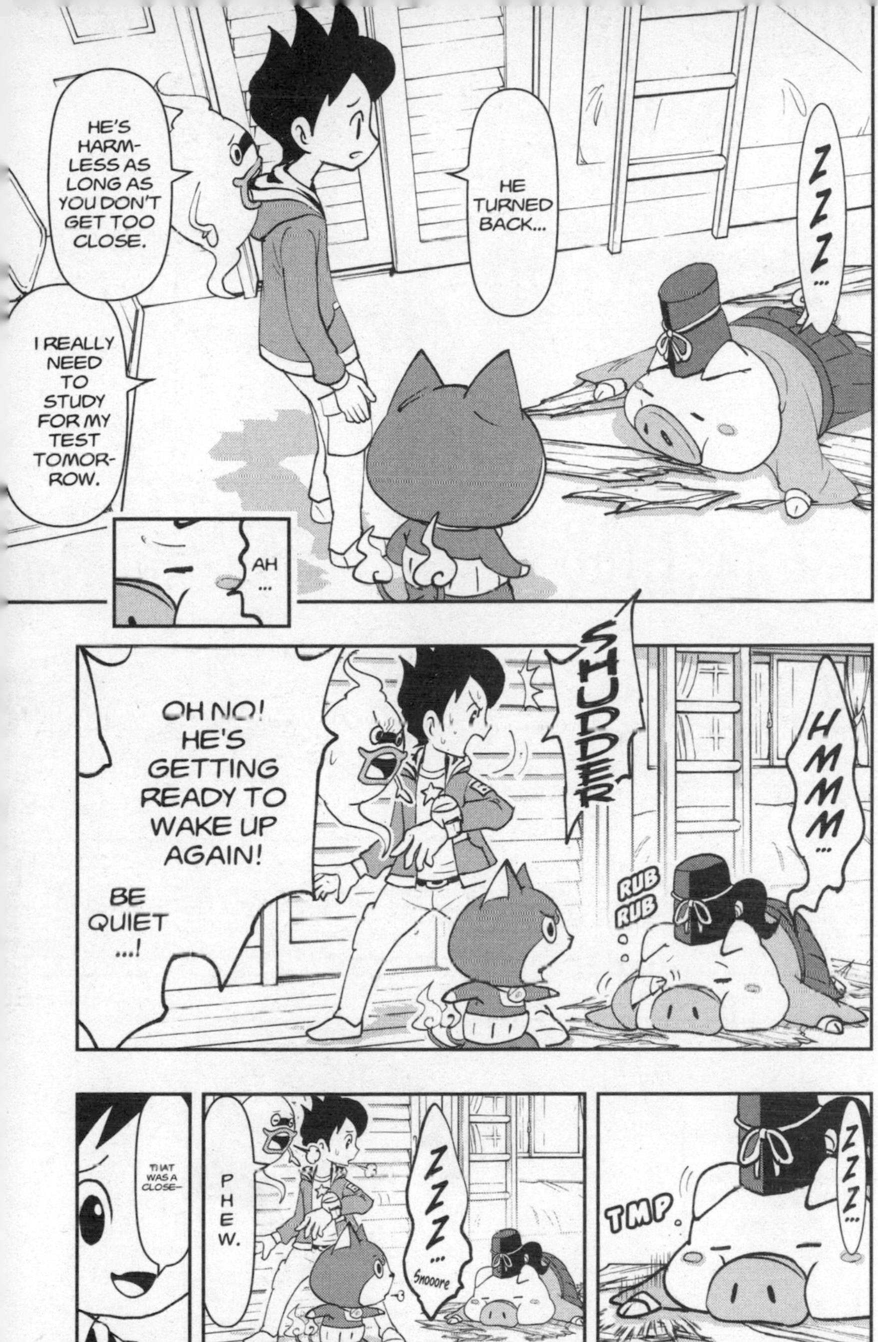
Z Z Z ...
HE TURNED BACK...
HE'S HARMLESS AS LONG AS YOU DON'T GET TOO CLOSE.
I REALLY NEED TO STUDY FOR MY TEST TOMORROW.
AH ...
HMMM...
RUB RUB
SHUDDER
OH NO! HE'S GETTING READY TO WAKE UP AGAIN!
BE QUIET ...!
ZZZ...
TMP
ZZZ...
Snooore
PHEW.
THAT WAS A CLOSE—

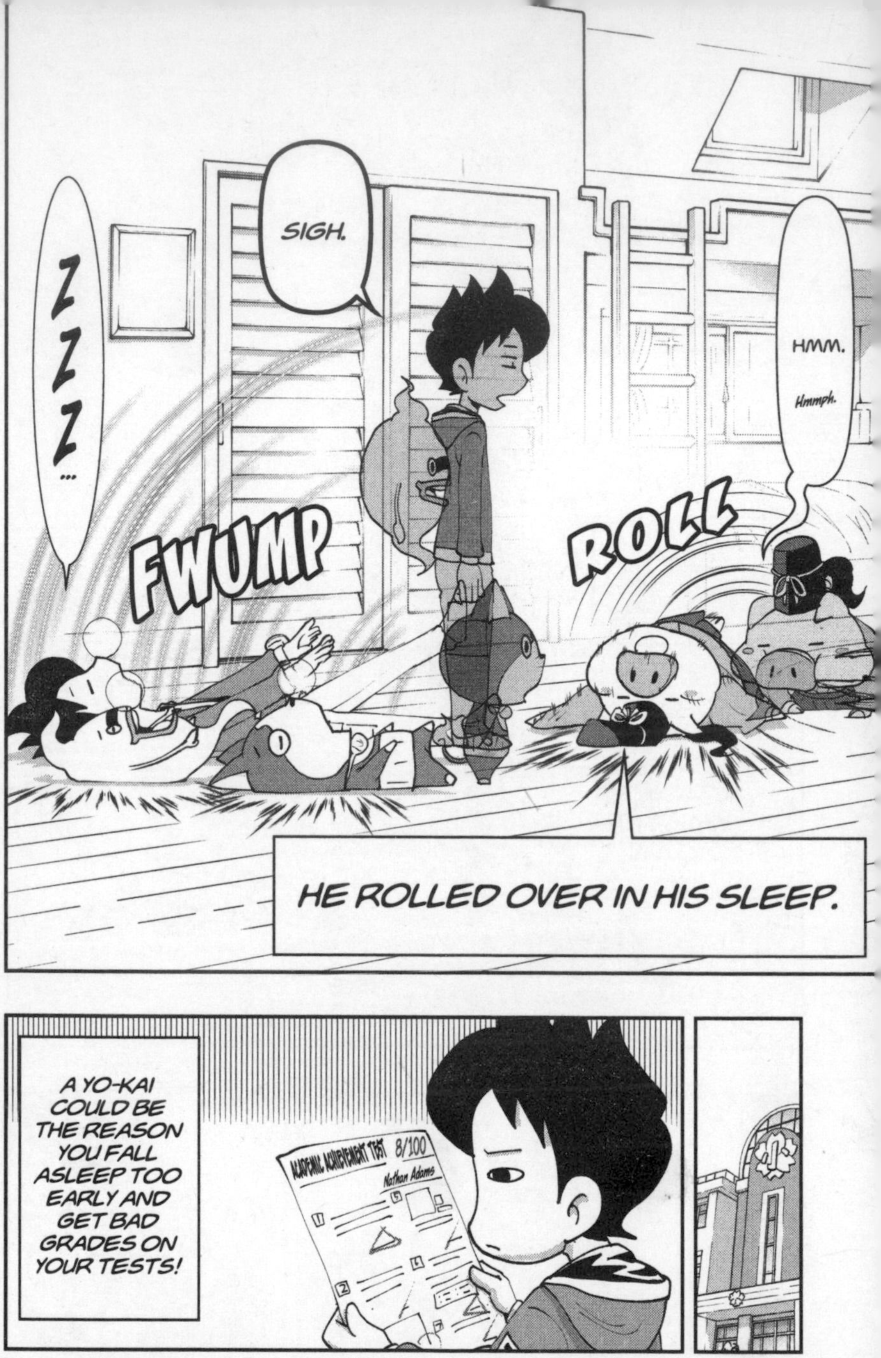
HMM.
Hmmph.
ROLL
SIGH.
FWUMP
ZZZ...
HE ROLLED OVER IN HIS SLEEP.
ACADEMIC ACHIEVEMENT TEST 8/100
Nathan Adams
A YO-KAI COULD BE THE REASON YOU FALL ASLEEP TOO EARLY AND GET BAD GRADES ON YOUR TESTS!

CHAPTER 211
THUNDER YO-KAI PAPA BOLT

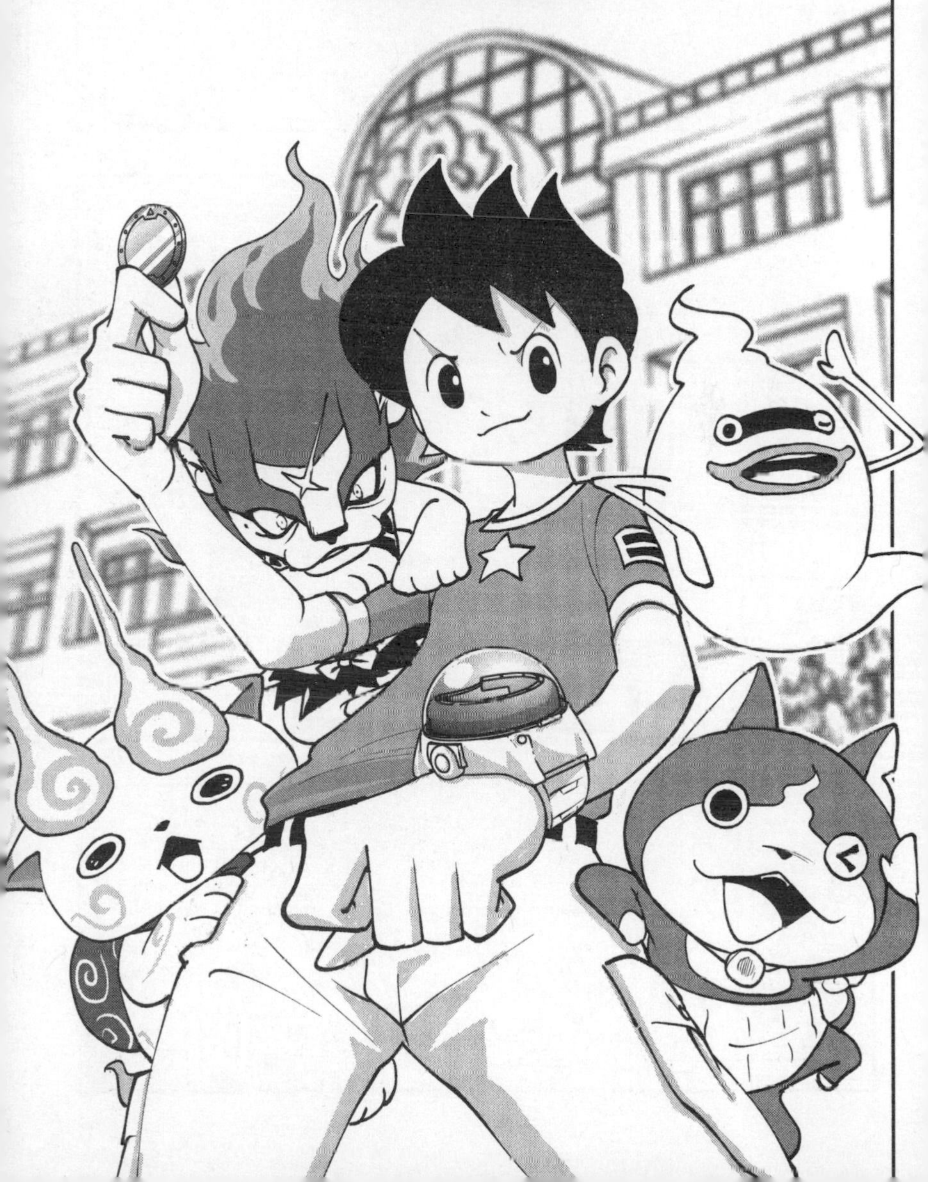

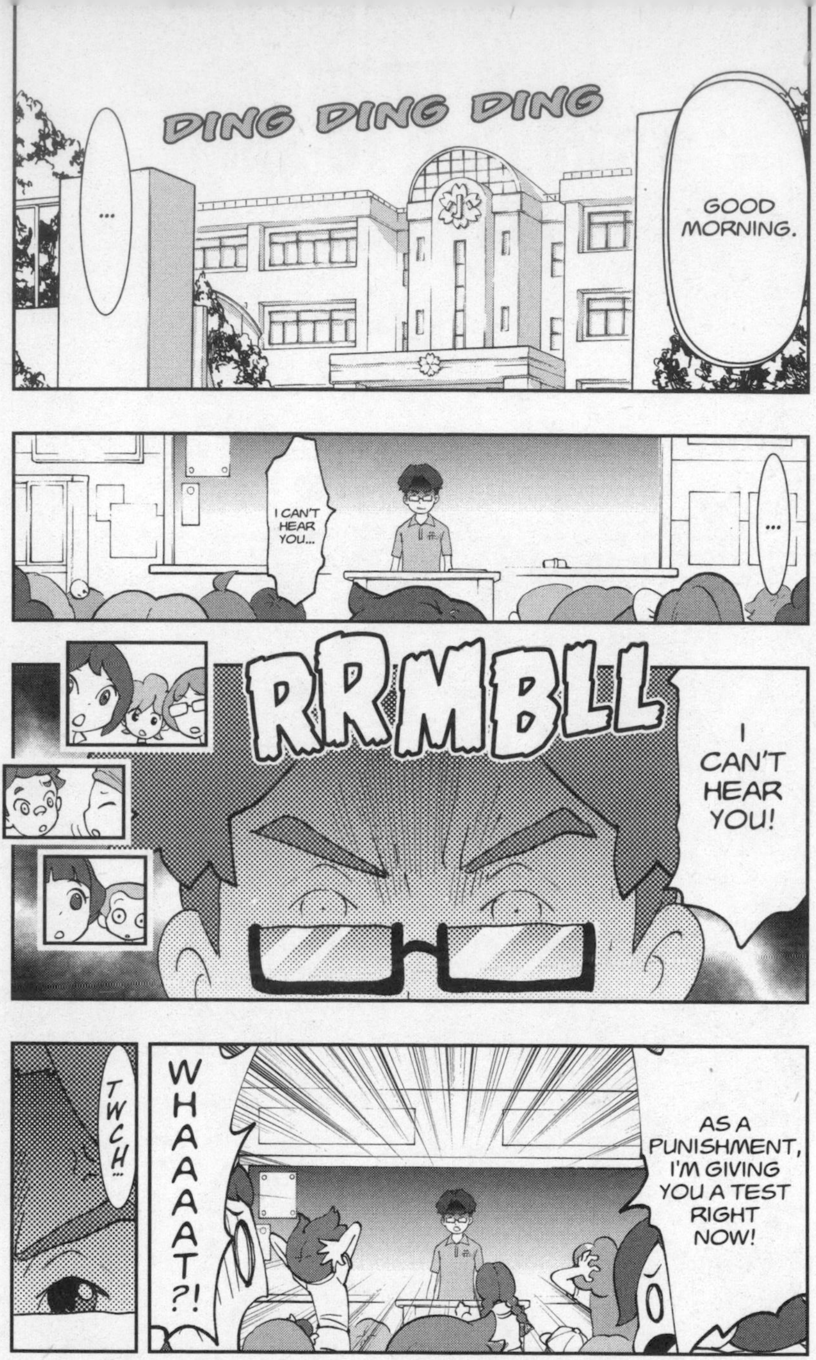
GOOD MORNING.
DING DING DING
...
...
I CAN'T HEAR YOU...
RRMBLL
I CAN'T HEAR YOU!
AS A PUNISHMENT, I'M GIVING YOU A TEST RIGHT NOW!
WHAAAAAT?!
TWCH...

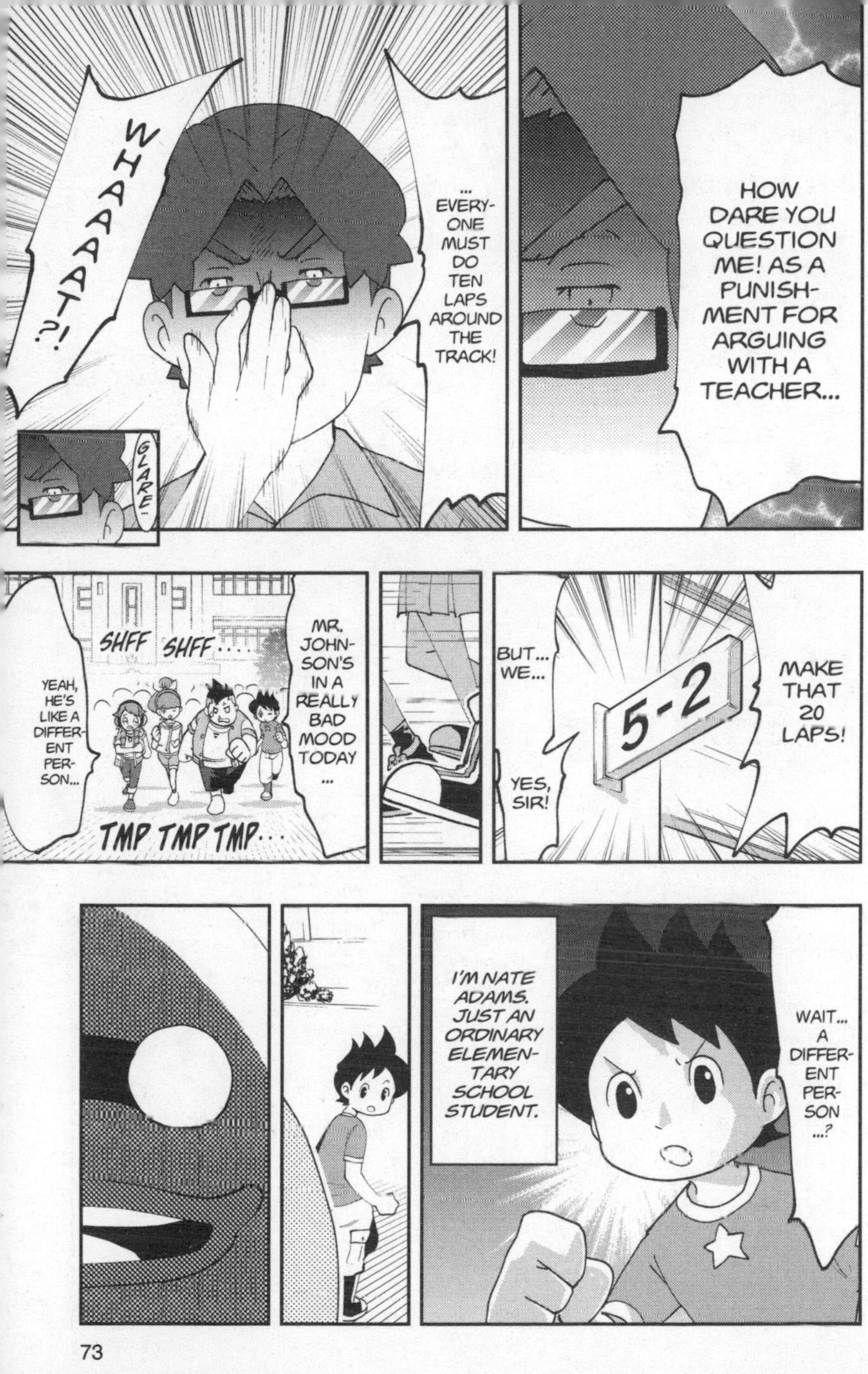
HOW DARE YOU QUESTION ME! AS A PUNISHMENT FOR ARGUING WITH A TEACHER...
...EVERYONE MUST DO TEN LAPS AROUND THE TRACK!
WHAAAAAT?!
GLARE...
MAKE THAT 20 LAPS!
BUT... WE...
YES, SIR!
MR. JOHNSON'S IN A REALLY BAD MOOD TODAY...
SHFF SHFF...
YEAH, HE'S LIKE A DIFFERENT PERSON...
TMP TMP TMP...
WAIT... A DIFFERENT PERSON...?
I'M NATE ADAMS. JUST AN ORDINARY ELEMENTARY SCHOOL STUDENT.

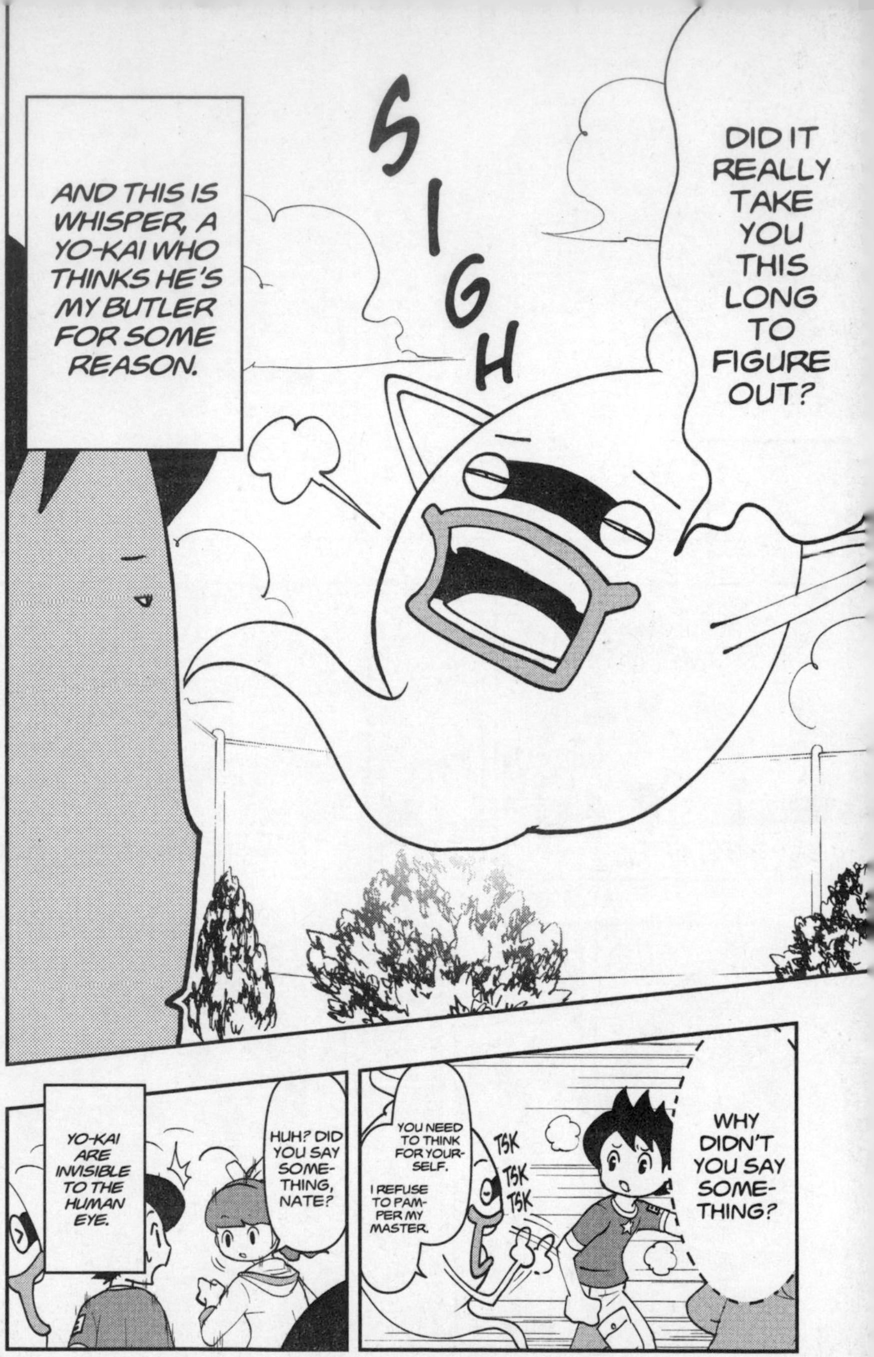
DID IT REALLY TAKE YOU THIS LONG TO FIGURE OUT?
SIGH
AND THIS IS WHISPER, A YO-KAI WHO THINKS HE'S MY BUTLER FOR SOME REASON.
WHY DIDN'T YOU SAY SOMETHING?
YOU NEED TO THINK FOR YOURSELF.
I REFUSE TO PAMPER MY MASTER.
TSK TSK TSK
HUH? DID YOU SAY SOMETHING, NATE?
YO-KAI ARE INVISIBLE TO THE HUMAN EYE.

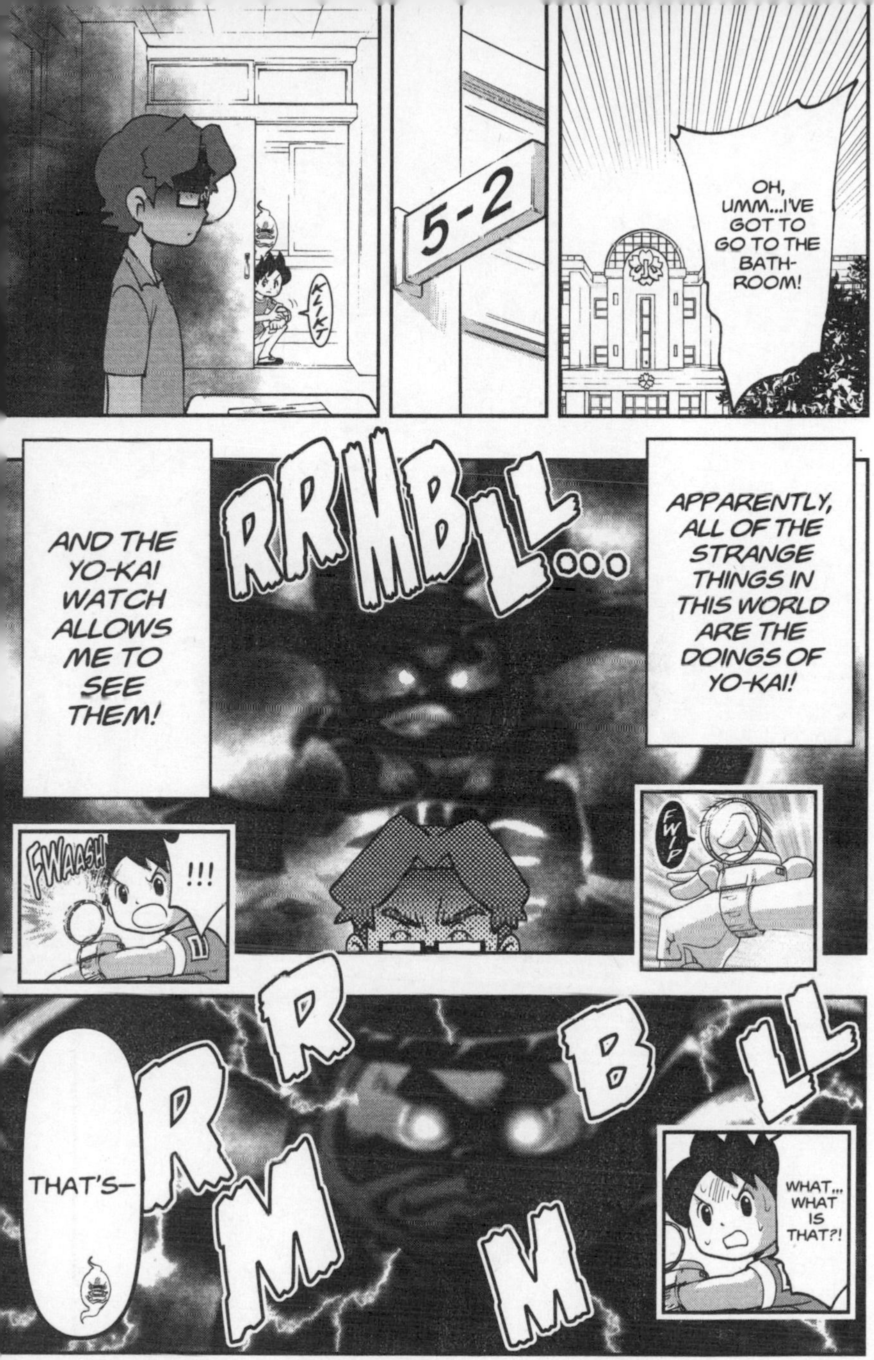
OH, UMM...I'VE GOT TO GO TO THE BATH-ROOM!
5-2
KLIKT
APPARENTLY, ALL OF THE STRANGE THINGS IN THIS WORLD ARE THE DOINGS OF YO-KAI!
RRMBLL...
AND THE YO-KAI WATCH ALLOWS ME TO SEE THEM!
FWIP
FWAASH
!!!
WHAT... WHAT IS THAT?!
RRMMBLL
THAT'S—

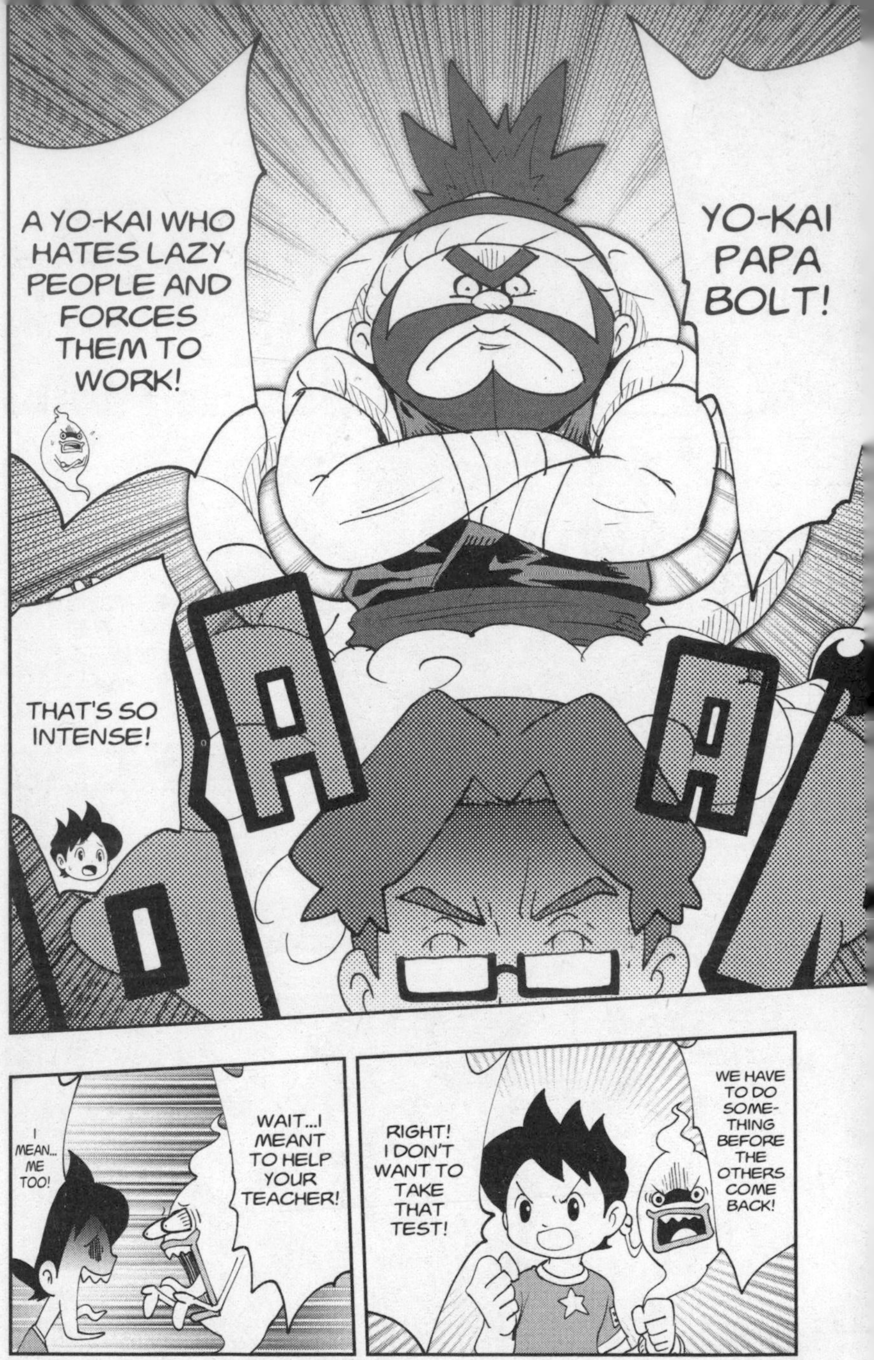
YO-KAI PAPA BOLT!
A YO-KAI WHO HATES LAZY PEOPLE AND FORCES THEM TO WORK!
THAT'S SO INTENSE!
WE HAVE TO DO SOME-THING BEFORE THE OTHERS COME BACK!
RIGHT! I DON'T WANT TO TAKE THAT TEST!
WAIT...I MEANT TO HELP YOUR TEACHER!
I MEAN... ME TOO!

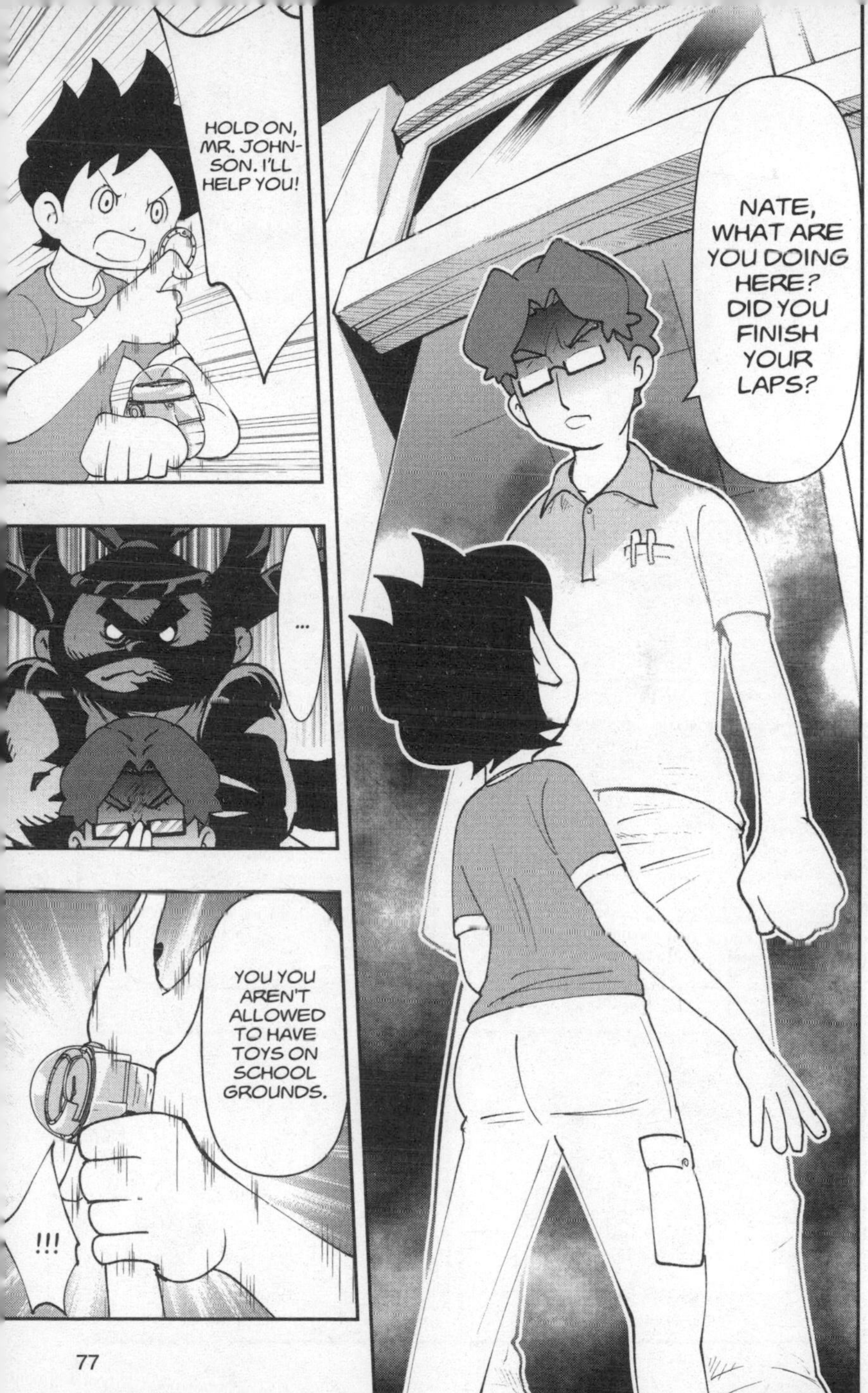
NATE, WHAT ARE YOU DOING HERE? DID YOU FINISH YOUR LAPS?
HOLD ON, MR. JOHN-SON. I'LL HELP YOU!
...
YOU YOU AREN'T ALLOWED TO HAVE TOYS ON SCHOOL GROUNDS.
!!!

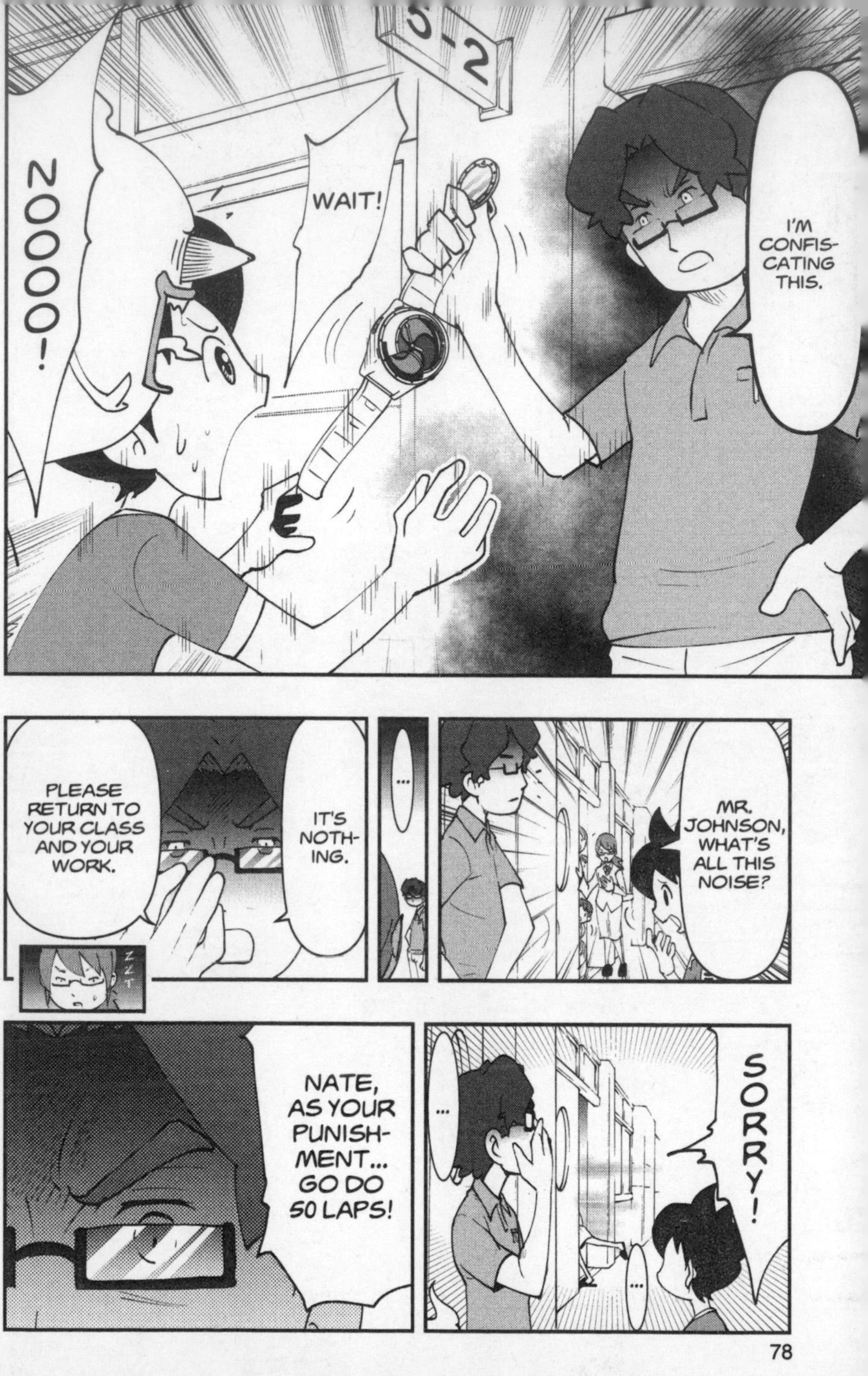
I'M CONFIS-
CATING THIS.
WAIT!
NOOOOO!
MR. JOHNSON, WHAT'S ALL THIS NOISE?
...
IT'S NOTH-ING.
PLEASE RETURN TO YOUR CLASS AND YOUR WORK.
SORRY!
...
...
NATE, AS YOUR PUNISH-MENT... GO DO 50 LAPS!

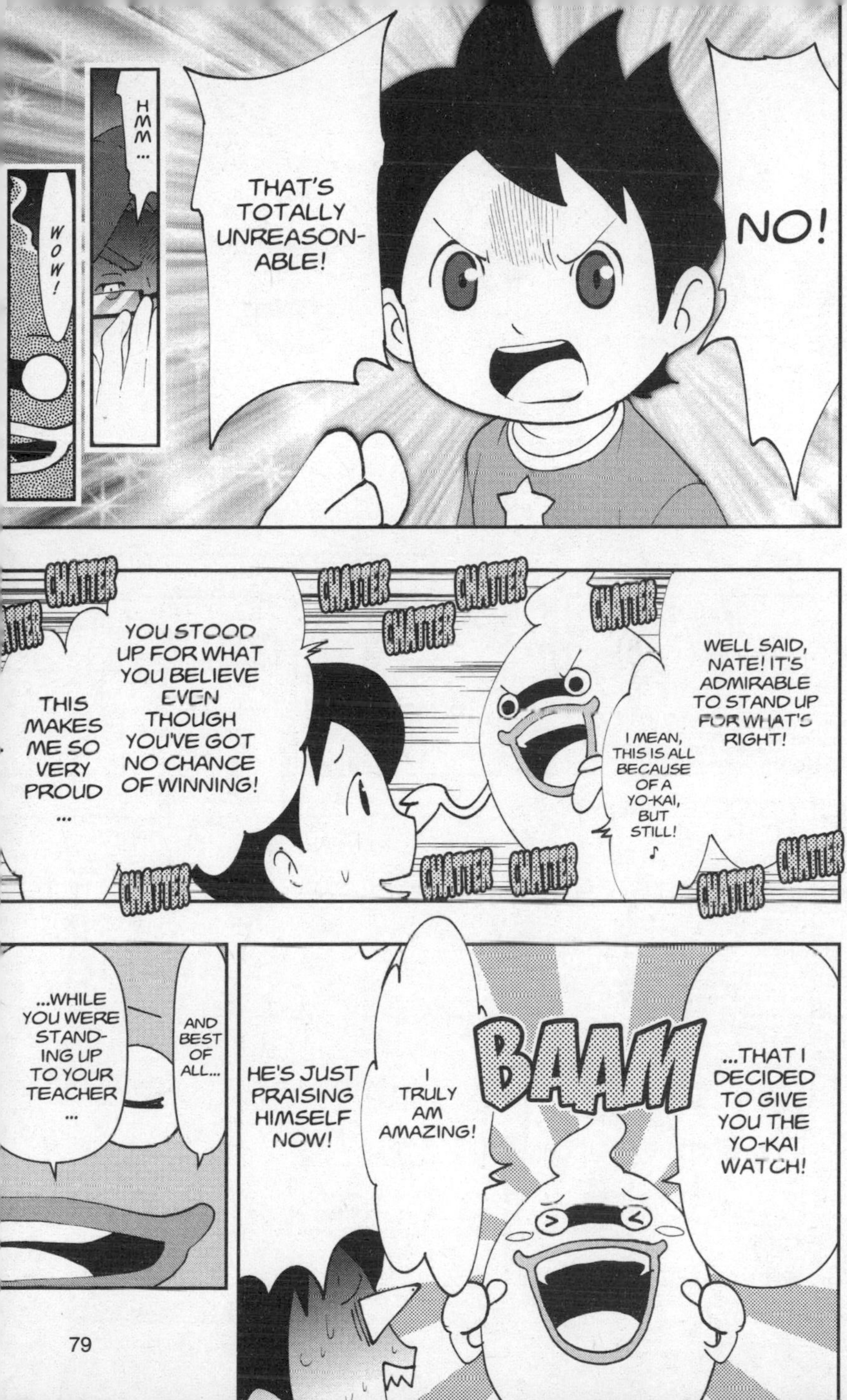
NO!
THAT'S TOTALLY UNREASON-ABLE!
HMM ...
WOW!
CHATTER
CHATTER
CHATTER
CHATTER
WELL SAID, NATE! IT'S ADMIRABLE TO STAND UP FOR WHAT'S RIGHT!
I MEAN, THIS IS ALL BECAUSE OF A YO-KAI, BUT STILL! ♪
YOU STOOD UP FOR WHAT YOU BELIEVE EVEN THOUGH YOU'VE GOT NO CHANCE OF WINNING!
THIS MAKES ME SO VERY PROUD ...
CHATTER
CHATTER
CHATTER
CHATTER
CHATTER
CHATTER
...THAT I DECIDED TO GIVE YOU THE YO-KAI WATCH!
BAAM
I TRULY AM AMAZING!
HE'S JUST PRAISING HIMSELF NOW!
AND BEST OF ALL...
...WHILE YOU WERE STAND-ING UP TO YOUR TEACHER ...

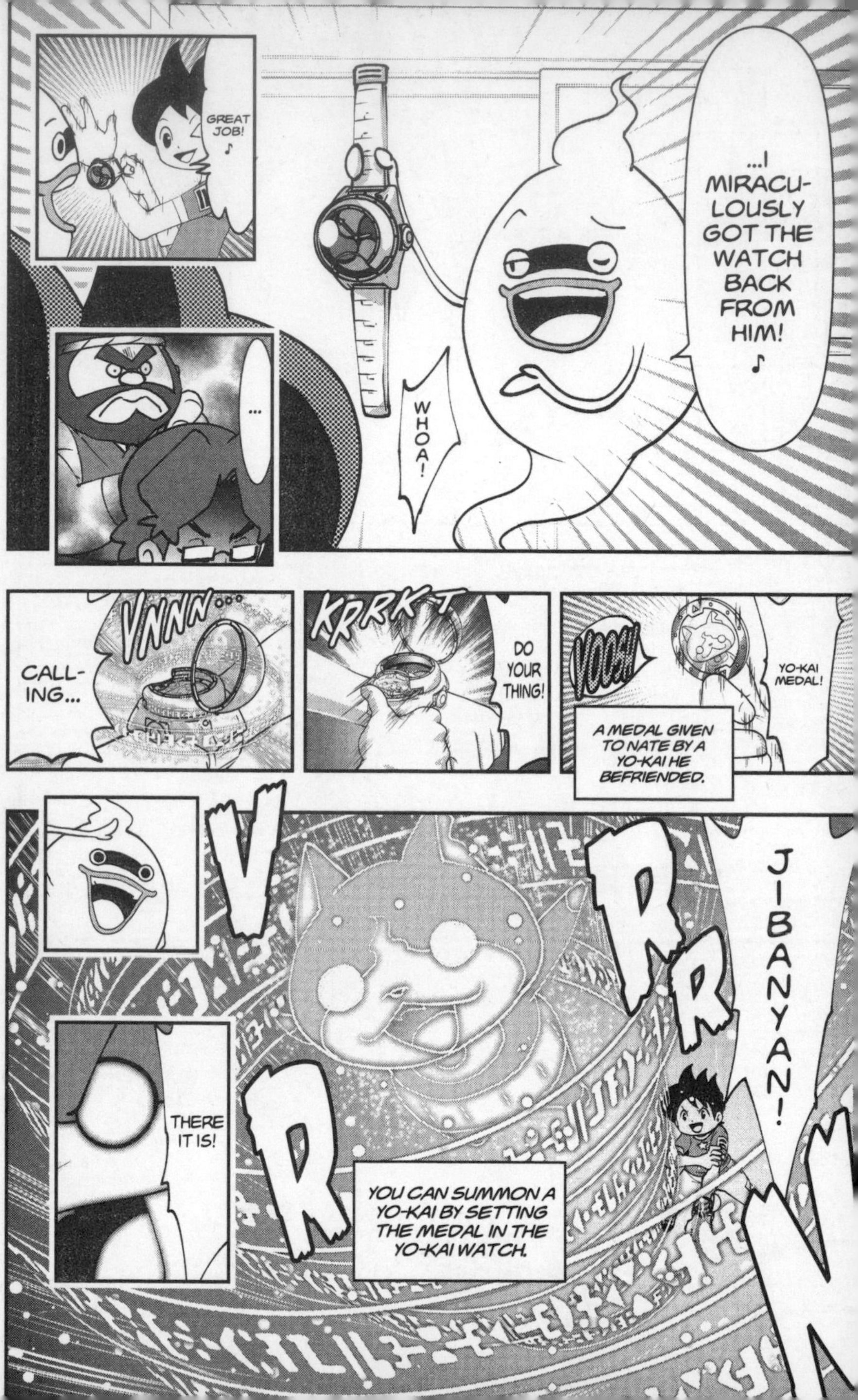
...I MIRACU-LOUSLY GOT THE WATCH BACK FROM HIM! ♪
WHOA!
GREAT JOB! ♪
...
YO-KAI MEDAL!
VOOSH!
A MEDAL GIVEN TO NATE BY A YO-KAI HE BEFRIENDED.
KRRKT
DO YOUR THING!
VNNN...
CALLING...
JIBANYAN!
VRRR
YOU CAN SUMMON A YO-KAI BY SETTING THE MEDAL IN THE YO-KAI WATCH.
THERE IT IS!

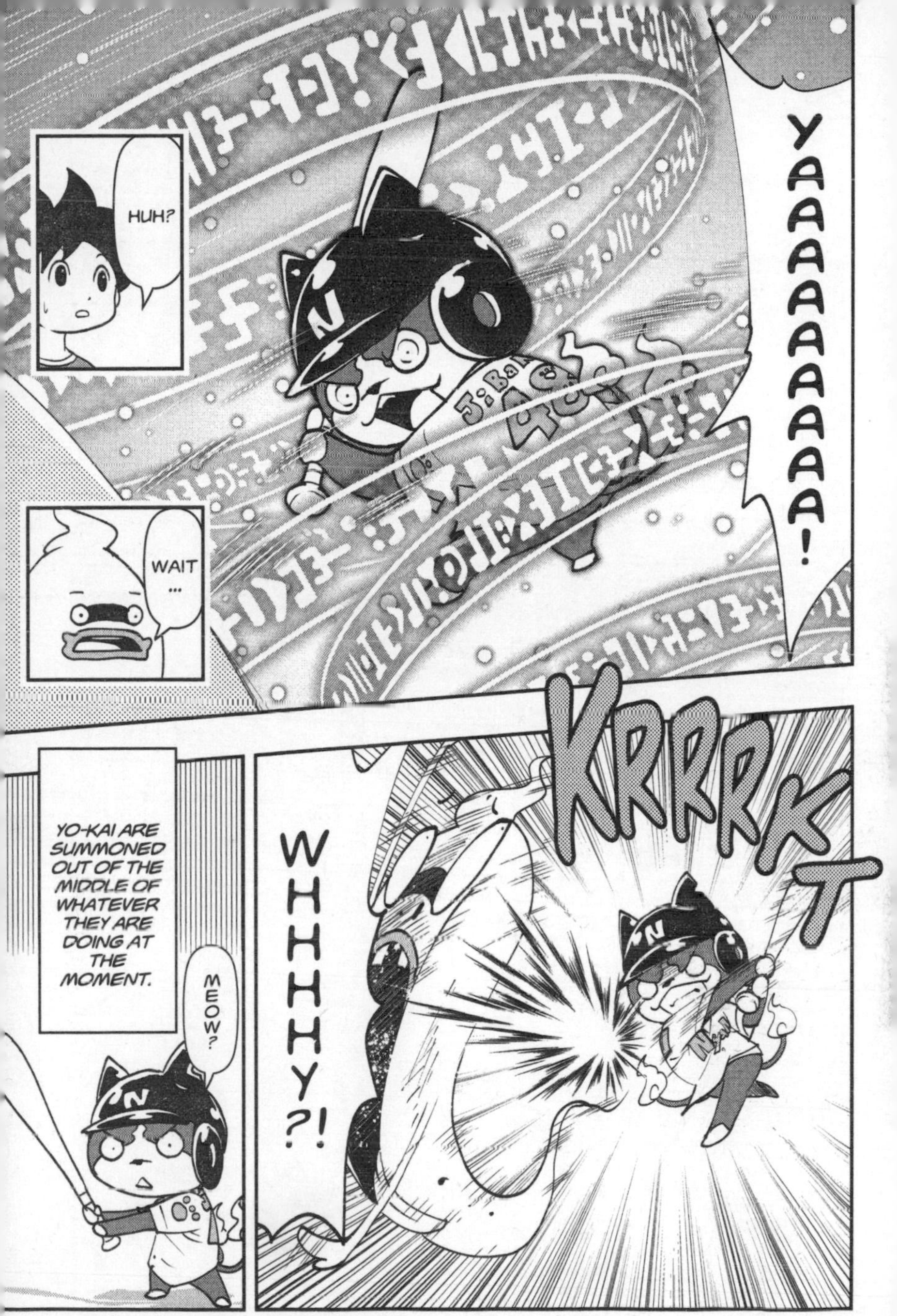
YAAAAAAAAAA!
HUH?
WAIT ...
KRRRKT
WHHHHY?!
YO-KAI ARE SUMMONED OUT OF THE MIDDLE OF WHATEVER THEY ARE DOING AT THE MOMENT.
MEOW?

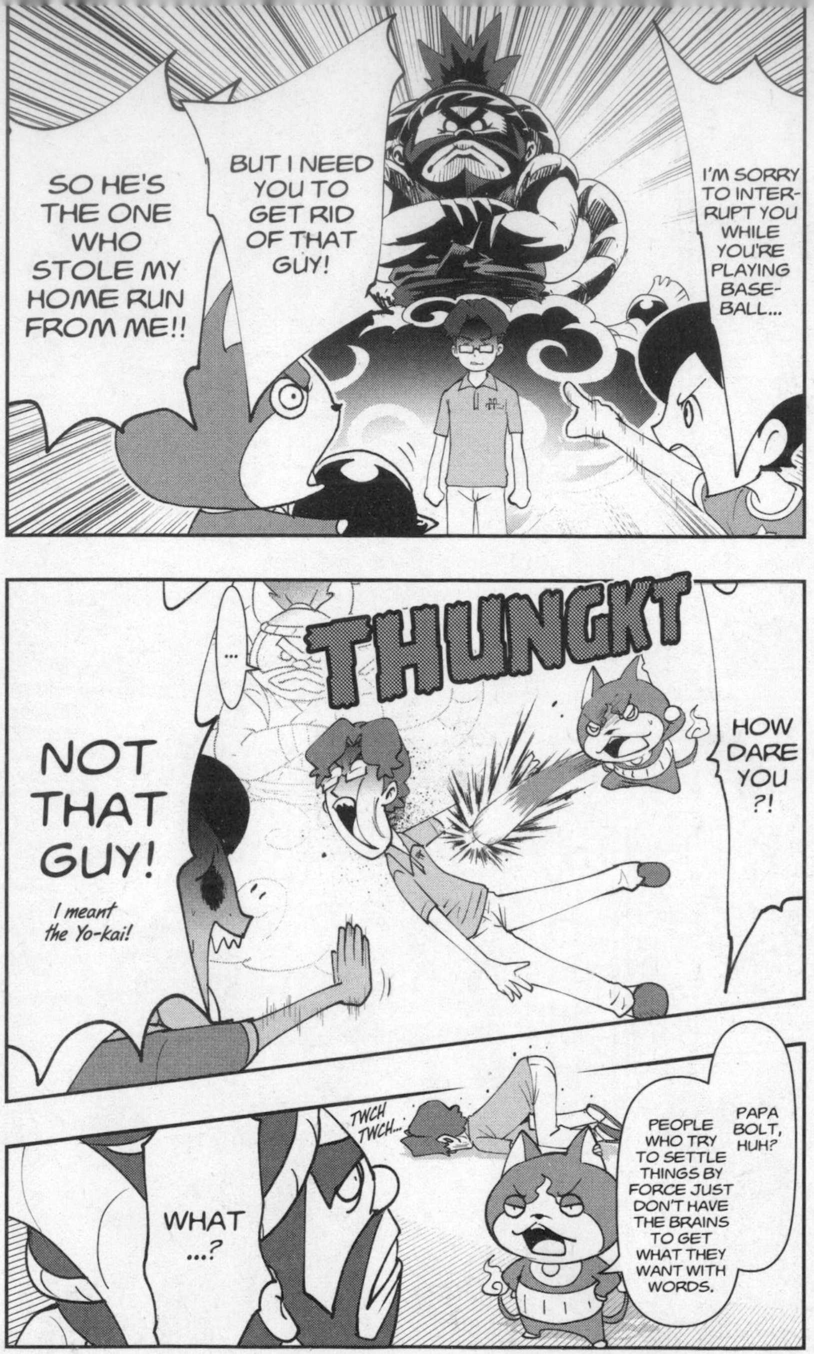

I'M SORRY TO INTERRUPT YOU WHILE YOU'RE PLAYING BASEBALL...
BUT I NEED YOU TO GET RID OF THAT GUY!
SO HE'S THE ONE WHO STOLE MY HOME RUN FROM ME!!
HOW DARE YOU?!
THUNGKT
...
NOT THAT GUY!
I meant the Yo-kai!
PAPA BOLT, HUH?
PEOPLE WHO TRY TO SETTLE THINGS BY FORCE JUST DON'T HAVE THE BRAINS TO GET WHAT THEY WANT WITH WORDS.
TWCH TWCH...
WHAT ...?

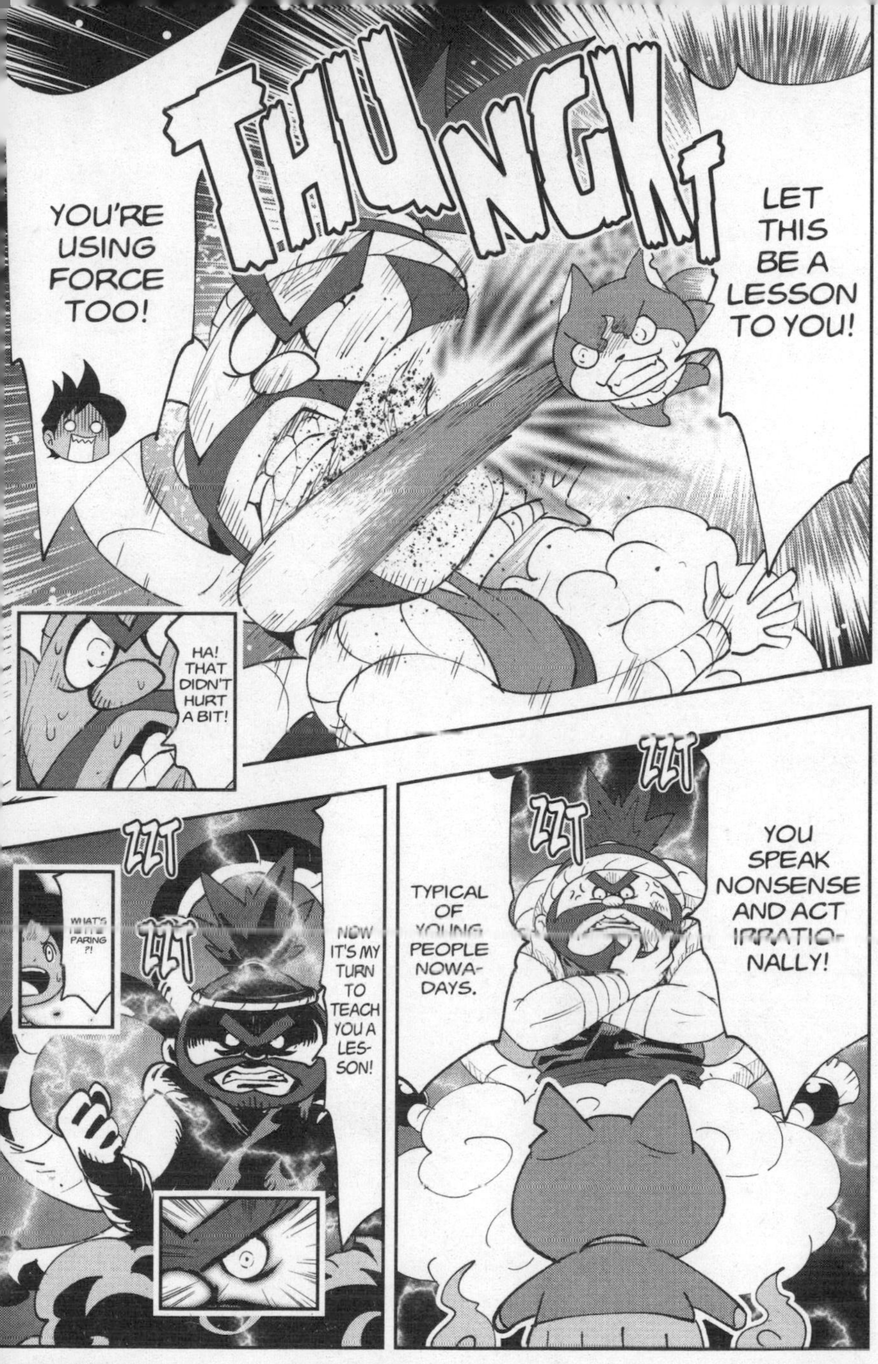
THUNGK
LET THIS BE A LESSON TO YOU!
YOU'RE USING FORCE TOO!
HA! THAT DIDN'T HURT A BIT!
ZZT
ZZT
YOU SPEAK NONSENSE AND ACT IRRATIO-NALLY!
TYPICAL OF YOUNG PEOPLE NOWA-DAYS.
ZZT
ZZT
NOW IT'S MY TURN TO TEACH YOU A LES-SON!
WHAT'S
PARING ?!

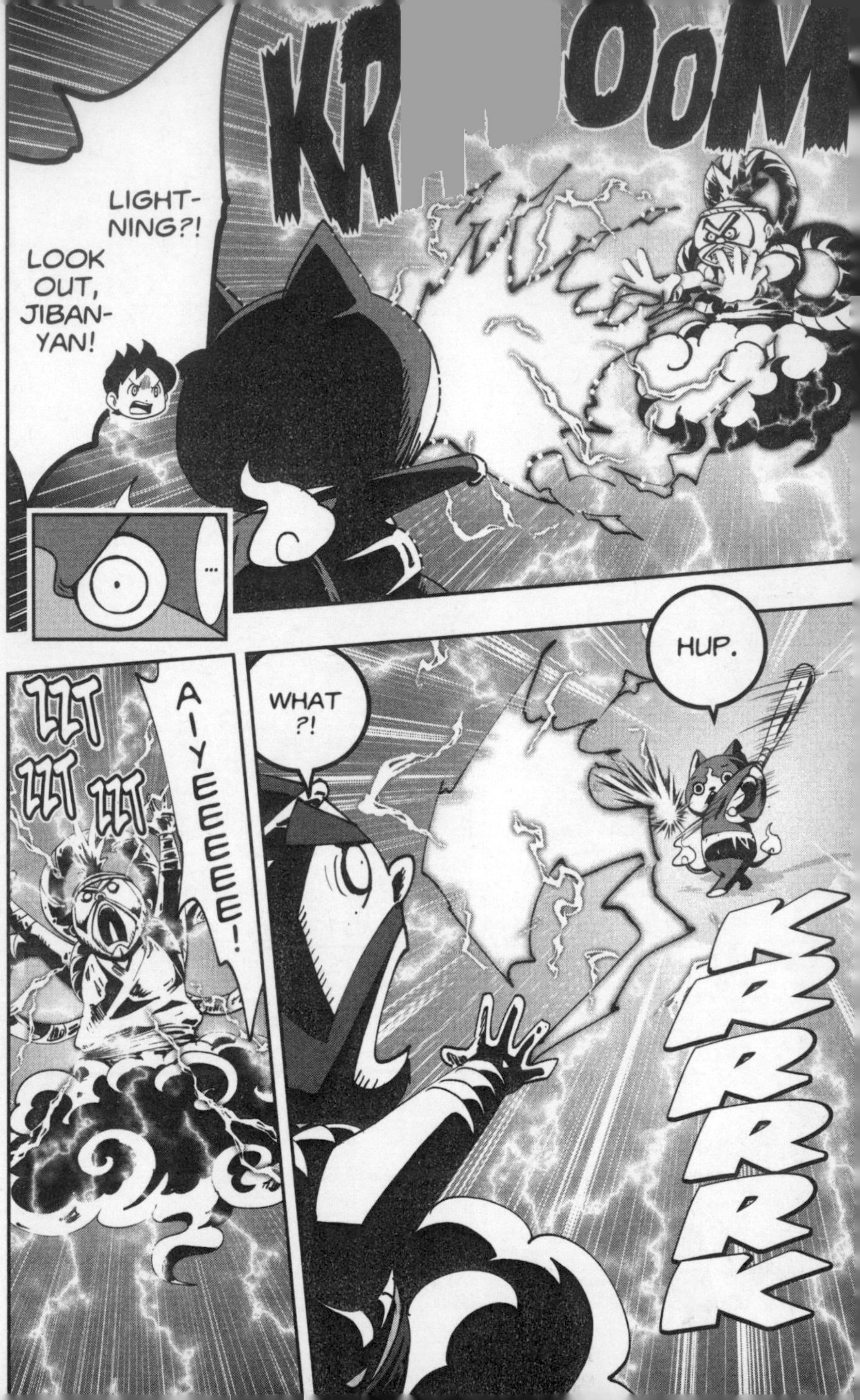
KR OOM
LIGHT-NING?!
LOOK OUT, JIBAN-YAN!
...
HUP.
KRRRRK
WHAT?!
AIYEEEEEE!
ZZT
ZZT
ZZT

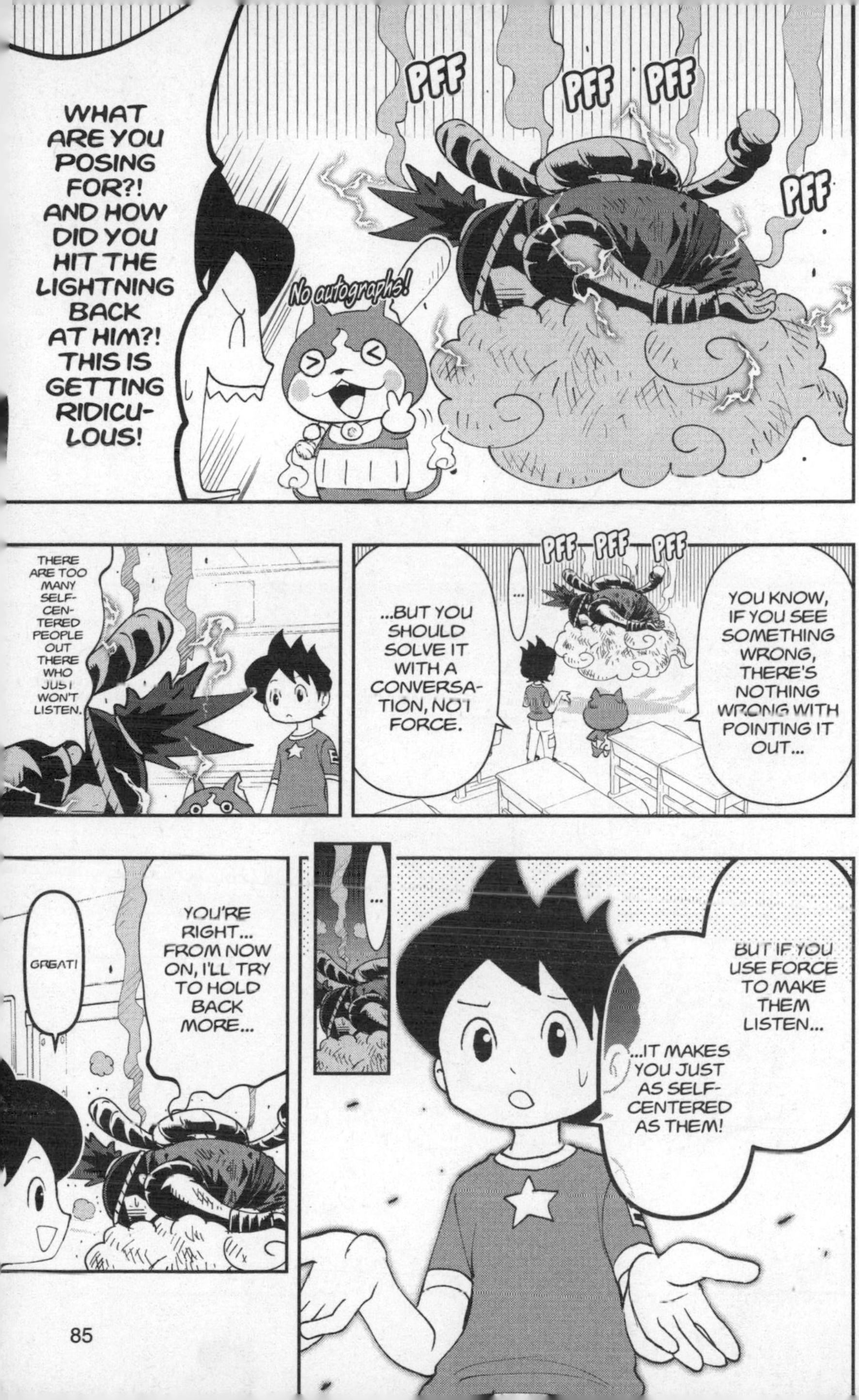
PFF
PFF
PFF
PFF
No autographs!
WHAT ARE YOU POSING FOR?! AND HOW DID YOU HIT THE LIGHTNING BACK AT HIM?! THIS IS GETTING RIDICULOUS!
YOU KNOW, IF YOU SEE SOMETHING WRONG, THERE'S NOTHING WRONG WITH POINTING IT OUT...
PFF PFF PFF
...
...BUT YOU SHOULD SOLVE IT WITH A CONVERSATION, NOT FORCE.
THERE ARE TOO MANY SELF-CENTERED PEOPLE OUT THERE WHO JUST WON'T LISTEN.
BUT IF YOU USE FORCE TO MAKE THEM LISTEN...
...IT MAKES YOU JUST AS SELF-CENTERED AS THEM!
...
YOU'RE RIGHT... FROM NOW ON, I'LL TRY TO HOLD BACK MORE...
GREAT!

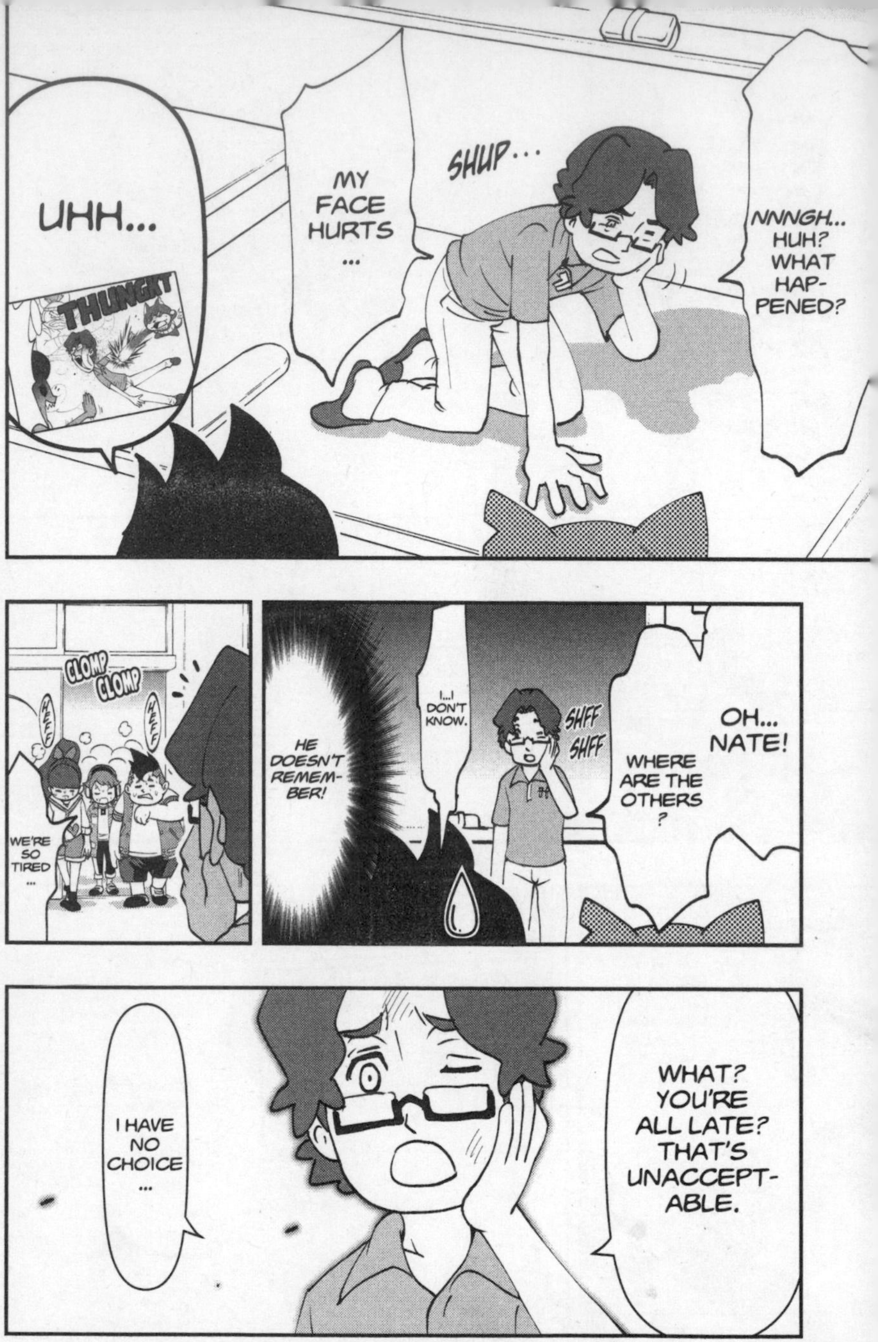
NNNGH... HUH? WHAT HAP-PENED?
SHUP...
MY FACE HURTS ...
UHH...
THUNGK
OH... NATE!
WHERE ARE THE OTHERS ?
SHFF SHFF
I...I DON'T KNOW.
HE DOESN'T REMEM-BER!
CLOMP CLOMP
HEFF
HEFF
WE'RE SO TIRED ...
WHAT? YOU'RE ALL LATE? THAT'S UNACCEPT-ABLE.
I HAVE NO CHOICE ...

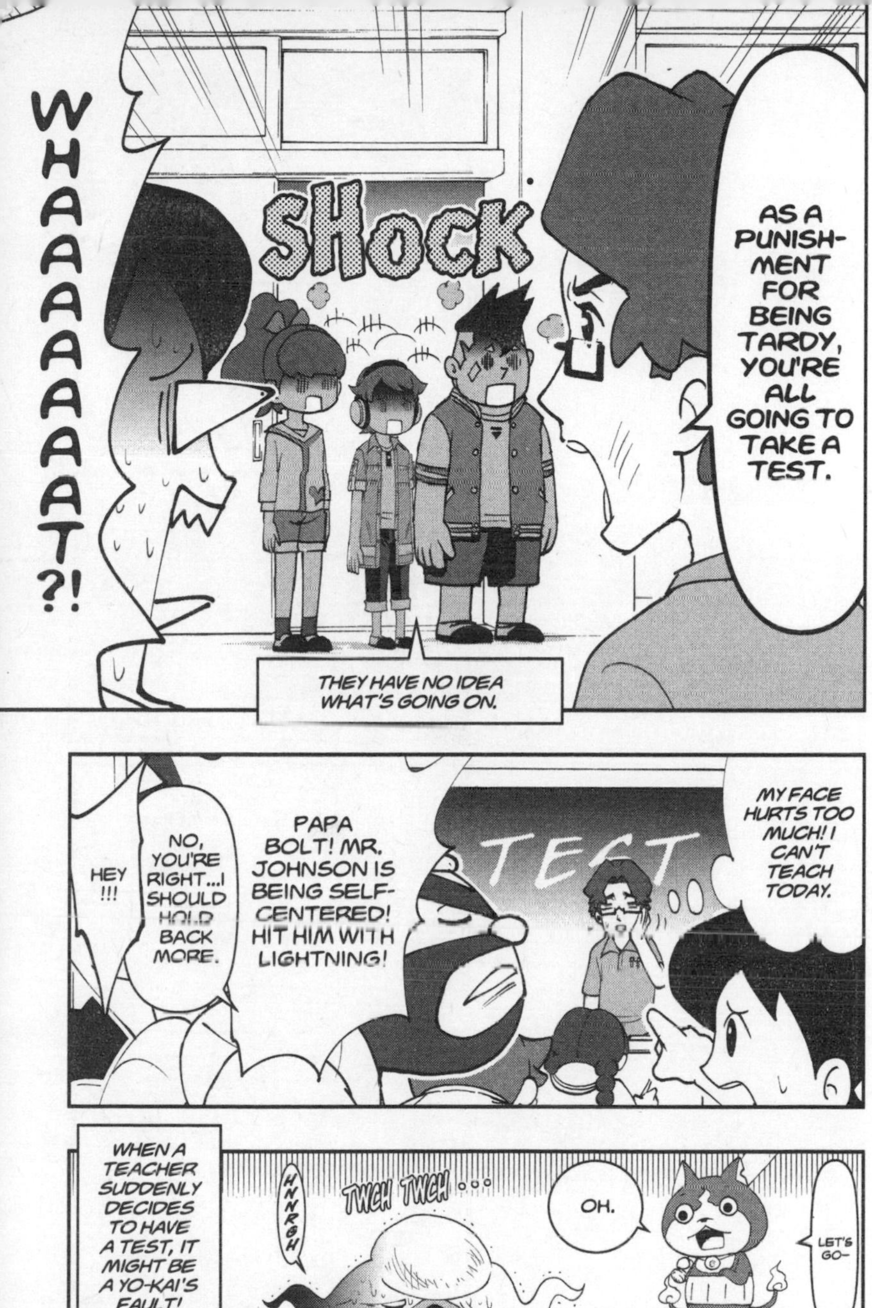
AS A PUNISHMENT FOR BEING TARDY, YOU'RE ALL GOING TO TAKE A TEST.
SHOCK
WHAAAAAAAT?!
THEY HAVE NO IDEA WHAT'S GOING ON.
MY FACE HURTS TOO MUCH! I CAN'T TEACH TODAY.
TEST
PAPA BOLT! MR. JOHNSON IS BEING SELF-CENTERED! HIT HIM WITH LIGHTNING!
NO, YOU'RE RIGHT...I SHOULD HOLD BACK MORE.
HEY!!!
LET'S GO—
OH.
TWCH TWCH...
HNNRGH
WHEN A TEACHER SUDDENLY DECIDES TO HAVE A TEST, IT MIGHT BE A YO-KAI'S FAULT!

FIST BUMP

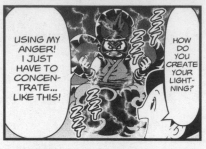

HOW DO YOU CREATE YOUR LIGHTNING?
USING MY ANGER! I JUST HAVE TO CONCENTRATE... LIKE THIS!
WOW! THAT'S INCREDIBLE! ♪
COULD YOU HELP ME WHEN THERE'S A BAD YO-KAI? ♪
SURE THING!
(FIST BUMP) A RITUAL TO RECEIVE THE YO-KAI MEDAL.
IT'S NICE TO MEET YOU! ♪
THE PLEASURE'S ALL MINE!
AIYEEE!
WHOOPS, SORRY! I FORGOT ABOUT THE LIGHTNING!

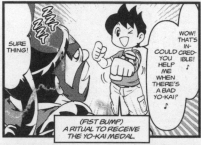

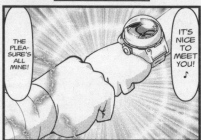

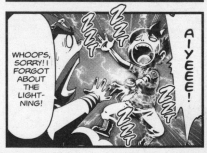

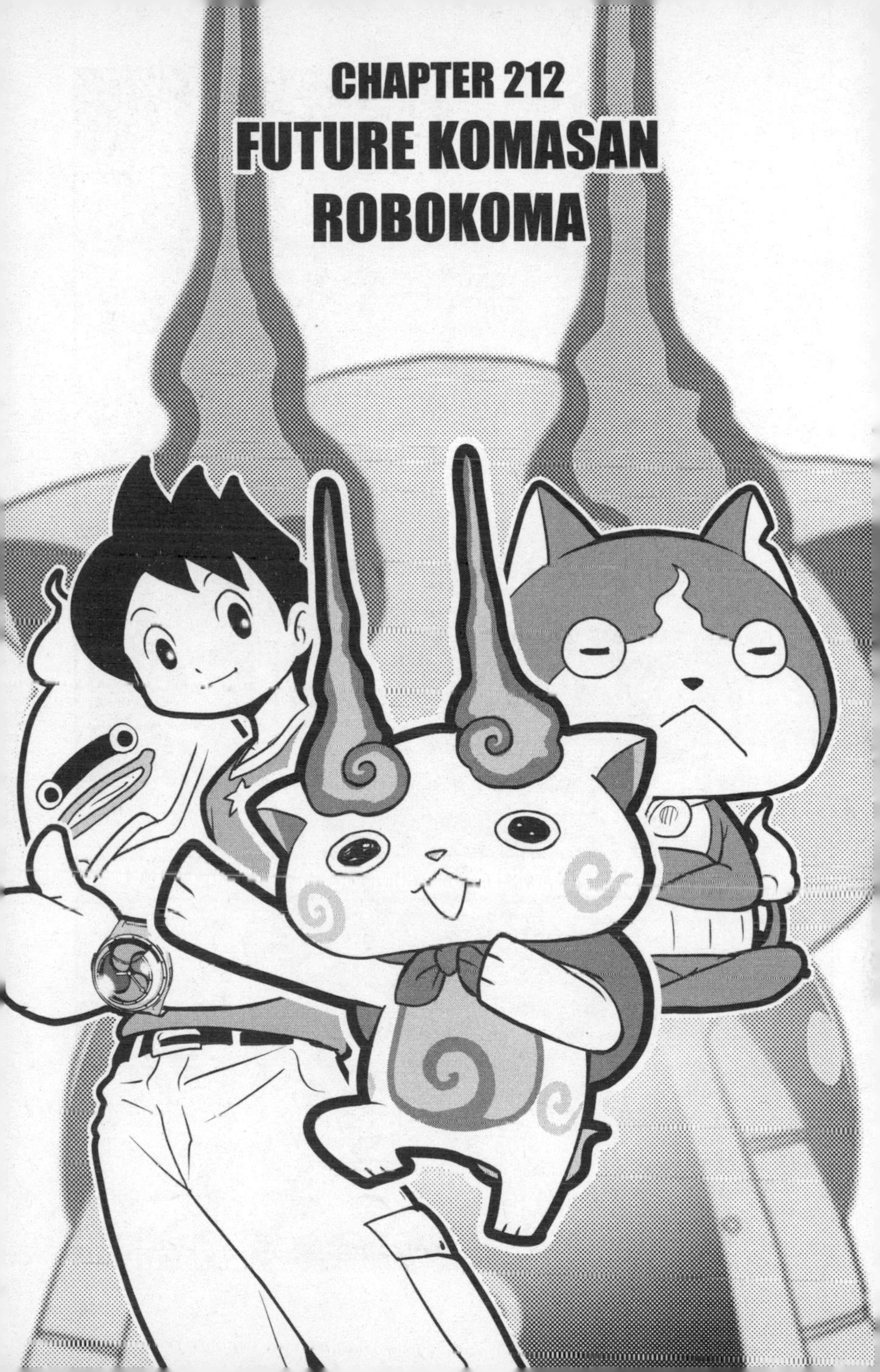
CHAPTER 212
FUTURE KOMASAN
ROBOKOMA

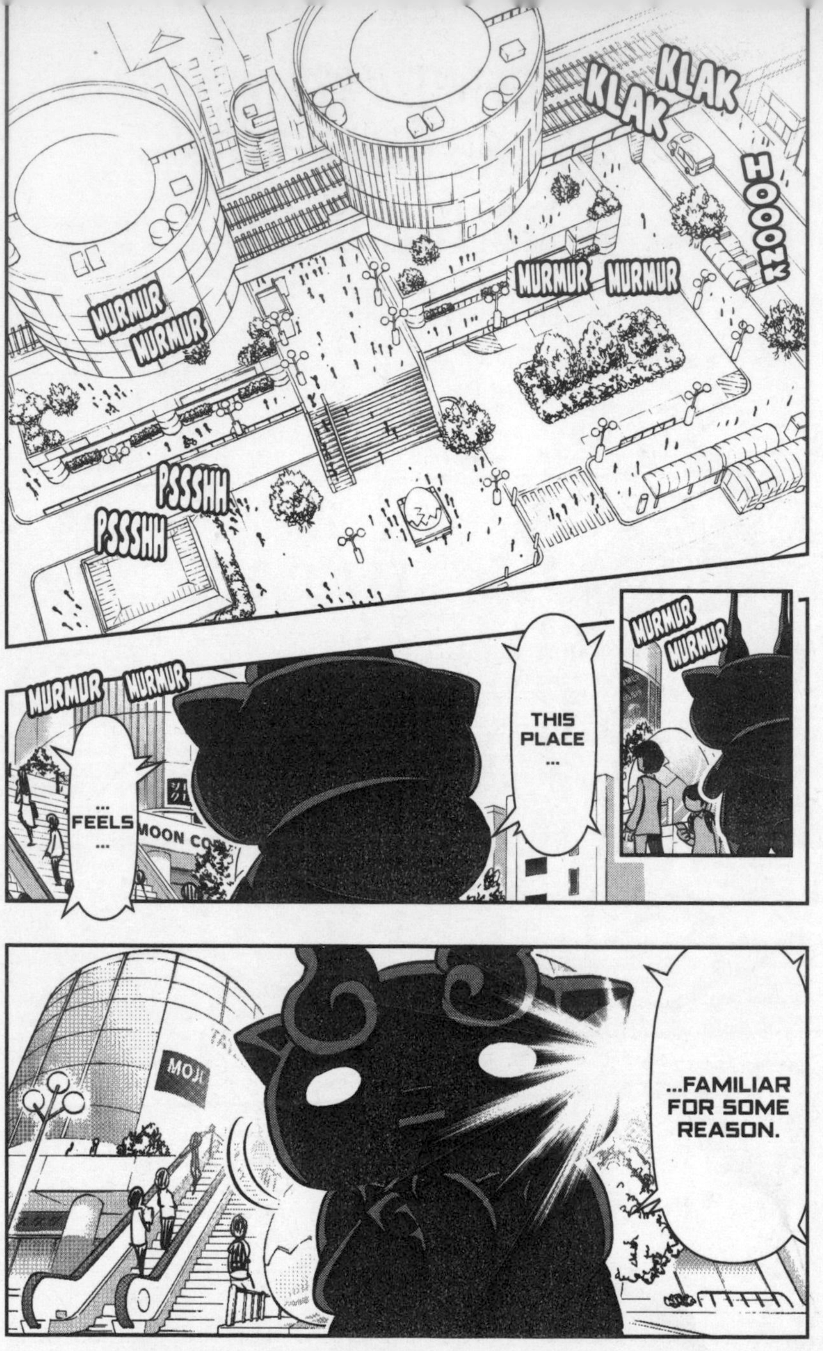
KLAK KLAK
HOOONK
MURMUR MURMUR
MURMUR MURMUR
PSSSHH PSSSHH
MURMUR MURMUR
THIS PLACE ...
MURMUR MURMUR
... FEELS ...
MOON CO
...FAMILIAR FOR SOME REASON.

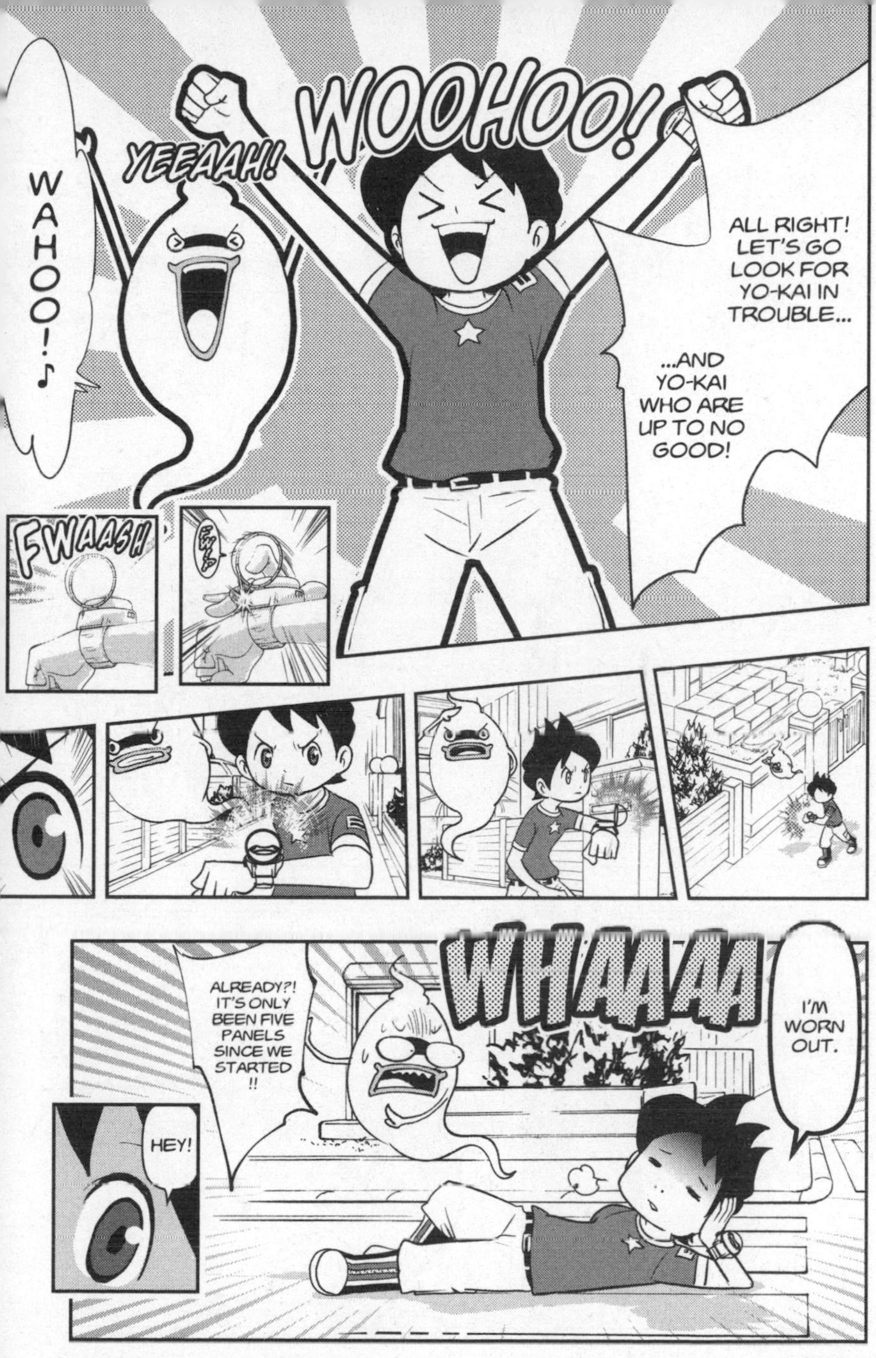
ALL RIGHT! LET'S GO LOOK FOR YO-KAI IN TROUBLE...
...AND YO-KAI WHO ARE UP TO NO GOOD!
WOOHOO!
YEEAAH!
WAHOO!♪
FWAASH
WHAAAA
I'M WORN OUT.
ALREADY?! IT'S ONLY BEEN FIVE PANELS SINCE WE STARTED !!
HEY!

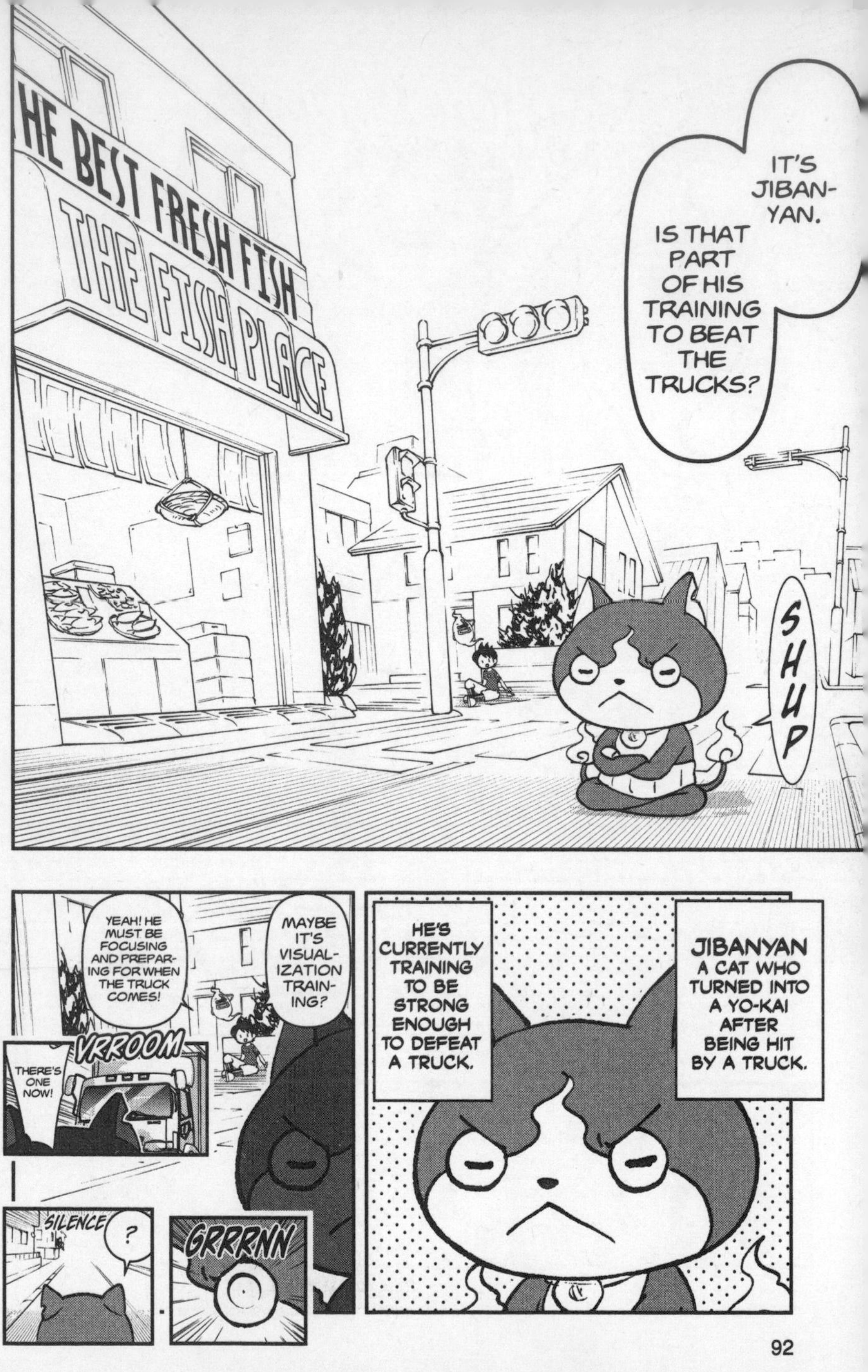
HE BEST FRESH FISH
THE FISH PLACE
IT'S JIBAN-YAN.
IS THAT PART OF HIS TRAINING TO BEAT THE TRUCKS?
SHUP
JIBANYAN A CAT WHO TURNED INTO A YO-KAI AFTER BEING HIT BY A TRUCK.
HE'S CURRENTLY TRAINING TO BE STRONG ENOUGH TO DEFEAT A TRUCK.
MAYBE IT'S VISUAL-IZATION TRAIN-ING?
YEAH! HE MUST BE FOCUSING AND PREPAR-ING FOR WHEN THE TRUCK COMES!
VRROOM
THERE'S ONE NOW!
GRRRNN
SILENCE
?

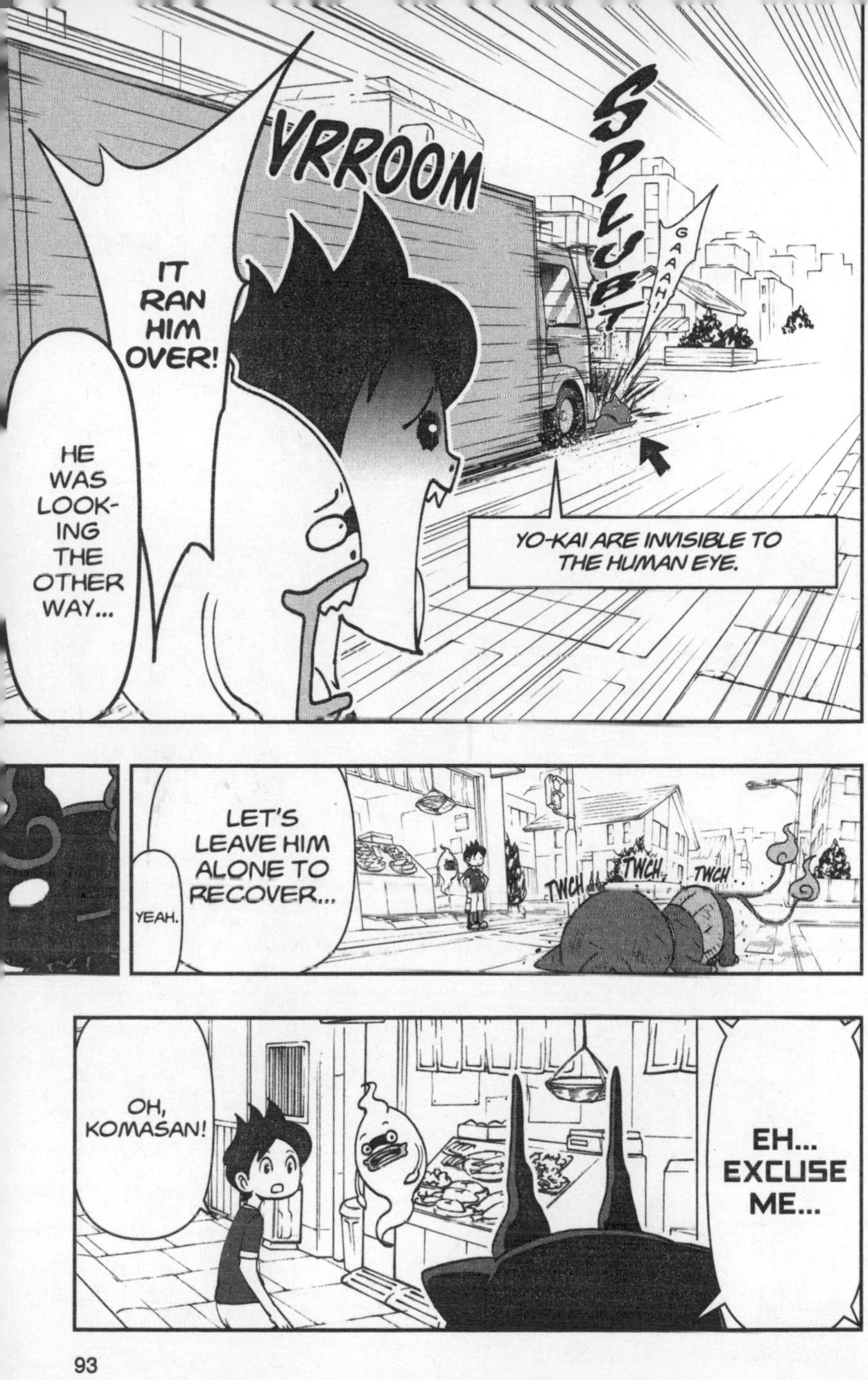
SPLUBT
GAAAH!
VRROOM
YO-KAI ARE INVISIBLE TO THE HUMAN EYE.
IT RAN HIM OVER!
HE WAS LOOKING THE OTHER WAY...
TWCH TWCH TWCH
LET'S LEAVE HIM ALONE TO RECOVER...
YEAH.
EH... EXCUSE ME...
OH, KOMASAN!

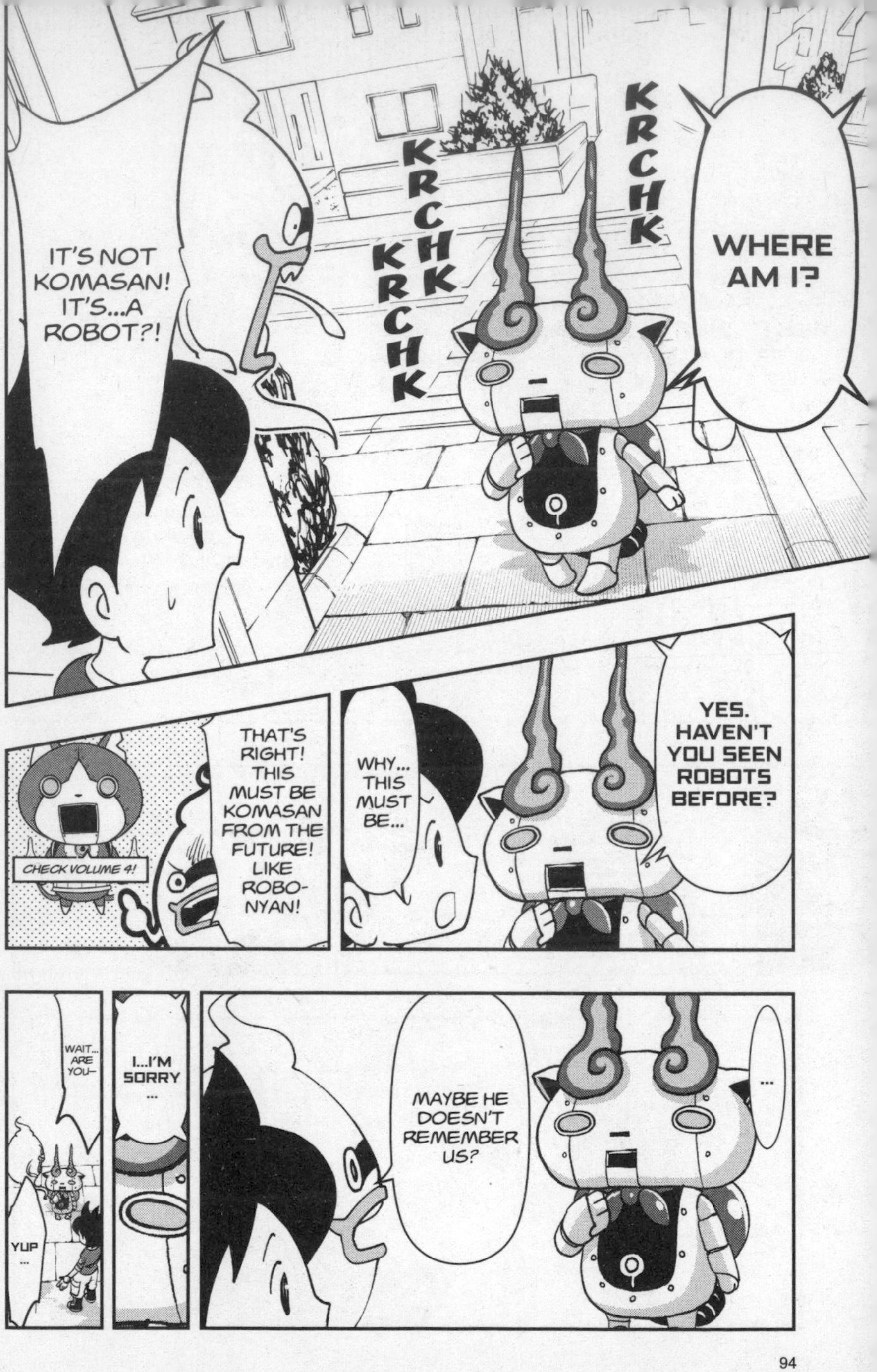
WHERE AM I?
KRCHK
KRCHK
KRCHK
IT'S NOT KOMASAN! IT'S...A ROBOT?!
YES. HAVEN'T YOU SEEN ROBOTS BEFORE?
WHY... THIS MUST BE...
THAT'S RIGHT! THIS MUST BE KOMASAN FROM THE FUTURE! LIKE ROBO-NYAN!
CHECK VOLUME 4!
...
MAYBE HE DOESN'T REMEMBER US?
I...I'M SORRY ...
WAIT... ARE YOU—
YUP ...

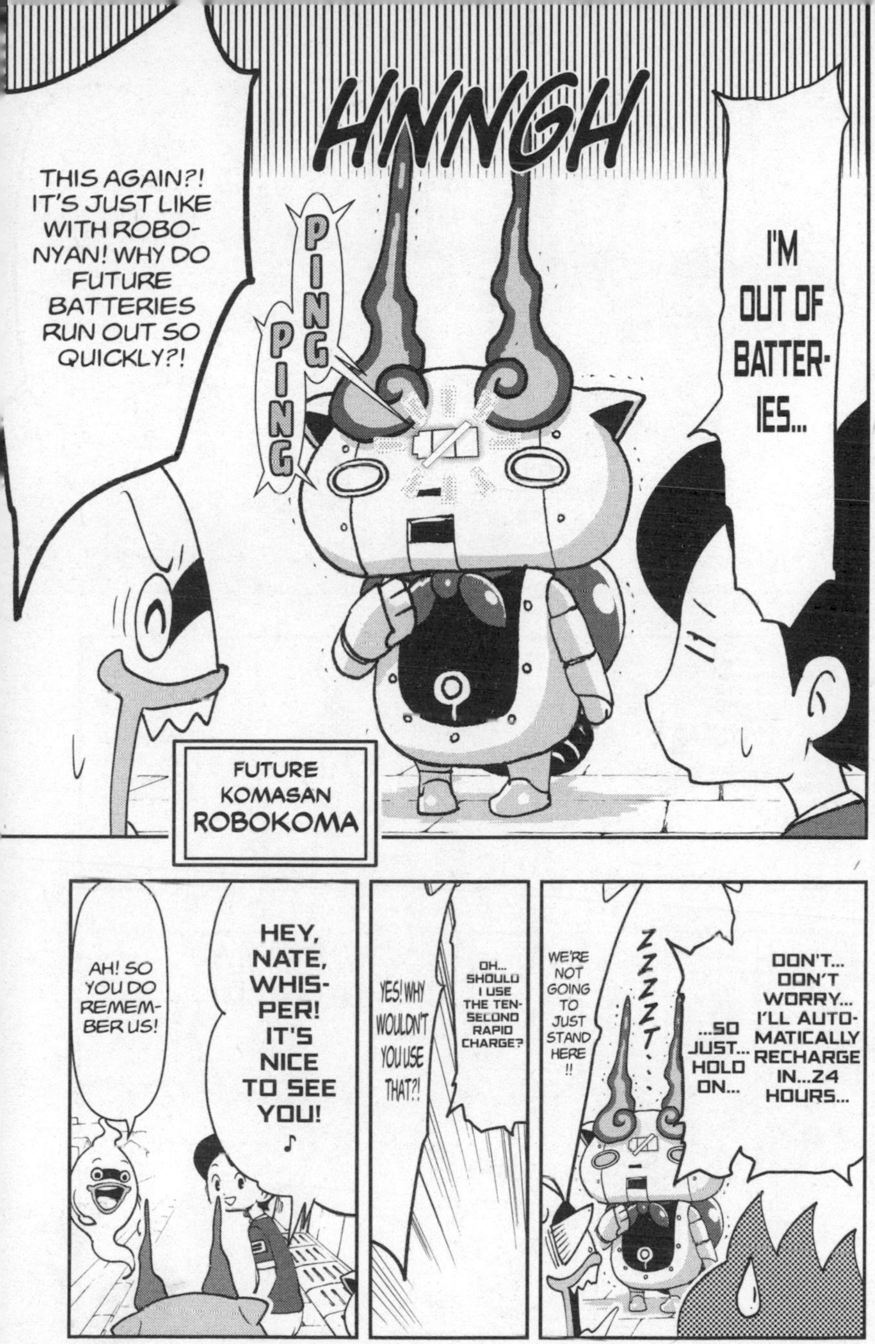
HNNGH
I'M OUT OF BATTER-IES...
PING PING
PING PING
THIS AGAIN?! IT'S JUST LIKE WITH ROBO-NYAN! WHY DO FUTURE BATTERIES RUN OUT SO QUICKLY?!
FUTURE KOMASAN ROBOKOMA
DON'T... DON'T WORRY... I'LL AUTO-MATICALLY RECHARGE IN...24 HOURS...
...SO JUST... HOLD ON...
ZZZZT...
WE'RE NOT GOING TO JUST STAND HERE!!
OH... SHOULD I USE THE TEN-SECOND RAPID CHARGE?
YES! WHY WOULDN'T YOU USE THAT?!
HEY, NATE, WHISPER! IT'S NICE TO SEE YOU! ♪
AH! SO YOU DO REMEMBER US!

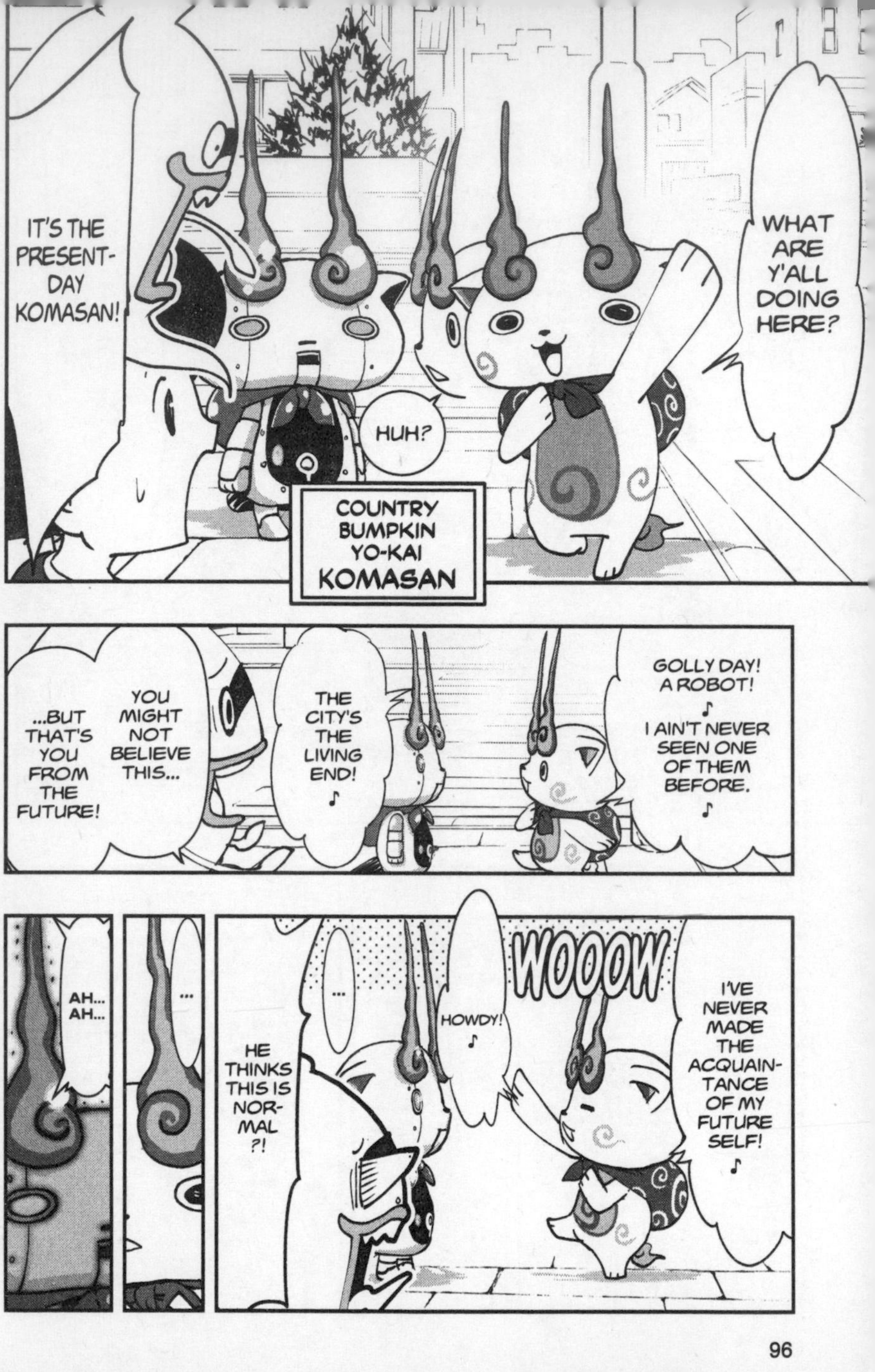
WHAT ARE Y'ALL DOING HERE?
IT'S THE PRESENT-DAY KOMASAN!
HUH?
COUNTRY BUMPKIN YO-KAI KOMASAN
GOLLY DAY! A ROBOT! ♪ I AIN'T NEVER SEEN ONE OF THEM BEFORE. ♪
THE CITY'S THE LIVING END! ♪
YOU MIGHT NOT BELIEVE THIS...
...BUT THAT'S YOU FROM THE FUTURE!
WOOOW
I'VE NEVER MADE THE ACQUAINTANCE OF MY FUTURE SELF! ♪
HOWDY! ♪
...
HE THINKS THIS IS NORMAL?!
...
AH... AH...

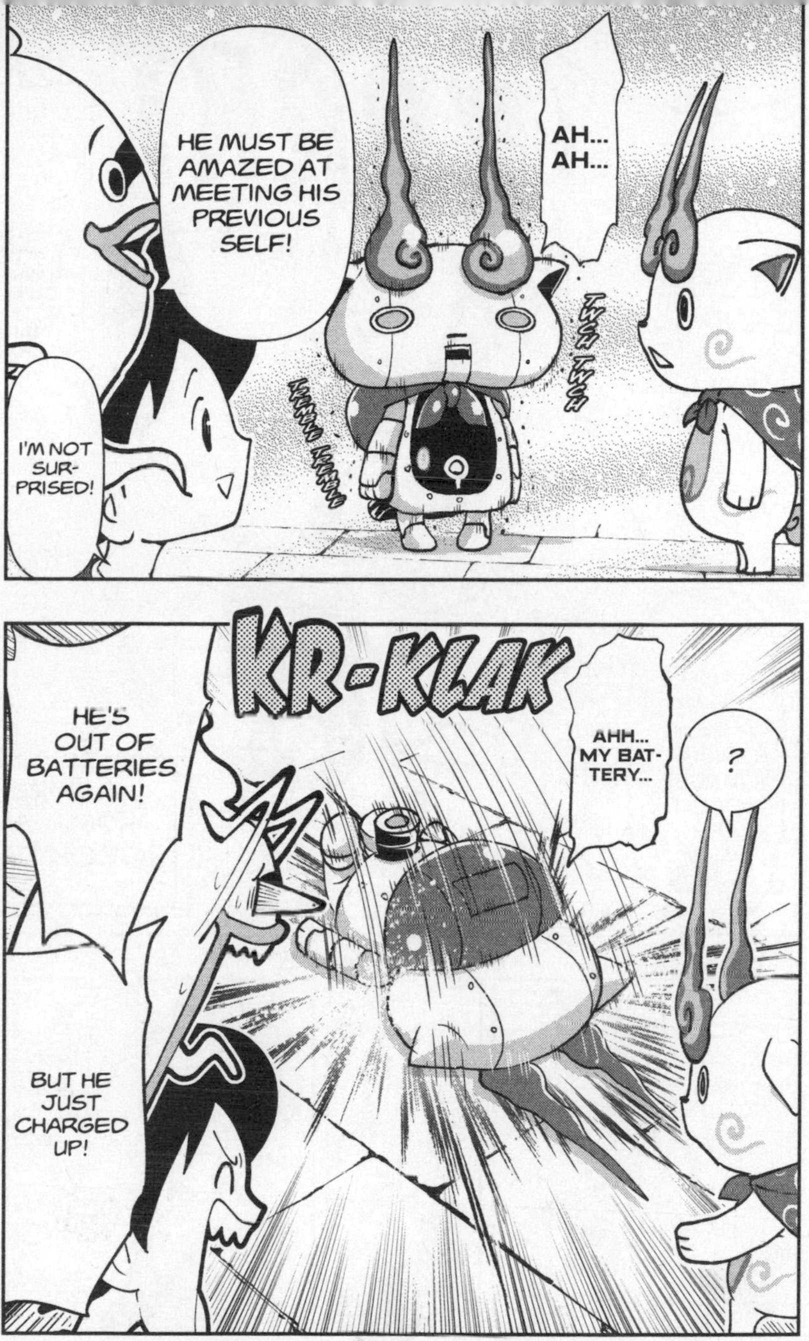
AH... AH...
TWCH TWCH
HE MUST BE AMAZED AT MEETING HIS PREVIOUS SELF!
I'M NOT SUR-PRISED!
?
AHH... MY BAT-TERY...
KR-KLAK
HE'S OUT OF BATTERIES AGAIN!
BUT HE JUST CHARGED UP!

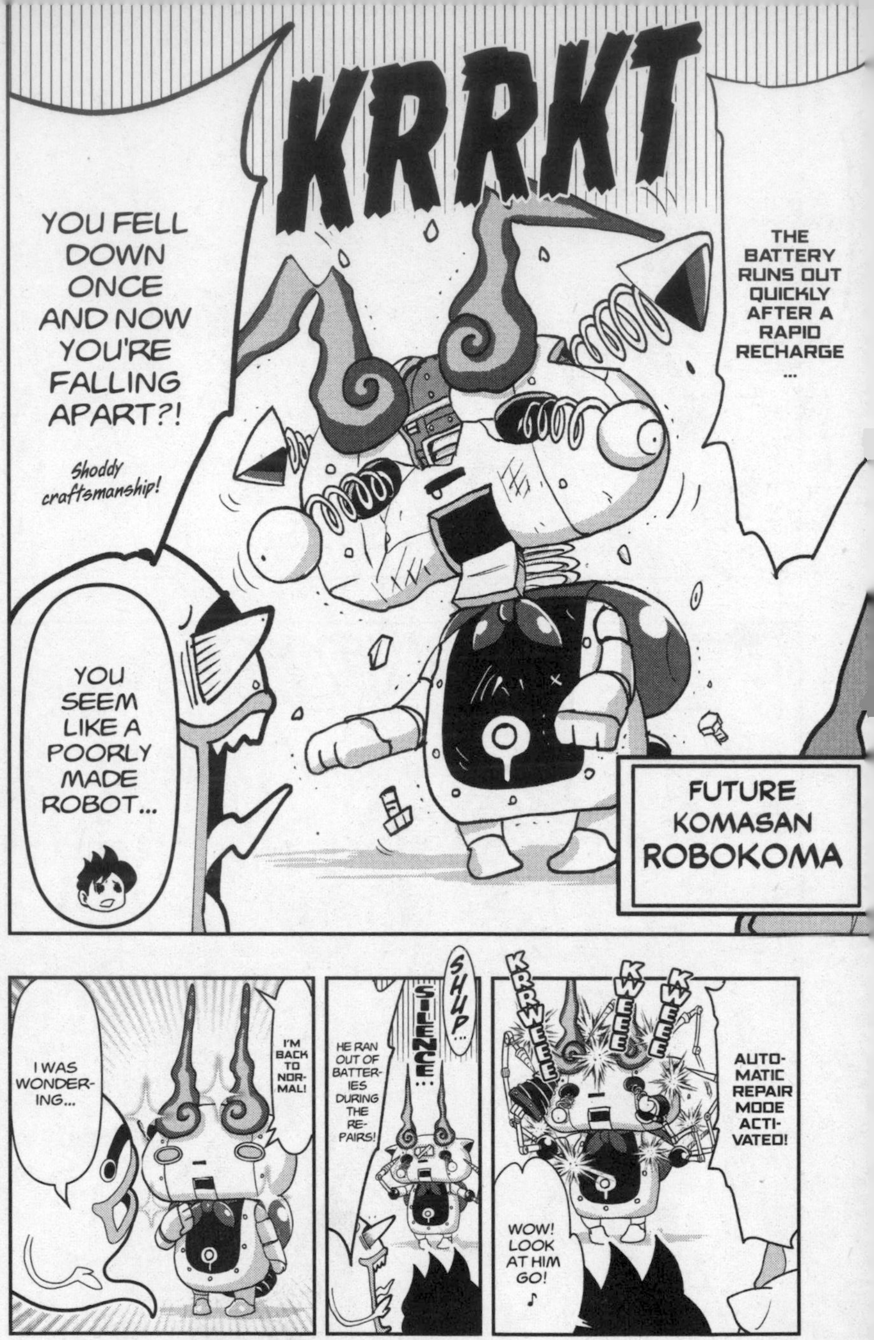
KRRKT
THE BATTERY RUNS OUT QUICKLY AFTER A RAPID RECHARGE ...
YOU FELL DOWN ONCE AND NOW YOU'RE FALLING APART?!
Shoddy craftsmanship!
FUTURE KOMASAN ROBOKOMA
YOU SEEM LIKE A POORLY MADE ROBOT...
KWEEE
KWEEE
KRRWEEE
AUTO-MATIC REPAIR MODE ACTI-VATED!
WOW! LOOK AT HIM GO! ♪
SHUP...
SILENCE...
HE RAN OUT OF BATTER-IES DURING THE RE-PAIRS!
I'M BACK TO NOR-MAL!
I WAS WONDER-ING...

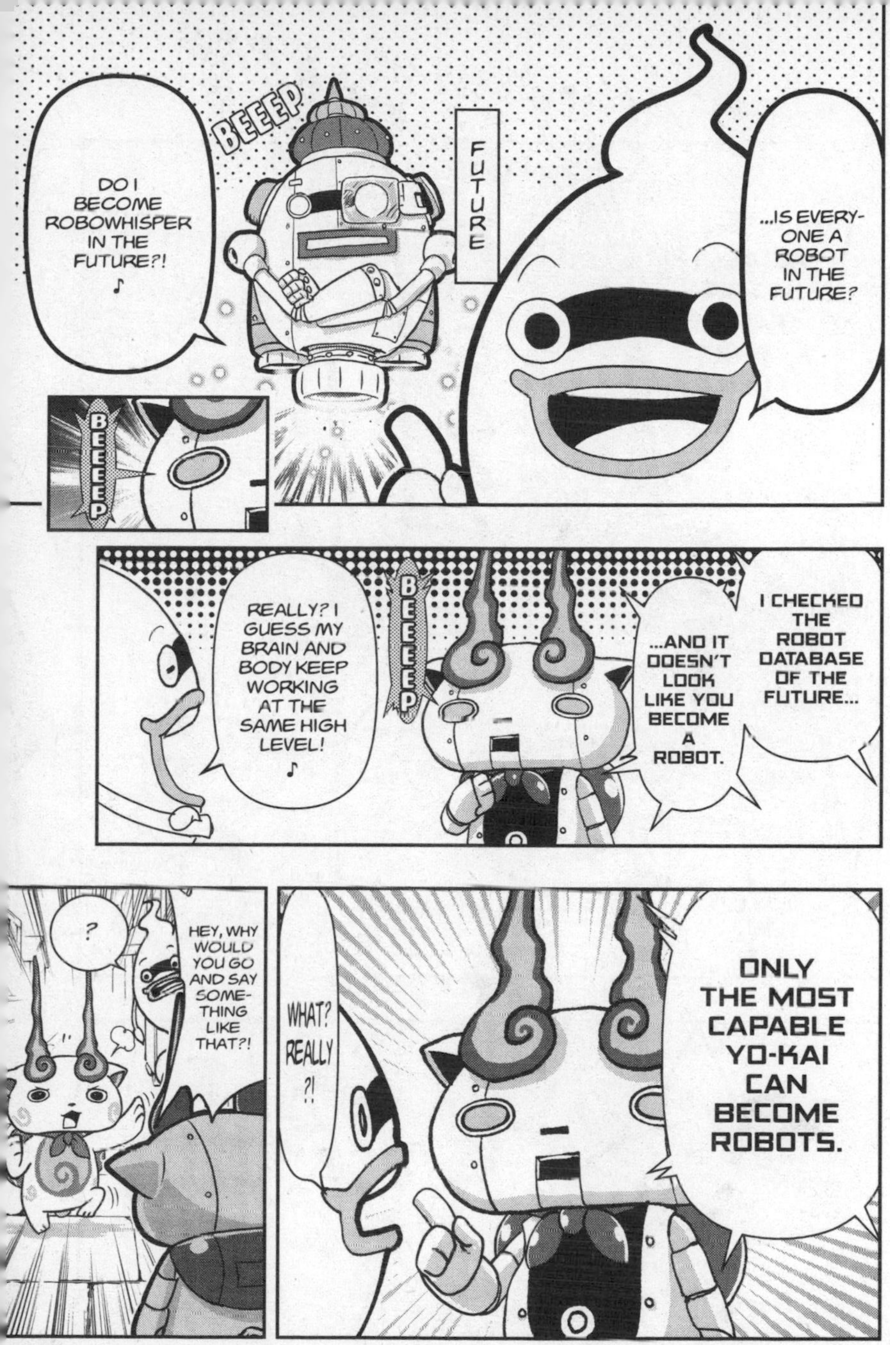

...IS EVERYONE A ROBOT IN THE FUTURE?
FUTURE
BEEEP
DO I BECOME ROBOWHISPER IN THE FUTURE?! ♪
BEEEEEP
I CHECKED THE ROBOT DATABASE OF THE FUTURE...
...AND IT DOESN'T LOOK LIKE YOU BECOME A ROBOT.
BEEEEEP
REALLY?! I GUESS MY BRAIN AND BODY KEEP WORKING AT THE SAME HIGH LEVEL! ♪
ONLY THE MOST CAPABLE YO-KAI CAN BECOME ROBOTS.
WHAT? REALLY?!
HEY, WHY WOULD YOU GO AND SAY SOMETHING LIKE THAT?!
?

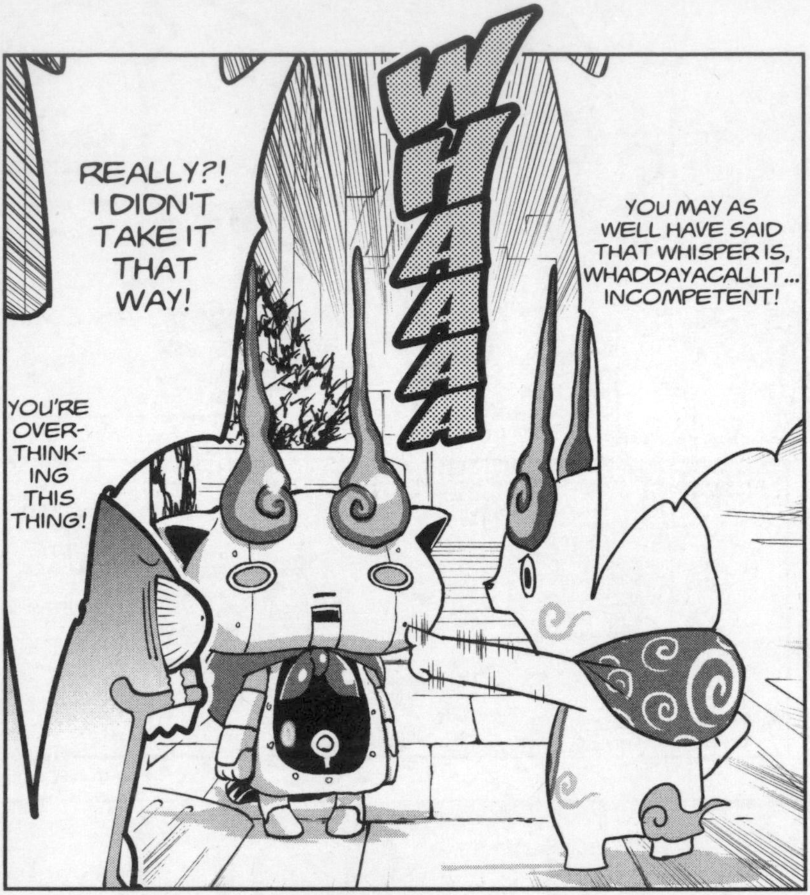
YOU MAY AS WELL HAVE SAID THAT WHISPER IS, WHADDAYACALLIT... INCOMPETENT!
WHAAAA
REALLY?! I DIDN'T TAKE IT THAT WAY!
YOU'RE OVER-THINK-ING THIS THING!
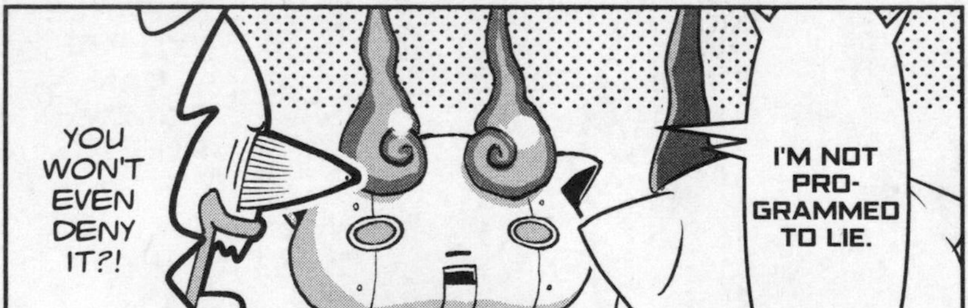
I'M NOT PRO-GRAMMED TO LIE.
YOU WON'T EVEN DENY IT?!

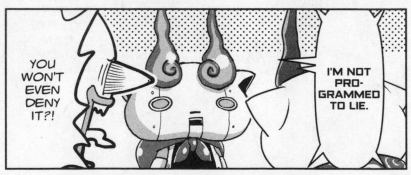

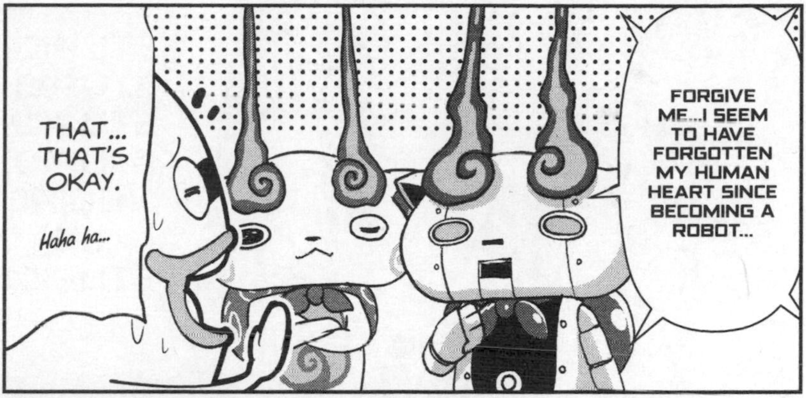
FORGIVE ME...I SEEM TO HAVE FORGOTTEN MY HUMAN HEART SINCE BECOMING A ROBOT...
THAT... THAT'S OKAY.
Haha ha...

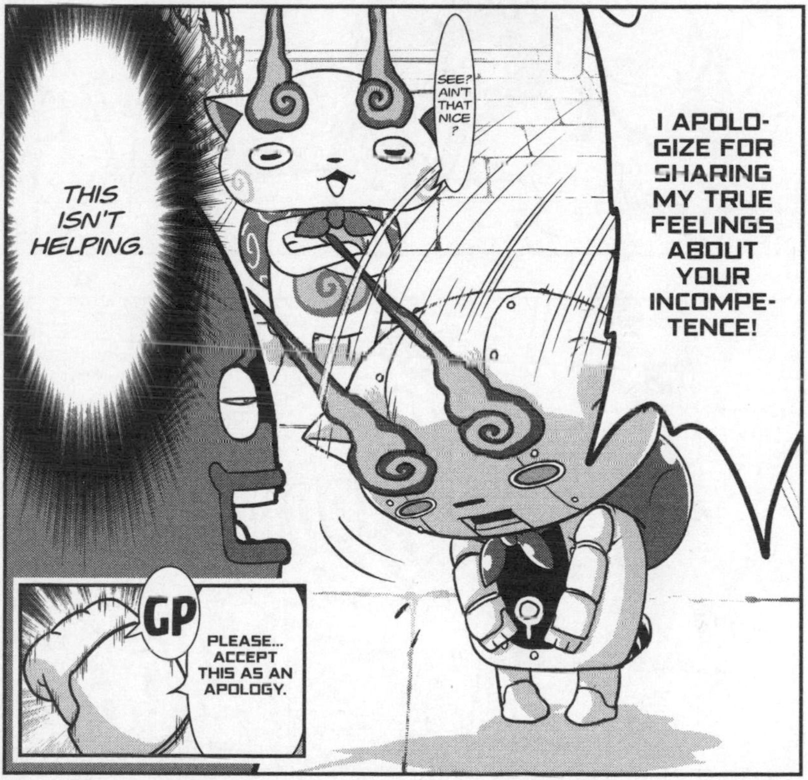
I APOLOGIZE FOR SHARING MY TRUE FEELINGS ABOUT YOUR INCOMPETENCE!
SEE? AIN'T THAT NICE?
THIS ISN'T HELPING.
GP
PLEASE... ACCEPT THIS AS AN APOLOGY.

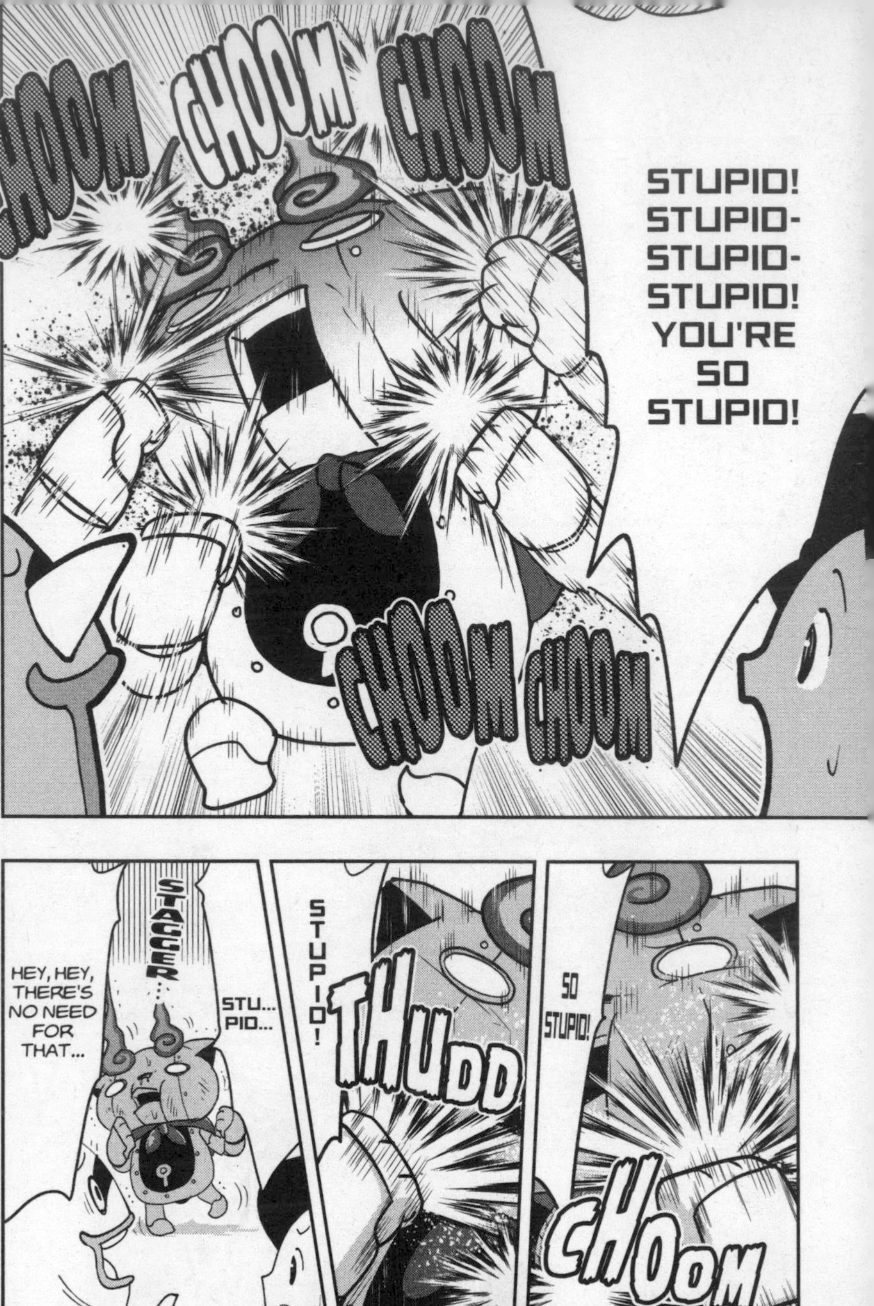
CHOOM CHOOM CHOOM
STUPID! STUPID-STUPID-STUPID! YOU'RE SO STUPID!
CHOOM CHOOM
SO STUPID!
CHOOM
STUPID!
THUDD
STU... PID...
STAGGER...
HEY, HEY, THERE'S NO NEED FOR THAT...

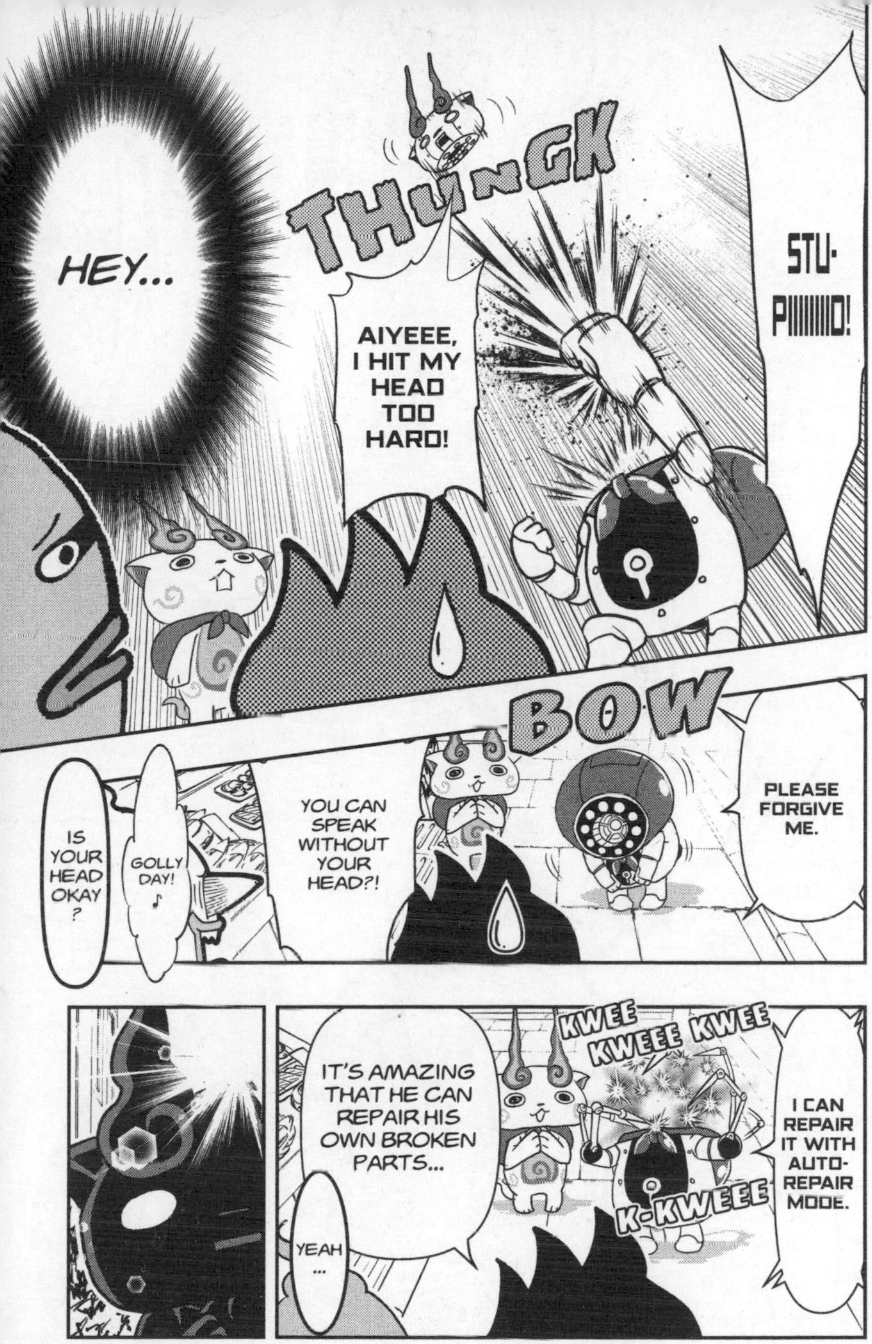
STU-PIIIIID!
THUNGK
AIYEEE, I HIT MY HEAD TOO HARD!
HEY...
PLEASE FORGIVE ME.
BOW
YOU CAN SPEAK WITHOUT YOUR HEAD?!
GOLLY DAY! ♪
IS YOUR HEAD OKAY?
I CAN REPAIR IT WITH AUTO-REPAIR MODE.
KWEE KWEEE KWEE
K-KWEEE
IT'S AMAZING THAT HE CAN REPAIR HIS OWN BROKEN PARTS...
YEAH...

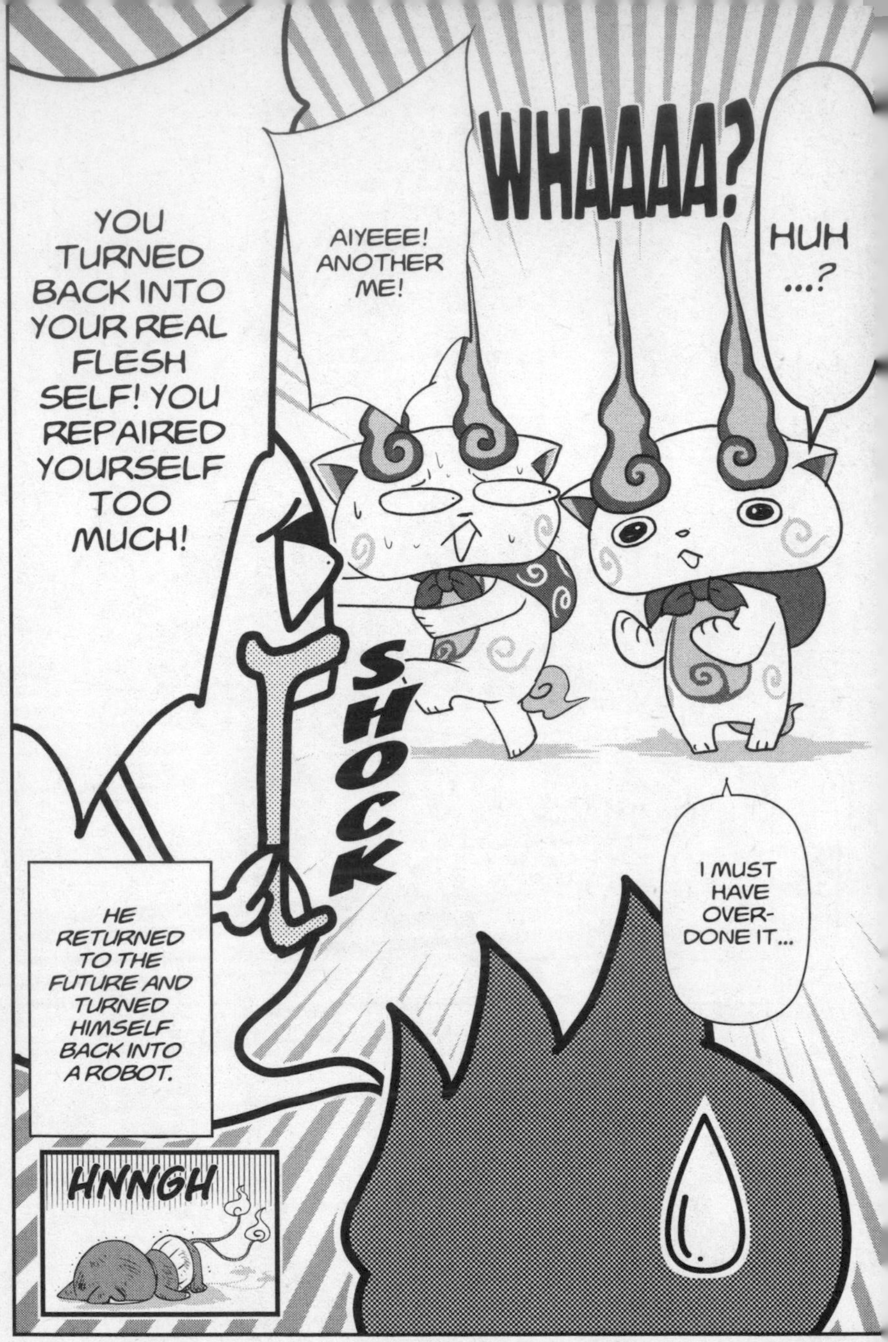
WHAAAA?
HUH ...?
AIYEEE! ANOTHER ME!
YOU TURNED BACK INTO YOUR REAL FLESH SELF! YOU REPAIRED YOURSELF TOO MUCH!
SHOCK
I MUST HAVE OVER-DONE IT...
HE RETURNED TO THE FUTURE AND TURNED HIMSELF BACK INTO A ROBOT.
HNNGH

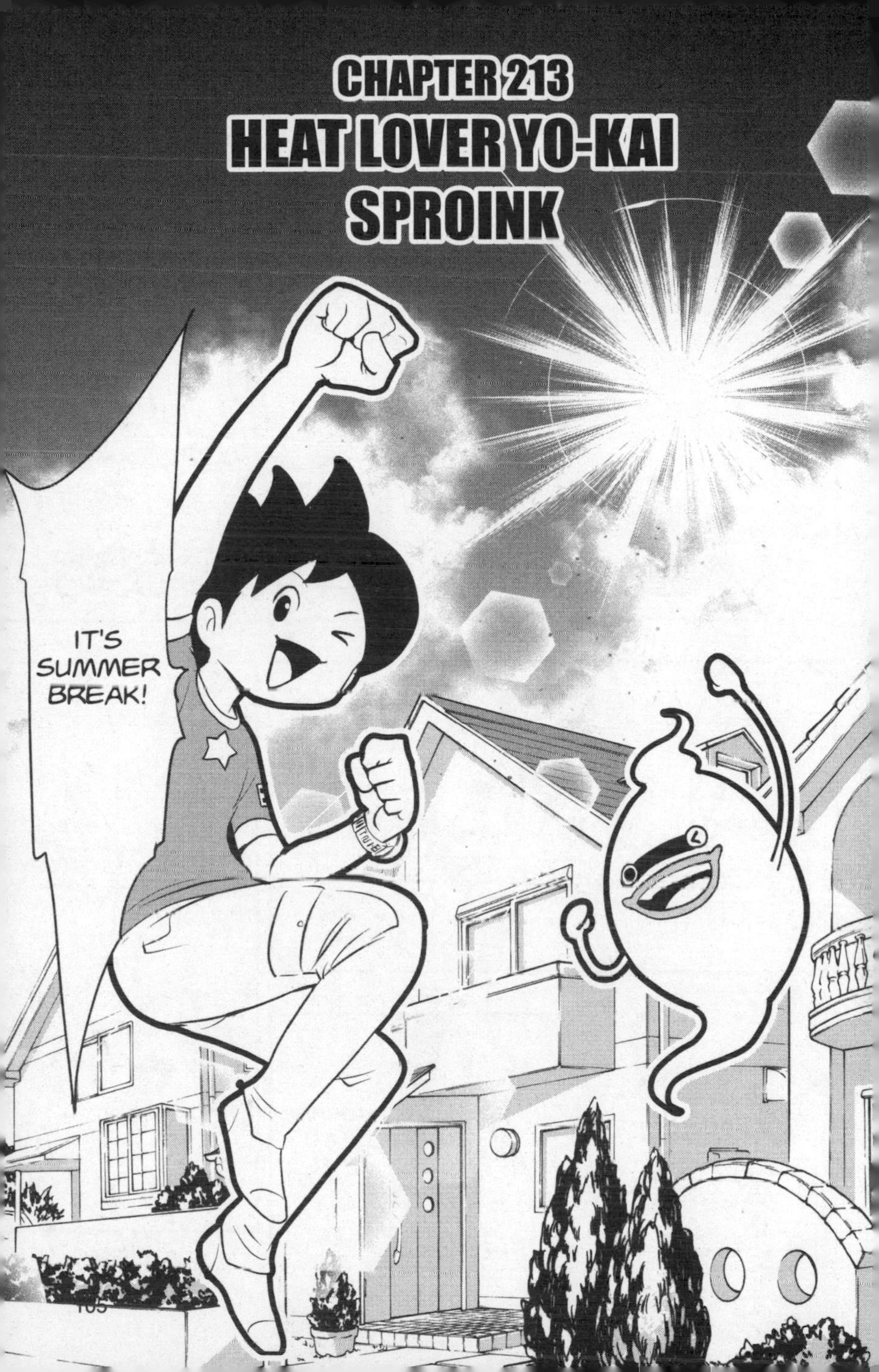
CHAPTER 213
HEAT LOVER YO-KAI
SPROINK
IT'S SUMMER BREAK!

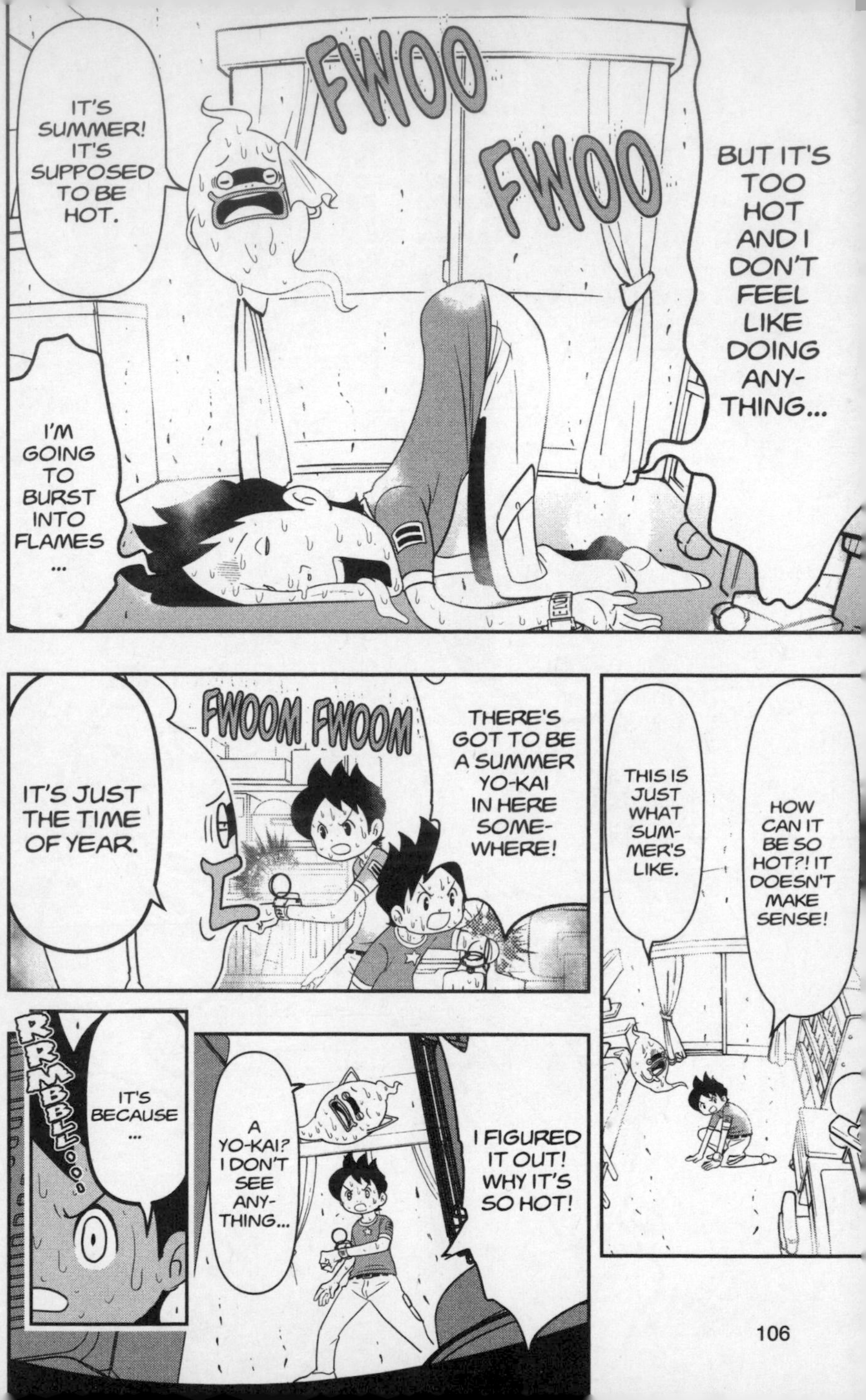

FWOO
FWOO
BUT IT'S TOO HOT AND I DON'T FEEL LIKE DOING ANY-THING...
IT'S SUMMER! IT'S SUPPOSED TO BE HOT.
I'M GOING TO BURST INTO FLAMES ...
HOW CAN IT BE SO HOT?! IT DOESN'T MAKE SENSE!
THIS IS JUST WHAT SUM-MER'S LIKE.
THERE'S GOT TO BE A SUMMER YO-KAI IN HERE SOME-WHERE!
FWOOM FWOOM
IT'S JUST THE TIME OF YEAR.
I FIGURED IT OUT! WHY IT'S SO HOT!
A YO-KAI? I DON'T SEE ANY-THING...
RRMBBLL...
IT'S BECAUSE ...

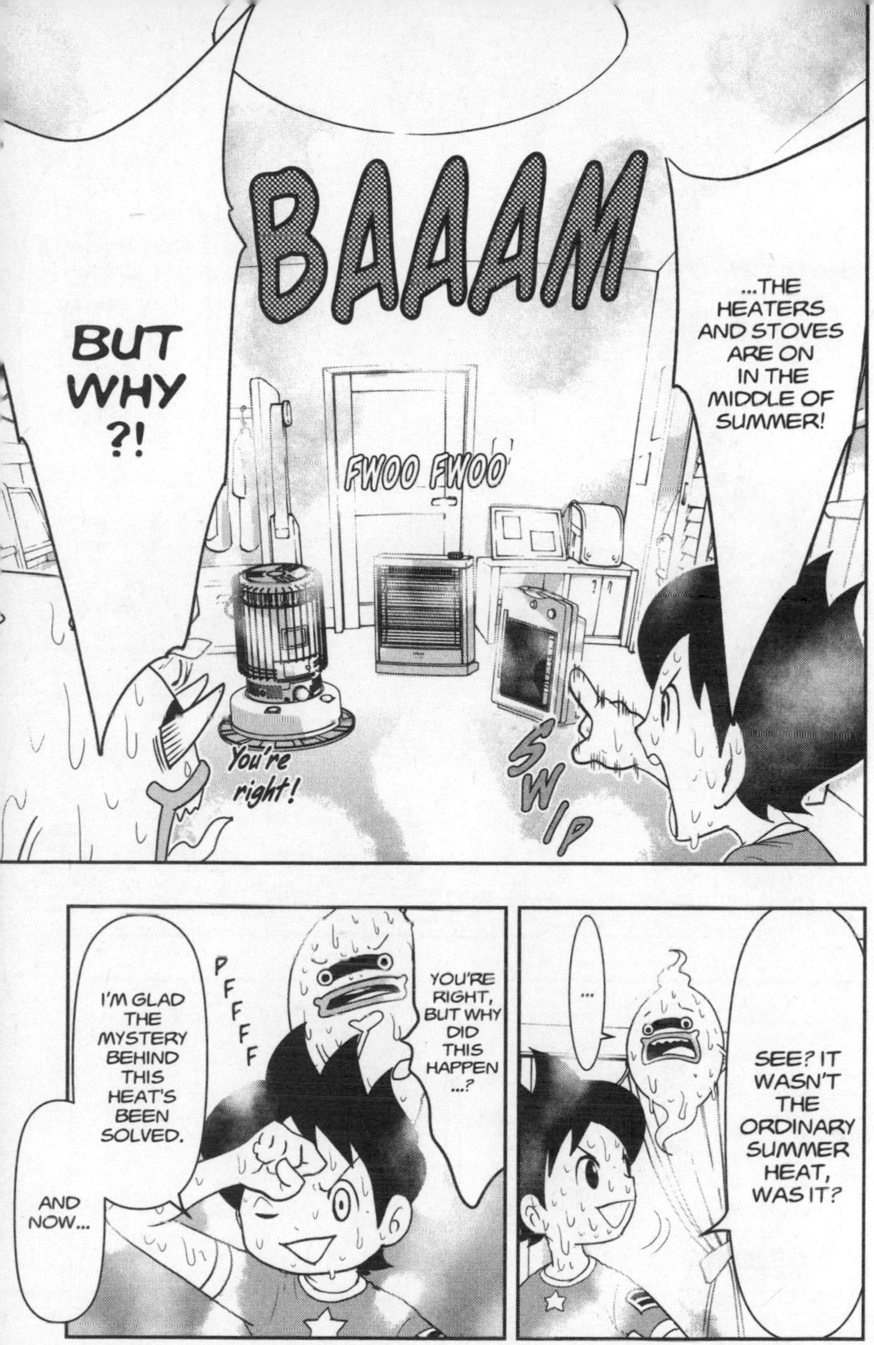
...THE HEATERS AND STOVES ARE ON IN THE MIDDLE OF SUMMER!
BAAAM
BUT WHY ?!
FWOO FWOO
SWIP
You're right!
SEE? IT WASN'T THE ORDINARY SUMMER HEAT, WAS IT?
...
YOU'RE RIGHT, BUT WHY DID THIS HAPPEN ...?
PFFFF
I'M GLAD THE MYSTERY BEHIND THIS HEAT'S BEEN SOLVED.
AND NOW...

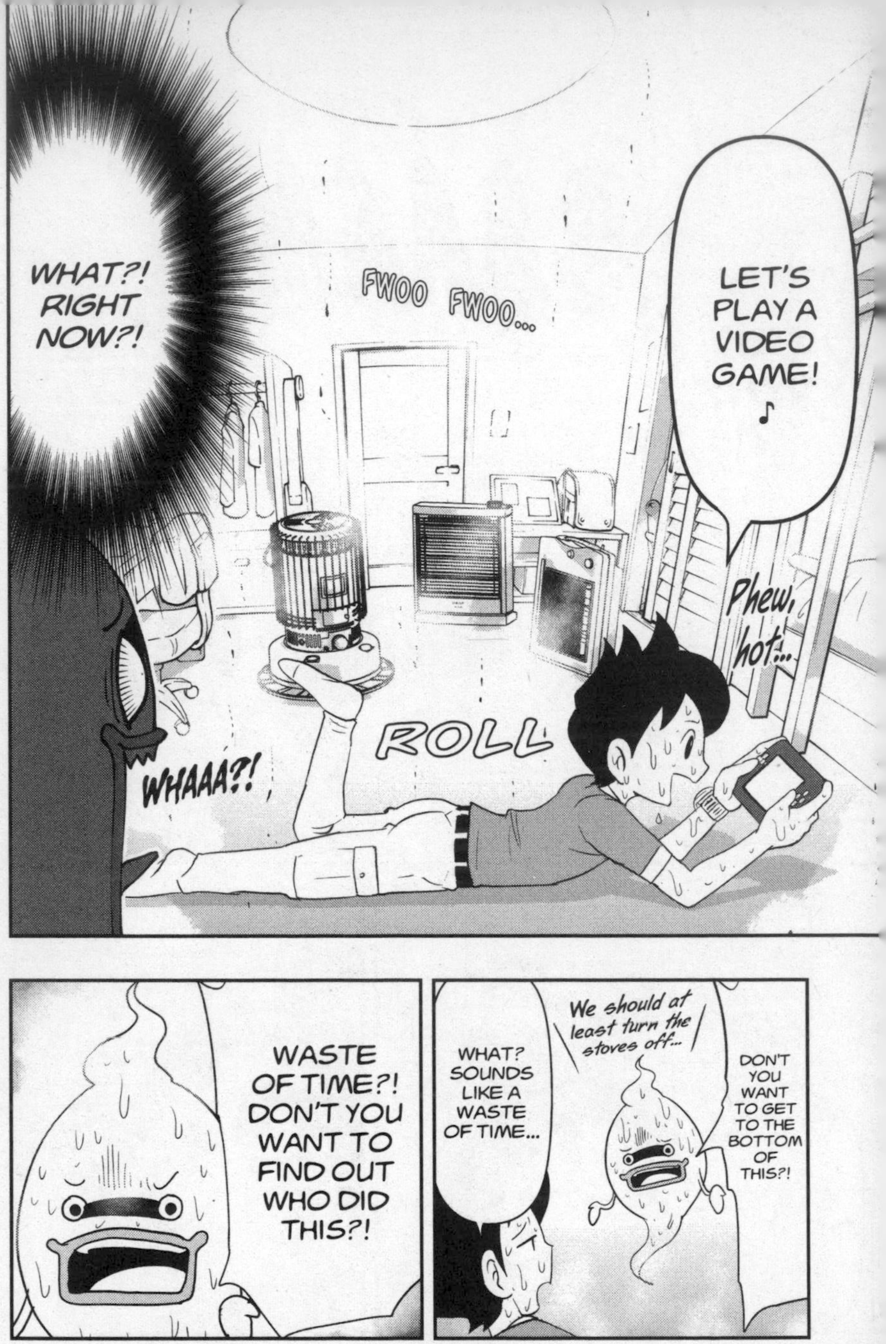
LET'S PLAY A VIDEO GAME! ♪
Phew, hot...
FWOO FWOO...
WHAT?! RIGHT NOW?!
ROLL
WHAAA?!
DON'T YOU WANT TO GET TO THE BOTTOM OF THIS?!
We should at least turn the stoves off...
WHAT? SOUNDS LIKE A WASTE OF TIME...
WASTE OF TIME?! DON'T YOU WANT TO FIND OUT WHO DID THIS?!

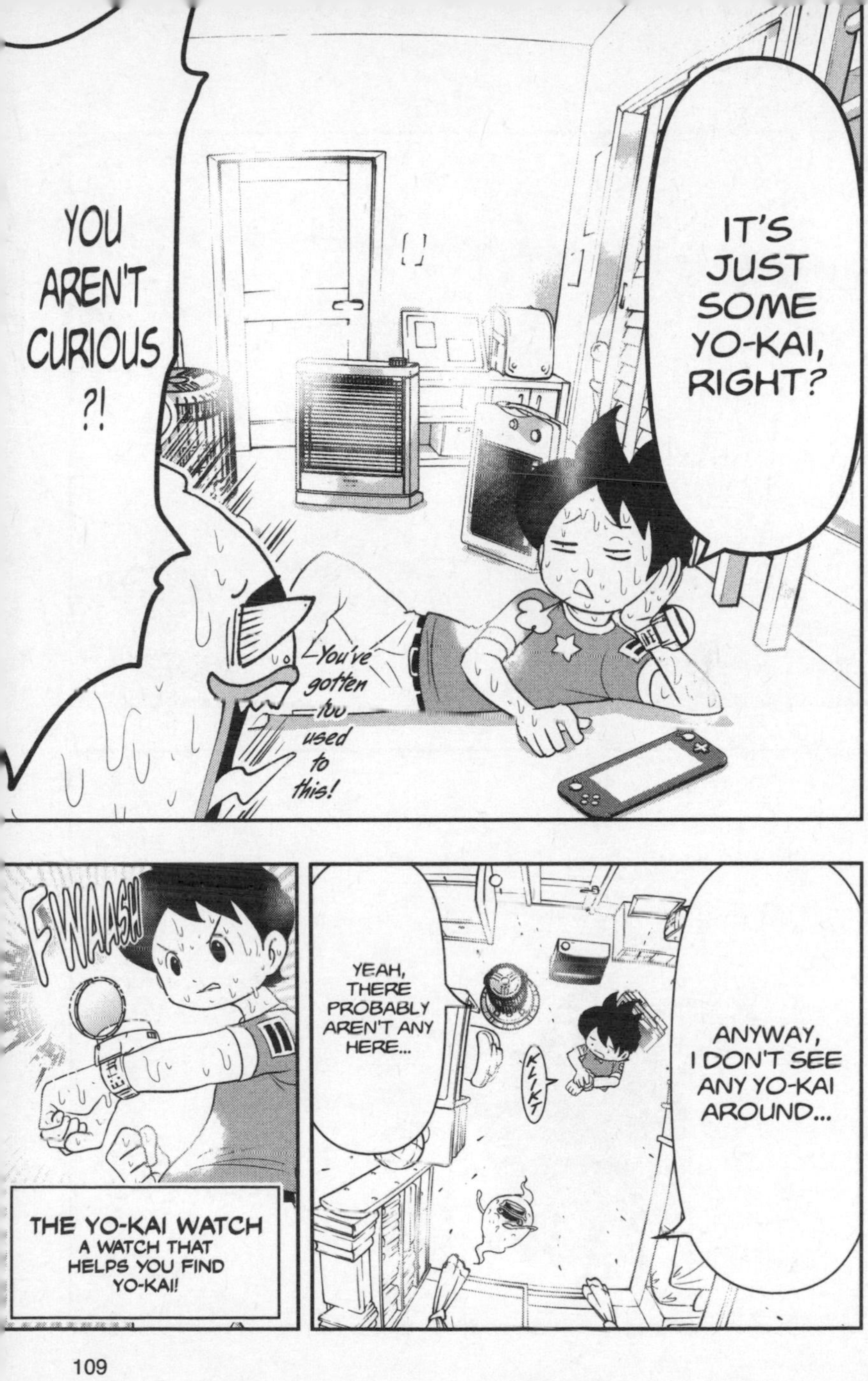
IT'S JUST SOME YO-KAI, RIGHT?
YOU AREN'T CURIOUS ?!
You've gotten too used to this!
ANYWAY, I DON'T SEE ANY YO-KAI AROUND...
KLIKT
YEAH, THERE PROBABLY AREN'T ANY HERE...
FWAASH
THE YO-KAI WATCH
A WATCH THAT HELPS YOU FIND YO-KAI!

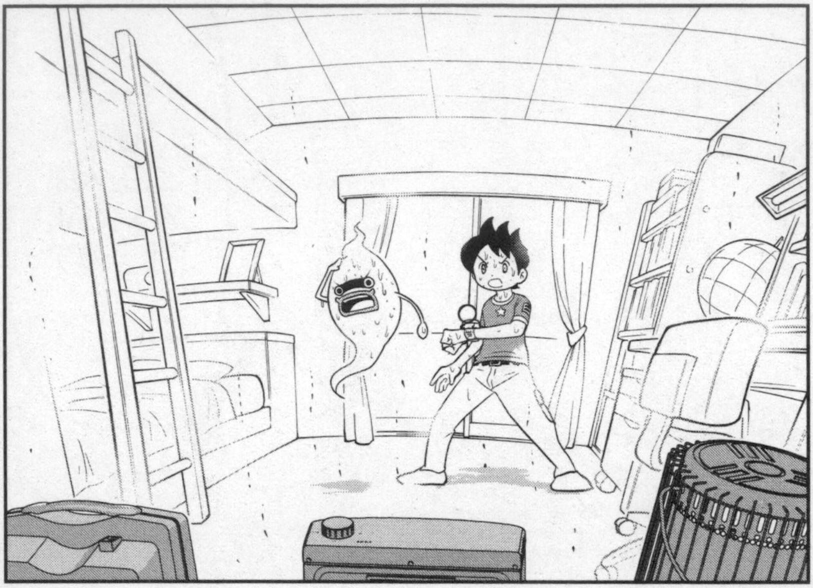

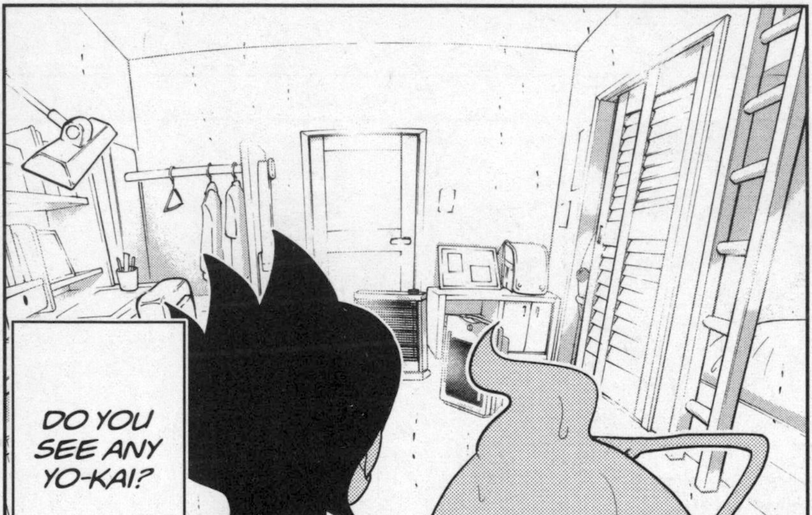
DO YOU SEE ANY YO-KAI?

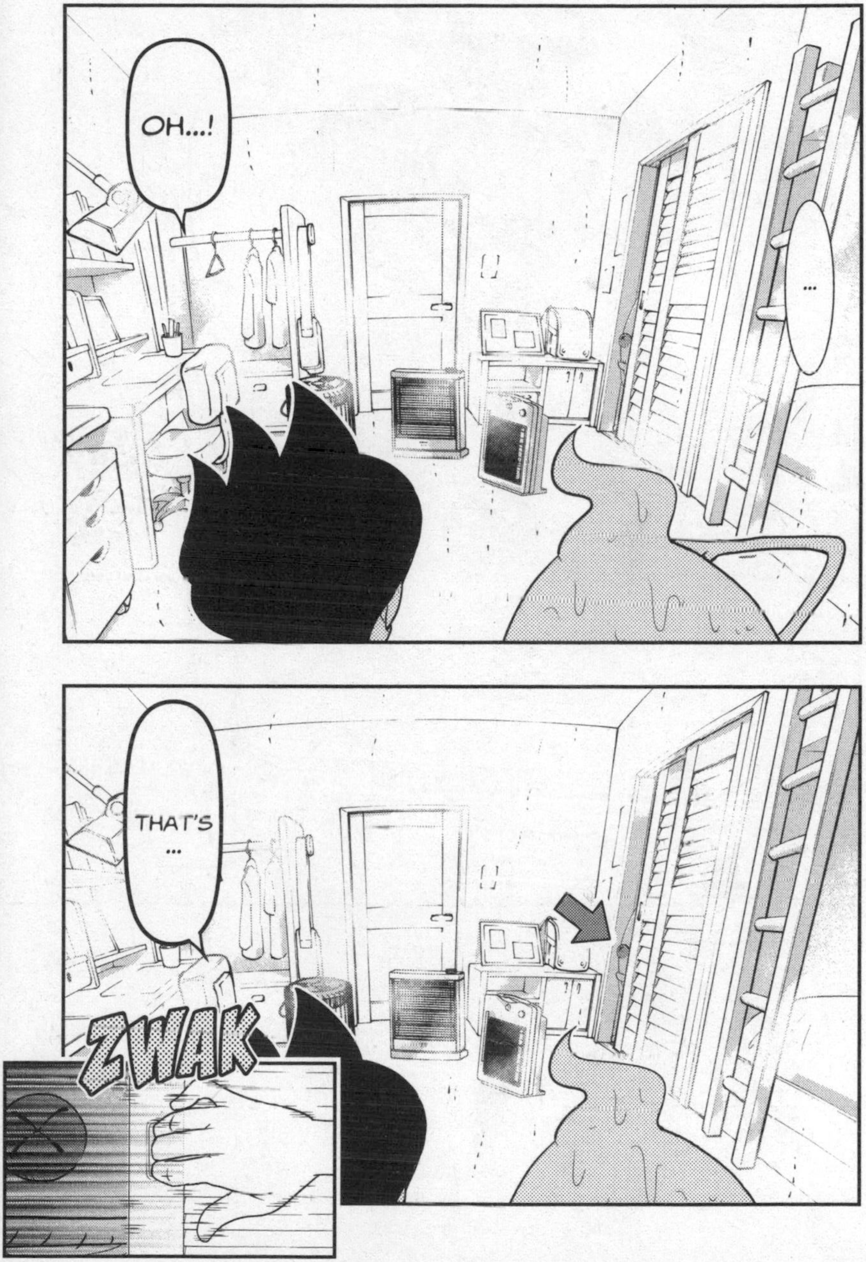
OH...!
...
THAT'S ...
ZWAK

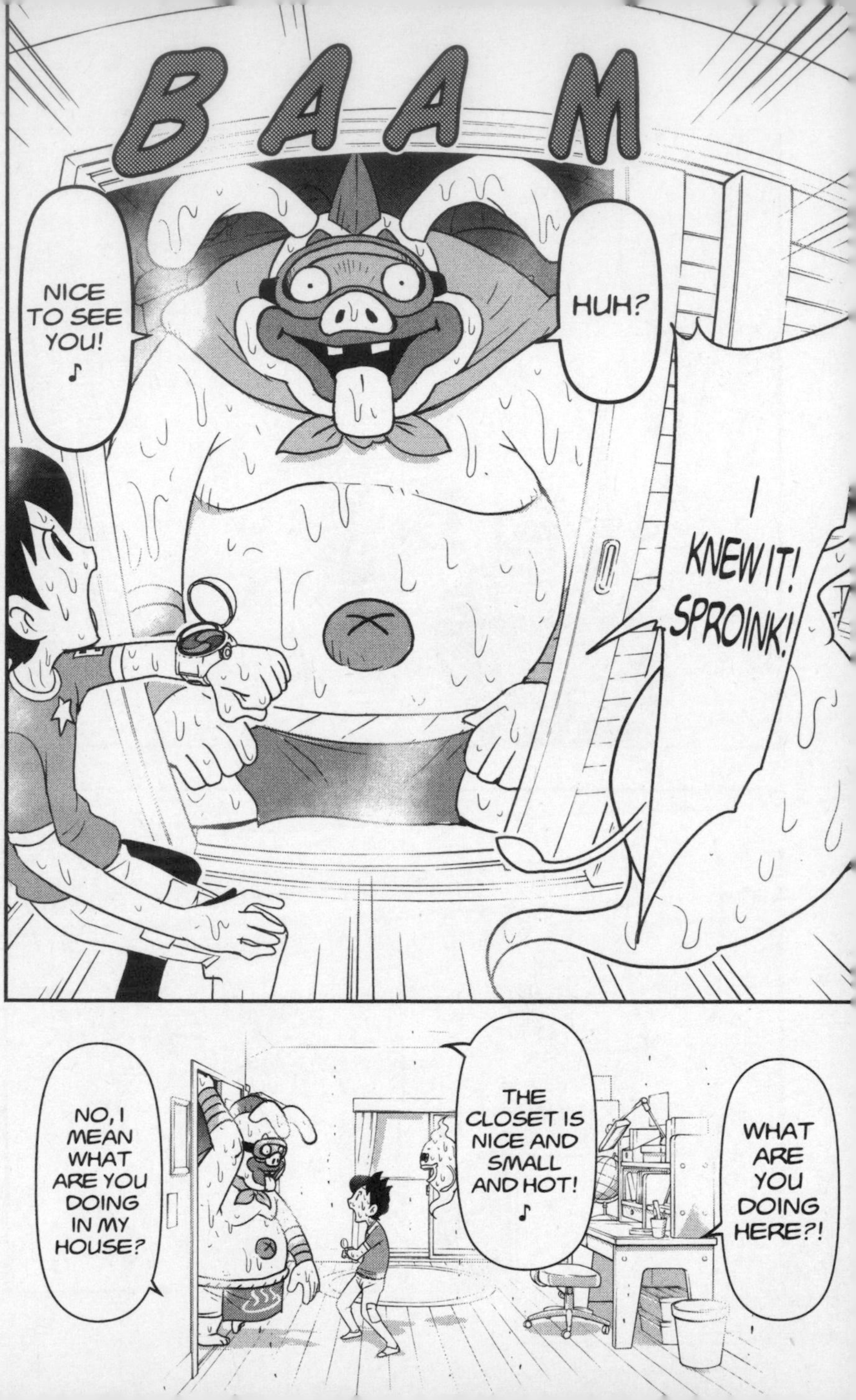
BAAM
HUH?
NICE TO SEE YOU! ♪
I KNEW IT! SPROINK!
WHAT ARE YOU DOING HERE?!
THE CLOSET IS NICE AND SMALL AND HOT! ♪
NO, I MEAN WHAT ARE YOU DOING IN MY HOUSE?

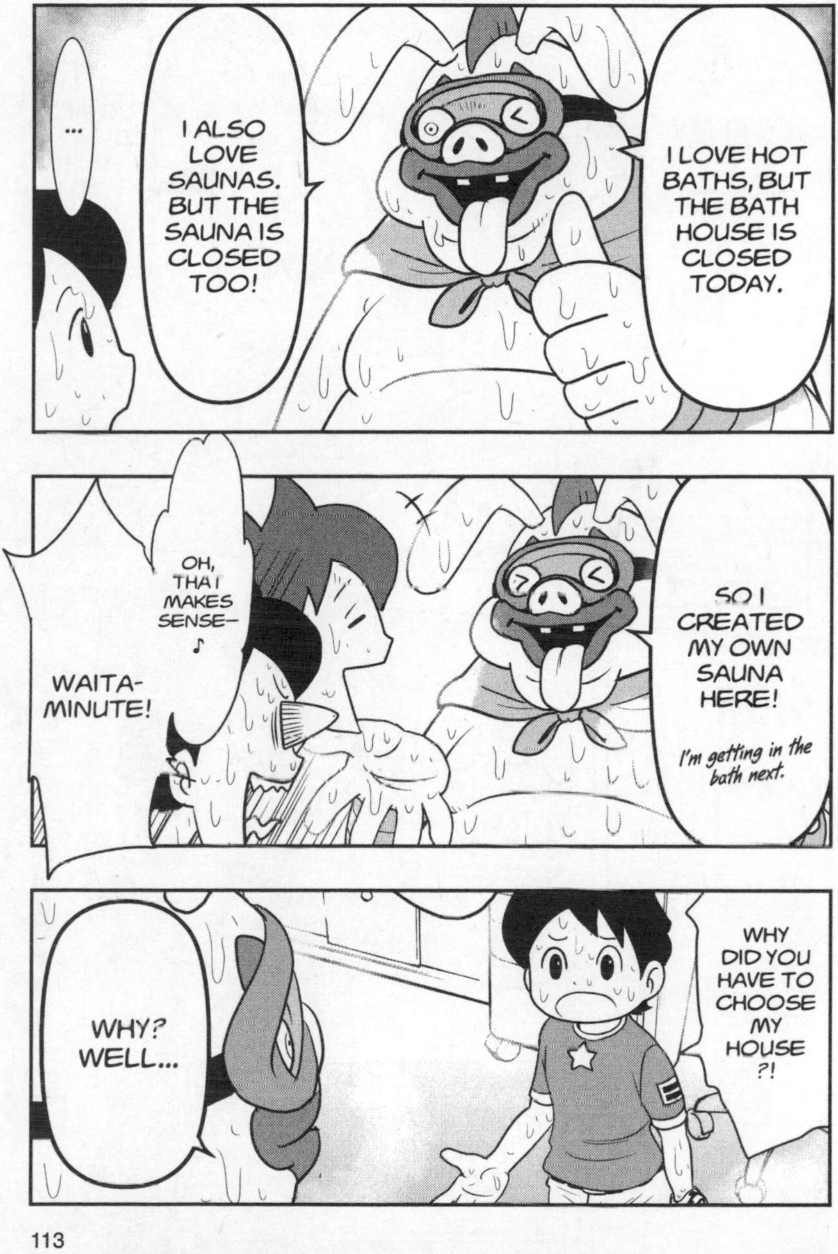
I LOVE HOT BATHS, BUT THE BATH HOUSE IS CLOSED TODAY.
I ALSO LOVE SAUNAS. BUT THE SAUNA IS CLOSED TOO!
...
SO I CREATED MY OWN SAUNA HERE!
I'm getting in the bath next.
OH, THAT MAKES SENSE-♪
WAITA-MINUTE!
WHY DID YOU HAVE TO CHOOSE MY HOUSE?!
WHY? WELL...

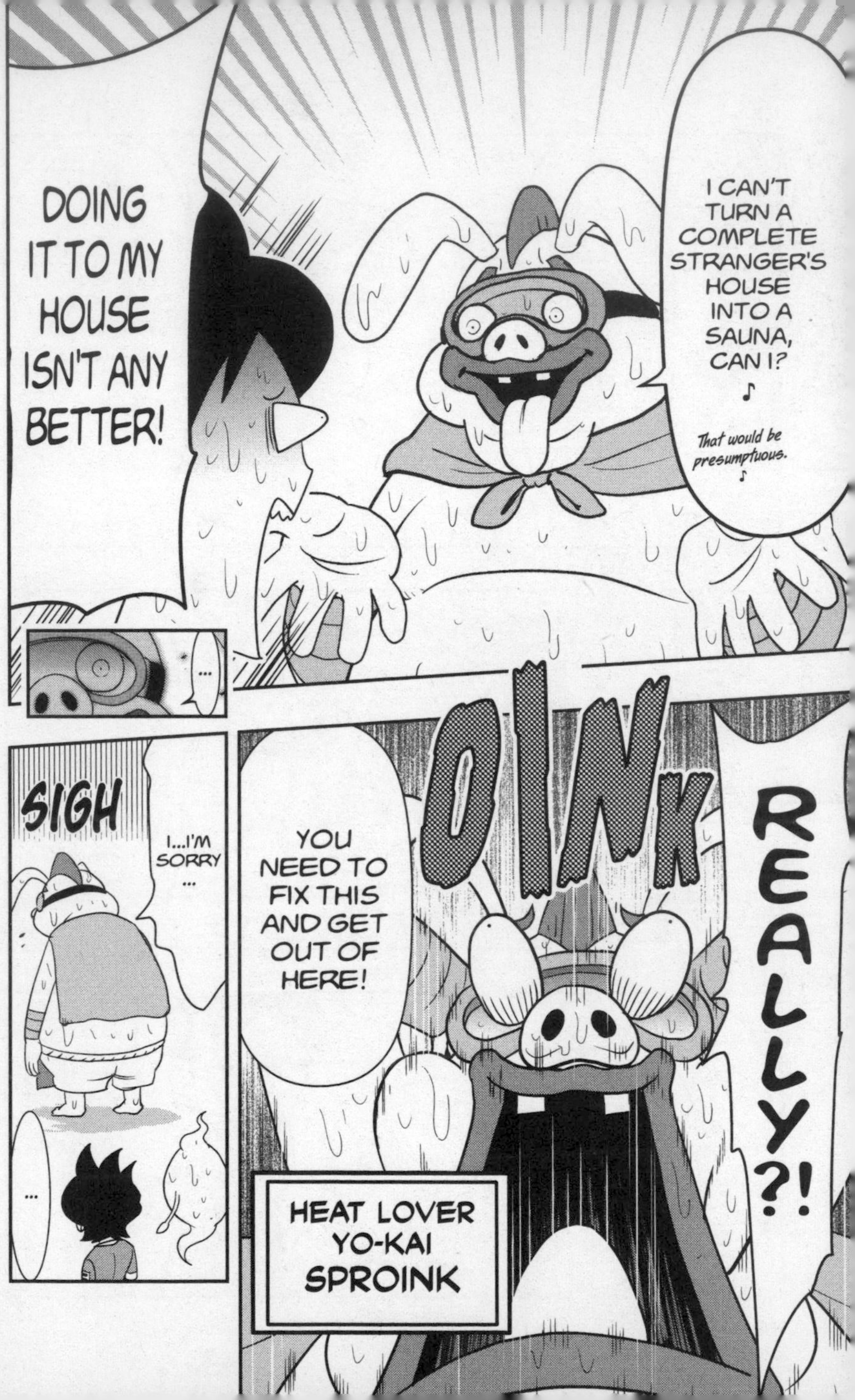
I CAN'T TURN A COMPLETE STRANGER'S HOUSE INTO A SAUNA, CAN I? ♪
That would be presumptuous. ♪
DOING IT TO MY HOUSE ISN'T ANY BETTER!
...
REALLY?!
OINK
YOU NEED TO FIX THIS AND GET OUT OF HERE!
HEAT LOVER YO-KAI SPROINK
SIGH
I...I'M SORRY...
...

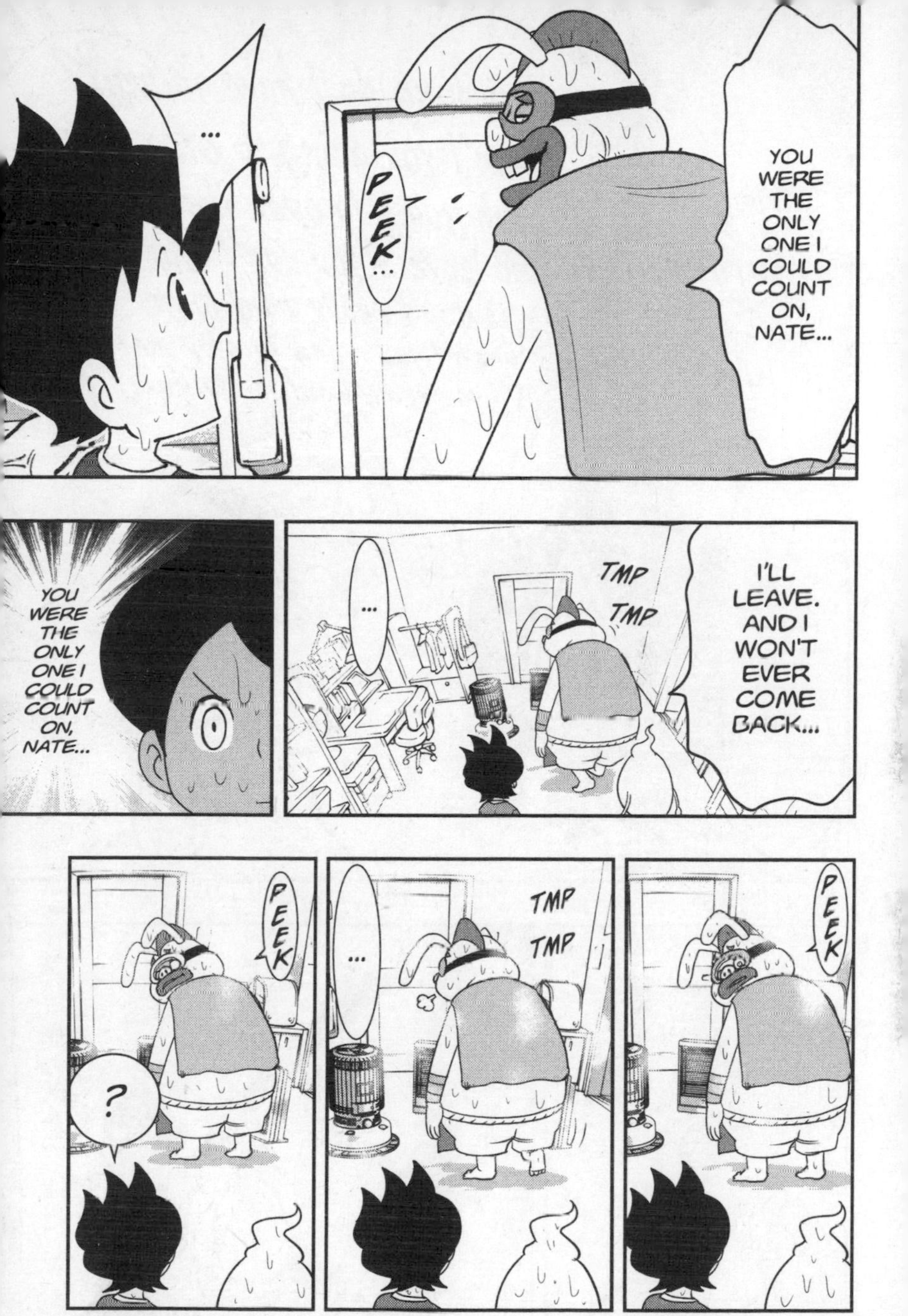
YOU WERE THE ONLY ONE I COULD COUNT ON, NATE...
PEEK...
...
I'LL LEAVE. AND I WON'T EVER COME BACK...
TMP
TMP
...
YOU WERE THE ONLY ONE I COULD COUNT ON, NATE...
PEEK
TMP
TMP
...
PEEK
?

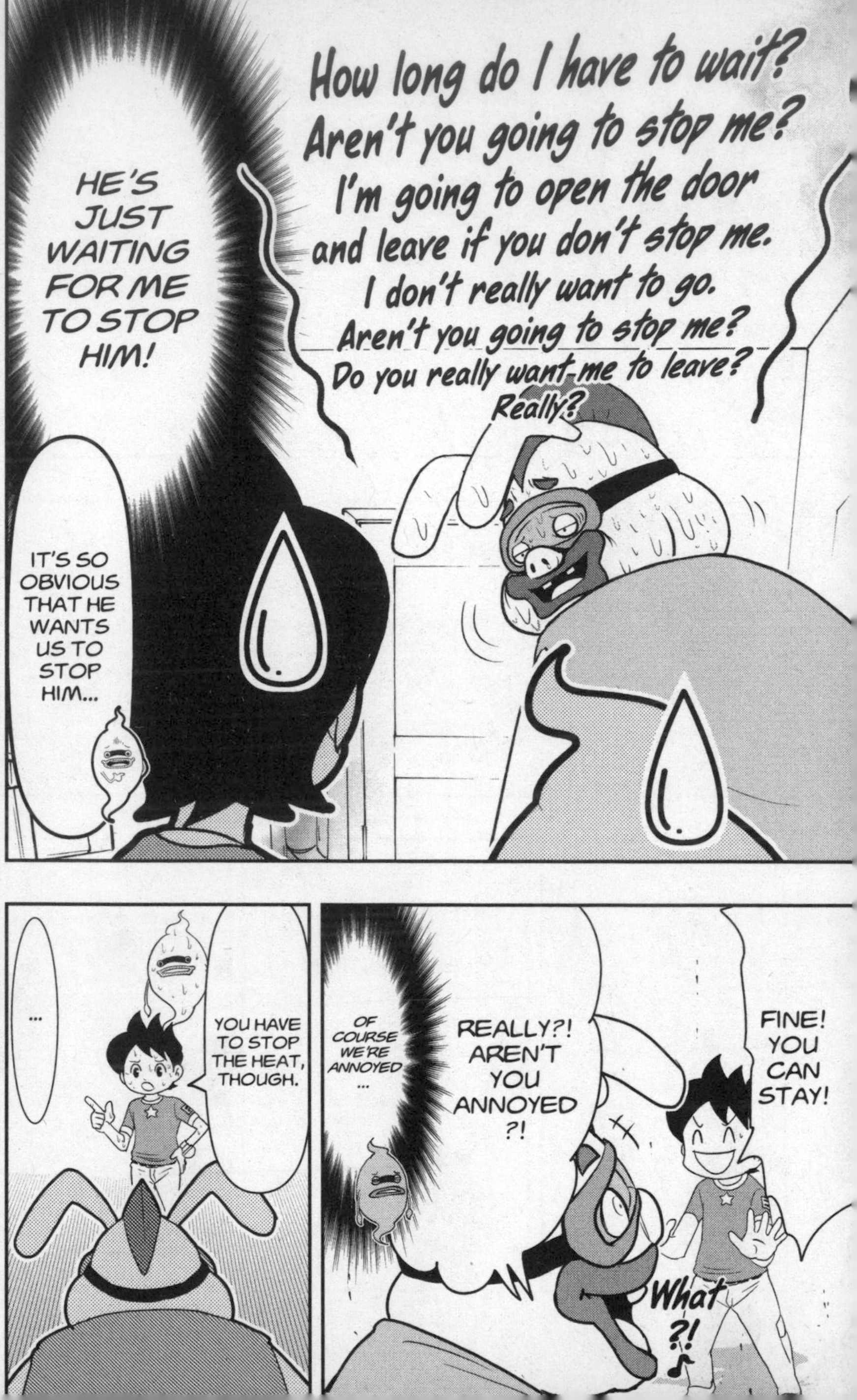
How long do I have to wait? Aren't you going to stop me? I'm going to open the door and leave if you don't stop me. I don't really want to go. Aren't you going to stop me? Do you really want me to leave? Really?
HE'S JUST WAITING FOR ME TO STOP HIM!
IT'S SO OBVIOUS THAT HE WANTS US TO STOP HIM...
FINE! YOU CAN STAY!
REALLY?! AREN'T YOU ANNOYED?!
What?!
OF COURSE WE'RE ANNOYED...
YOU HAVE TO STOP THE HEAT, THOUGH.
...

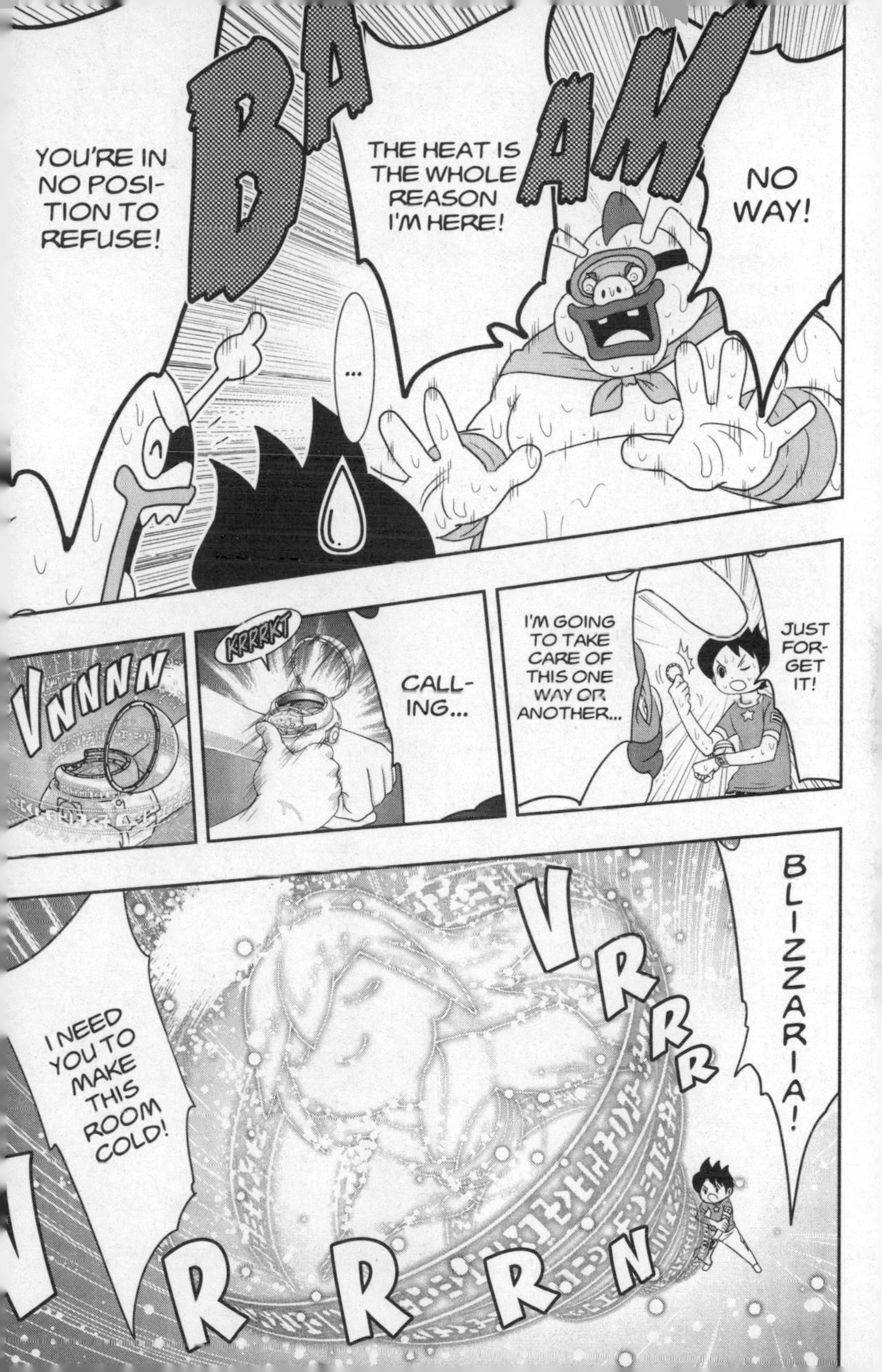
NO WAY!
THE HEAT IS THE WHOLE REASON I'M HERE!
BAAM
YOU'RE IN NO POSI-TION TO REFUSE!
...
JUST FOR-GET IT!
I'M GOING TO TAKE CARE OF THIS ONE WAY OR ANOTHER...
KRRRKT
CALL-ING...
VNNNN
BLIZZARIA!
VRRR
I NEED YOU TO MAKE THIS ROOM COLD!
VRRRRN

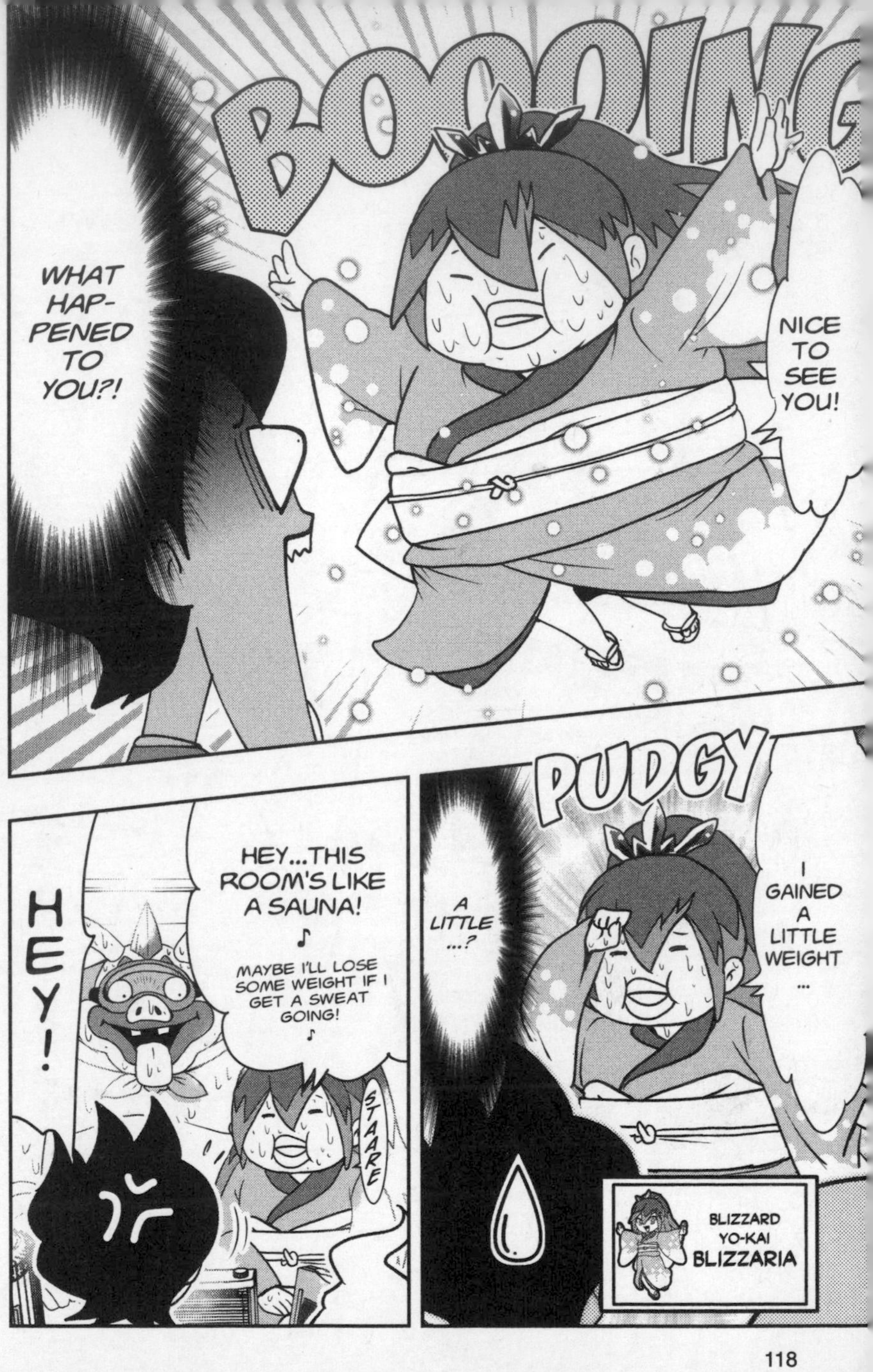
BOOOING
NICE TO SEE YOU!
WHAT HAPPENED TO YOU?!
PUDGY
I GAINED A LITTLE WEIGHT...
A LITTLE...?
BLIZZARD YO-KAI BLIZZARIA
HEY...THIS ROOM'S LIKE A SAUNA! ♪
MAYBE I'LL LOSE SOME WEIGHT IF I GET A SWEAT GOING! ♪
HEY!
STAARE

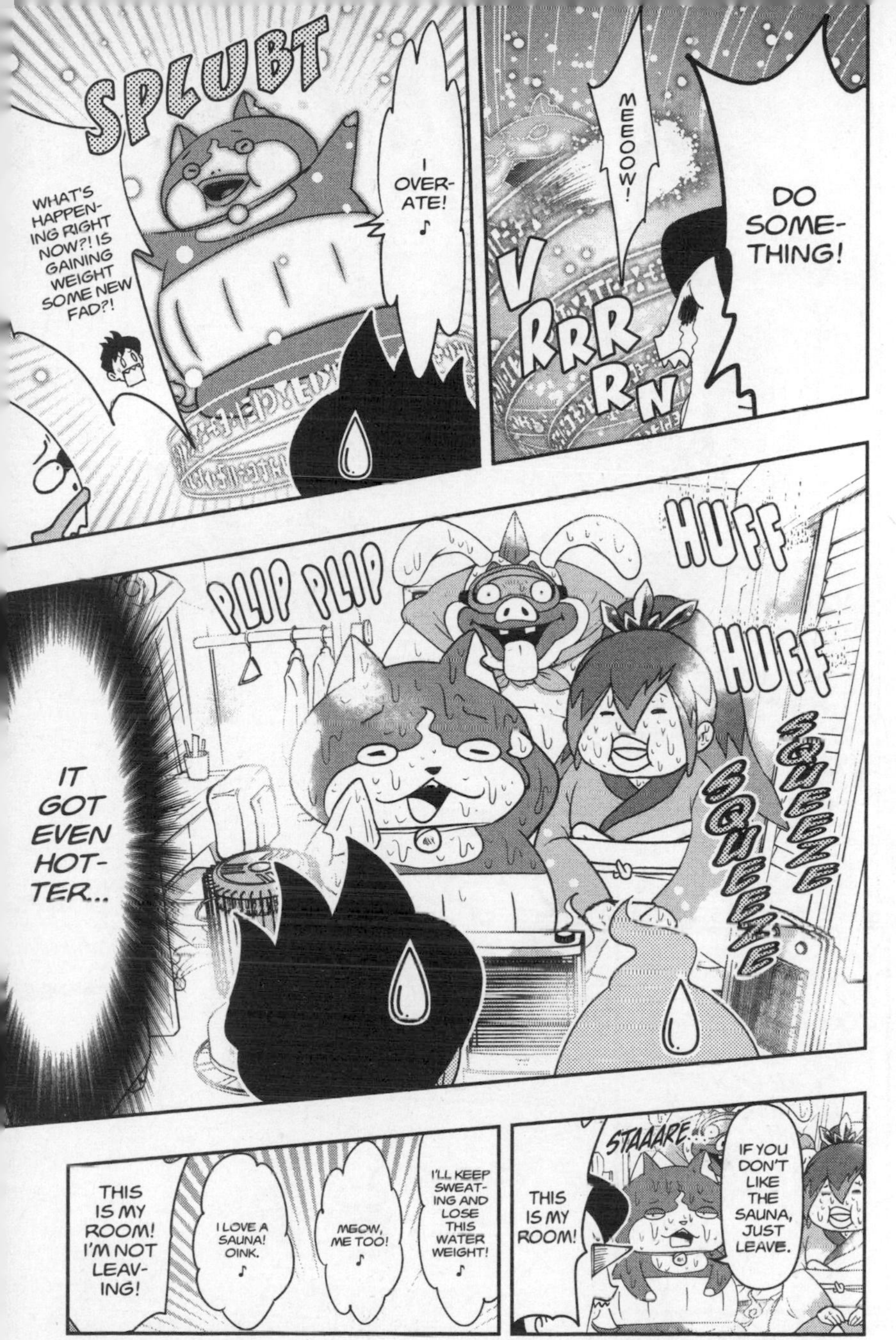
MEEOOW!
DO SOME-THING!
VRRRRN
SPLUBT
I OVER-ATE! ♪
WHAT'S HAPPEN-ING RIGHT NOW?! IS GAINING WEIGHT SOME NEW FAD?!
HUFF HUFF
SQUEEEZE SQUEEEZE
PLIP PLIP
IT GOT EVEN HOT-TER...
STAAARE...
IF YOU DON'T LIKE THE SAUNA, JUST LEAVE.
THIS IS MY ROOM!
I'LL KEEP SWEAT-ING AND LOSE THIS WATER WEIGHT! ♪
MEOW, ME TOO! ♪
I LOVE A SAUNA! OINK. ♪
THIS IS MY ROOM! I'M NOT LEAV-ING!

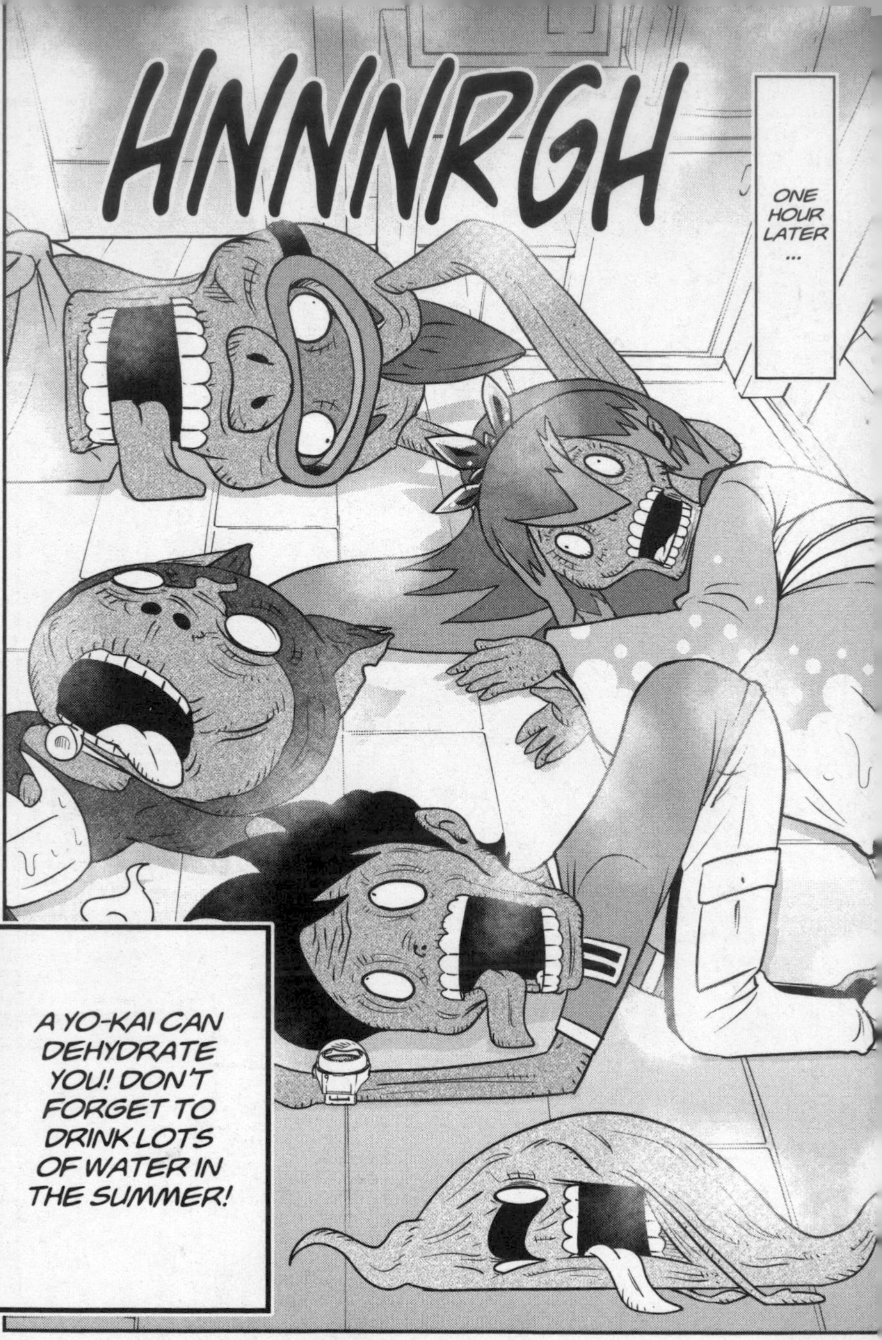
ONE HOUR LATER ...
HNNNRGH
A YO-KAI CAN DEHYDRATE YOU! DON'T FORGET TO DRINK LOTS OF WATER IN THE SUMMER!

CHAPTER 214

TROUBLEMAKER HUNTER YO-KAI VENOCT

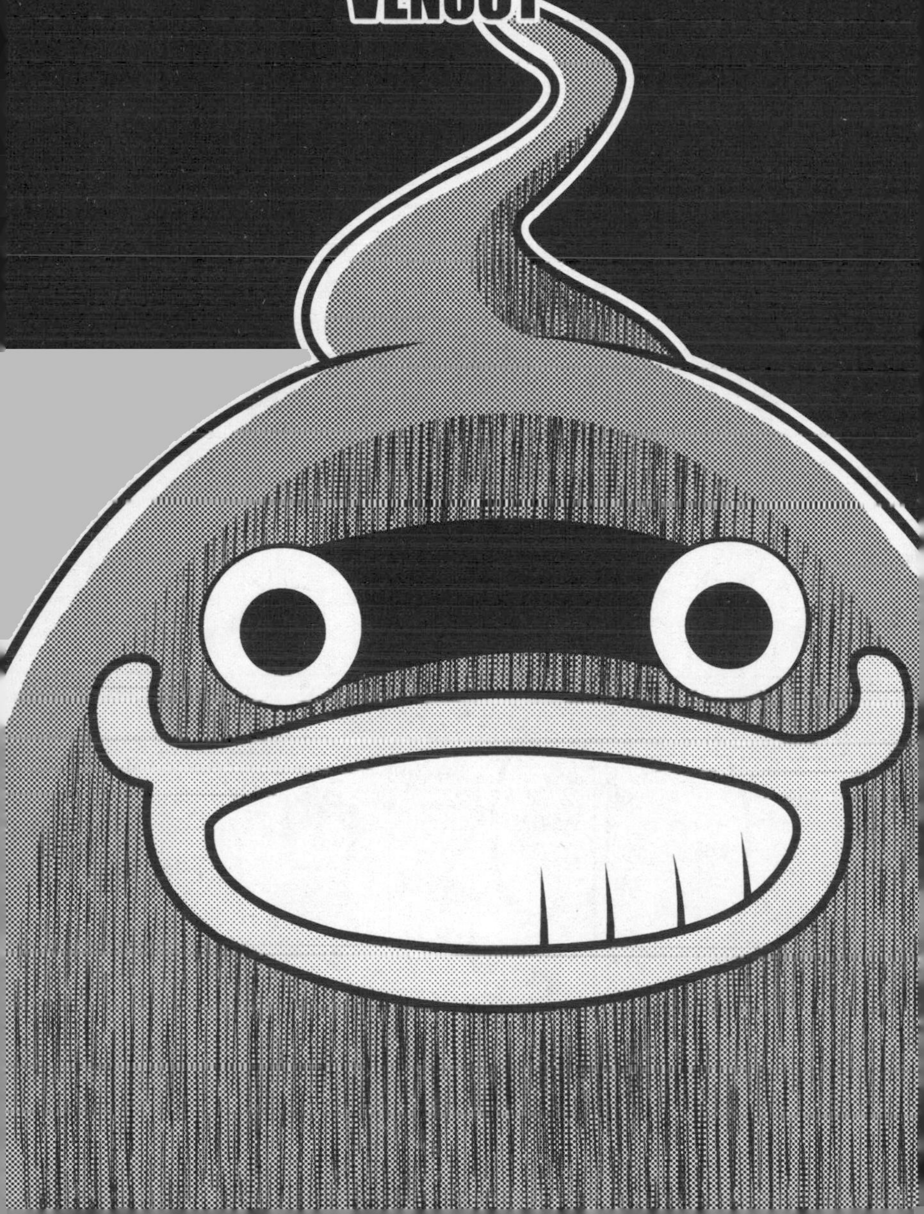

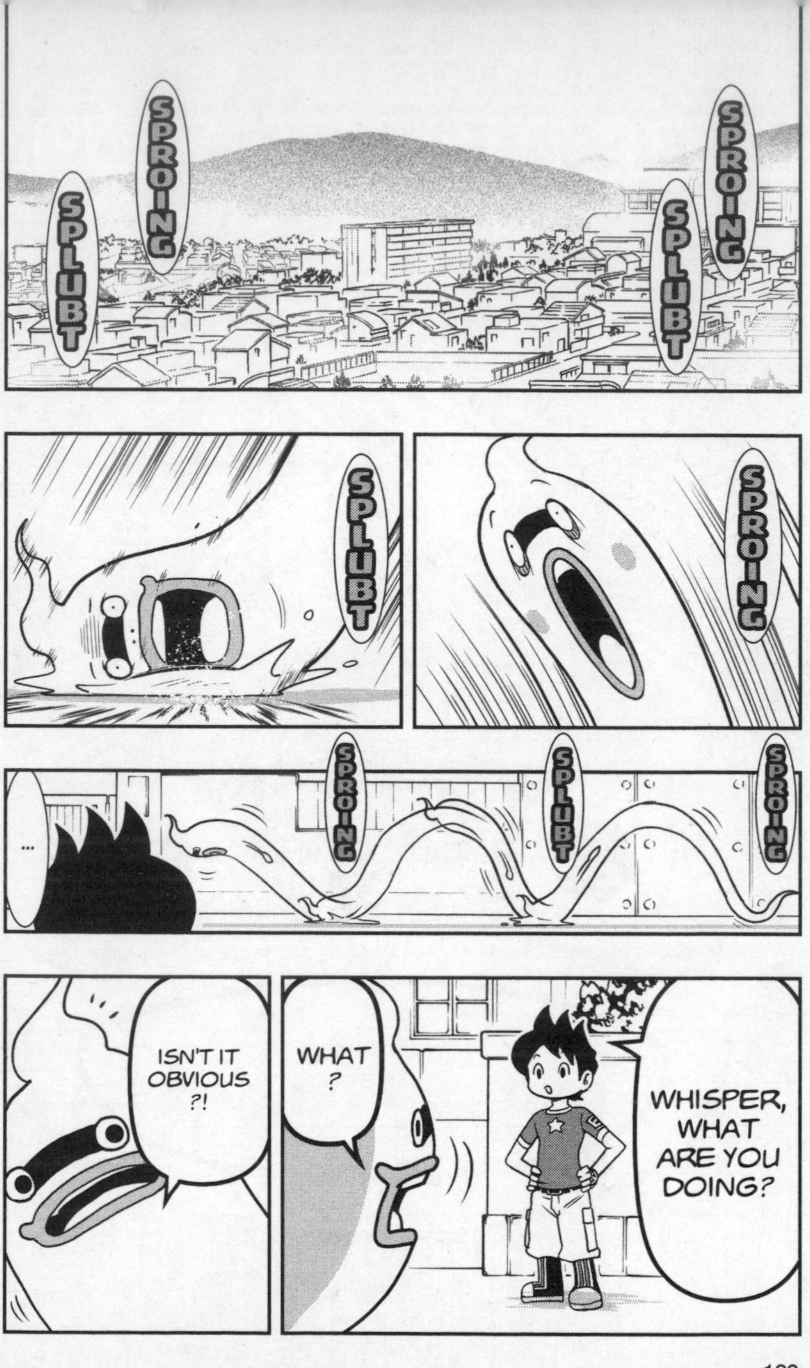
SPROING
SPLUBT
SPROING
SPLUBT
SPROING
SPLUBT
SPROING
SPLUBT
SPROING
...
WHISPER, WHAT ARE YOU DOING?
WHAT ?
ISN'T IT OBVIOUS ?!

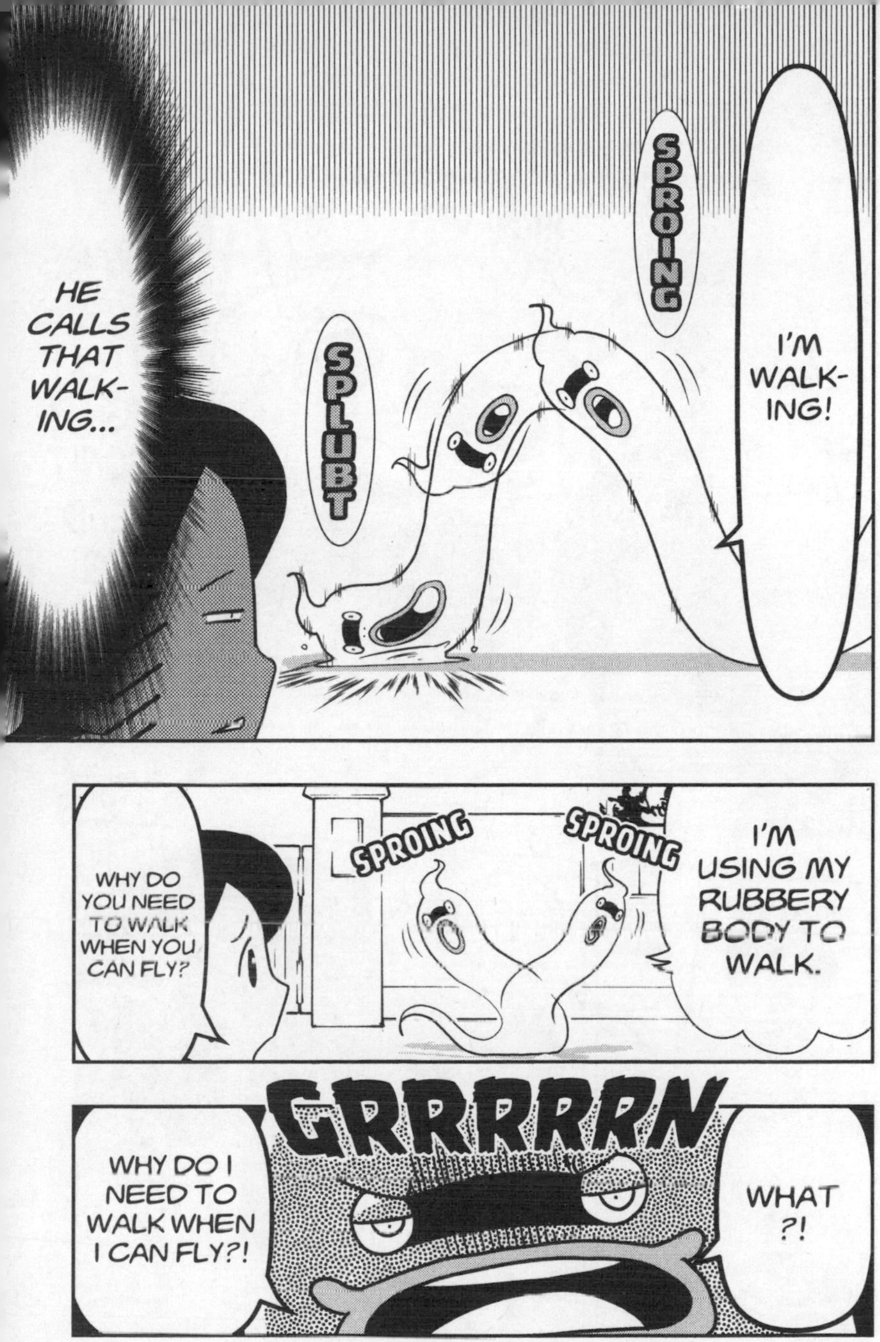
I'M WALKING!
SPROING
SPLUBT
HE CALLS THAT WALKING...
I'M USING MY RUBBERY BODY TO WALK.
SPROING
SPROING
WHY DO YOU NEED TO WALK WHEN YOU CAN FLY?
WHAT?!
GRRRRRN
WHY DO I NEED TO WALK WHEN I CAN FLY?!

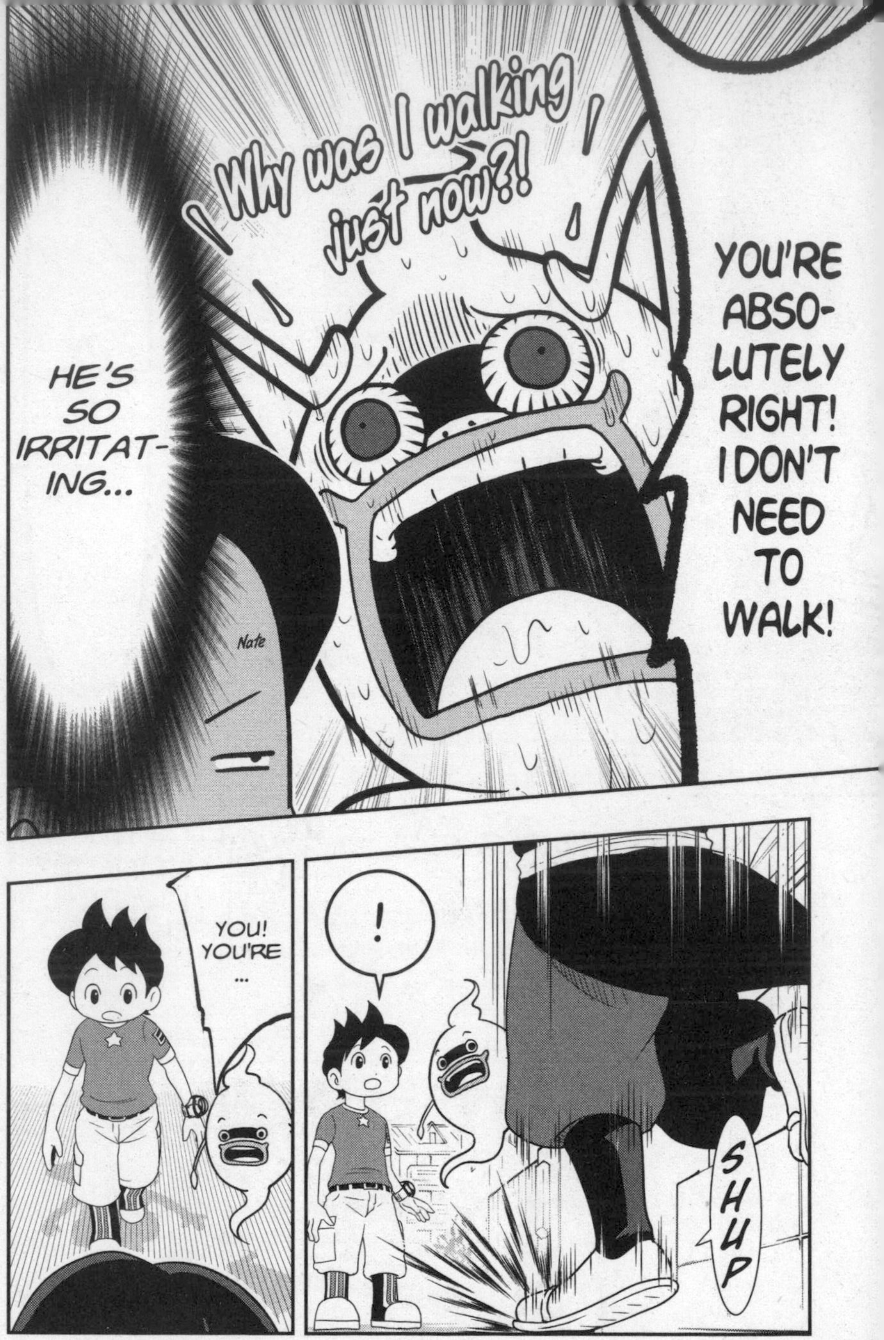
YOU'RE ABSO-LUTELY RIGHT! I DON'T NEED TO WALK!
Why was I walking just now?!
HE'S SO IRRITAT-ING...
Nate
SHUP
!
YOU! YOU'RE ...

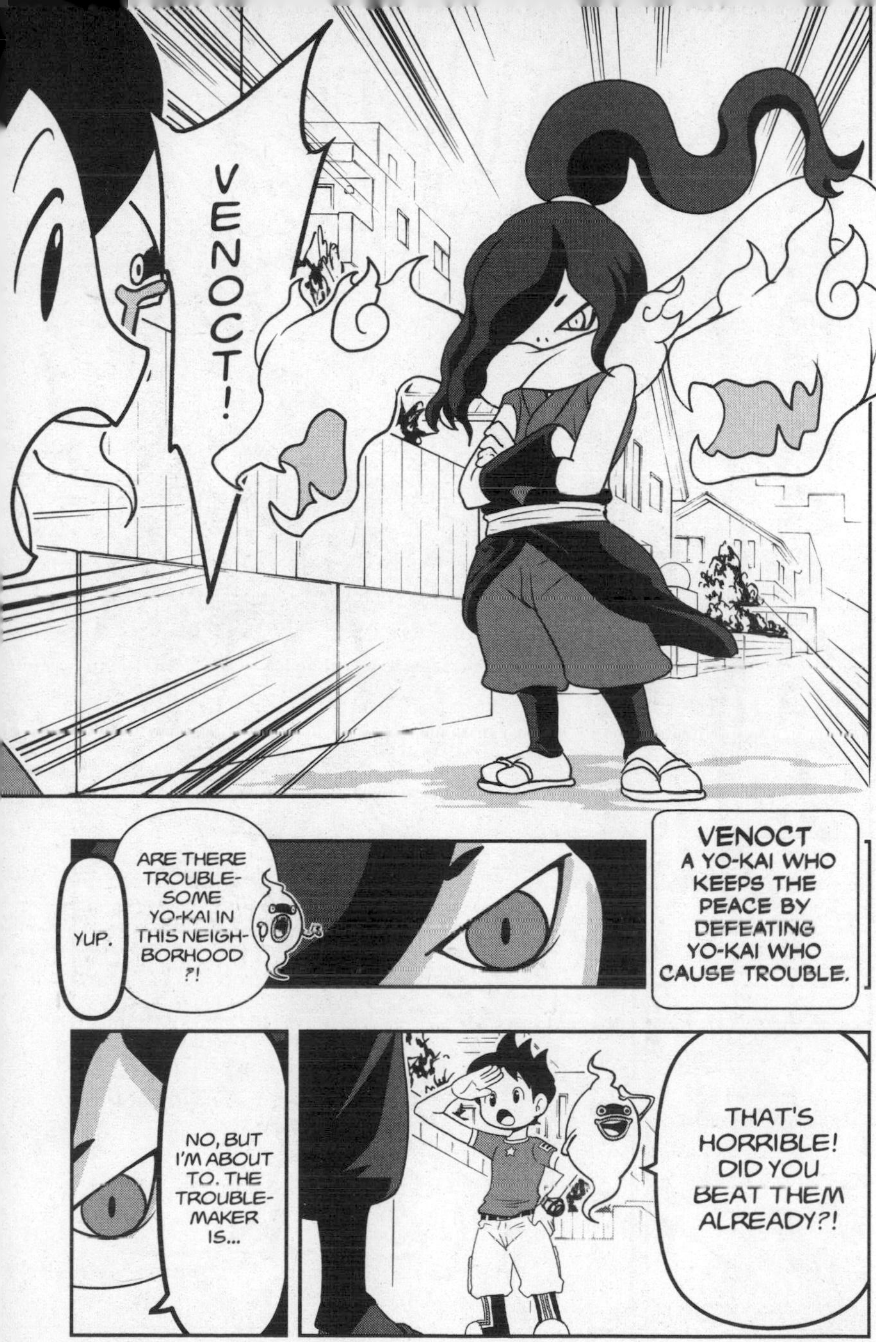
VENOCT!
VENOCT
A YO-KAI WHO KEEPS THE PEACE BY DEFEATING YO-KAI WHO CAUSE TROUBLE.
ARE THERE TROUBLESOME YO-KAI IN THIS NEIGHBORHOOD?!
YUP.
THAT'S HORRIBLE! DID YOU BEAT THEM ALREADY?!
NO, BUT I'M ABOUT TO. THE TROUBLEMAKER IS...

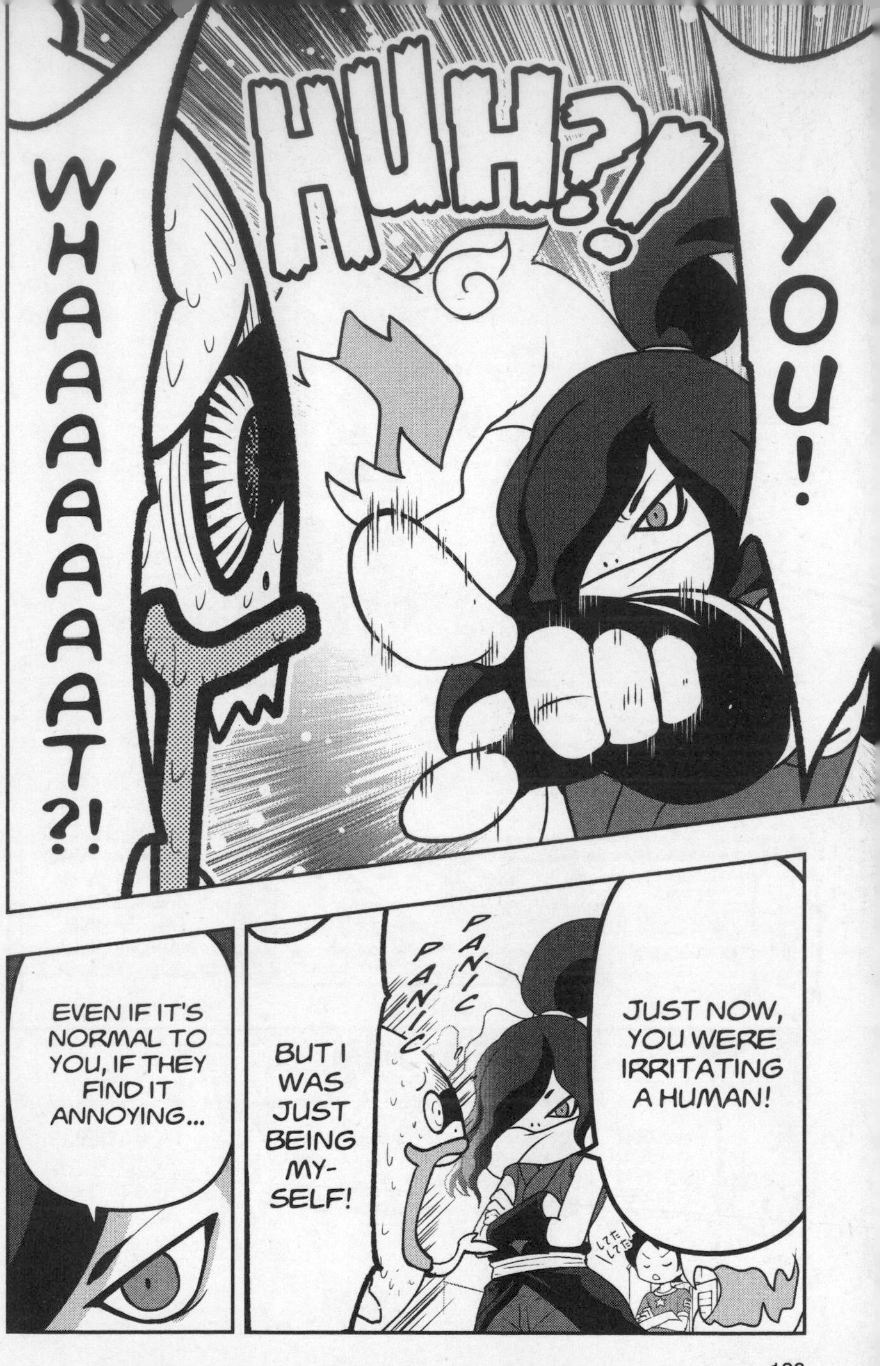
YOU!
HUH?!
WHAAAAAAAT?!
JUST NOW, YOU WERE IRRITATING A HUMAN!
PANIC PANIC
BUT I WAS JUST BEING MY-SELF!
EVEN IF IT'S NORMAL TO YOU, IF THEY FIND IT ANNOYING...

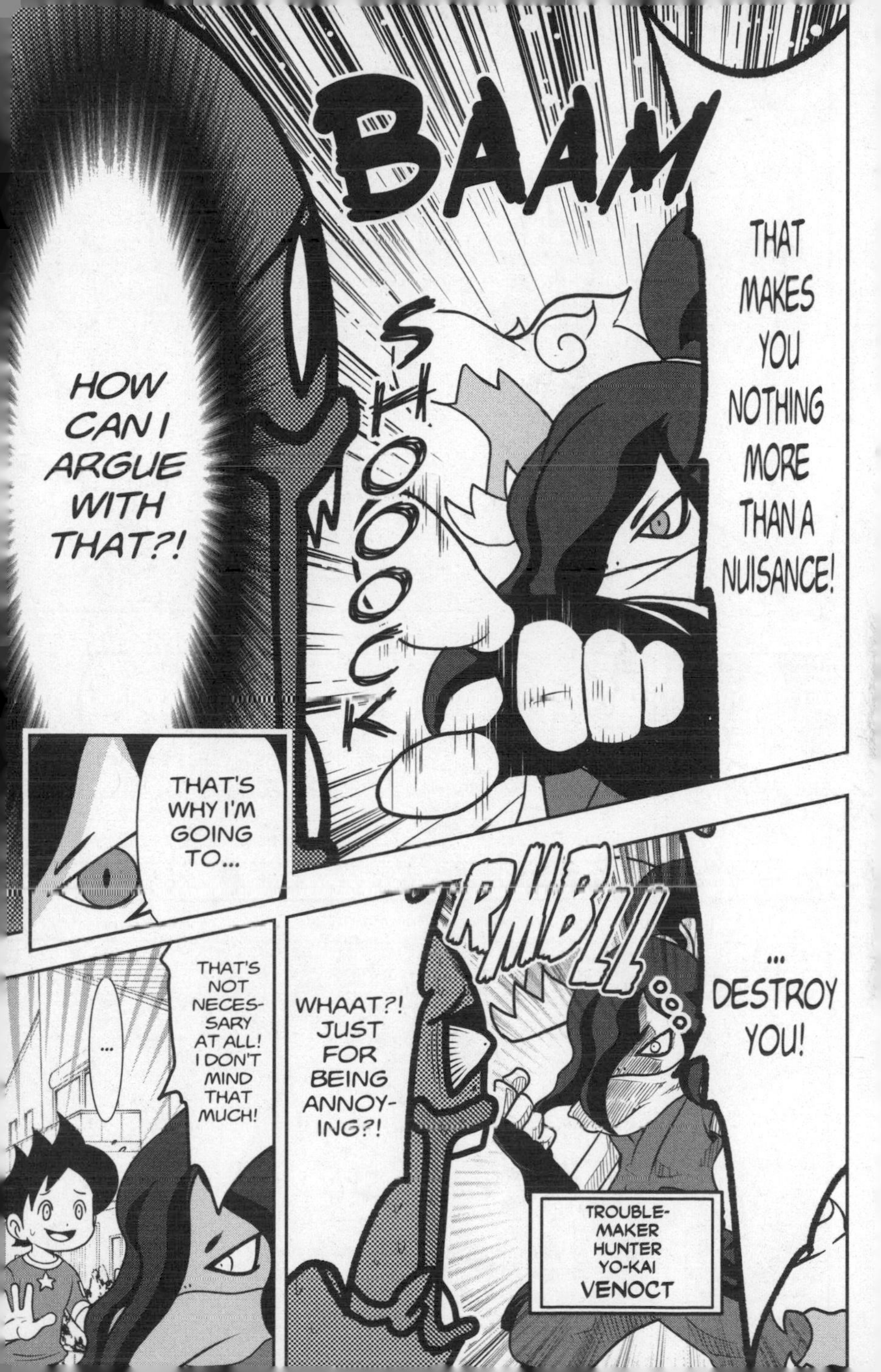
BAAM
THAT MAKES YOU NOTHING MORE THAN A NUISANCE!
SHOOOOCK
HOW CAN I ARGUE WITH THAT?!
THAT'S WHY I'M GOING TO...
RMBLL
...DESTROY YOU!
WHAAT?! JUST FOR BEING ANNOY-ING?!
TROUBLE-MAKER HUNTER YO-KAI VENOCT
THAT'S NOT NECES-SARY AT ALL! I DON'T MIND THAT MUCH!
...

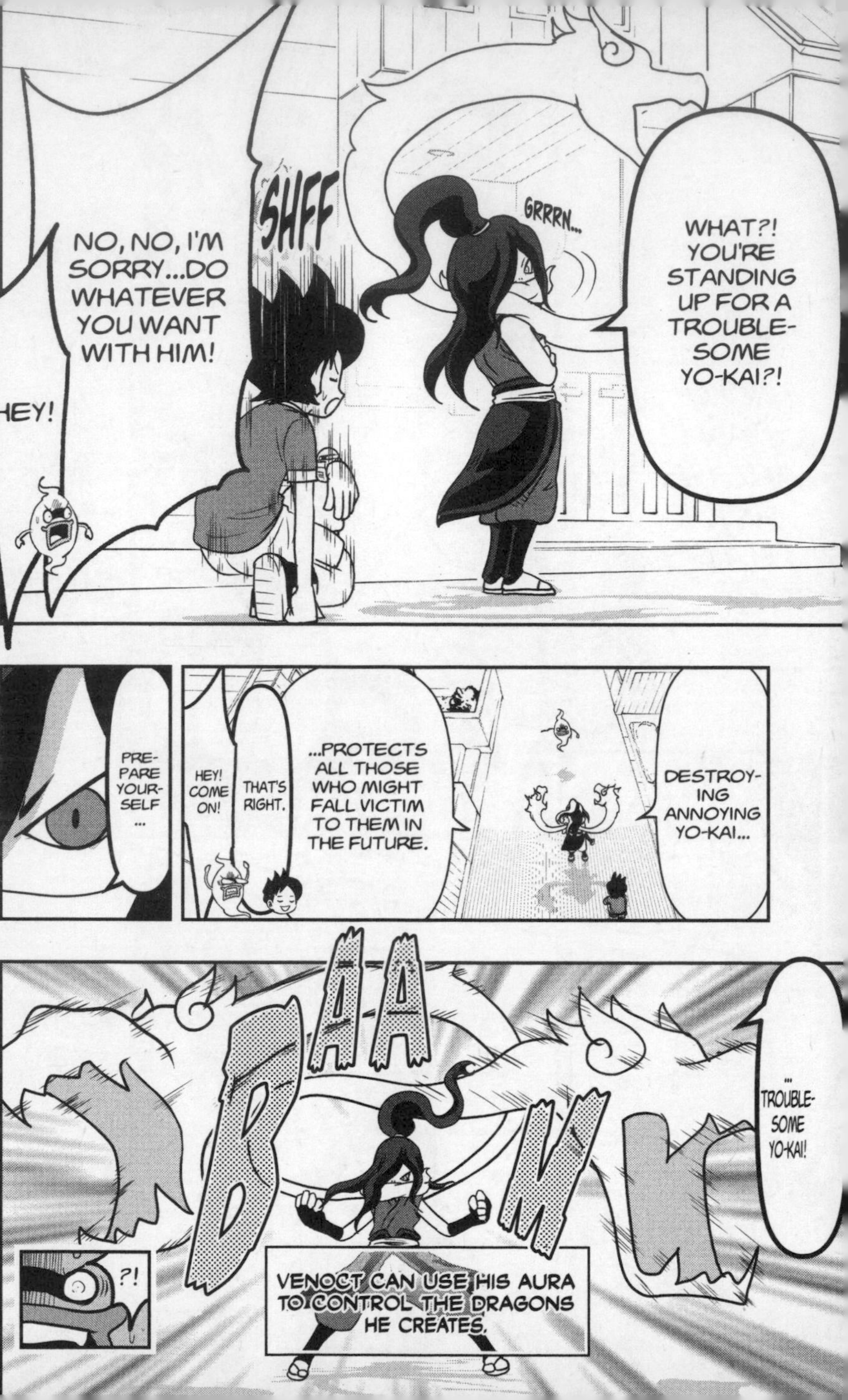
WHAT?! YOU'RE STANDING UP FOR A TROUBLE-SOME YO-KAI?!
GRRRN...
SHFF
NO, NO, I'M SORRY...DO WHATEVER YOU WANT WITH HIM!
HEY!
DESTROY-ING ANNOYING YO-KAI...
...PROTECTS ALL THOSE WHO MIGHT FALL VICTIM TO THEM IN THE FUTURE.
THAT'S RIGHT.
HEY! COME ON!
PRE-PARE YOUR-SELF...
...TROUBLE-SOME YO-KAI!
BAAM
VENOCT CAN USE HIS AURA TO CONTROL THE DRAGONS HE CREATES.
?!

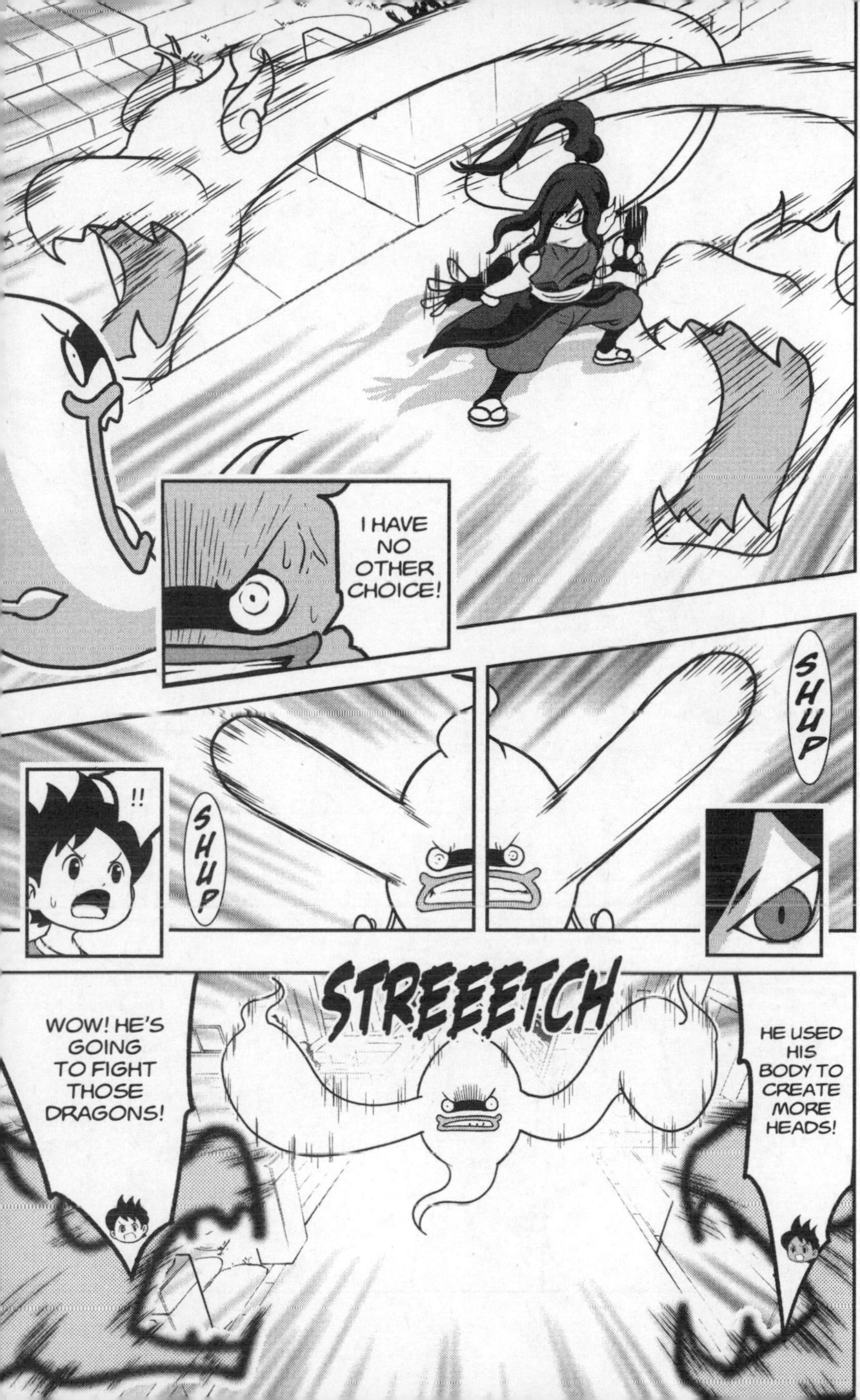
I HAVE NO OTHER CHOICE!
SHUP
SHUP
!!
STREEETCH
HE USED HIS BODY TO CREATE MORE HEADS!
WOW! HE'S GOING TO FIGHT THOSE DRAGONS!

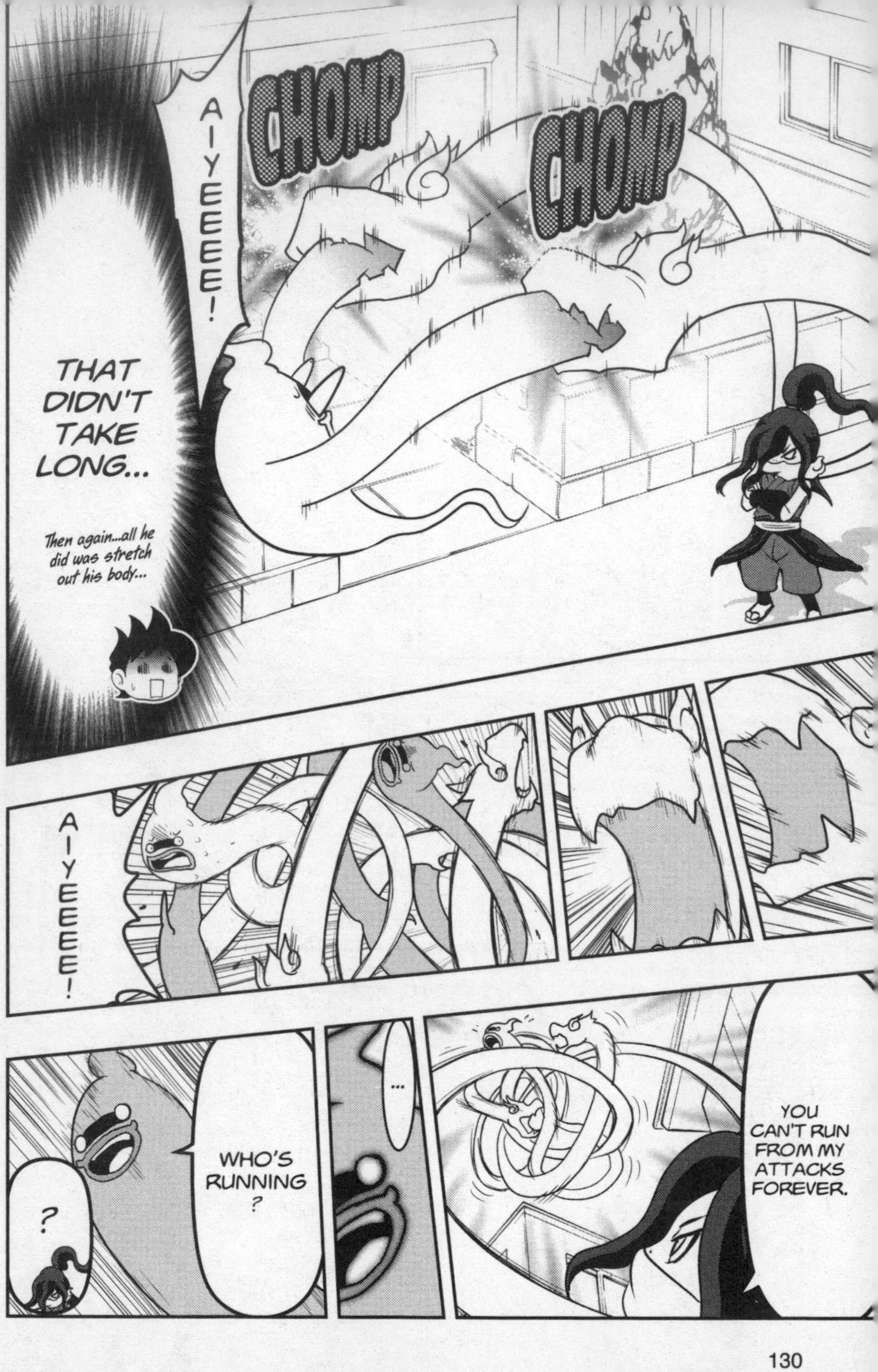
CHOMP
CHOMP
AIYEEEEE!
THAT DIDN'T TAKE LONG...
Then again...all he did was stretch out his body...
AIYEEEEE!
YOU CAN'T RUN FROM MY ATTACKS FOREVER.
...
WHO'S RUNNING?
?

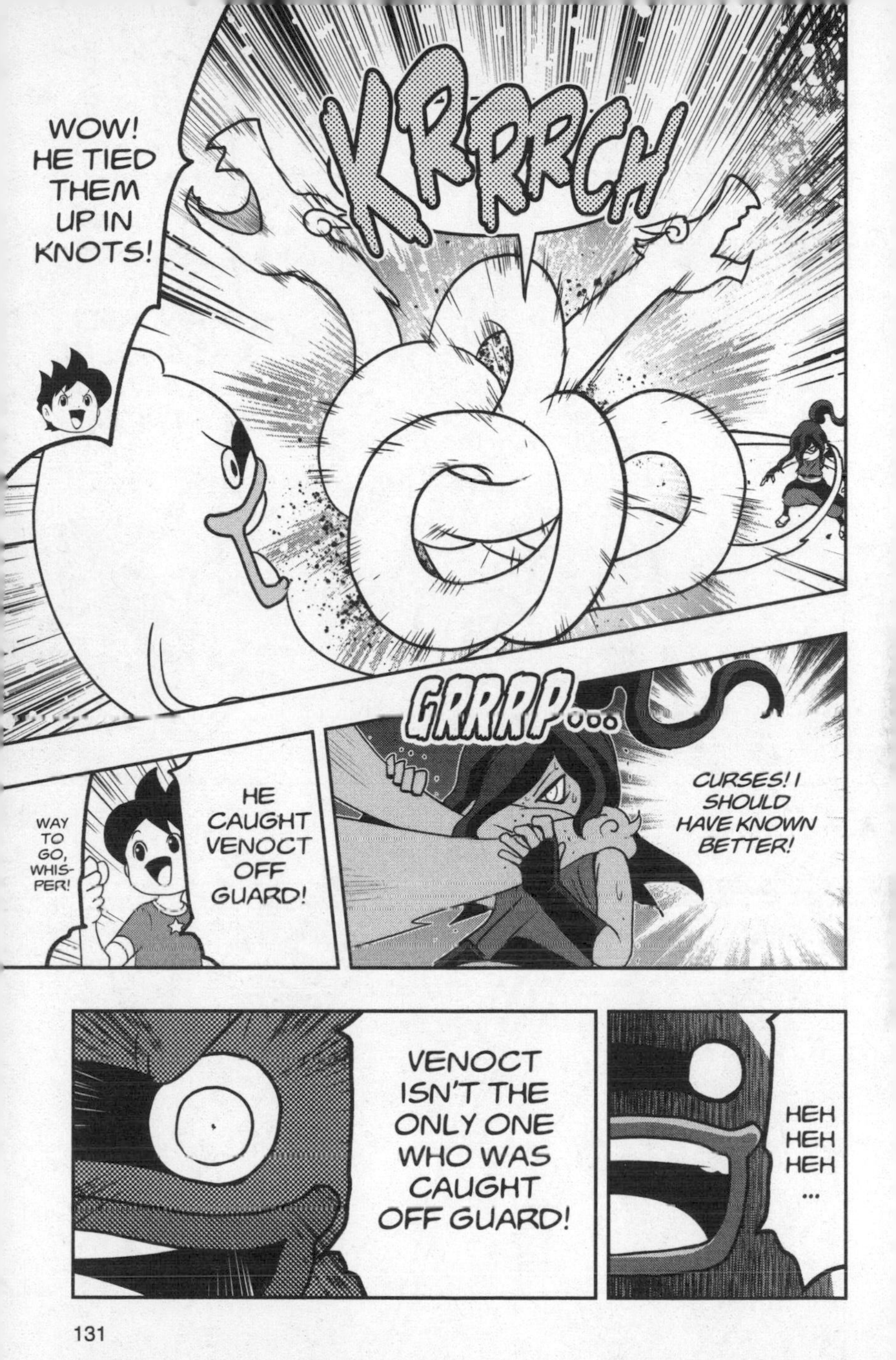
KRRRCH
WOW! HE TIED THEM UP IN KNOTS!
GRRRP...
CURSES! I SHOULD HAVE KNOWN BETTER!
HE CAUGHT VENOCT OFF GUARD!
WAY TO GO, WHISPER!
HEH HEH HEH ...
VENOCT ISN'T THE ONLY ONE WHO WAS CAUGHT OFF GUARD!

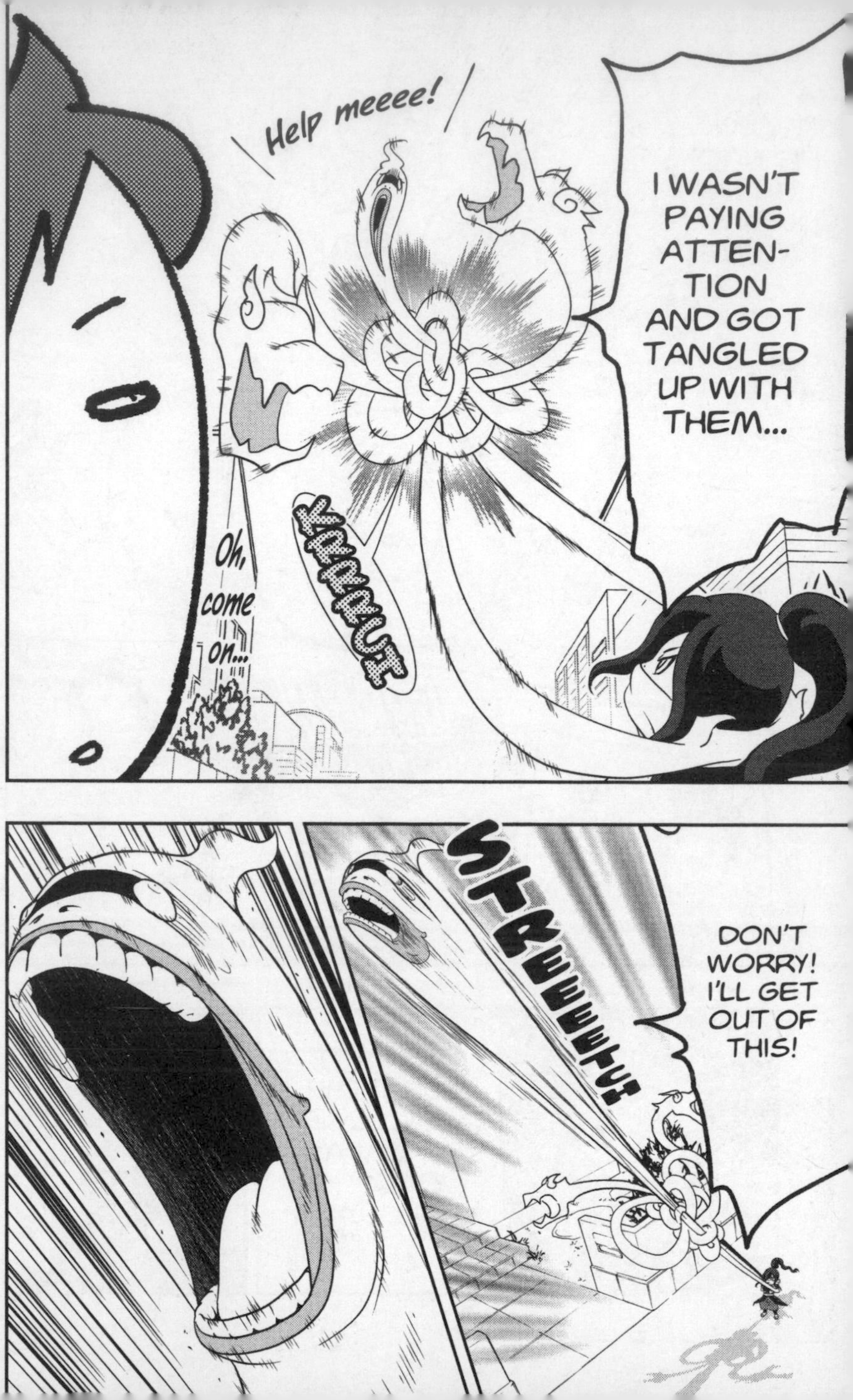
I WASN'T PAYING ATTEN-TION AND GOT TANGLED UP WITH THEM...
Help meeee!
Oh, come on...
DON'T WORRY! I'LL GET OUT OF THIS!
STREEEETCH!

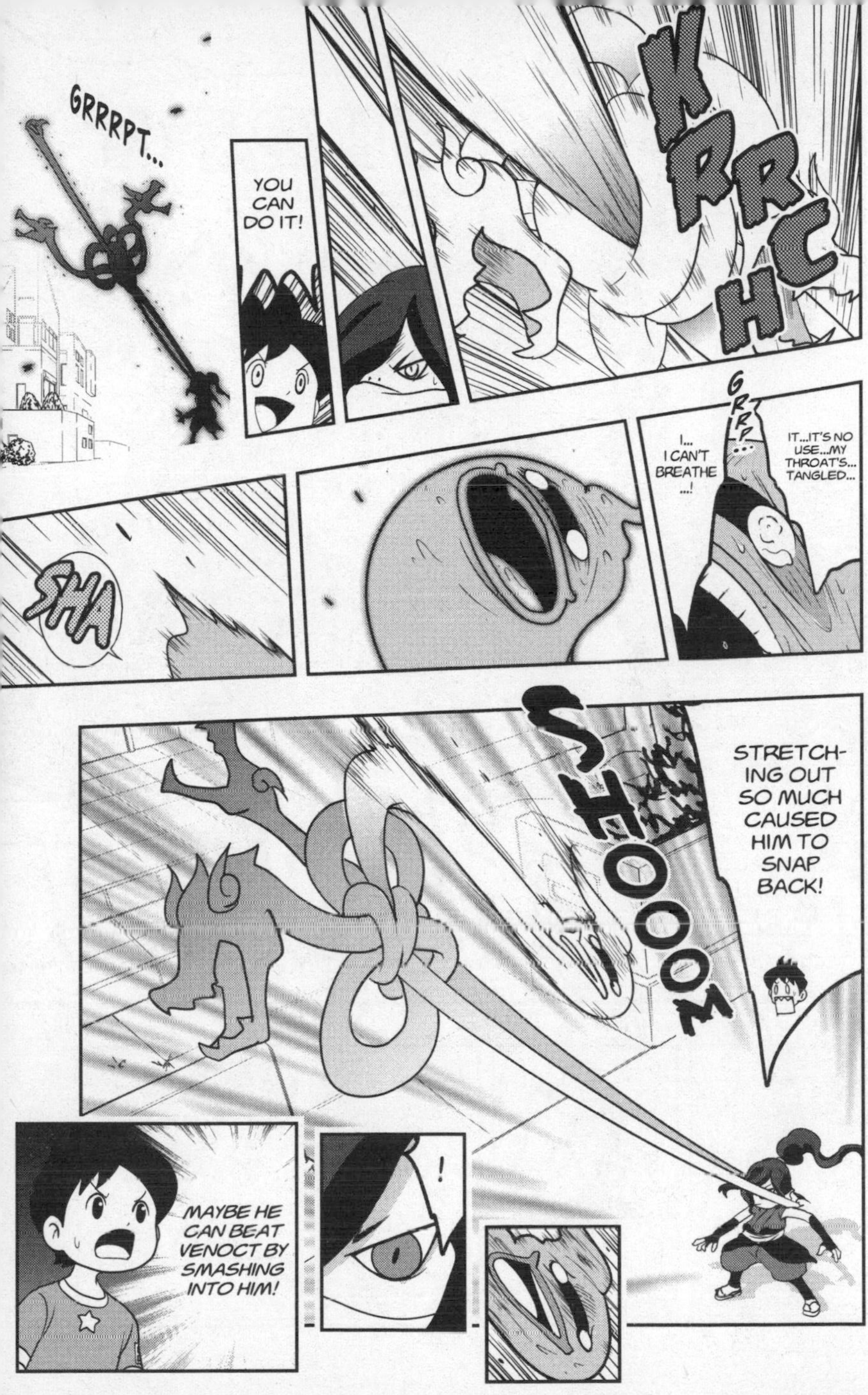
KRRCHH
YOU CAN DO IT!
GRRRPT...
IT...IT'S NO USE...MY THROAT'S... TANGLED...
GRRP...
I... I CAN'T BREATHE...!
SHA
STRETCHING OUT SO MUCH CAUSED HIM TO SNAP BACK!
SHOOOOM
!
MAYBE HE CAN BEAT VENOCT BY SMASHING INTO HIM!

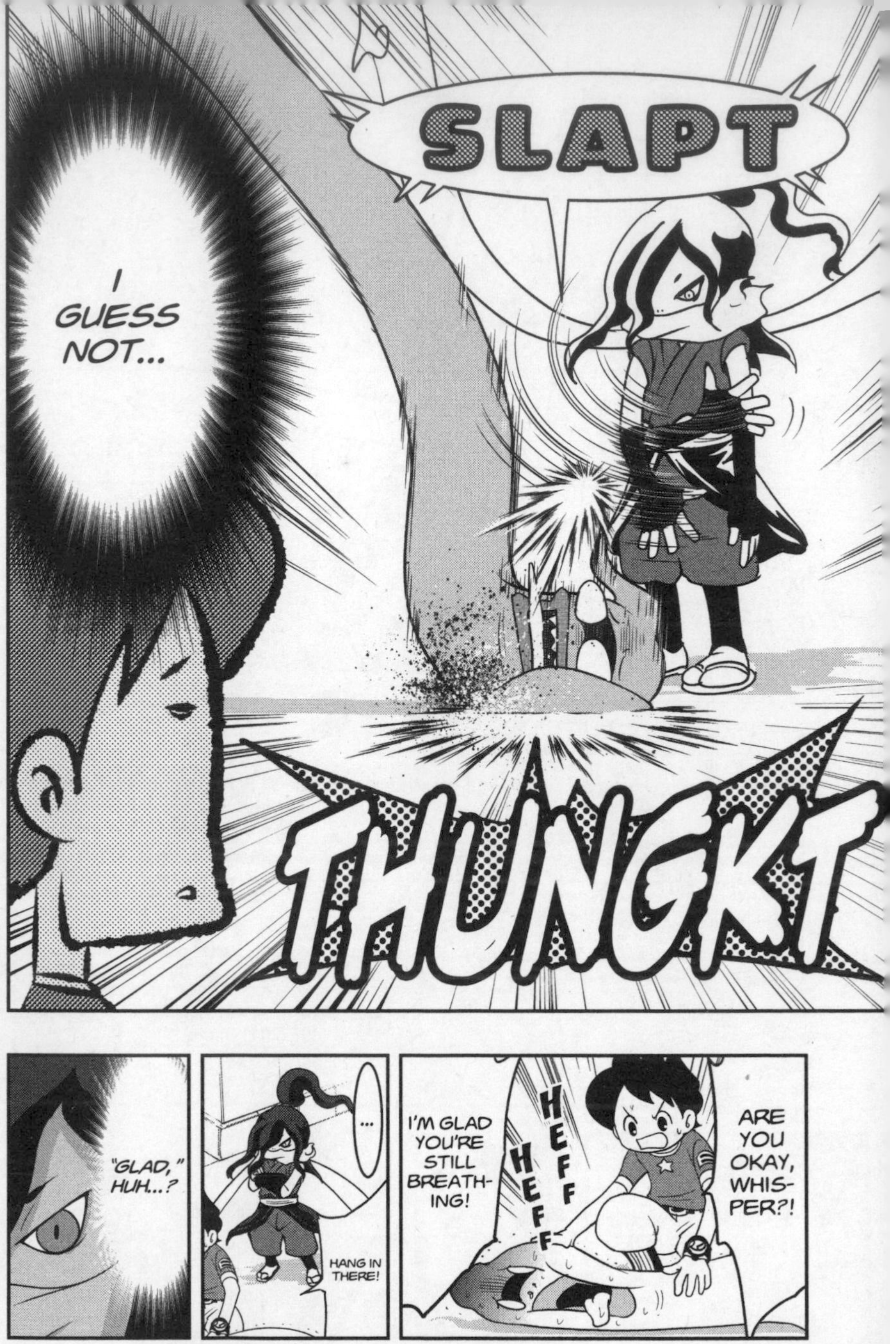
SLAPT
I GUESS NOT...
THUNGKT
ARE YOU OKAY, WHISPER?!
HEFF HEFF
HEFF HEFF
I'M GLAD YOU'RE STILL BREATHING!
...
HANG IN THERE!
"GLAD," HUH...?

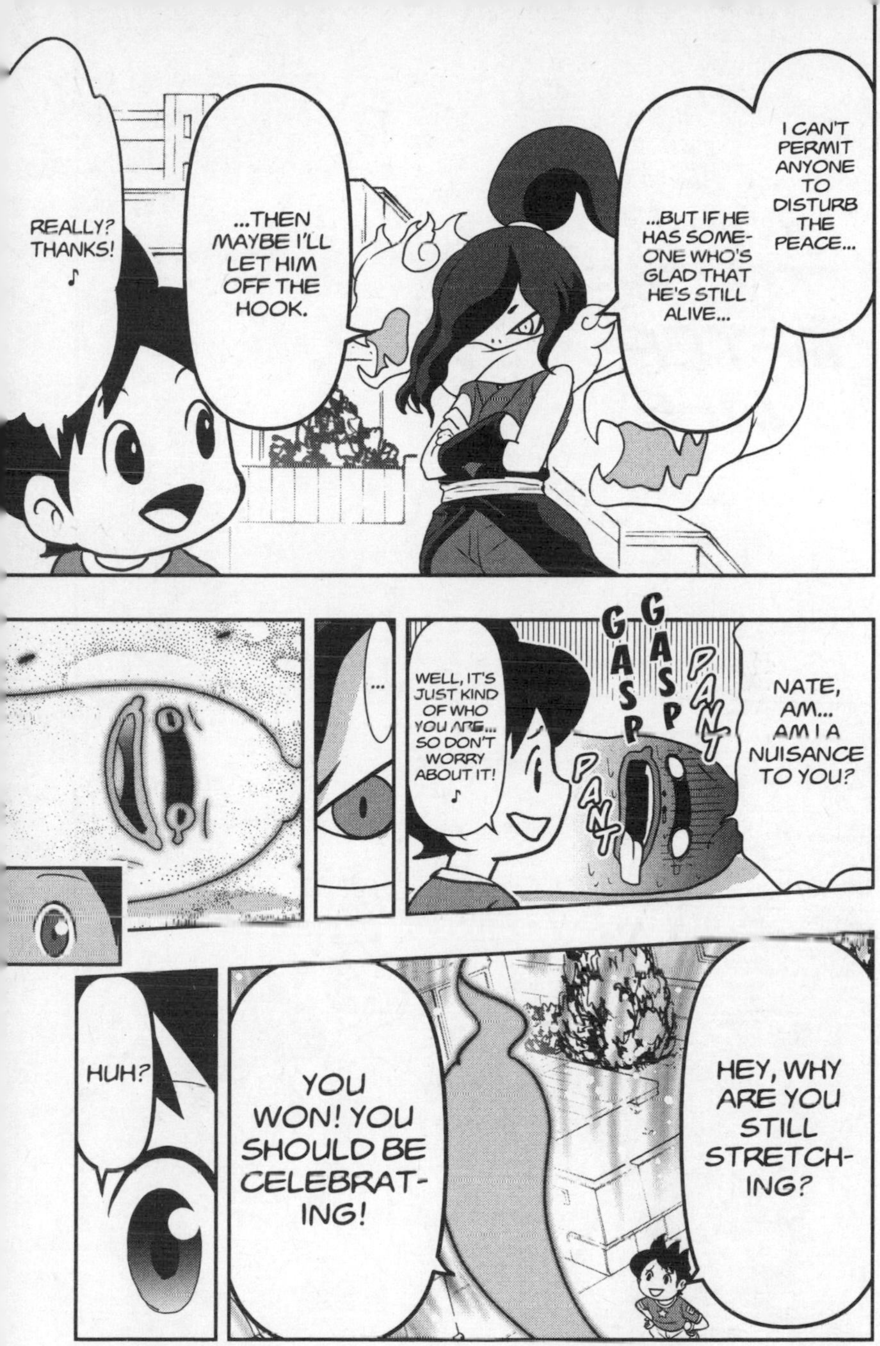
I CAN'T PERMIT ANYONE TO DISTURB THE PEACE...
...BUT IF HE HAS SOME-ONE WHO'S GLAD THAT HE'S STILL ALIVE...
...THEN MAYBE I'LL LET HIM OFF THE HOOK.
REALLY? THANKS! ♪
NATE, AM... AM I A NUISANCE TO YOU?
GASP GASP
PANT PANT
WELL, IT'S JUST KIND OF WHO YOU ARE... SO DON'T WORRY ABOUT IT! ♪
...
HEY, WHY ARE YOU STILL STRETCH-ING?
YOU WON! YOU SHOULD BE CELEBRAT-ING!
HUH?

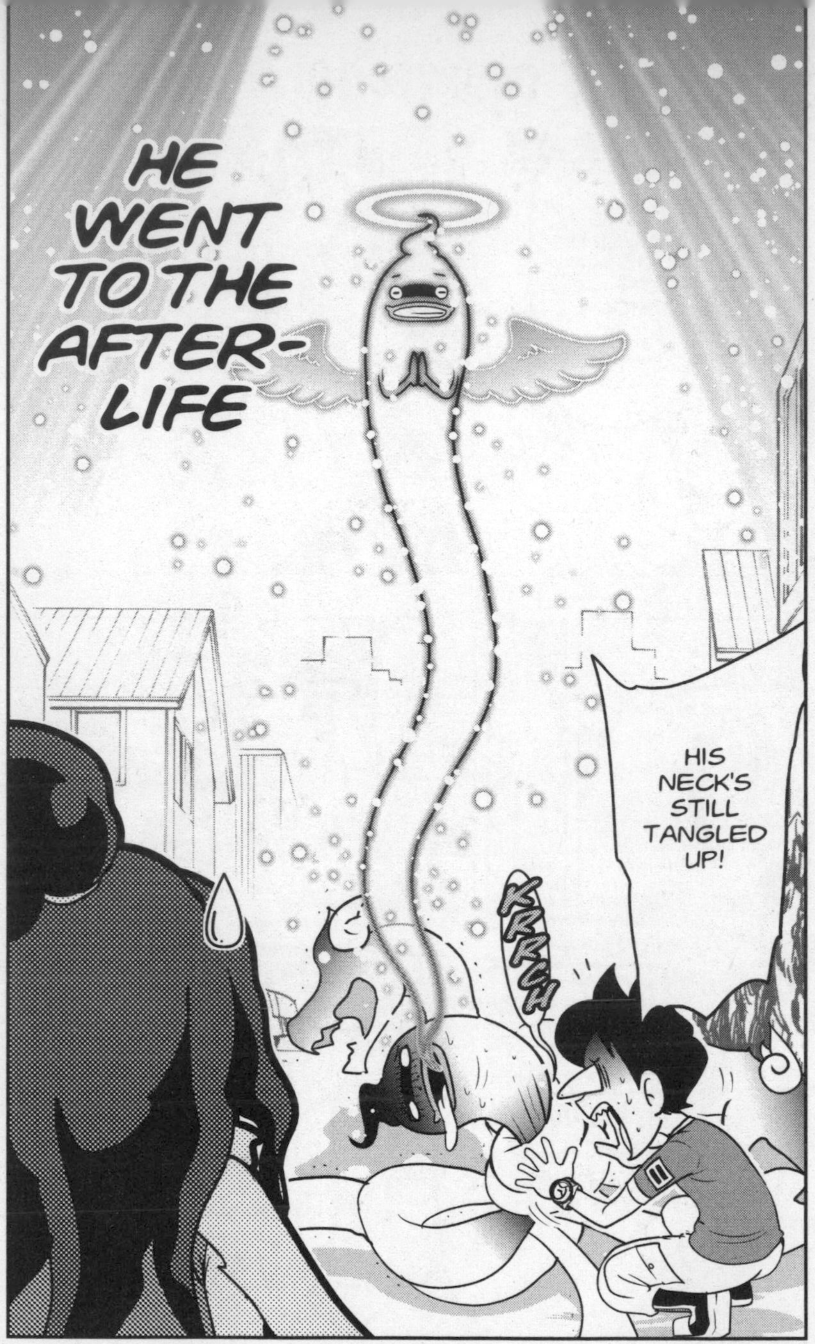
HE WENT TO THE AFTER-LIFE
HIS NECK'S STILL TANGLED UP!
KRRCH

CHAPTER 215
BLANK MIND YO-KAI DAIZ

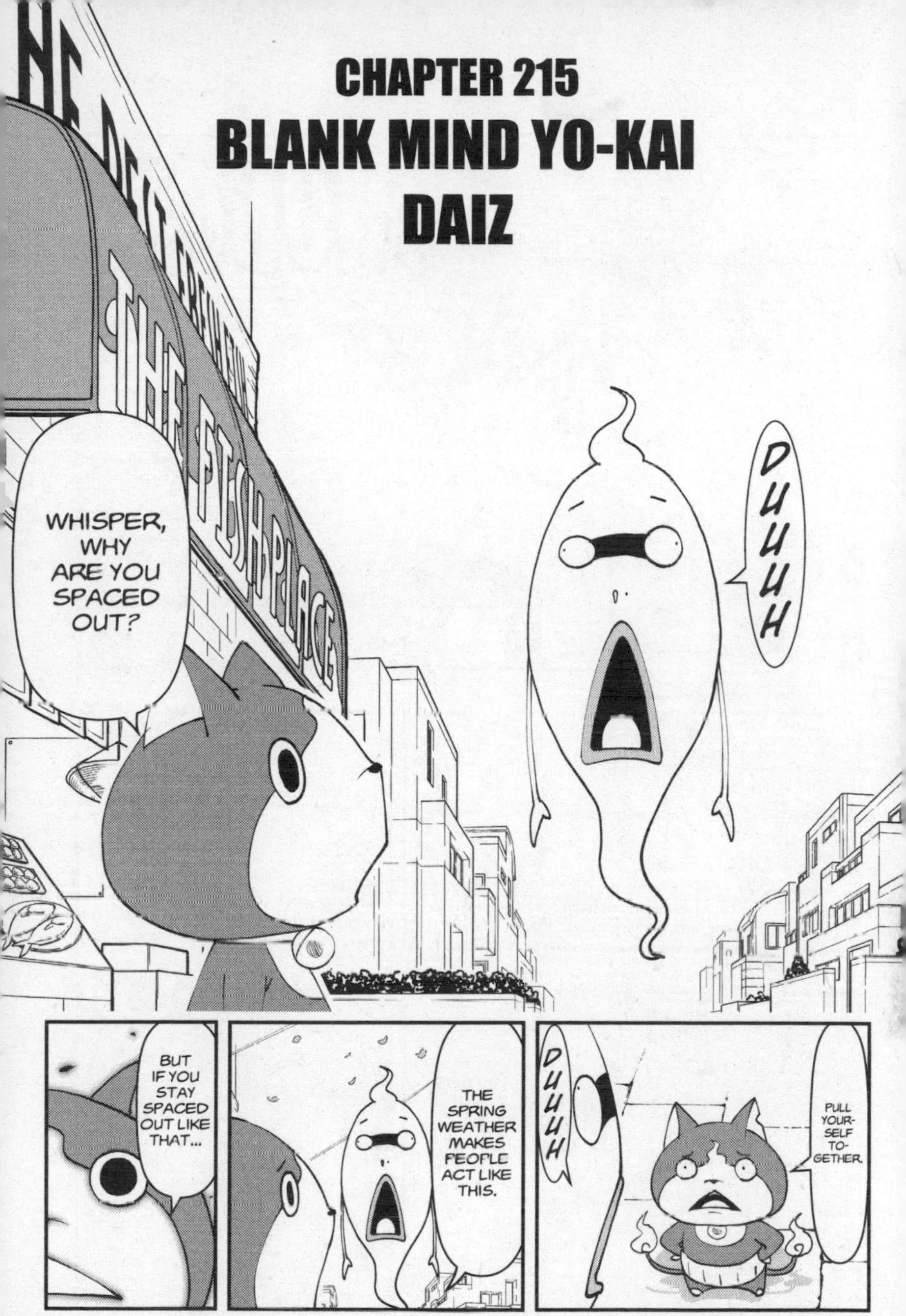
THE FISH PLACE
DUUUH
WHISPER, WHY ARE YOU SPACED OUT?
PULL YOURSELF TOGETHER.
DUUUH
THE SPRING WEATHER MAKES PEOPLE ACT LIKE THIS.
BUT IF YOU STAY SPACED OUT LIKE THAT...

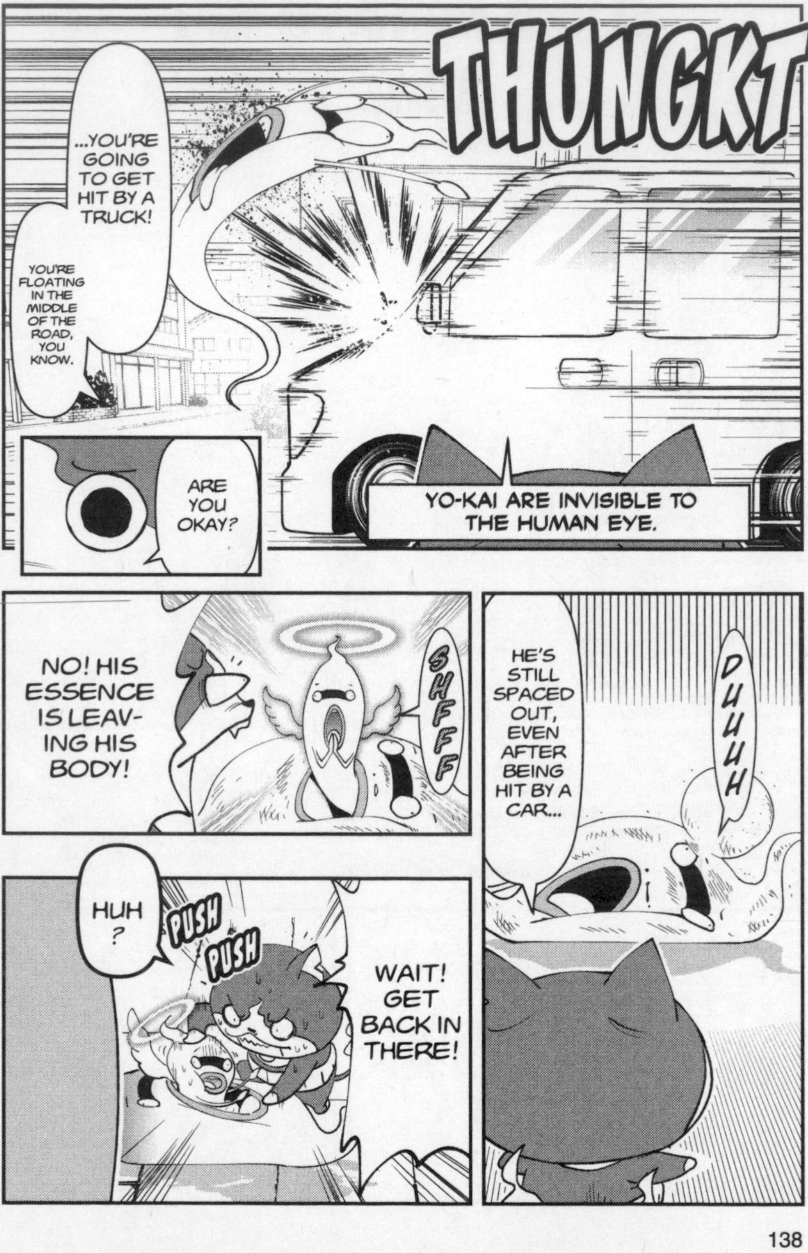
THUNGKT
...YOU'RE GOING TO GET HIT BY A TRUCK!
YOU'RE FLOATING IN THE MIDDLE OF THE ROAD, YOU KNOW.
YO-KAI ARE INVISIBLE TO THE HUMAN EYE.
ARE YOU OKAY?
DUUUH
HE'S STILL SPACED OUT, EVEN AFTER BEING HIT BY A CAR...
SHFFF
NO! HIS ESSENCE IS LEAVING HIS BODY!
WAIT! GET BACK IN THERE!
PUSH
PUSH
HUH?

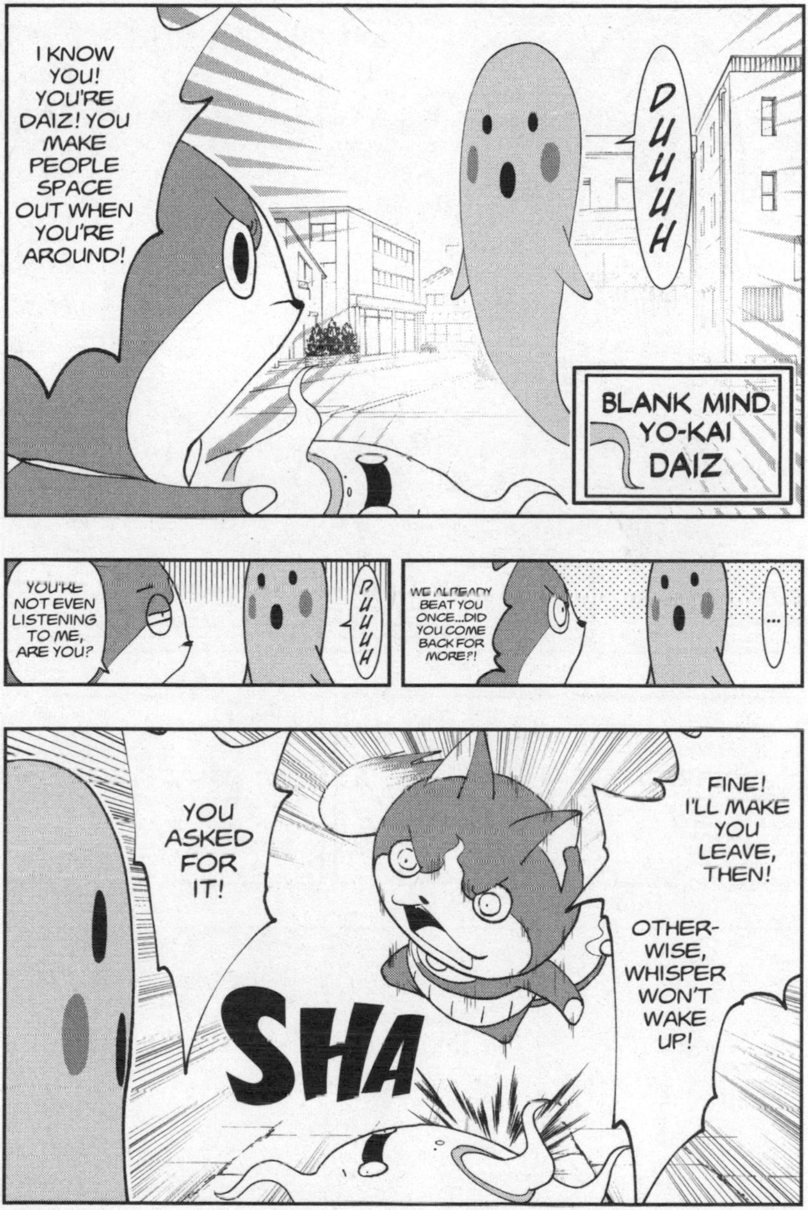
DUUUH
I KNOW YOU! YOU'RE DAIZ! YOU MAKE PEOPLE SPACE OUT WHEN YOU'RE AROUND!
BLANK MIND YO-KAI DAIZ
...
WE ALREADY BEAT YOU ONCE...DID YOU COME BACK FOR MORE?!
DUUUH
YOU'RE NOT EVEN LISTENING TO ME, ARE YOU?
FINE! I'LL MAKE YOU LEAVE, THEN!
OTHER-WISE, WHISPER WON'T WAKE UP!
YOU ASKED FOR IT!
SHA

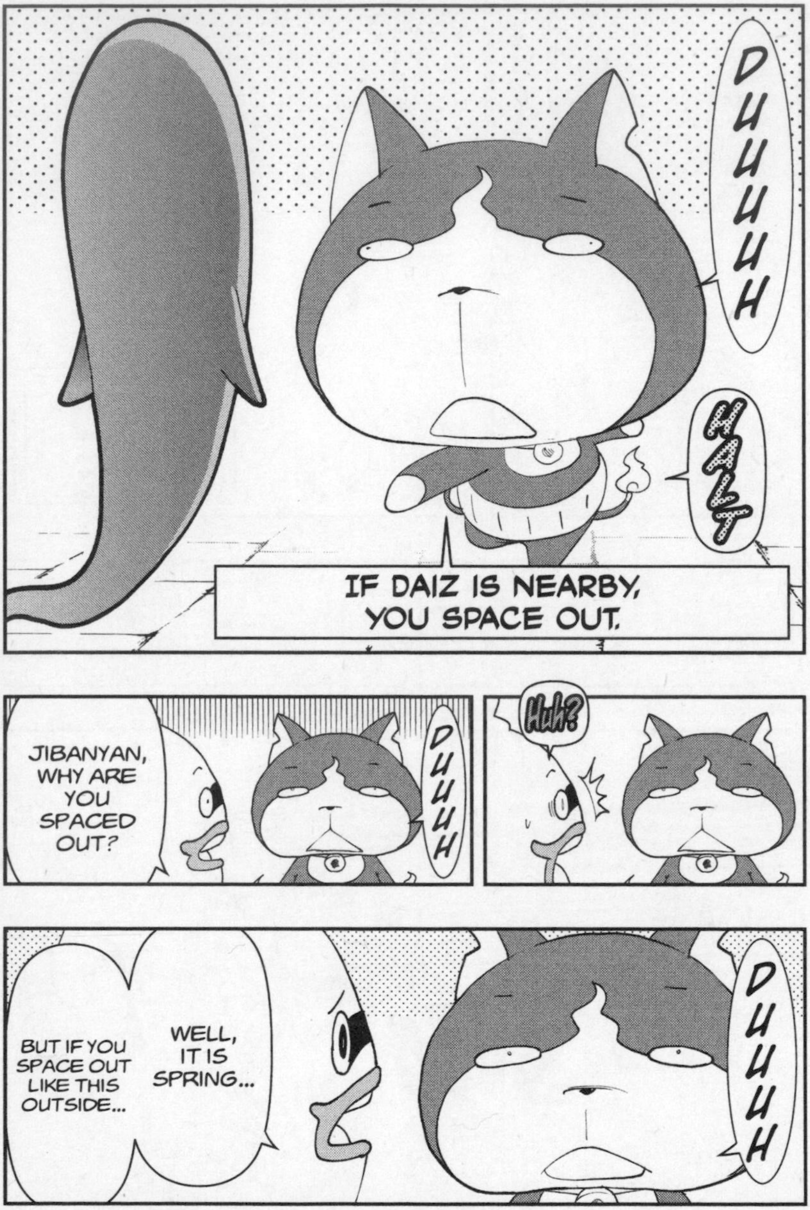
DUUUUUH
HAZY
IF DAIZ IS NEARBY, YOU SPACE OUT.
Huh?
DUUUUH
JIBANYAN, WHY ARE YOU SPACED OUT?
DUUUUH
WELL, IT IS SPRING...
BUT IF YOU SPACE OUT LIKE THIS OUTSIDE...

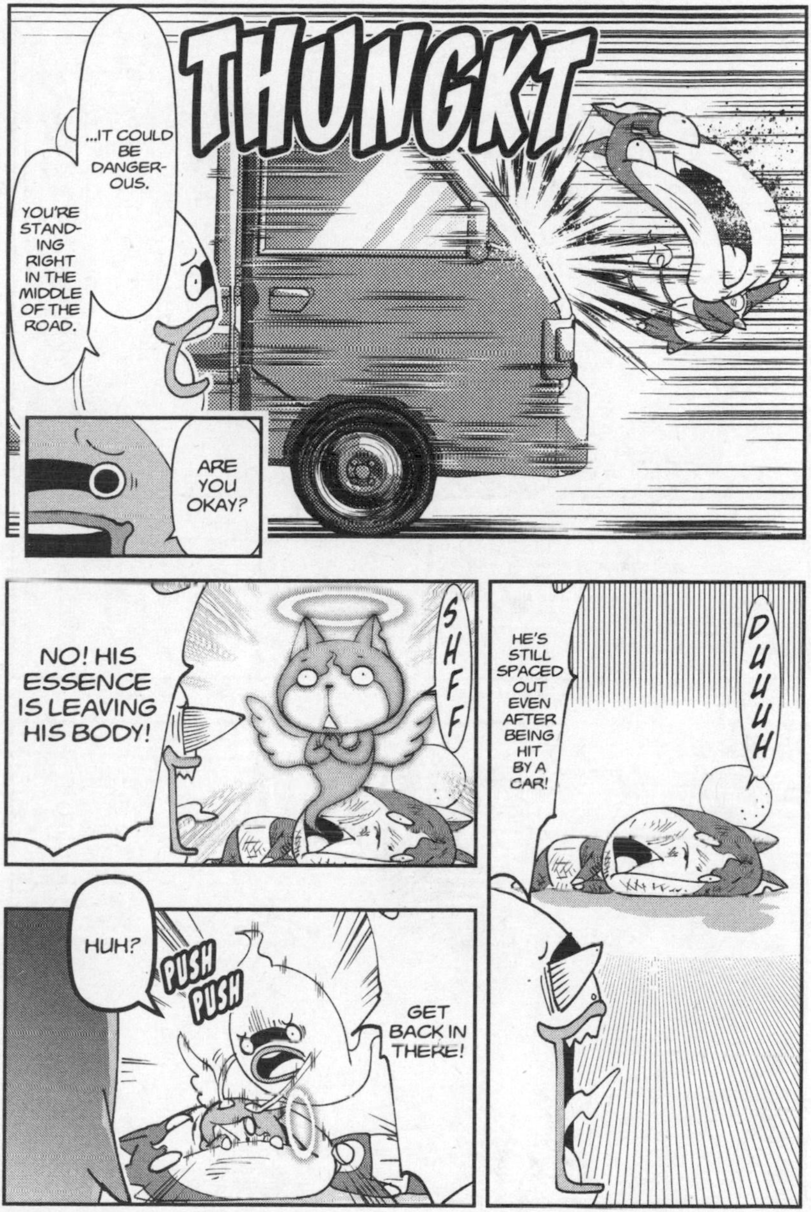
THUNGKT
...IT COULD BE DANGER-OUS.
YOU'RE STAND-ING RIGHT IN THE MIDDLE OF THE ROAD.
ARE YOU OKAY?
DUUUH
HE'S STILL SPACED OUT EVEN AFTER BEING HIT BY A CAR!
SHFF
NO! HIS ESSENCE IS LEAVING HIS BODY!
HUH?
PUSH PUSH
GET BACK IN THERE!

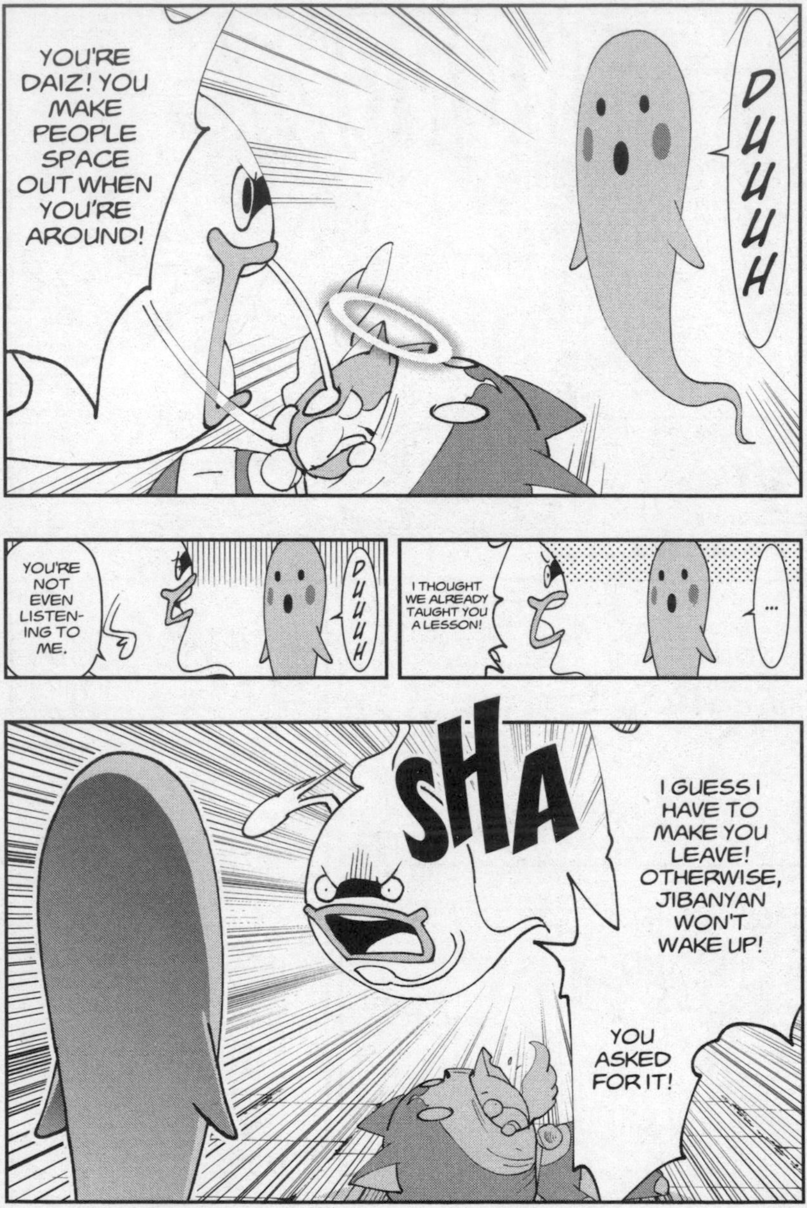
DUUUH
YOU'RE DAIZ! YOU MAKE PEOPLE SPACE OUT WHEN YOU'RE AROUND!
...
I THOUGHT WE ALREADY TAUGHT YOU A LESSON!
DUUUH
YOU'RE NOT EVEN LISTENING TO ME.
I GUESS I HAVE TO MAKE YOU LEAVE! OTHERWISE, JIBANYAN WON'T WAKE UP!
SHA
YOU ASKED FOR IT!

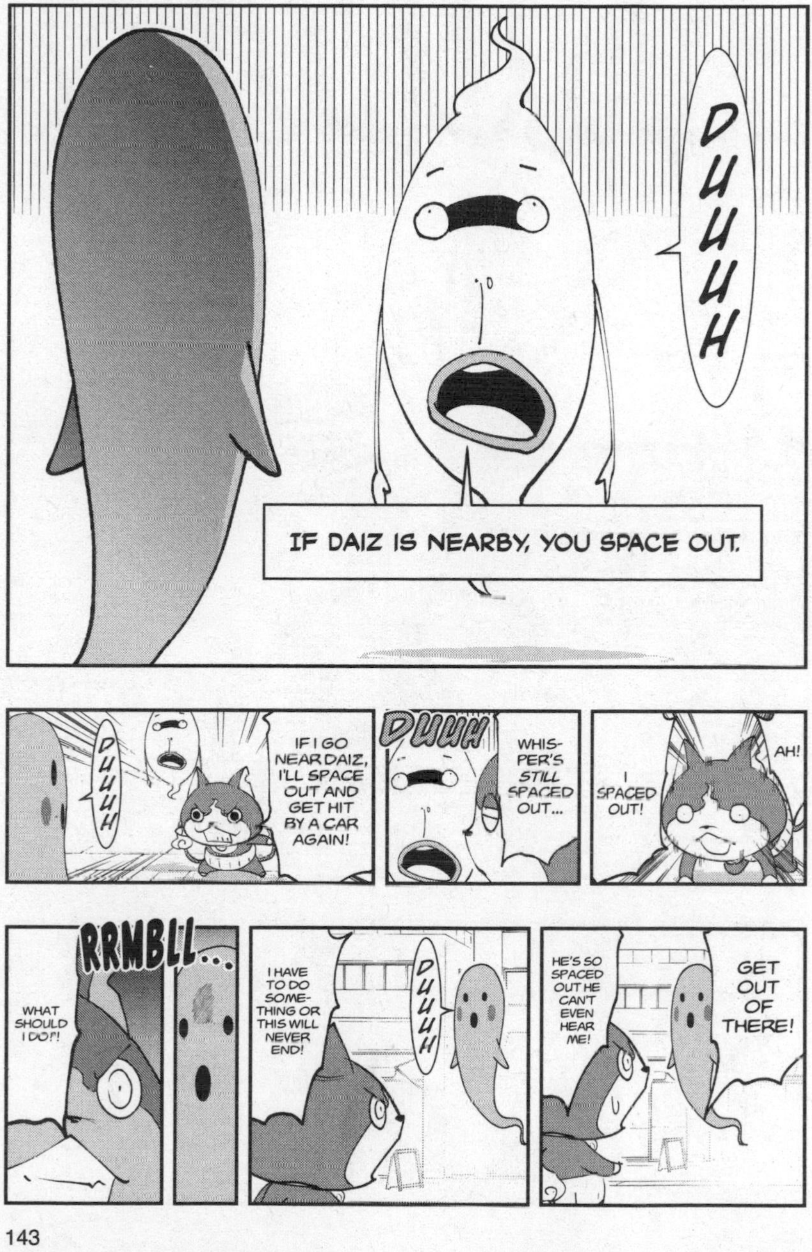
DUUUH
IF DAIZ IS NEARBY, YOU SPACE OUT.
AH!
I SPACED OUT!
DUUH
WHISPER'S STILL SPACED OUT...
IF I GO NEAR DAIZ, I'LL SPACE OUT AND GET HIT BY A CAR AGAIN!
DUUUH
GET OUT OF THERE!
HE'S SO SPACED OUT HE CAN'T EVEN HEAR ME!
DUUUH
I HAVE TO DO SOMETHING OR THIS WILL NEVER END!
RRMBLL...
WHAT SHOULD I DO?!

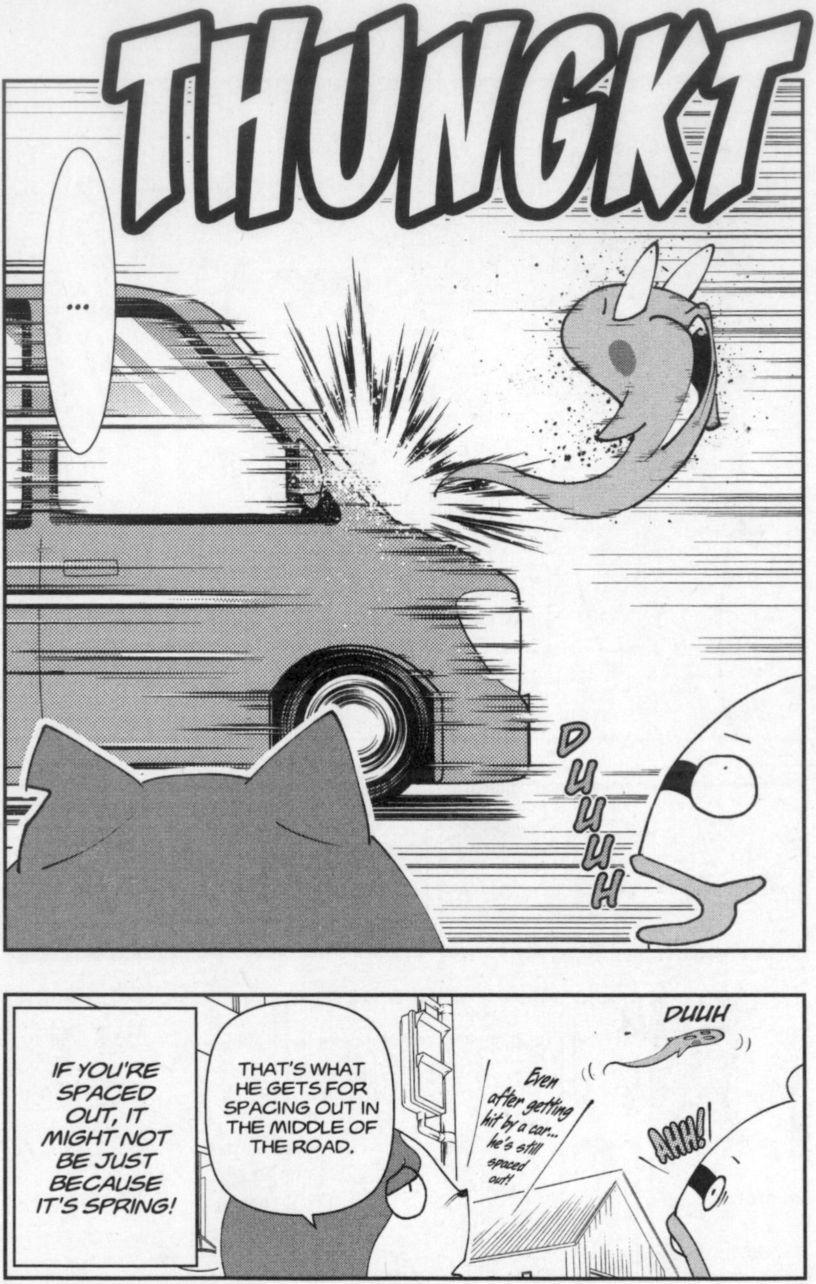
THUNGKT
...
DUUUH
DUUH
AHH!
Even after getting hit by a car... he's still spaced out!
THAT'S WHAT HE GETS FOR SPACING OUT IN THE MIDDLE OF THE ROAD.
IF YOU'RE SPACED OUT, IT MIGHT NOT BE JUST BECAUSE IT'S SPRING!

CHAPTER 216
HEART-THROBBING YO-KAI STARRYCANE

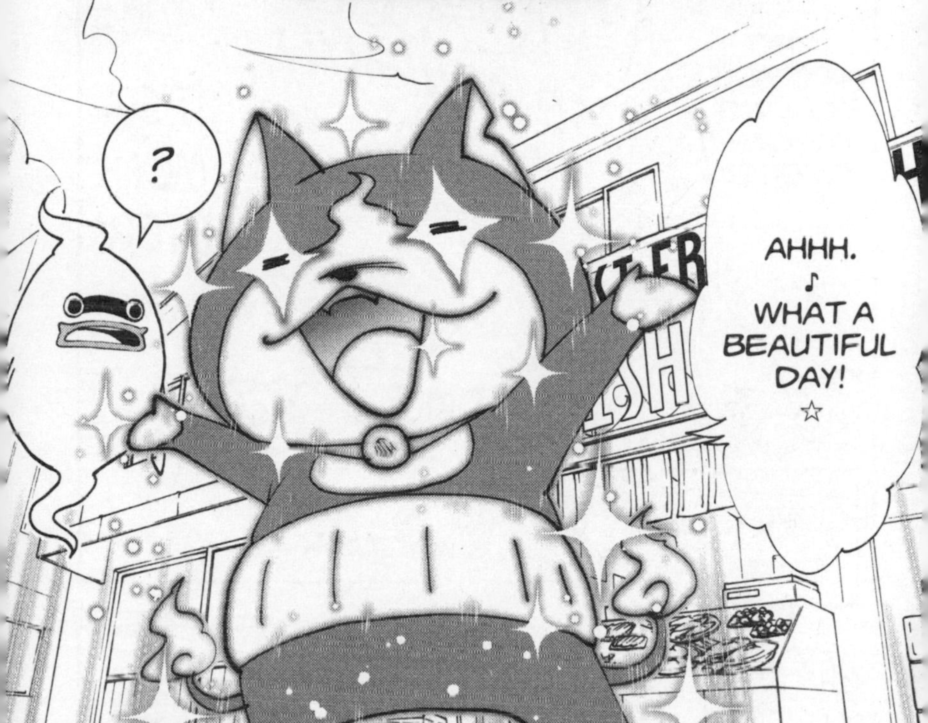
AHHH. ♪ WHAT A BEAUTIFUL DAY! ☆
?

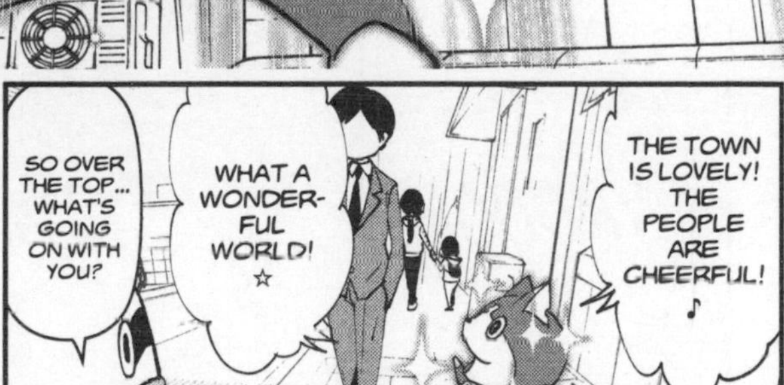
THE TOWN IS LOVELY! THE PEOPLE ARE CHEERFUL! ♪
WHAT A WONDER-FUL WORLD! ☆
SO OVER THE TOP... WHAT'S GOING ON WITH YOU?

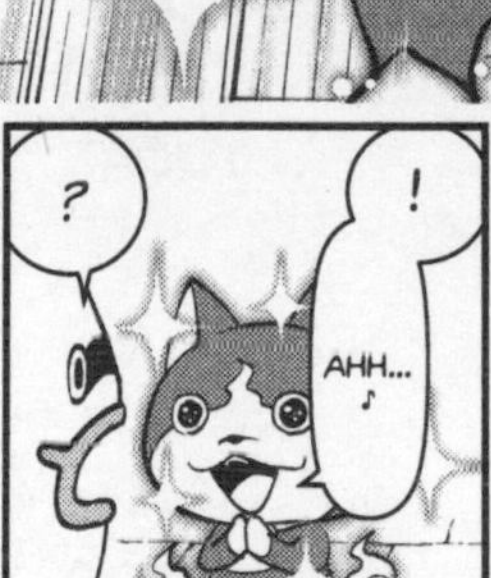
!
AHH... ♪
?

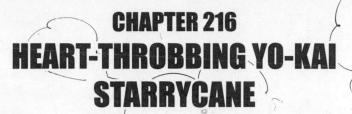

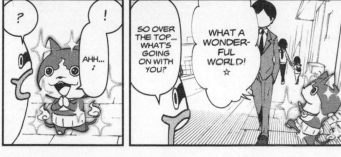

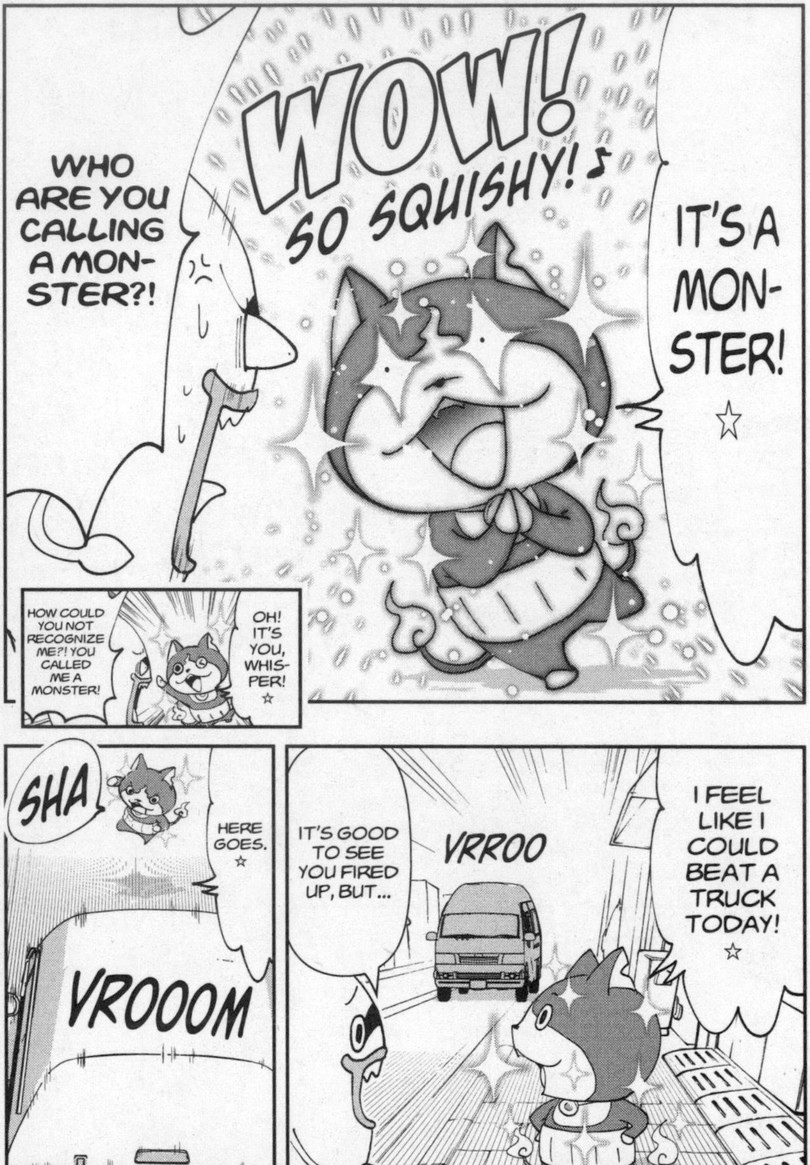
IT'S A MONSTER! ☆
WOW! SO SQUISHY! ♪
WHO ARE YOU CALLING A MONSTER?!
OH! IT'S YOU, WHISPER! ☆
HOW COULD YOU NOT RECOGNIZE ME?! YOU CALLED ME A MONSTER!
I FEEL LIKE I COULD BEAT A TRUCK TODAY! ☆
VRROO
IT'S GOOD TO SEE YOU FIRED UP, BUT...
HERE GOES. ☆
SHA
VROOOM

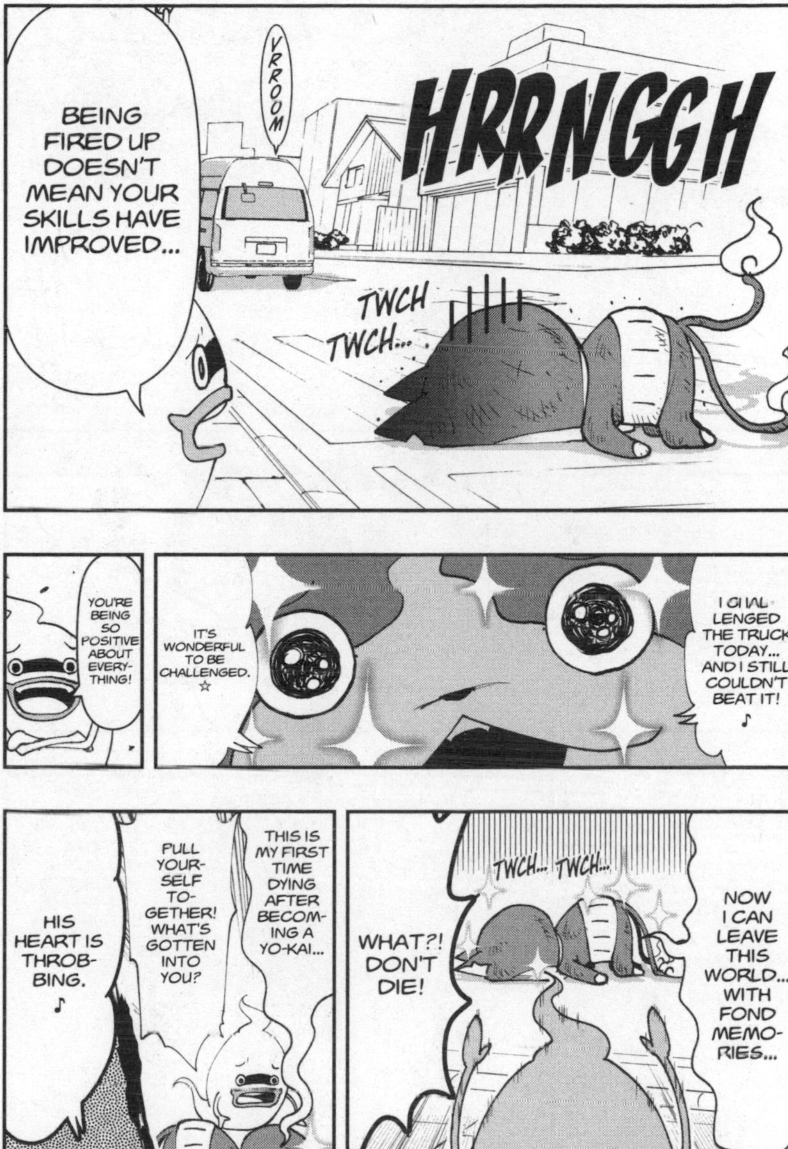
HRRNGGH
VRROOM
BEING FIRED UP DOESN'T MEAN YOUR SKILLS HAVE IMPROVED...
TWCH TWCH...
I CHALLENGED THE TRUCK TODAY... AND I STILL COULDN'T BEAT IT! ♪
IT'S WONDERFUL TO BE CHALLENGED. ☆
YOU'RE BEING SO POSITIVE ABOUT EVERYTHING!
NOW I CAN LEAVE THIS WORLD... WITH FOND MEMORIES...
TWCH... TWCH...
WHAT?! DON'T DIE!
THIS IS MY FIRST TIME DYING AFTER BECOMING A YO-KAI...
PULL YOURSELF TOGETHER! WHAT'S GOTTEN INTO YOU?
HIS HEART IS THROBBING. ♪

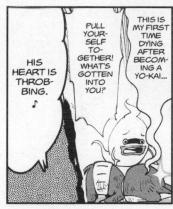

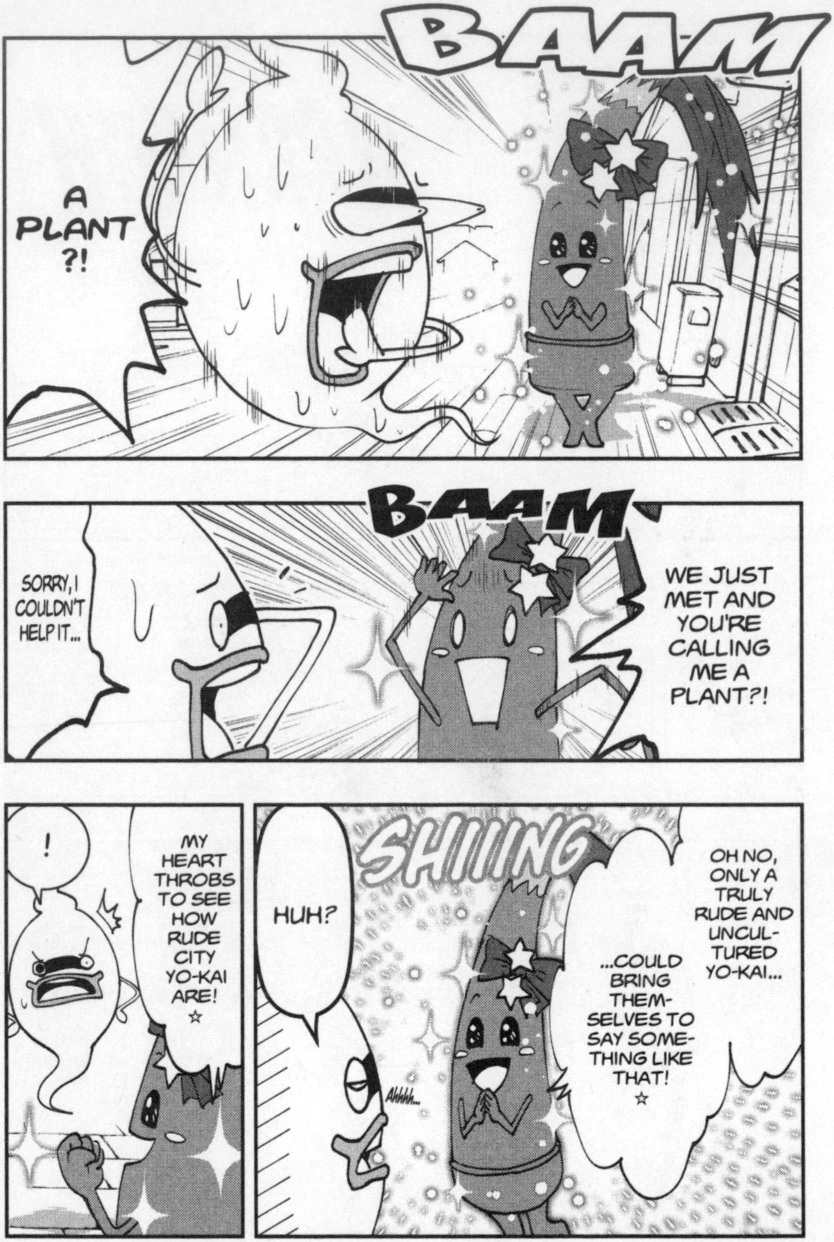
BAAM
A PLANT?!
BAAM
WE JUST MET AND YOU'RE CALLING ME A PLANT?!
SORRY, I COULDN'T HELP IT...
SHIIING
OH NO, ONLY A TRULY RUDE AND UNCULTURED YO-KAI...
...COULD BRING THEMSELVES TO SAY SOMETHING LIKE THAT! ☆
HUH?
Ahhhh...
MY HEART THROBS TO SEE HOW RUDE CITY YO-KAI ARE! ☆
!

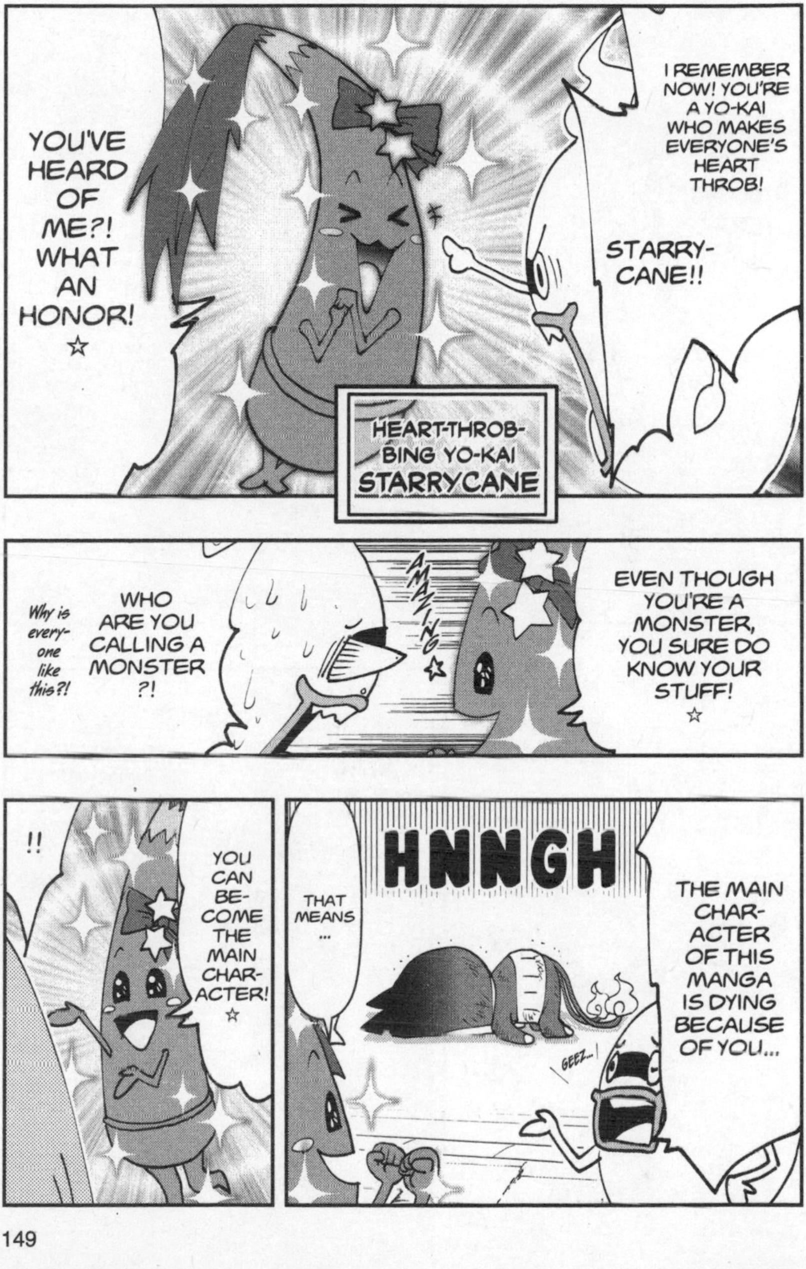
I REMEMBER NOW! YOU'RE A YO-KAI WHO MAKES EVERYONE'S HEART THROB!
STARRY-CANE!!
YOU'VE HEARD OF ME?! WHAT AN HONOR! ☆
HEART-THROBBING YO-KAI STARRYCANE
EVEN THOUGH YOU'RE A MONSTER, YOU SURE DO KNOW YOUR STUFF! ☆
AMAZING ☆
WHO ARE YOU CALLING A MONSTER?!
Why is everyone like this?!
THE MAIN CHARACTER OF THIS MANGA IS DYING BECAUSE OF YOU...
GEEZ...!
HNNGH
THAT MEANS ...
!!
YOU CAN BECOME THE MAIN CHARACTER! ☆

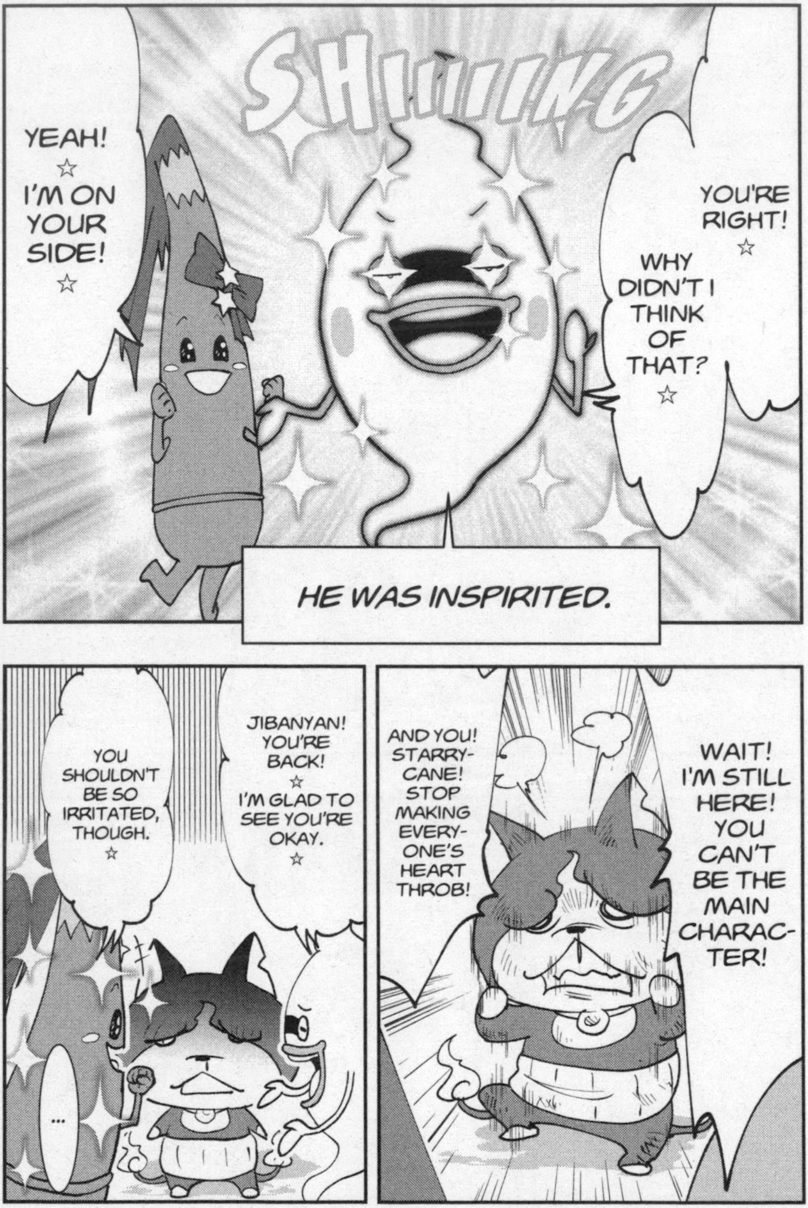
SHIIIIING
YOU'RE RIGHT! ☆ WHY DIDN'T I THINK OF THAT? ☆
YEAH! ☆ I'M ON YOUR SIDE! ☆
HE WAS INSPIRITED.
WAIT! I'M STILL HERE! YOU CAN'T BE THE MAIN CHARAC-TER!
AND YOU! STARRY-CANE! STOP MAKING EVERY-ONE'S HEART THROB!
JIBANYAN! YOU'RE BACK! ☆ I'M GLAD TO SEE YOU'RE OKAY. ☆
YOU SHOULDN'T BE SO IRRITATED, THOUGH. ☆
...

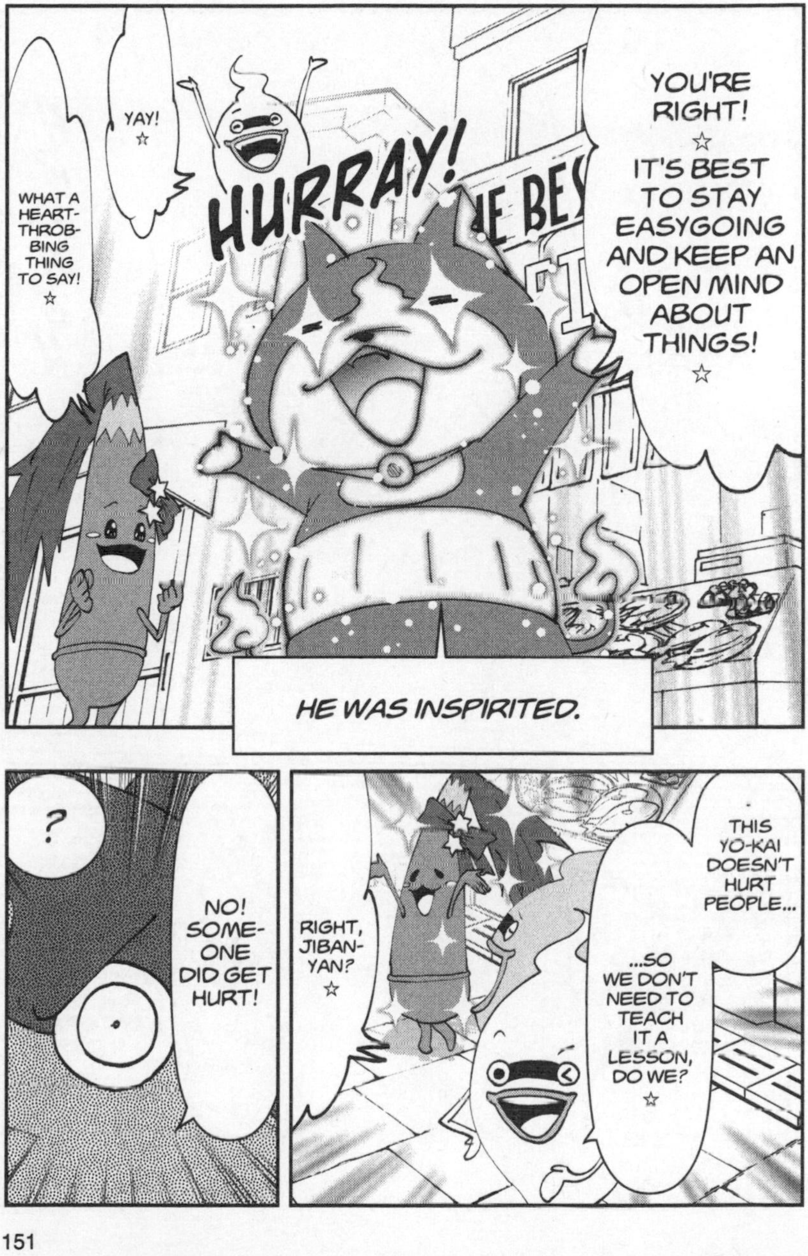
YOU'RE RIGHT! ☆ IT'S BEST TO STAY EASYGOING AND KEEP AN OPEN MIND ABOUT THINGS! ☆
HURRAY!
YAY! ☆
WHAT A HEART-THROBBING THING TO SAY! ☆
HE WAS INSPIRITED.
THIS YO-KAI DOESN'T HURT PEOPLE...
...SO WE DON'T NEED TO TEACH IT A LESSON, DO WE? ☆
RIGHT, JIBAN-YAN? ☆
?
NO! SOMEONE DID GET HURT!

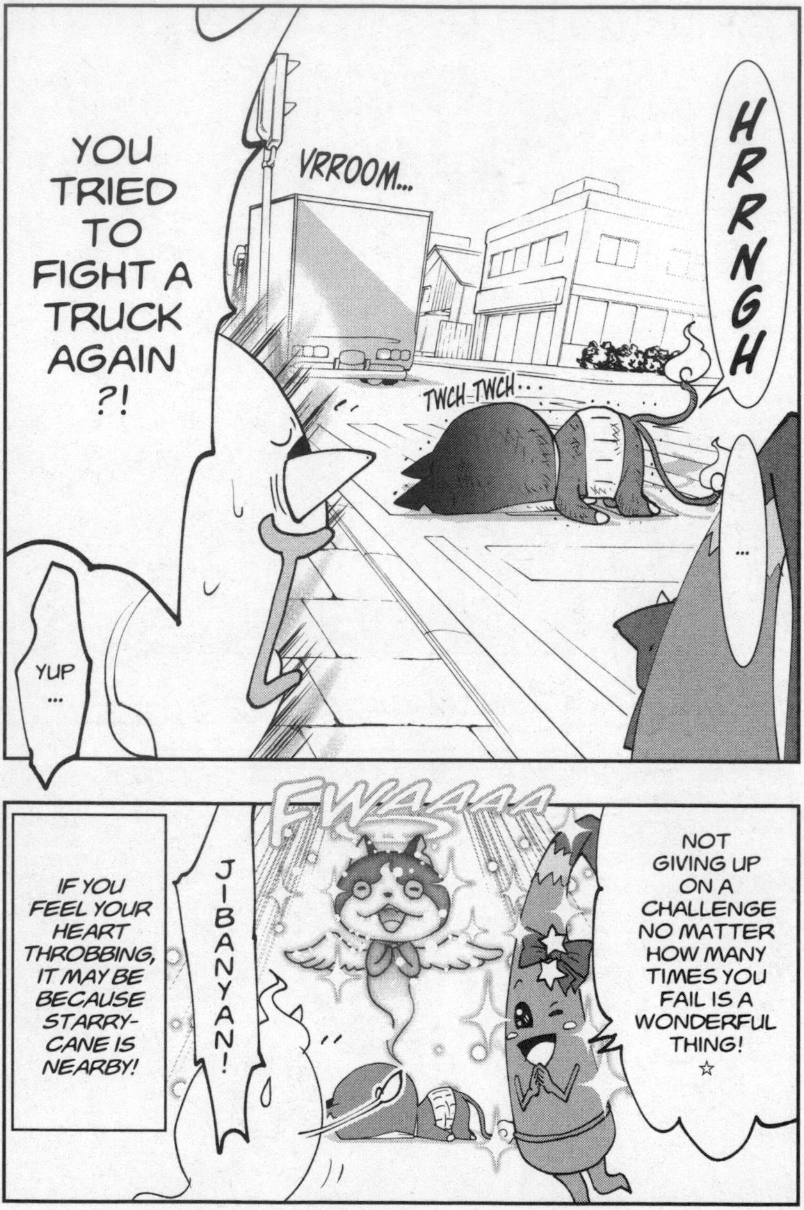
HRRNGH
VRROOM...
YOU TRIED TO FIGHT A TRUCK AGAIN?!
TWCH-TWCH...
...
YUP...
FWAAAA
NOT GIVING UP ON A CHALLENGE NO MATTER HOW MANY TIMES YOU FAIL IS A WONDERFUL THING! ☆
JIBANYAN!
IF YOU FEEL YOUR HEART THROBBING, IT MAY BE BECAUSE STARRYCANE IS NEARBY!

CHAPTER 217
SEVEN GODS OF FORTUNE YO-KAI EBISUISH

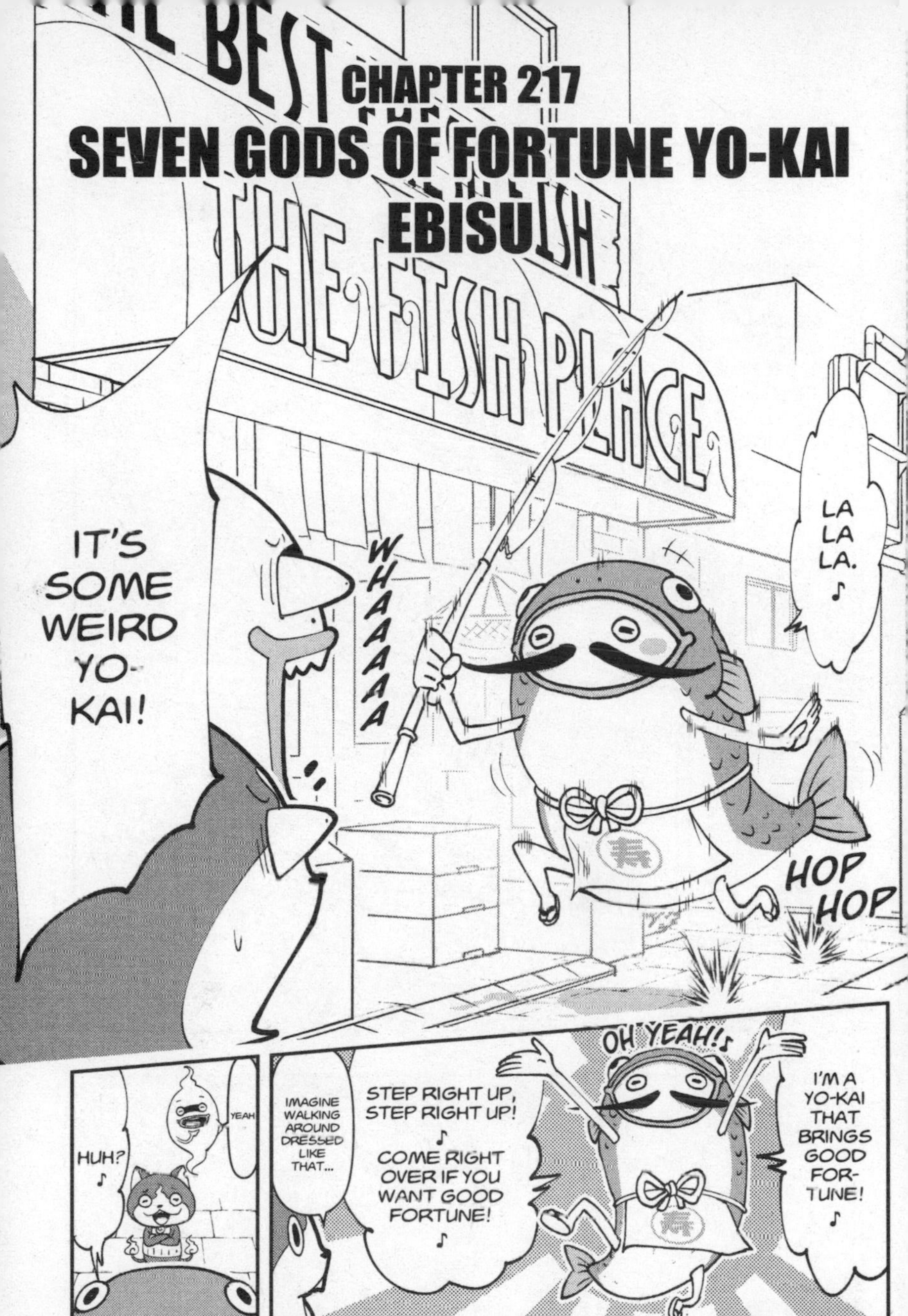

THE FISH PLACE
LA LA LA. ♪
HOP HOP
WHAAAAAA
IT'S SOME WEIRD YO-KAI!
OH YEAH! ♪
I'M A YO-KAI THAT BRINGS GOOD FORTUNE! ♪
STEP RIGHT UP, STEP RIGHT UP! ♪
COME RIGHT OVER IF YOU WANT GOOD FORTUNE! ♪
IMAGINE WALKING AROUND DRESSED LIKE THAT...
YEAH
HUH? ♪

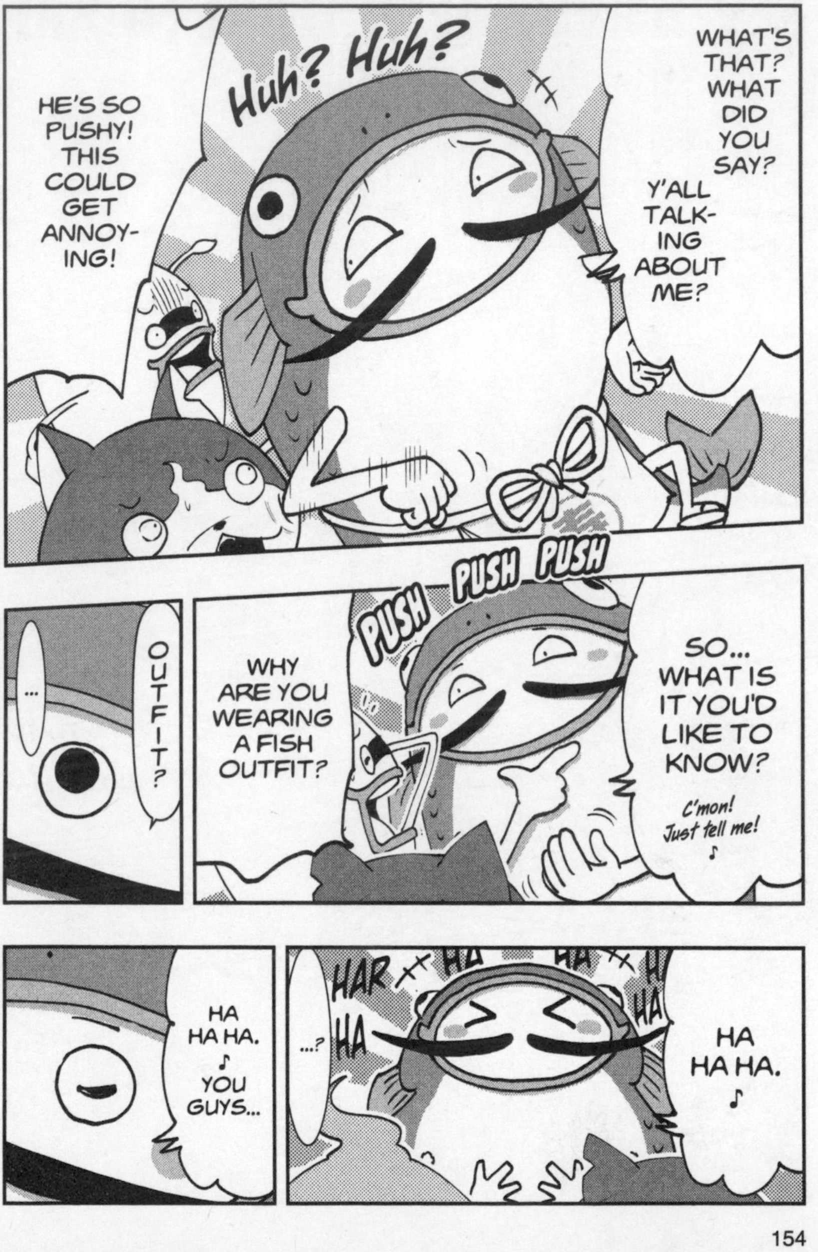
WHAT'S THAT? WHAT DID YOU SAY?
Y'ALL TALKING ABOUT ME?
Huh? Huh?
HE'S SO PUSHY! THIS COULD GET ANNOYING!
PUSH PUSH PUSH
SO... WHAT IS IT YOU'D LIKE TO KNOW?
C'mon! Just tell me! ♪
WHY ARE YOU WEARING A FISH OUTFIT?
OUTFIT?
...
HA HA HA. ♪
HAR HA HA
...?
HA HA HA. ♪ YOU GUYS...

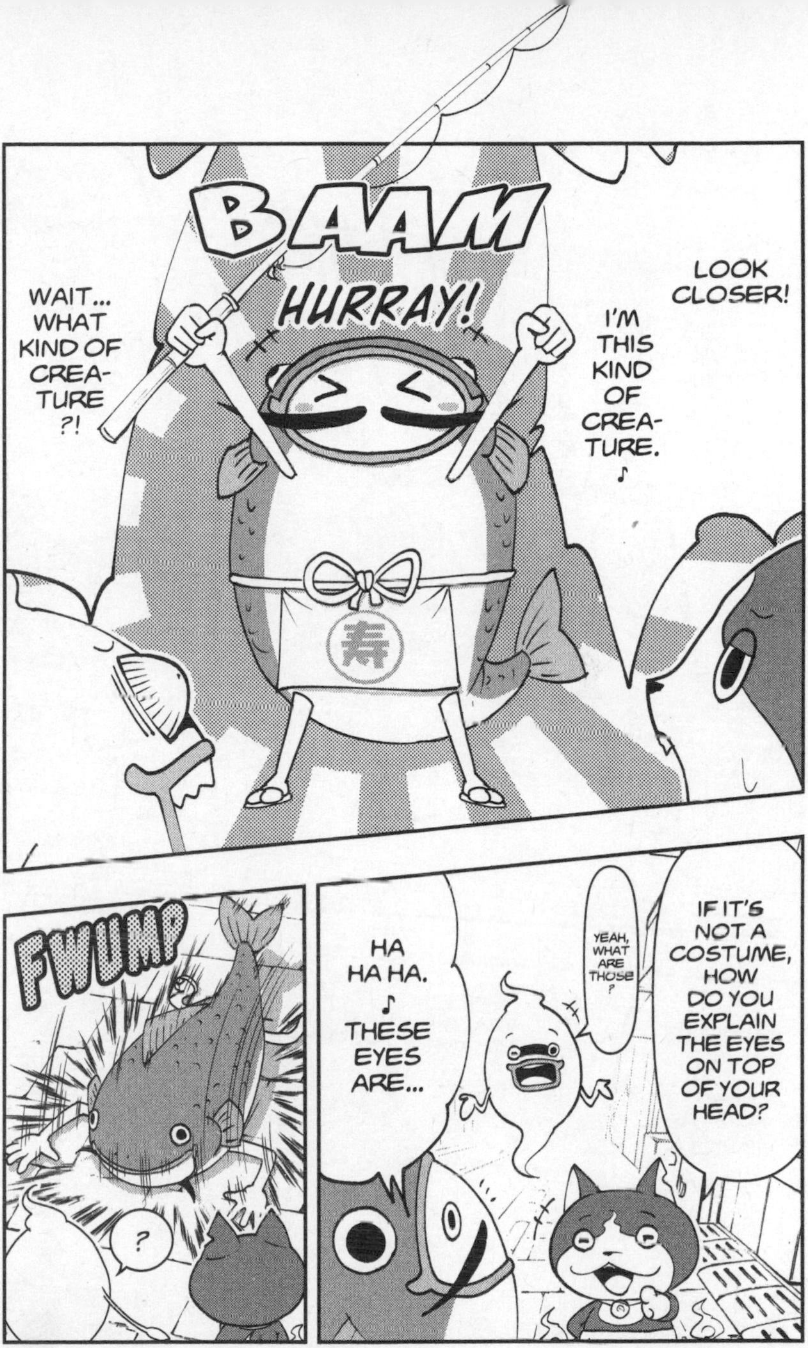
BAAM
LOOK CLOSER!
I'M THIS KIND OF CREA-TURE. ♪
HURRAY!
WAIT... WHAT KIND OF CREA-TURE ?!
IF IT'S NOT A COSTUME, HOW DO YOU EXPLAIN THE EYES ON TOP OF YOUR HEAD?
YEAH, WHAT ARE THOSE ?
HA HA HA. ♪ THESE EYES ARE...
FWUMP
?

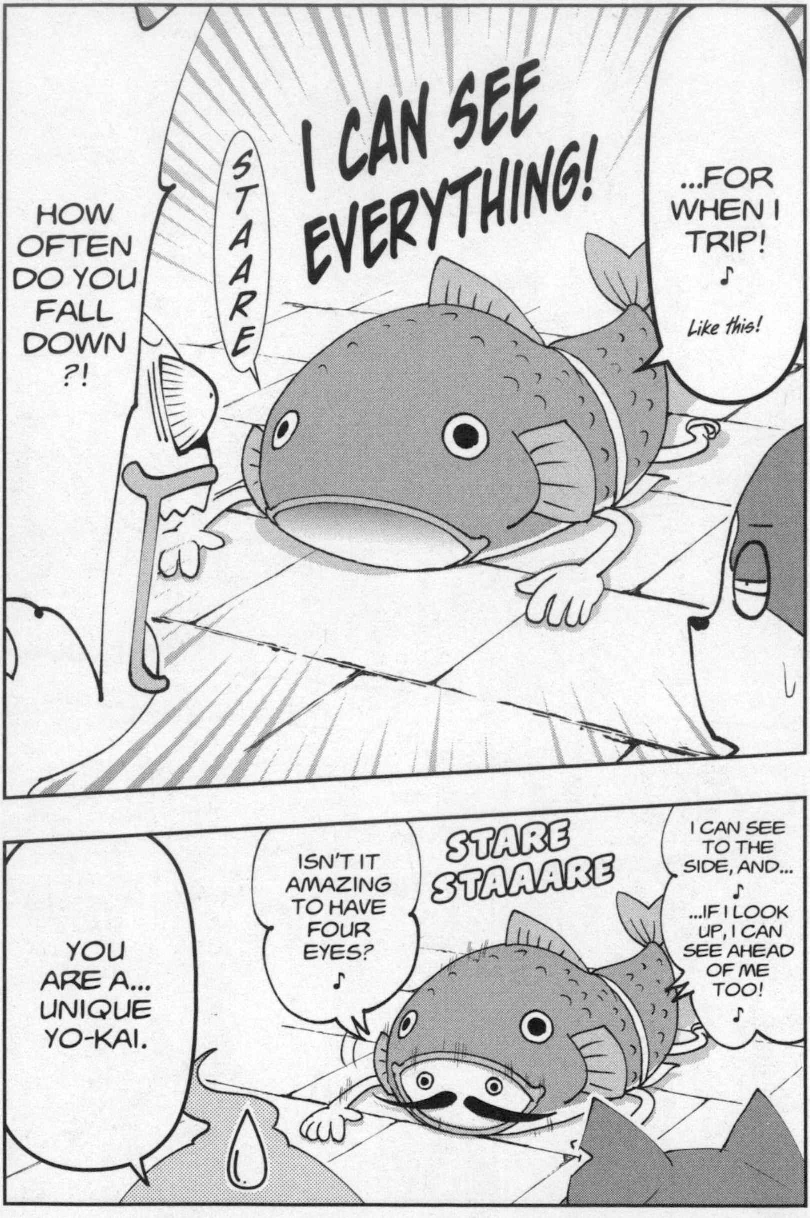
...FOR WHEN I TRIP! ♪
Like this!
I CAN SEE EVERYTHING!
STAARE
HOW OFTEN DO YOU FALL DOWN?!
I CAN SEE TO THE SIDE, AND... ♪ ...IF I LOOK UP, I CAN SEE AHEAD OF ME TOO! ♪
STARE STAAAARE
ISN'T IT AMAZING TO HAVE FOUR EYES? ♪
YOU ARE A... UNIQUE YO-KAI.

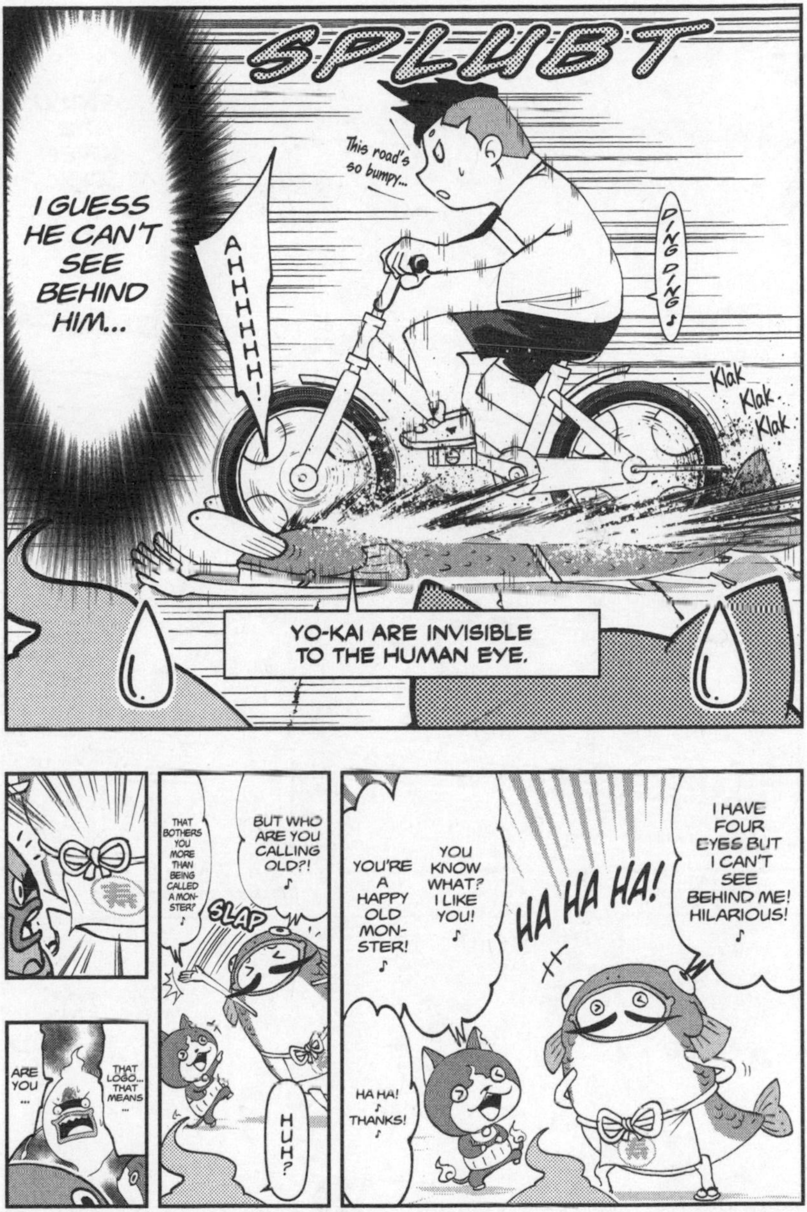
SPLUBT
This road's so bumpy...
DING DING ♪
Klak Klak Klak
AHHHHHH!
I GUESS HE CAN'T SEE BEHIND HIM...
YO-KAI ARE INVISIBLE TO THE HUMAN EYE.
I HAVE FOUR EYES BUT I CAN'T SEE BEHIND ME! HILARIOUS! ♪
HA HA HA!
YOU KNOW WHAT? I LIKE YOU! ♪
YOU'RE A HAPPY OLD MONSTER! ♪
HA HA! ♪ THANKS! ♪
BUT WHO ARE YOU CALLING OLD?! ♪
THAT BOTHERS YOU MORE THAN BEING CALLED A MONSTER? ♪
SLAP
HUH?
THAT LOGO... THAT MEANS ...
ARE YOU ...

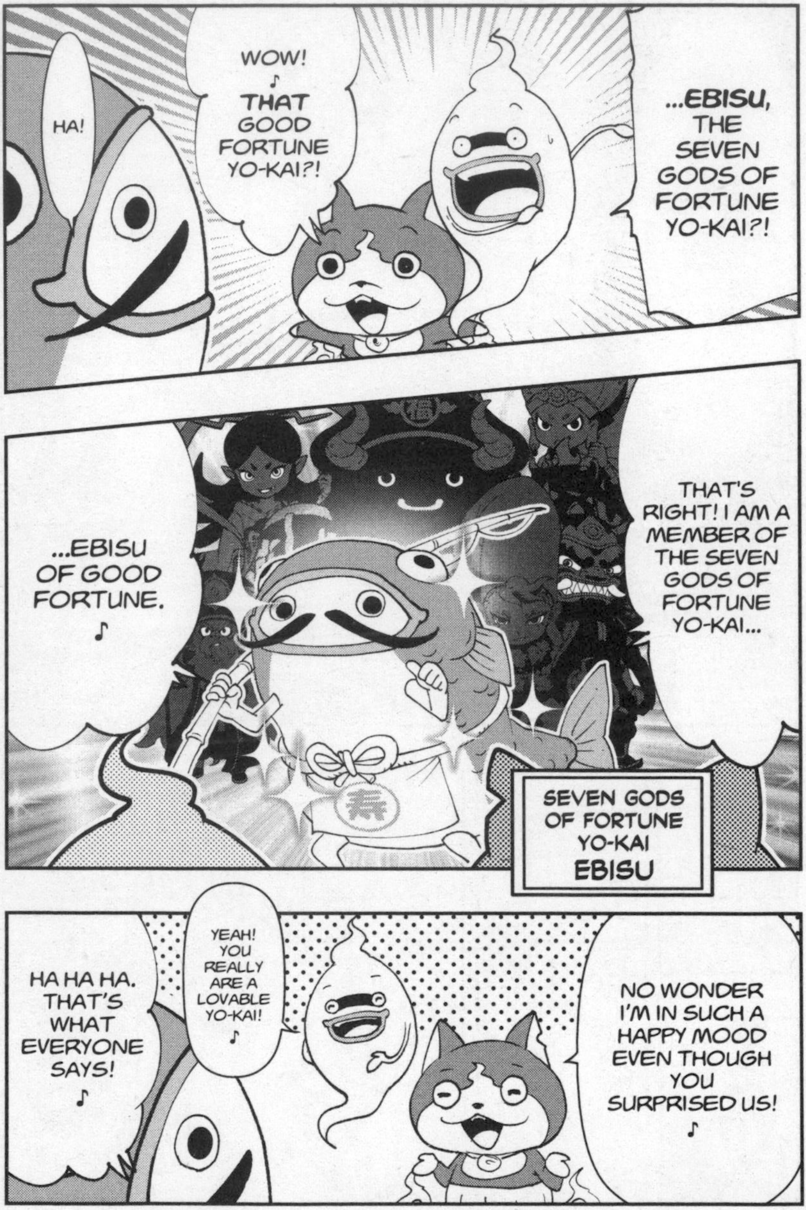
...EBISU, THE SEVEN GODS OF FORTUNE YO-KAI?!
WOW! ♪ THAT GOOD FORTUNE YO-KAI?!
HA!
THAT'S RIGHT! I AM A MEMBER OF THE SEVEN GODS OF FORTUNE YO-KAI...
...EBISU OF GOOD FORTUNE. ♪
SEVEN GODS OF FORTUNE YO-KAI EBISU
NO WONDER I'M IN SUCH A HAPPY MOOD EVEN THOUGH YOU SURPRISED US! ♪
YEAH! YOU REALLY ARE A LOVABLE YO-KAI! ♪
HA HA HA. THAT'S WHAT EVERYONE SAYS! ♪

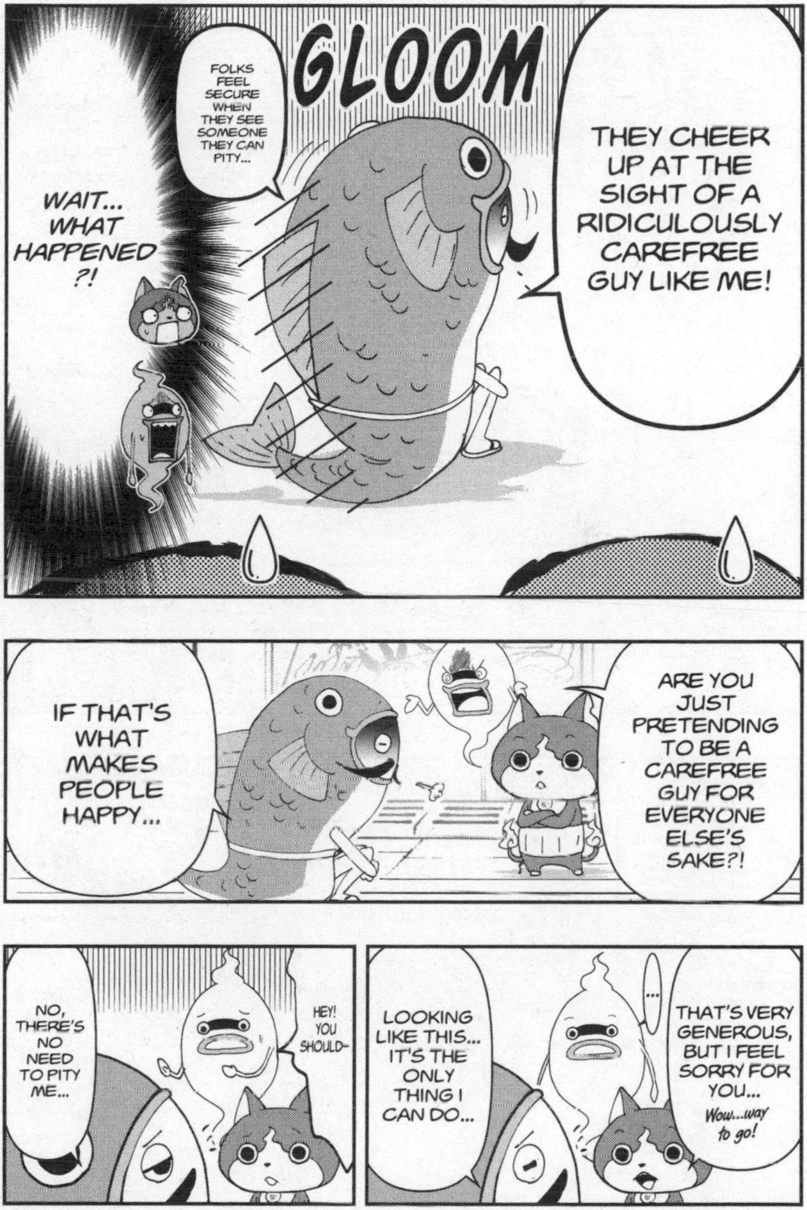
THEY CHEER UP AT THE SIGHT OF A RIDICULOUSLY CAREFREE GUY LIKE ME!
GLOOM
FOLKS FEEL SECURE WHEN THEY SEE SOMEONE THEY CAN PITY...
WAIT... WHAT HAPPENED?!
ARE YOU JUST PRETENDING TO BE A CAREFREE GUY FOR EVERYONE ELSE'S SAKE?!
IF THAT'S WHAT MAKES PEOPLE HAPPY...
THAT'S VERY GENEROUS, BUT I FEEL SORRY FOR YOU...
Wow...way to go!
...
LOOKING LIKE THIS... IT'S THE ONLY THING I CAN DO...
HEY! YOU SHOULD-
NO, THERE'S NO NEED TO PITY ME...

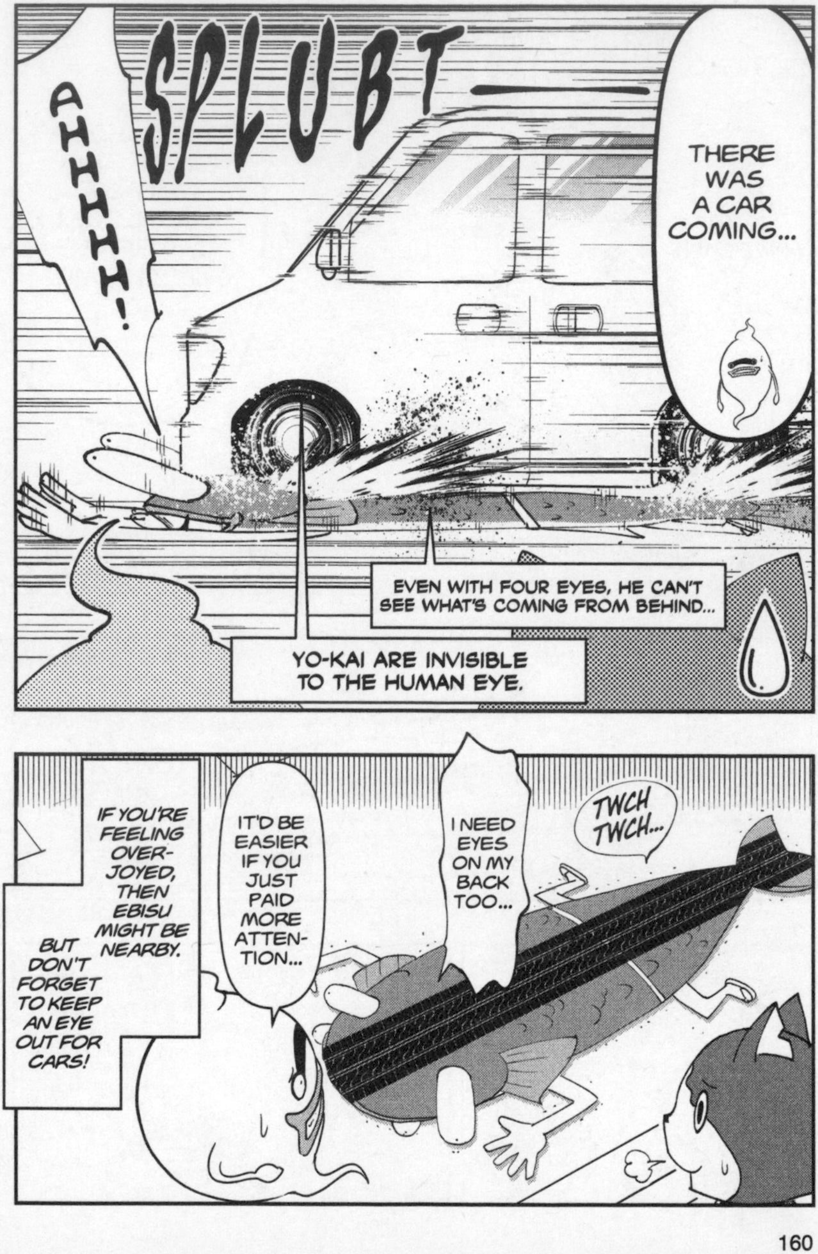
THERE WAS A CAR COMING...
SPLUBT
AHHHH!
EVEN WITH FOUR EYES, HE CAN'T SEE WHAT'S COMING FROM BEHIND...
YO-KAI ARE INVISIBLE TO THE HUMAN EYE.
TWCH TWCH...
I NEED EYES ON MY BACK TOO...
IT'D BE EASIER IF YOU JUST PAID MORE ATTEN-TION...
IF YOU'RE FEELING OVER-JOYED, THEN EBISU MIGHT BE NEARBY.
BUT DON'T FORGET TO KEEP AN EYE OUT FOR CARS!

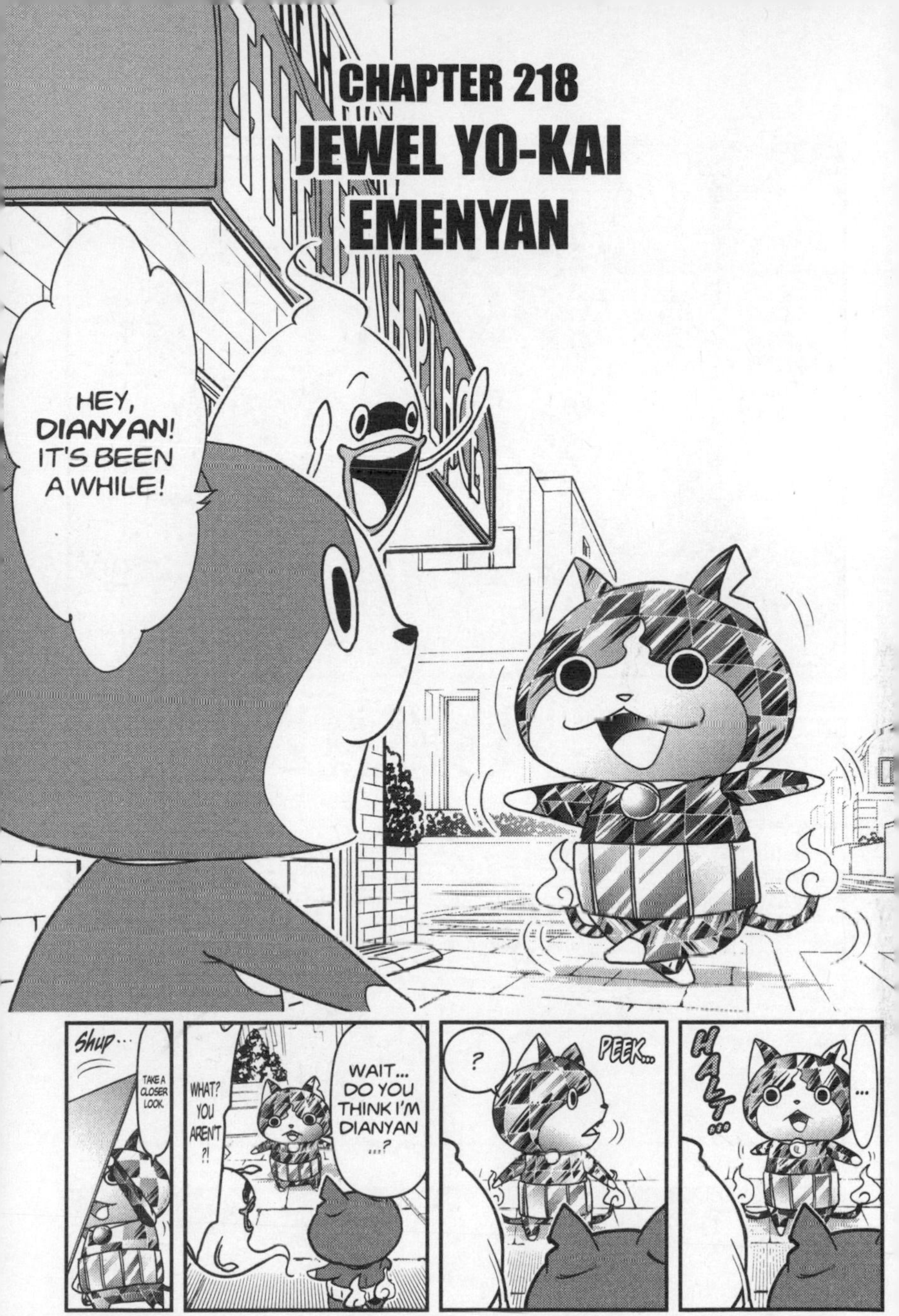
CHAPTER 218
JEWEL YO-KAI EMENYAN
HEY, DIANYAN! IT'S BEEN A WHILE!
...
HALT...
PEEK...
?
WAIT... DO YOU THINK I'M DIANYAN ...?
WHAT? YOU AREN'T ?!
TAKE A CLOSER LOOK.
Shup...

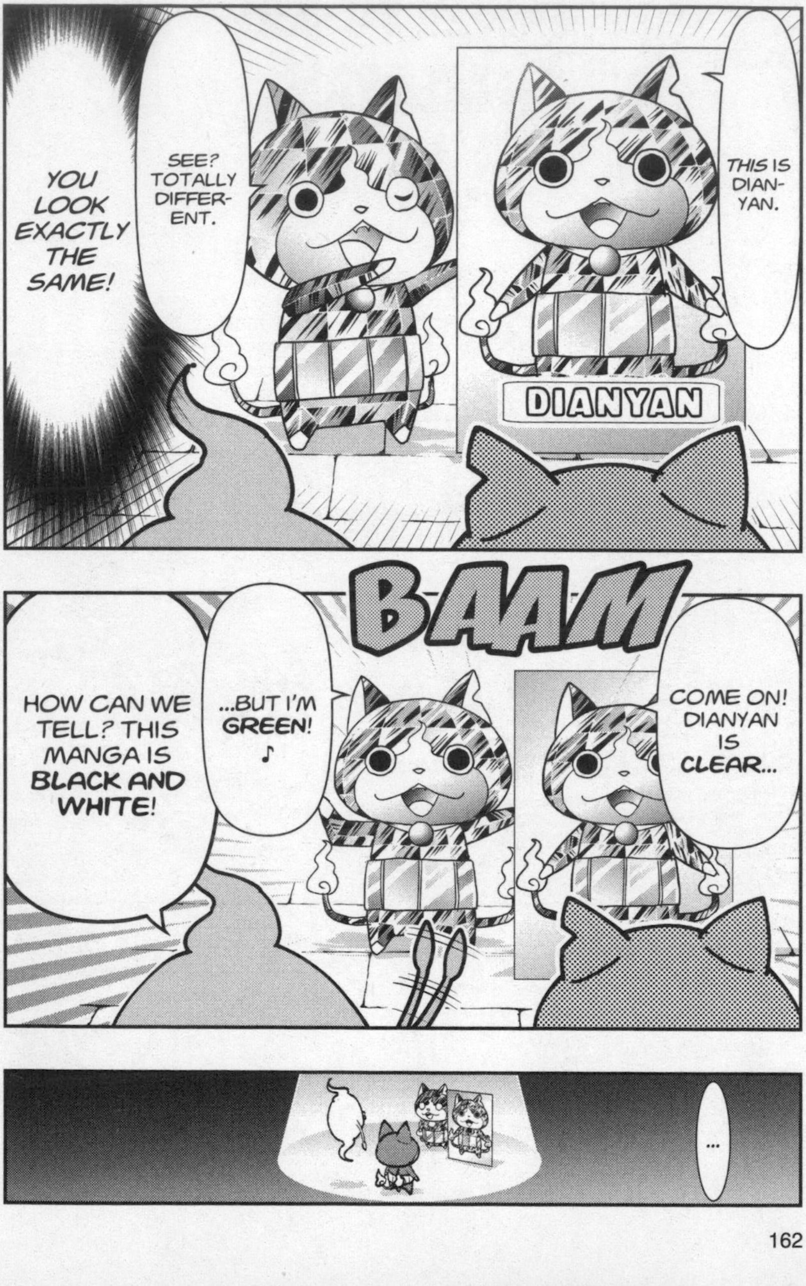
THIS IS DIAN-YAN.
DIANYAN
SEE? TOTALLY DIFFER-ENT.
YOU LOOK EXACTLY THE SAME!
BAAM
COME ON! DIANYAN IS CLEAR...
...BUT I'M GREEN! ♪
HOW CAN WE TELL? THIS MANGA IS BLACK AND WHITE!
...

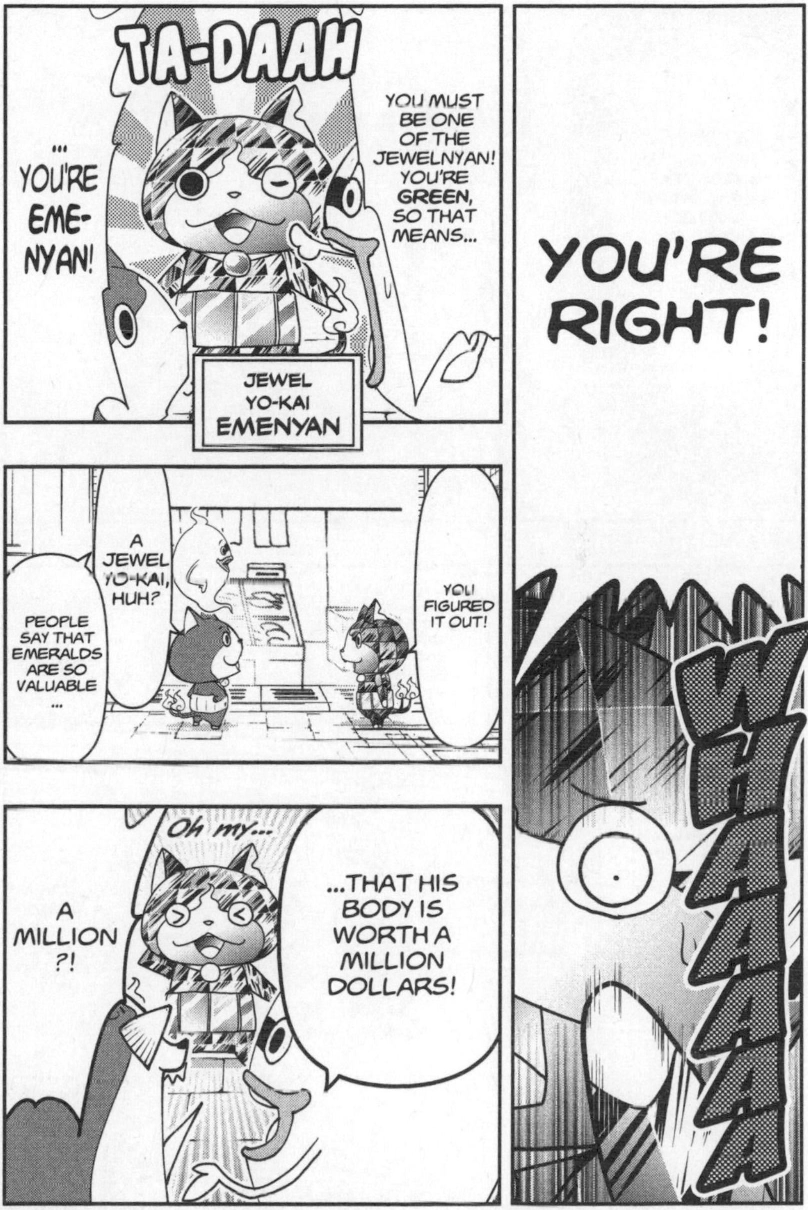
YOU'RE RIGHT!
WHAAAAA
TA-DAAH
YOU MUST BE ONE OF THE JEWELNYAN! YOU'RE GREEN, SO THAT MEANS...
... YOU'RE EME-NYAN!
JEWEL YO-KAI EMENYAN
YOU FIGURED IT OUT!
A JEWEL YO-KAI, HUH?
PEOPLE SAY THAT EMERALDS ARE SO VALUABLE ...
Oh my...
...THAT HIS BODY IS WORTH A MILLION DOLLARS!
A MILLION ?!

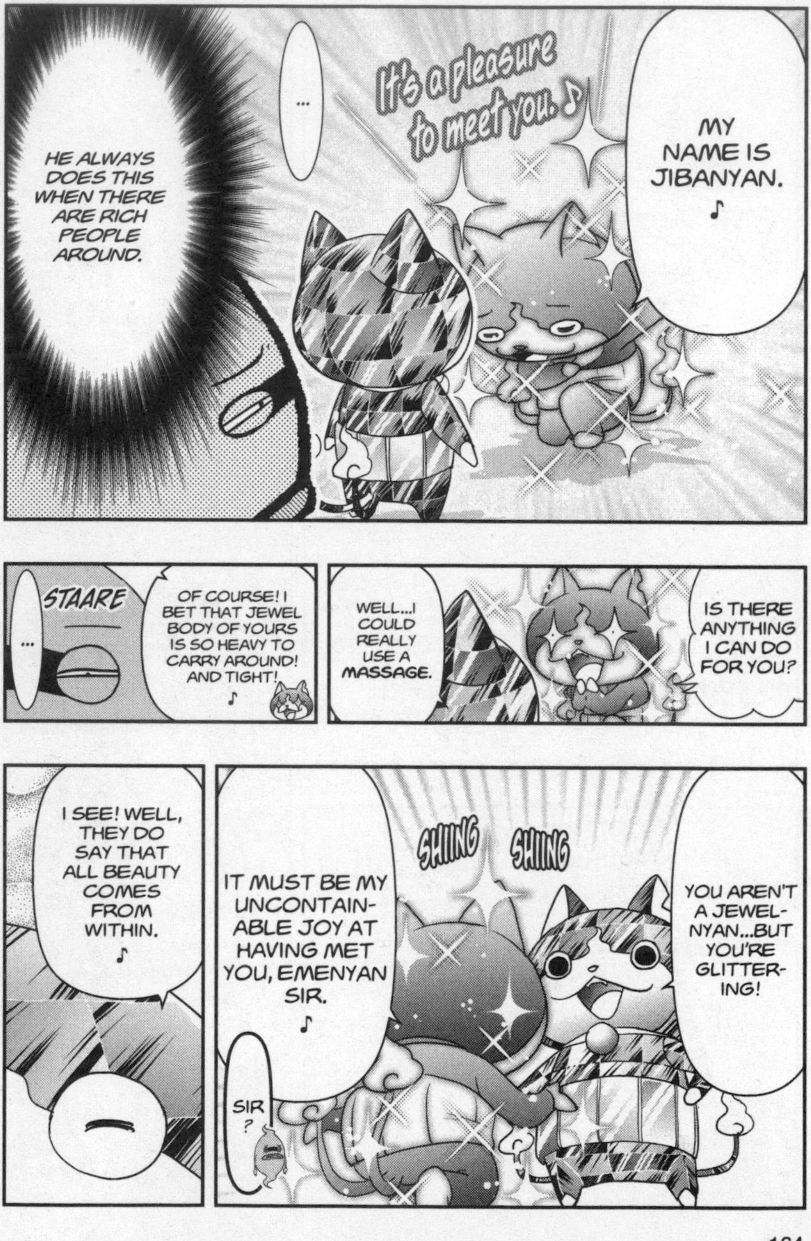
MY NAME IS JIBANYAN. ♪
It's a pleasure to meet you. ♪
...
HE ALWAYS DOES THIS WHEN THERE ARE RICH PEOPLE AROUND.
IS THERE ANYTHING I CAN DO FOR YOU?
WELL...I COULD REALLY USE A MASSAGE.
OF COURSE! I BET THAT JEWEL BODY OF YOURS IS SO HEAVY TO CARRY AROUND! AND TIGHT! ♪
STAARE
...
YOU AREN'T A JEWEL-NYAN...BUT YOU'RE GLITTER-ING!
SHIING
SHIING
IT MUST BE MY UNCONTAIN-ABLE JOY AT HAVING MET YOU, EMENYAN SIR. ♪
SIR?
I SEE! WELL, THEY DO SAY THAT ALL BEAUTY COMES FROM WITHIN. ♪

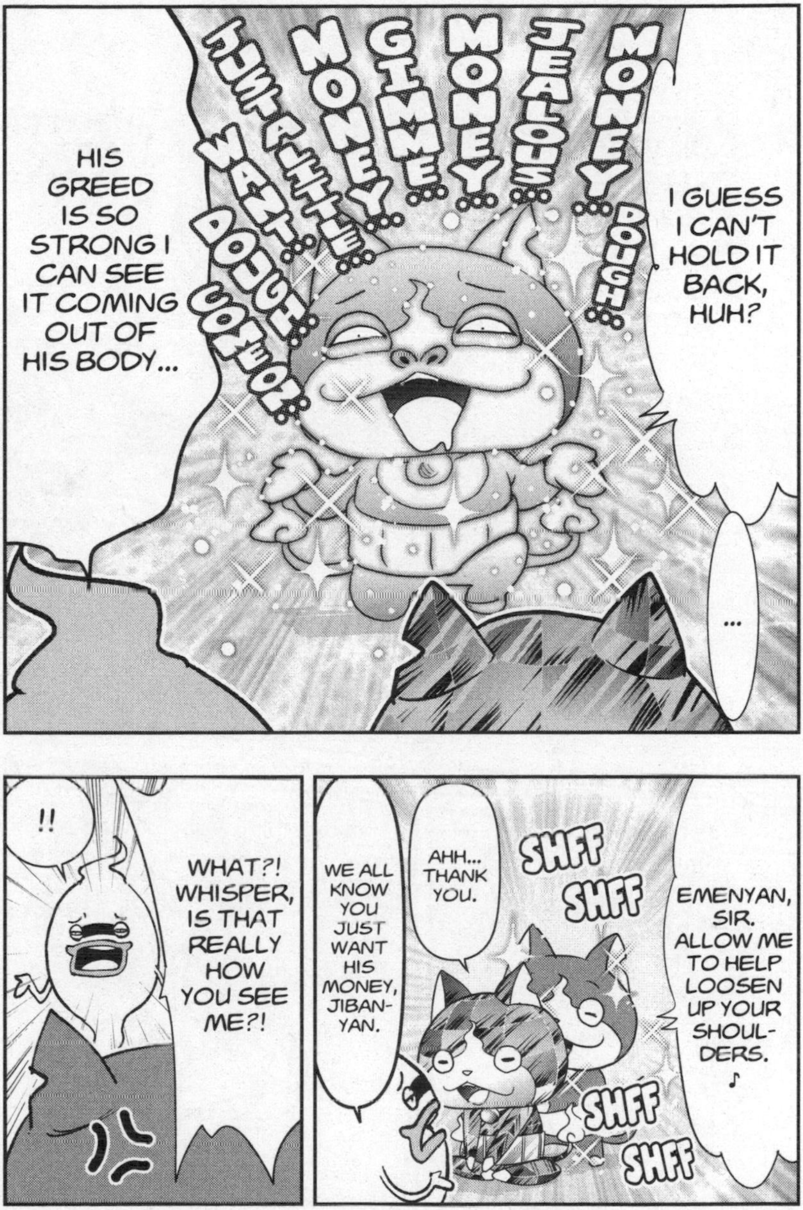
MONEY... DOUGH...
JEALOUS...
MONEY...
GIMME...
MONEY...
JUST A LITTLE...
WANT... DOUGH... COME ON...
I GUESS I CAN'T HOLD IT BACK, HUH?
HIS GREED IS SO STRONG I CAN SEE IT COMING OUT OF HIS BODY...
...
EMENYAN, SIR. ALLOW ME TO HELP LOOSEN UP YOUR SHOULDERS. ♪
SHFF
SHFF
AHH... THANK YOU.
WE ALL KNOW YOU JUST WANT HIS MONEY, JIBANYAN.
SHFF
SHFF
!!
WHAT?! WHISPER, IS THAT REALLY HOW YOU SEE ME?!

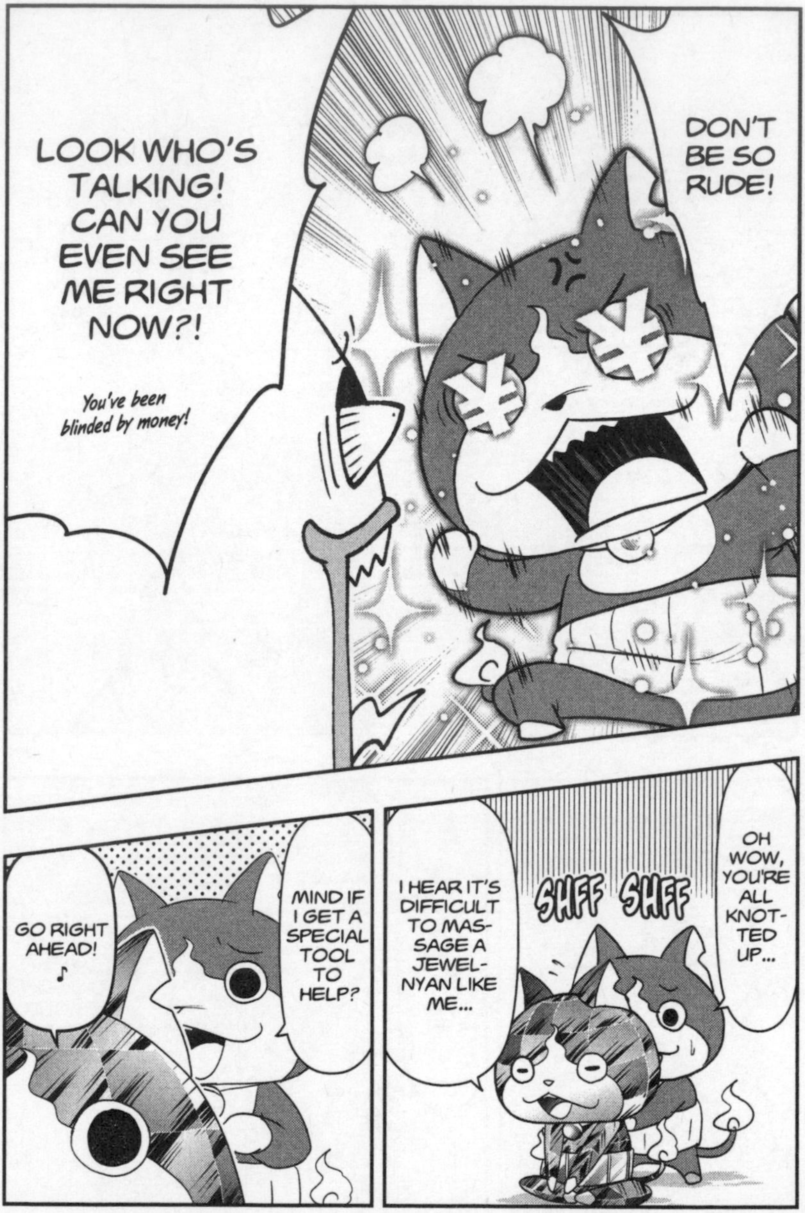
DON'T BE SO RUDE!
LOOK WHO'S TALKING! CAN YOU EVEN SEE ME RIGHT NOW?!
You've been blinded by money!
OH WOW, YOU'RE ALL KNOTTED UP...
SHFF SHFF
I HEAR IT'S DIFFICULT TO MASSAGE A JEWELNYAN LIKE ME...
MIND IF I GET A SPECIAL TOOL TO HELP?
GO RIGHT AHEAD! ♪

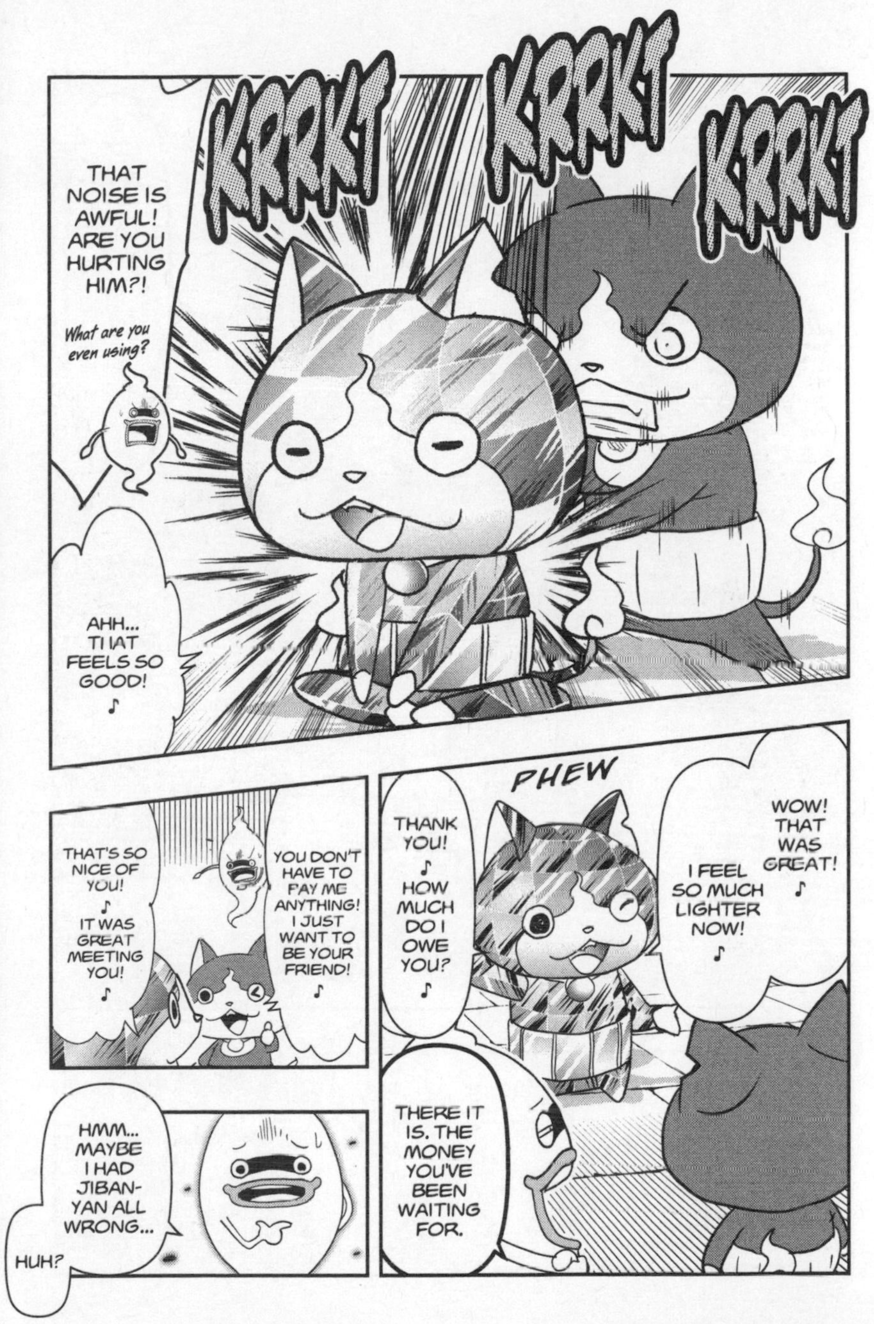
KRRKT
KRRKT
KRRKT
THAT NOISE IS AWFUL! ARE YOU HURTING HIM?!
What are you even using?
AHH... THAT FEELS SO GOOD! ♪
PHEW
WOW! THAT WAS GREAT! ♪
I FEEL SO MUCH LIGHTER NOW! ♪
THANK YOU! ♪ HOW MUCH DO I OWE YOU? ♪
THERE IT IS. THE MONEY YOU'VE BEEN WAITING FOR.
YOU DON'T HAVE TO PAY ME ANYTHING! I JUST WANT TO BE YOUR FRIEND! ♪
THAT'S SO NICE OF YOU! ♪ IT WAS GREAT MEETING YOU! ♪
HMM... MAYBE I HAD JIBAN-YAN ALL WRONG...
HUH?

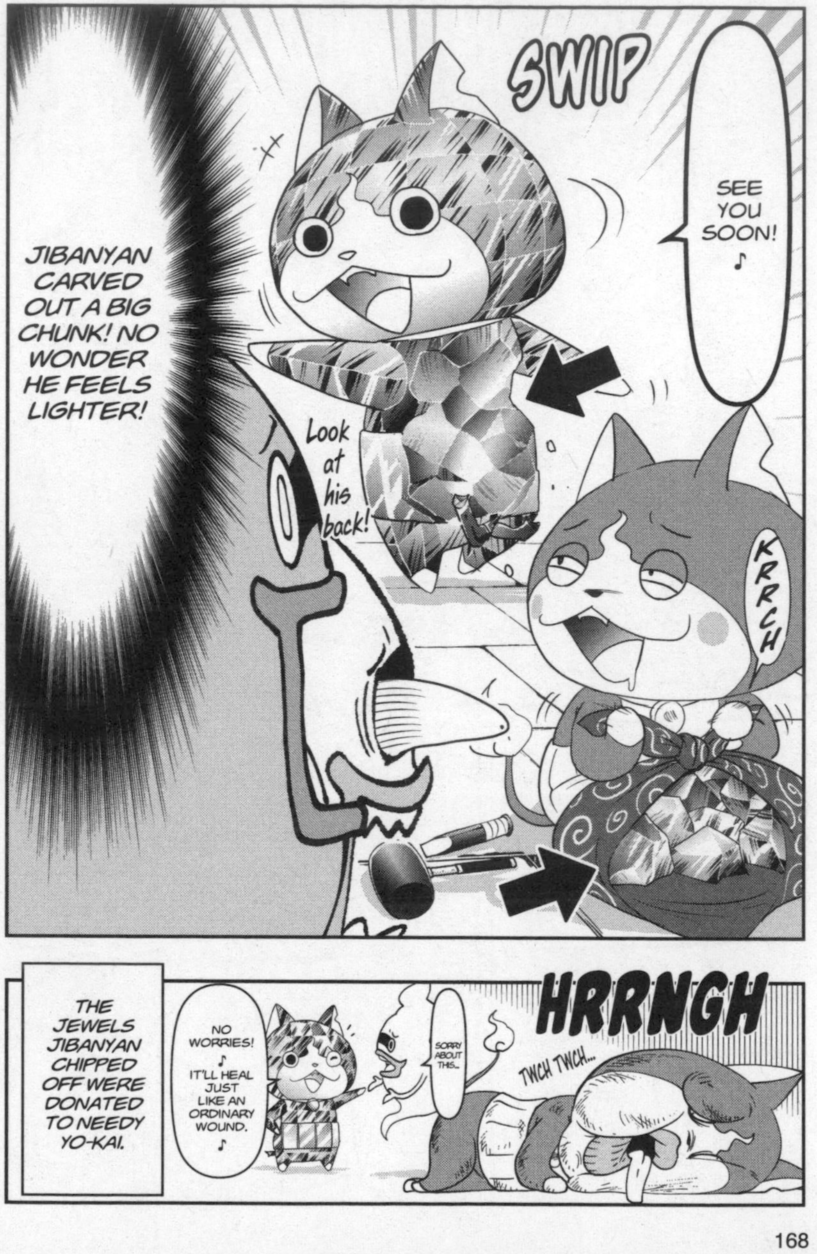
SEE YOU SOON! ♪
SWIP
KRRCH
Look at his back!
JIBANYAN CARVED OUT A BIG CHUNK! NO WONDER HE FEELS LIGHTER!
HRRNGH
TWCH TWCH...
SORRY ABOUT THIS...
NO WORRIES! ♪ IT'LL HEAL JUST LIKE AN ORDINARY WOUND. ♪
THE JEWELS JIBANYAN CHIPPED OFF WERE DONATED TO NEEDY YO-KAI.

CHAPTER 219
RECLUSE YO-KAI ABODABAT

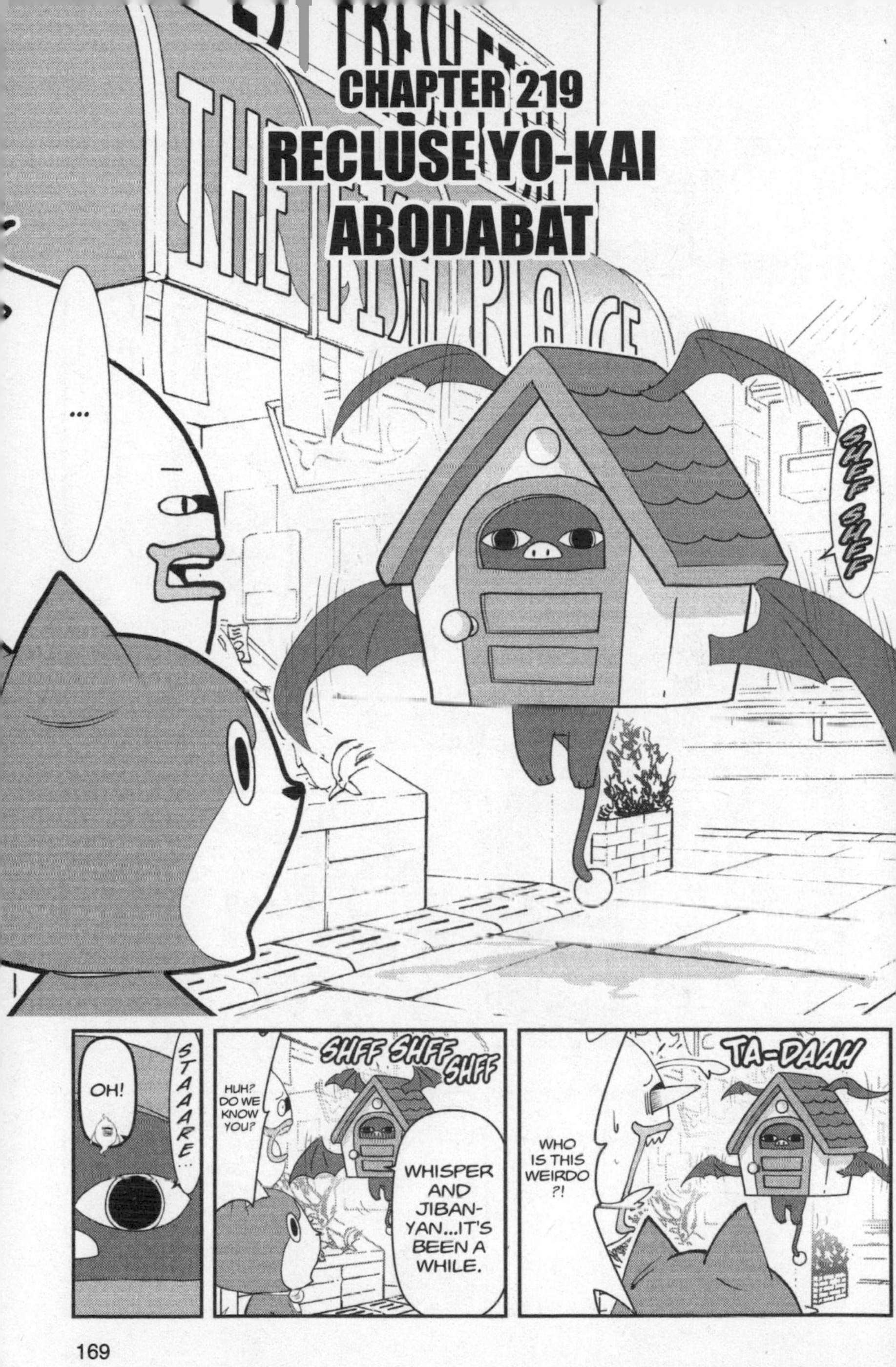

...
SHFF SHFF
TA-DAAH
WHO IS THIS WEIRDO?!
SHFF SHFF SHFF
HUH? DO WE KNOW YOU?
WHISPER AND JIBAN-YAN...IT'S BEEN A WHILE.
STAAARE...
OH!

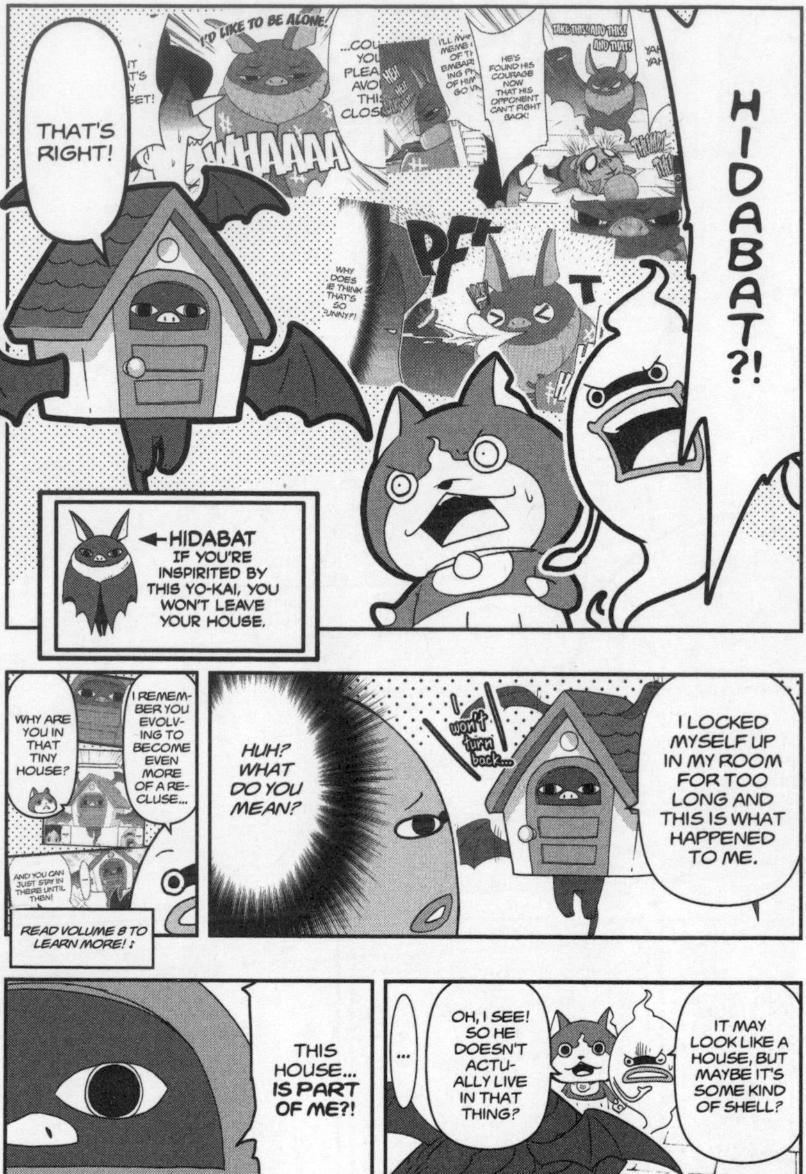
HIDABAT?!
TAKE THIS! AND THIS! AND THAT!
HE'S FOUND HIS COURAGE NOW THAT HIS OPPONENT CAN'T FIGHT BACK!
I'D LIKE TO BE ALONE!
WHAAAA
PFFT
THAT'S RIGHT!
←HIDABAT IF YOU'RE INSPIRITED BY THIS YO-KAI, YOU WON'T LEAVE YOUR HOUSE.
I LOCKED MYSELF UP IN MY ROOM FOR TOO LONG AND THIS IS WHAT HAPPENED TO ME.
I won't turn back...
HUH? WHAT DO YOU MEAN?
I REMEMBER YOU EVOLVING TO BECOME EVEN MORE OF A RECLUSE...
WHY ARE YOU IN THAT TINY HOUSE?
AND YOU CAN JUST STAY IN THERE UNTIL THEN!
READ VOLUME 8 TO LEARN MORE! ♪
IT MAY LOOK LIKE A HOUSE, BUT MAYBE IT'S SOME KIND OF SHELL?
OH, I SEE! SO HE DOESN'T ACTUALLY LIVE IN THAT THING?
...
THIS HOUSE... IS PART OF ME?!

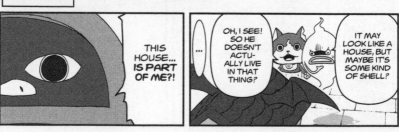

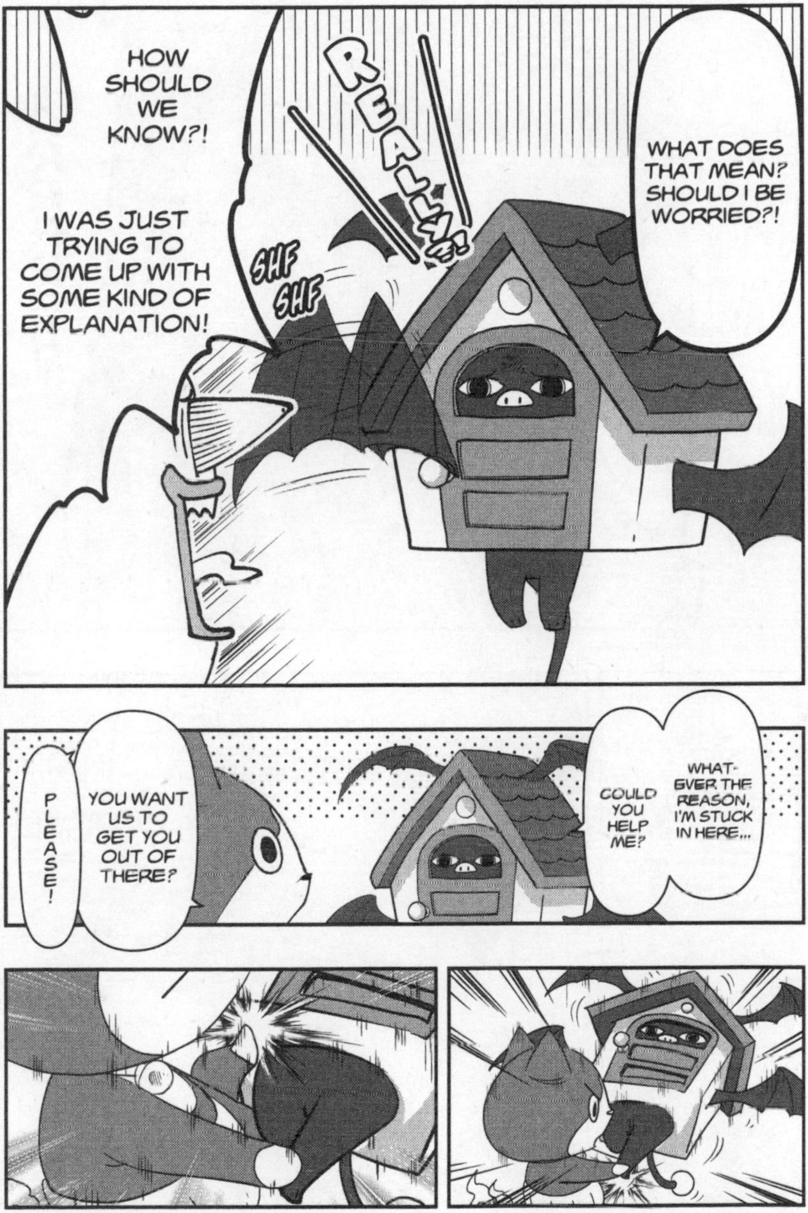
WHAT DOES THAT MEAN? SHOULD I BE WORRIED?!
REALLY?!
SHF SHF
HOW SHOULD WE KNOW?!
I WAS JUST TRYING TO COME UP WITH SOME KIND OF EXPLANATION!
WHATEVER THE REASON, I'M STUCK IN HERE...
COULD YOU HELP ME?
YOU WANT US TO GET YOU OUT OF THERE?
PLEASE!

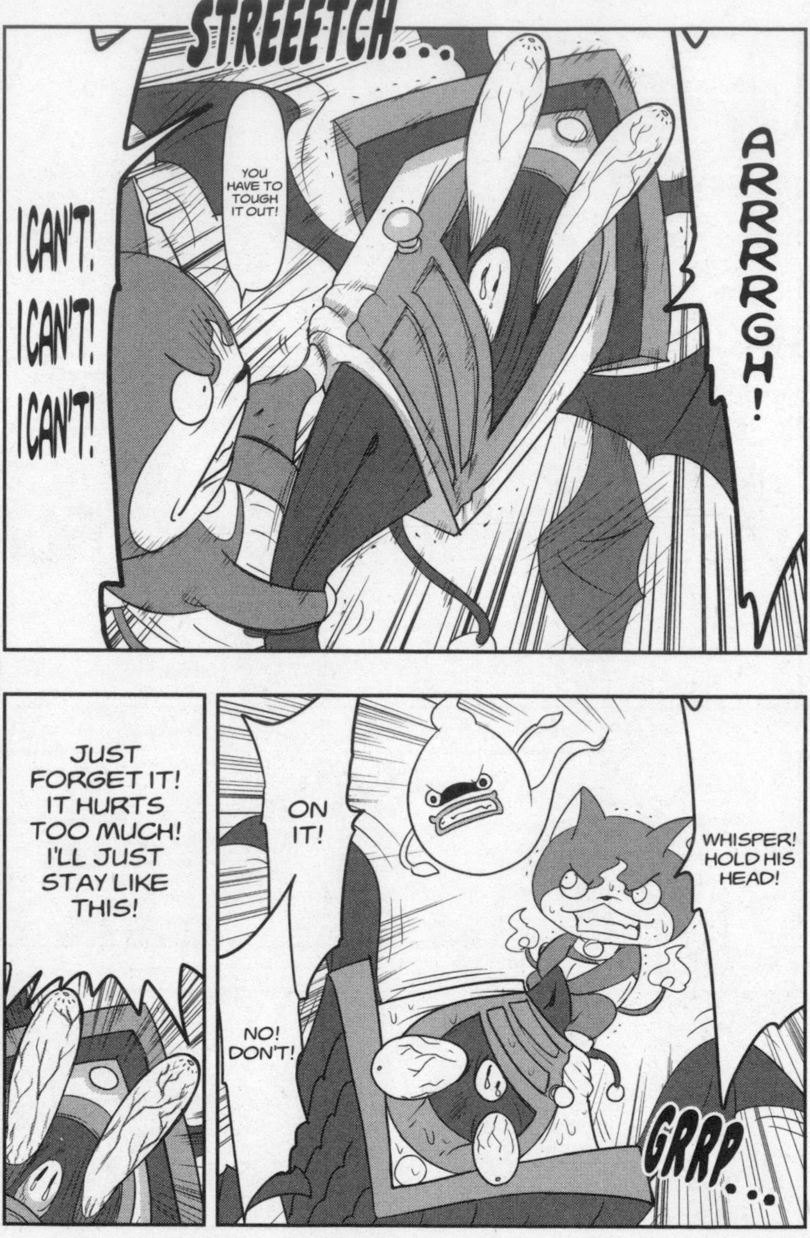

STREEETCH...
YOU HAVE TO TOUGH IT OUT!
ARRRRGH!
I CAN'T! I CAN'T! I CAN'T!
WHISPER! HOLD HIS HEAD!
ON IT!
NO! DON'T!
GRRP...
JUST FORGET IT! IT HURTS TOO MUCH! I'LL JUST STAY LIKE THIS!

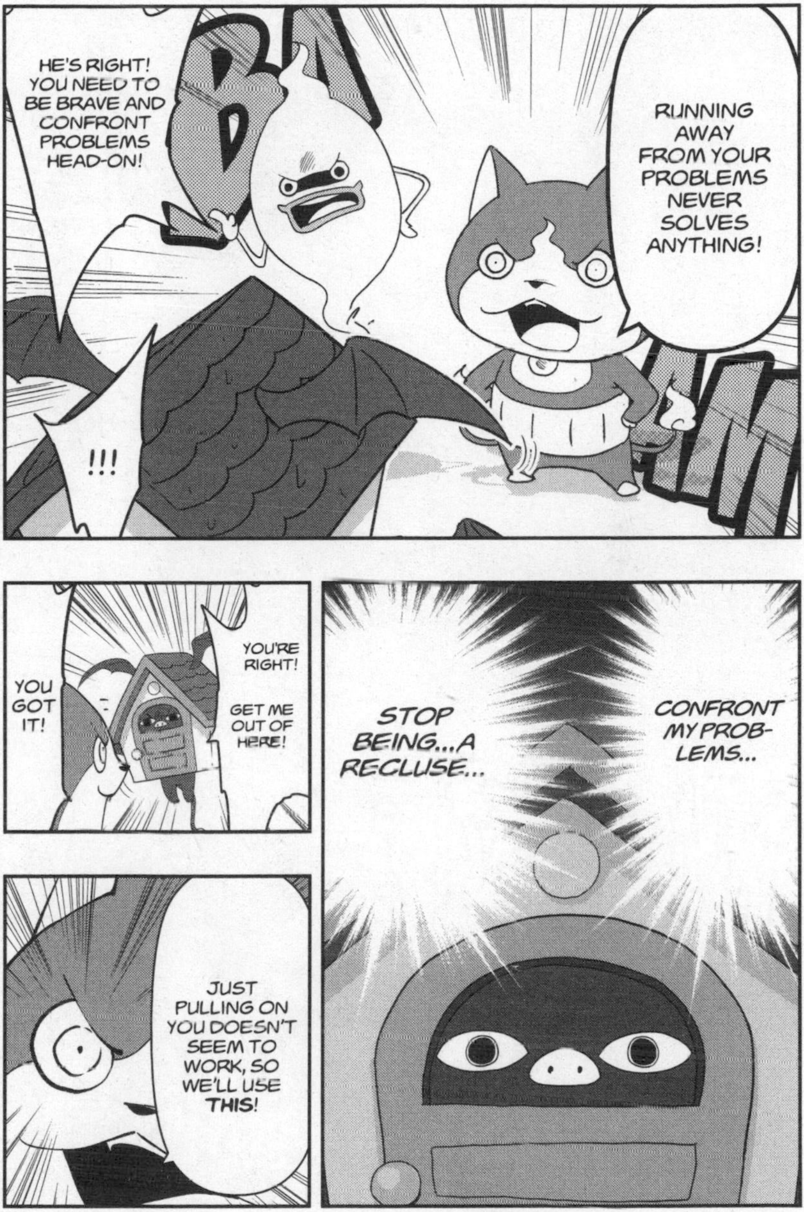
RUNNING AWAY FROM YOUR PROBLEMS NEVER SOLVES ANYTHING!
HE'S RIGHT! YOU NEED TO BE BRAVE AND CONFRONT PROBLEMS HEAD-ON!
!!!
CONFRONT MY PROB-LEMS...
STOP BEING...A RECLUSE...
YOU'RE RIGHT!
GET ME OUT OF HERE!
YOU GOT IT!
JUST PULLING ON YOU DOESN'T SEEM TO WORK, SO WE'LL USE THIS!

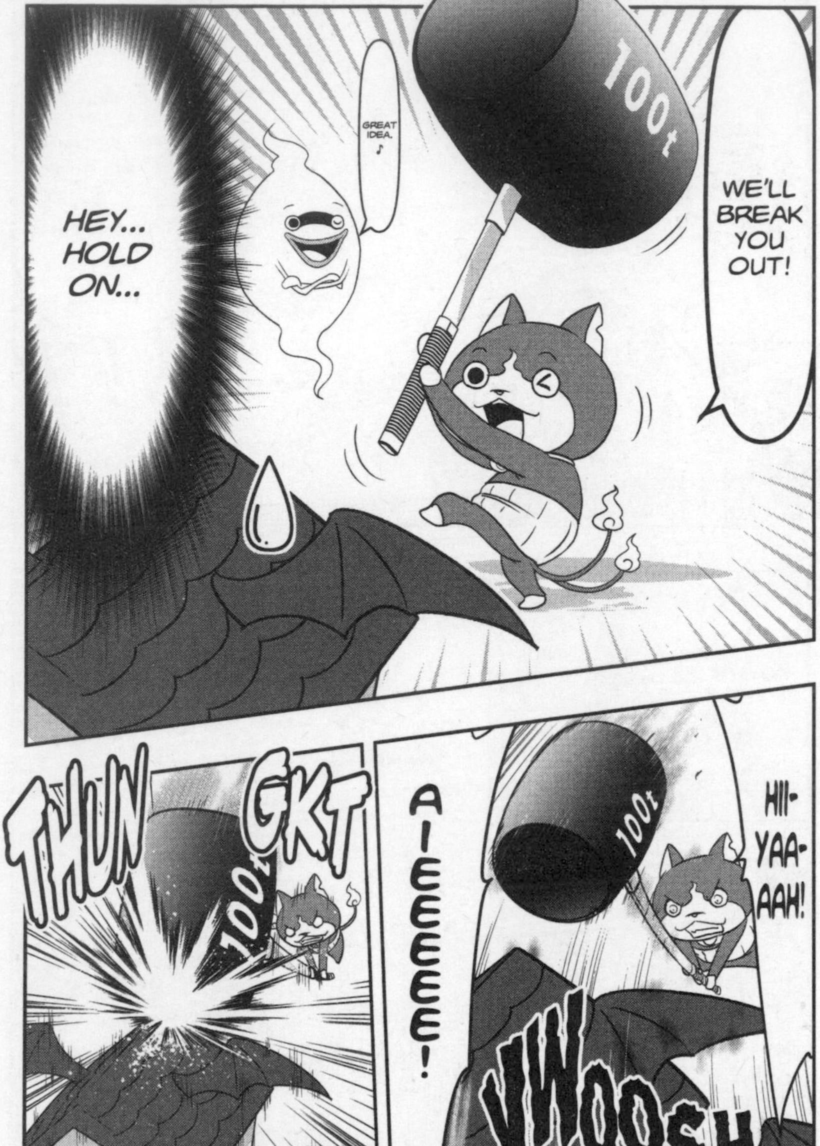
100t
WE'LL BREAK YOU OUT!
GREAT IDEA. ♪
HEY... HOLD ON...
HII-YAAA-AAH!
100t
AIEEEEEE!
VWOOSH
THUNGKT
100t

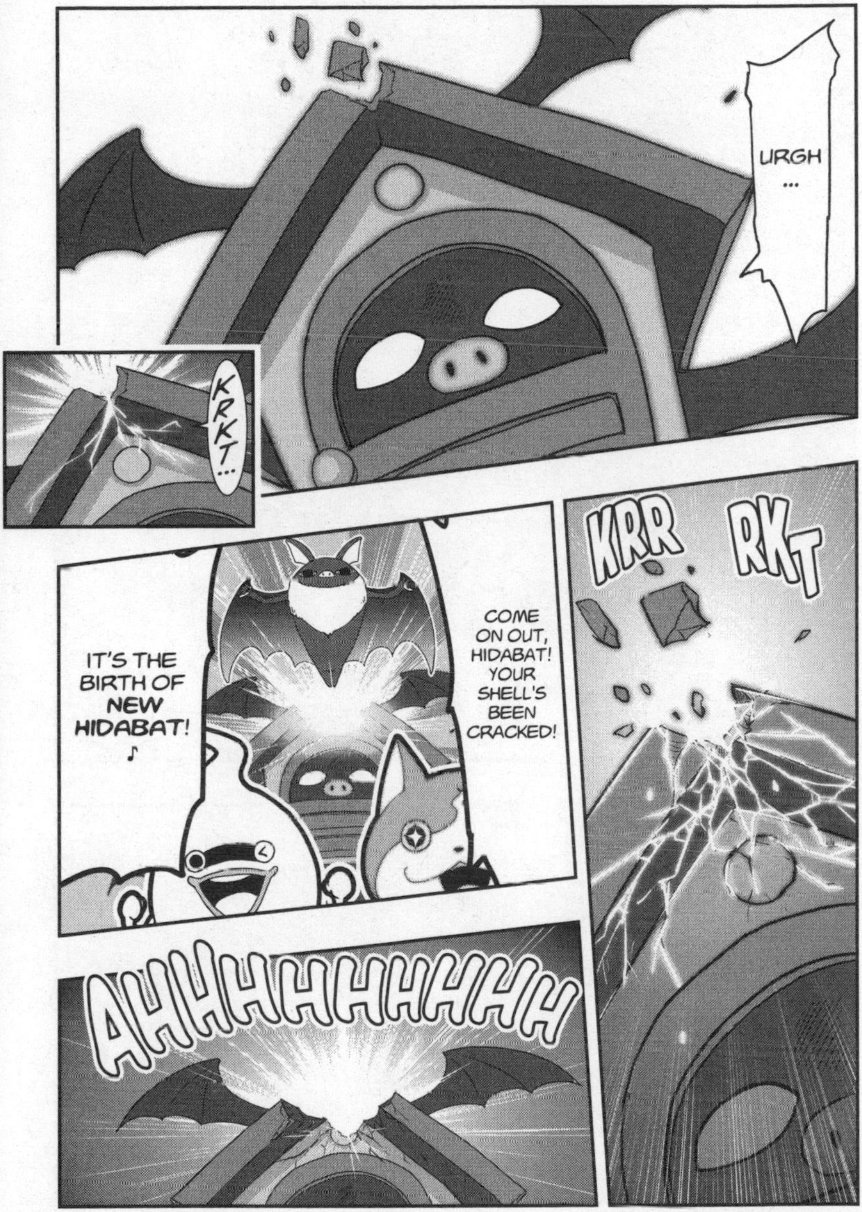
URGH ...
KRKT...
KRR RKT
COME ON OUT, HIDABAT! YOUR SHELL'S BEEN CRACKED!
IT'S THE BIRTH OF NEW HIDABAT! ♪
AHHHHHHHHHH

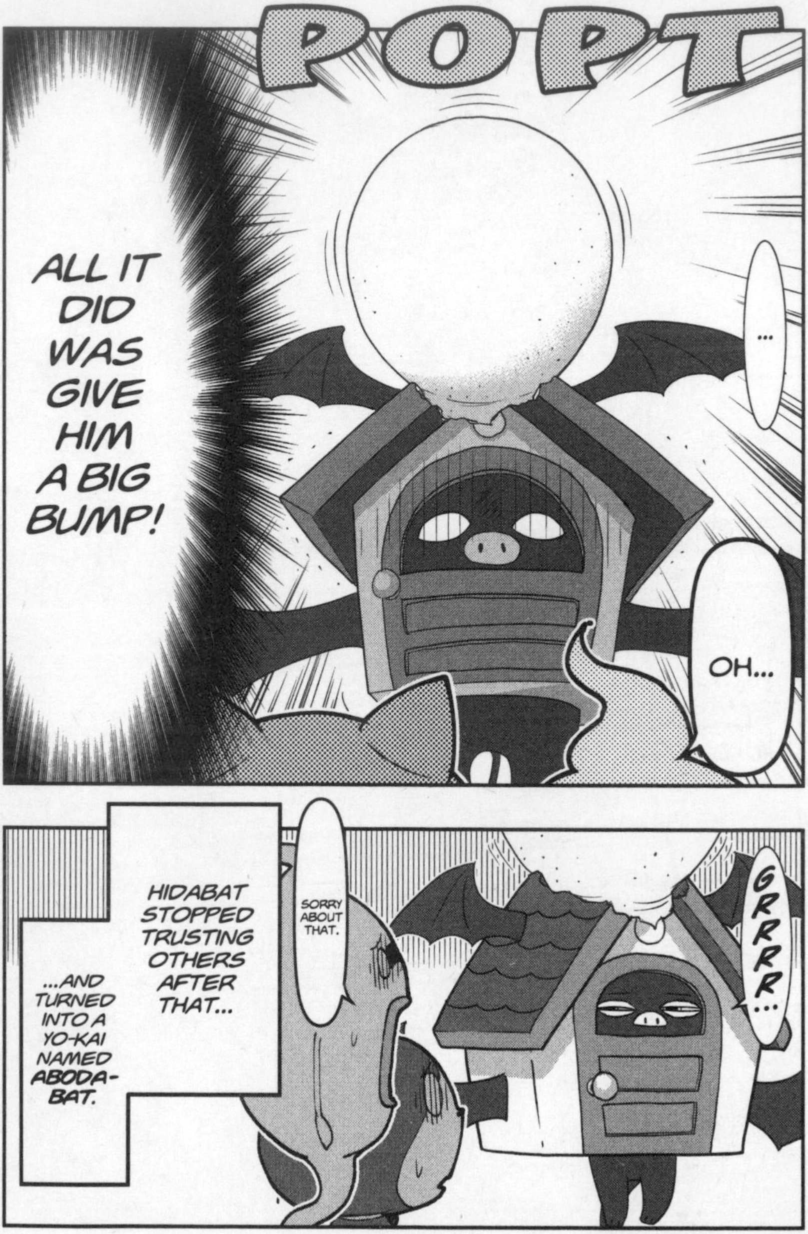
POPT
...
OH...
ALL IT DID WAS GIVE HIM A BIG BUMP!
GRRRR...
SORRY ABOUT THAT.
HIDABAT STOPPED TRUSTING OTHERS AFTER THAT...
...AND TURNED INTO A YO-KAI NAMED ABODA-BAT.

CHAPTER 220
WIBBLE WOBBLE YO-KAI WOBBLENYAN

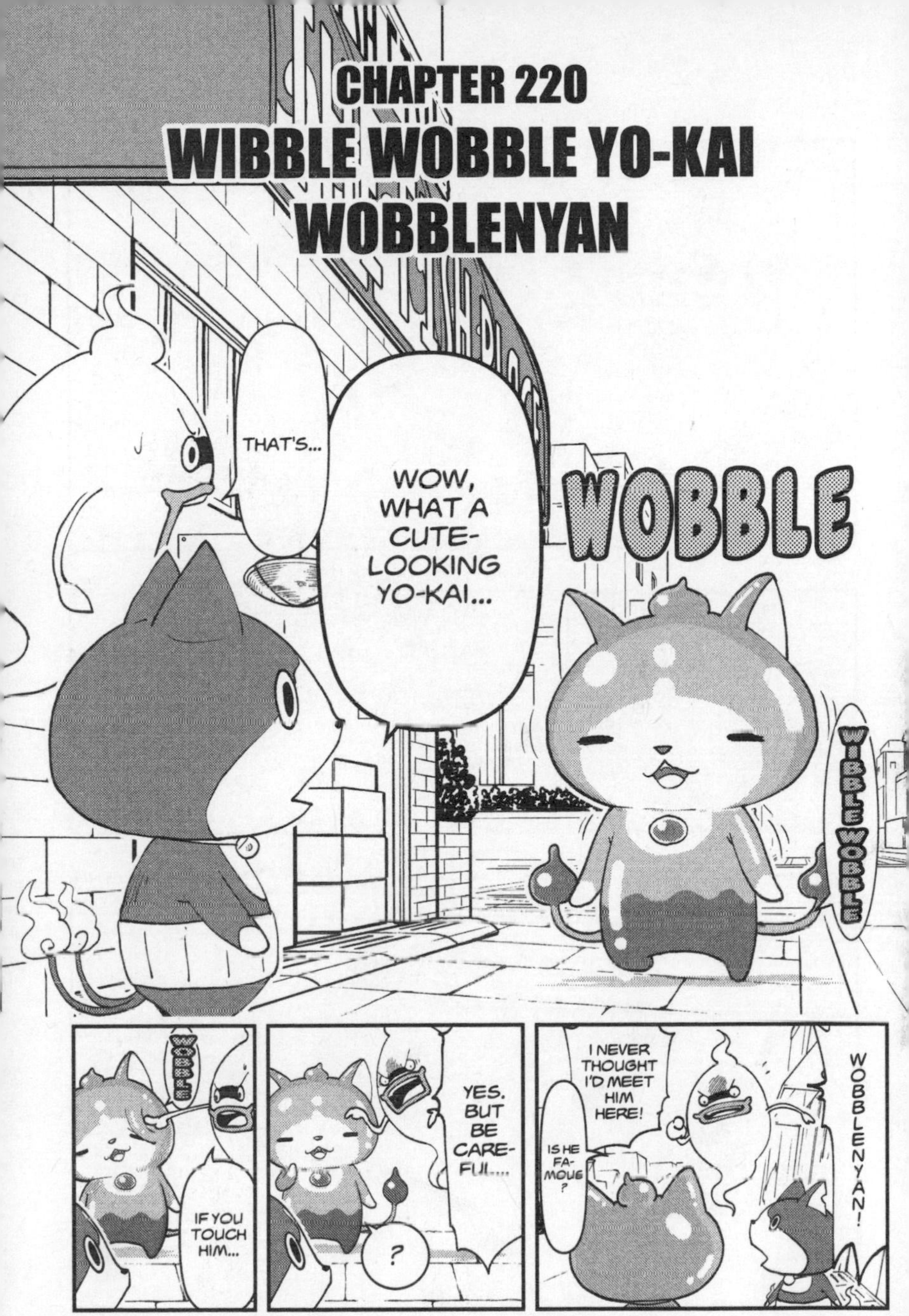

WOBBLE
WIBBLE WOBBLE
WOW, WHAT A CUTE-LOOKING YO-KAI...
THAT'S...
WOBBLENYAN!
I NEVER THOUGHT I'D MEET HIM HERE!
IS HE FAMOUS?
YES. BUT BE CAREFUL....
?
WOBBLE
IF YOU TOUCH HIM...

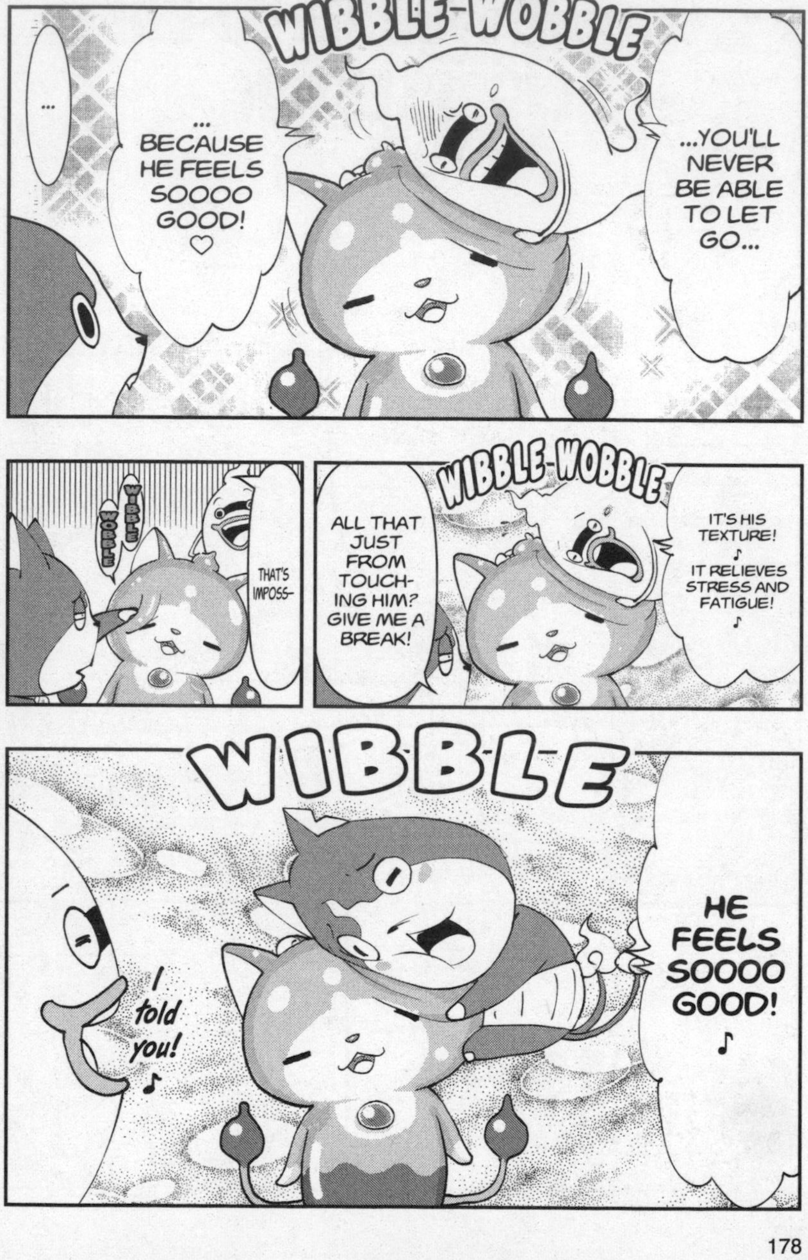
...YOU'LL NEVER BE ABLE TO LET GO...
WIBBLE-WOBBLE
... BECAUSE HE FEELS SOOOO GOOD! ♡
...
IT'S HIS TEXTURE! ♪ IT RELIEVES STRESS AND FATIGUE! ♪
WIBBLE-WOBBLE
ALL THAT JUST FROM TOUCHING HIM? GIVE ME A BREAK!
THAT'S IMPOSS-
WIBBLE
WOBBLE
WIBBLE
HE FEELS SOOOO GOOD! ♪
I told you! ♪

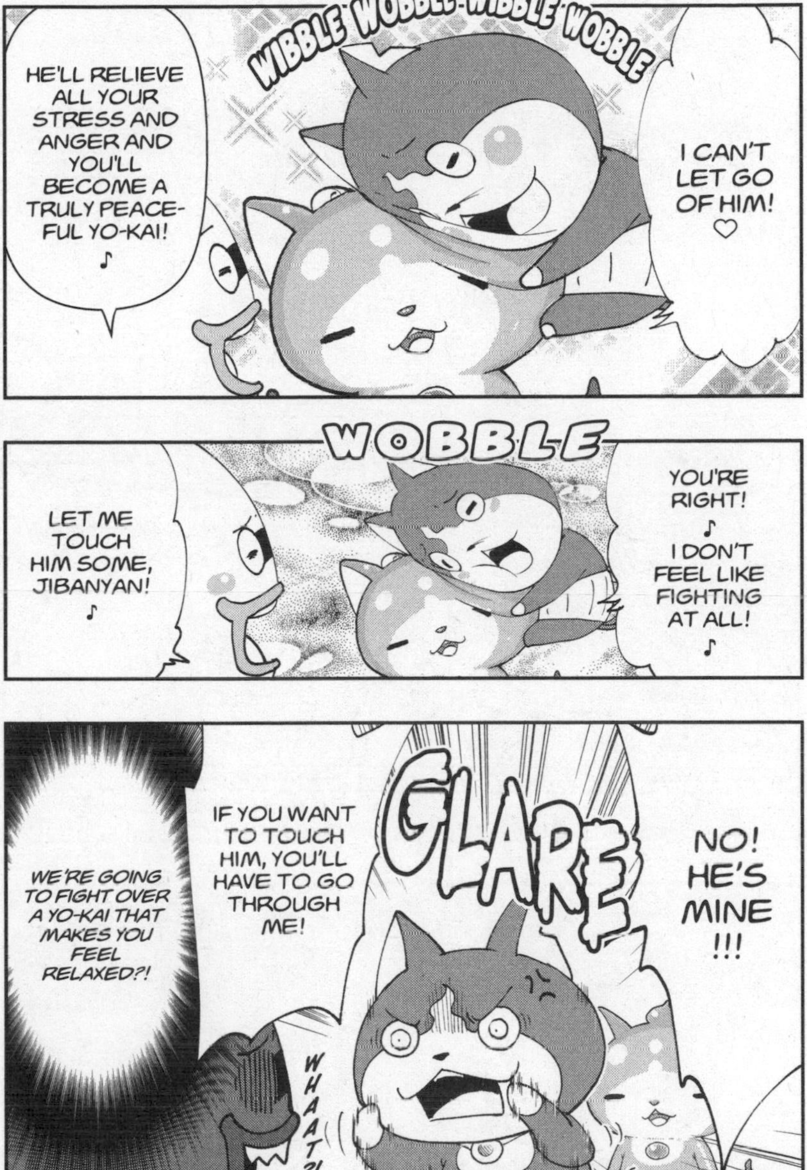
WIBBLE WOBBLE WIBBLE WOBBLE
I CAN'T LET GO OF HIM! ♡
HE'LL RELIEVE ALL YOUR STRESS AND ANGER AND YOU'LL BECOME A TRULY PEACE-FUL YO-KAI! ♪
WOBBLE
YOU'RE RIGHT! ♪ I DON'T FEEL LIKE FIGHTING AT ALL! ♪
LET ME TOUCH HIM SOME, JIBANYAN! ♪
NO! HE'S MINE !!!
GLARE
IF YOU WANT TO TOUCH HIM, YOU'LL HAVE TO GO THROUGH ME!
WE'RE GOING TO FIGHT OVER A YO-KAI THAT MAKES YOU FEEL RELAXED?!
WHAAAT?!

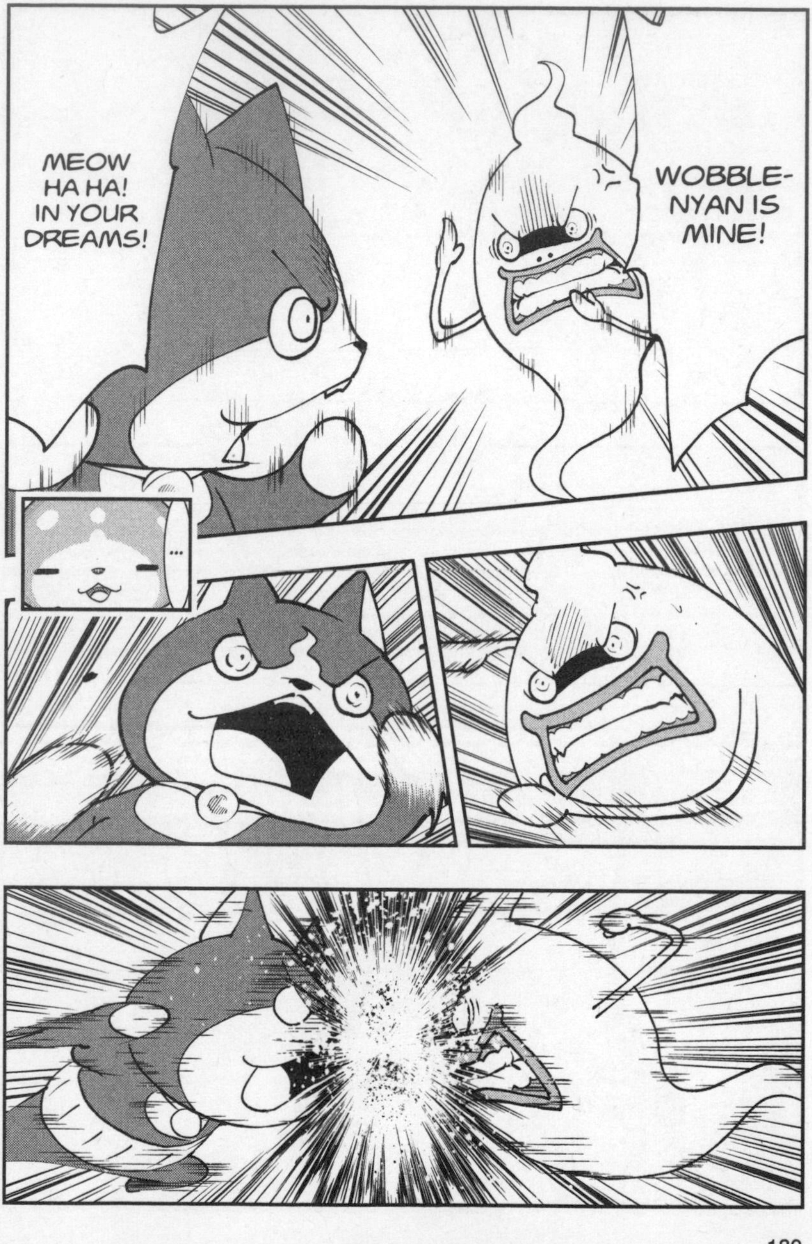
WOBBLE-NYAN IS MINE!
MEOW HA HA! IN YOUR DREAMS!
...

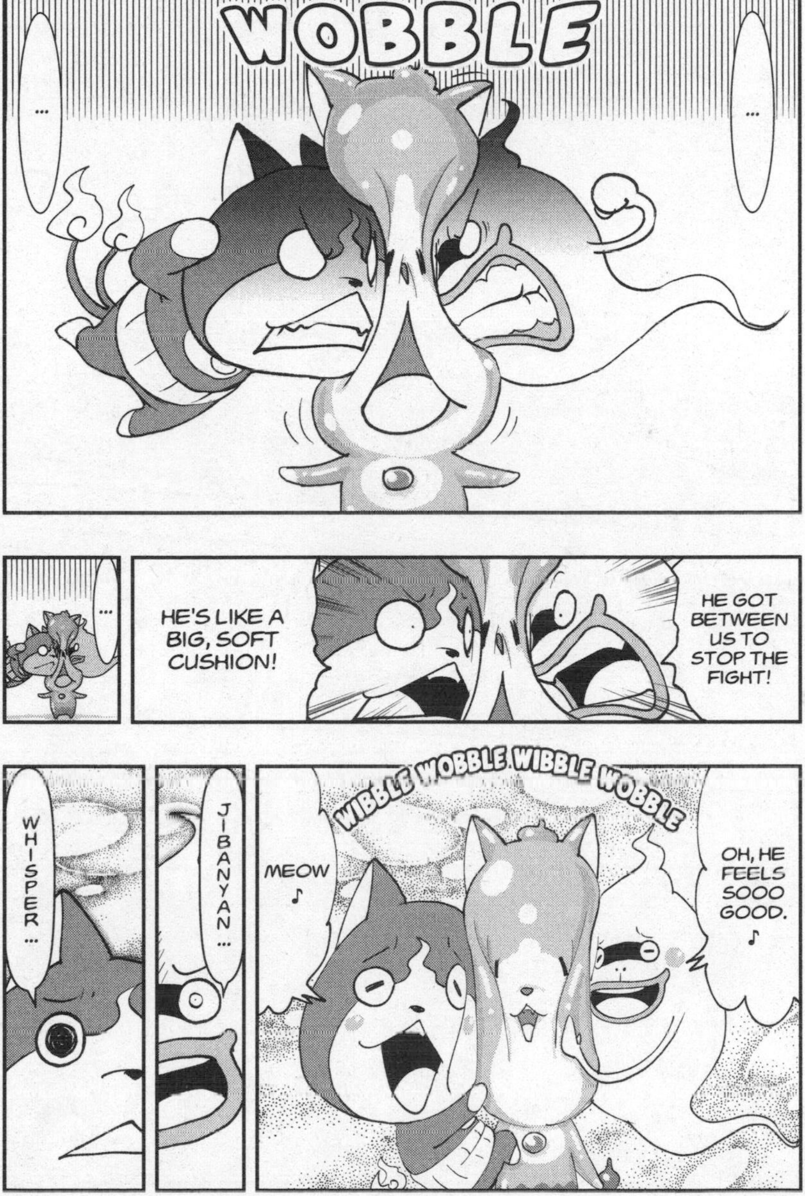
WOBBLE
...
...
HE GOT BETWEEN US TO STOP THE FIGHT!
HE'S LIKE A BIG, SOFT CUSHION!
...
WIBBLE WOBBLE WIBBLE WOBBLE
OH, HE FEELS SOOO GOOD. ♪
MEOW ♪
JIBANYAN...
WHISPER...

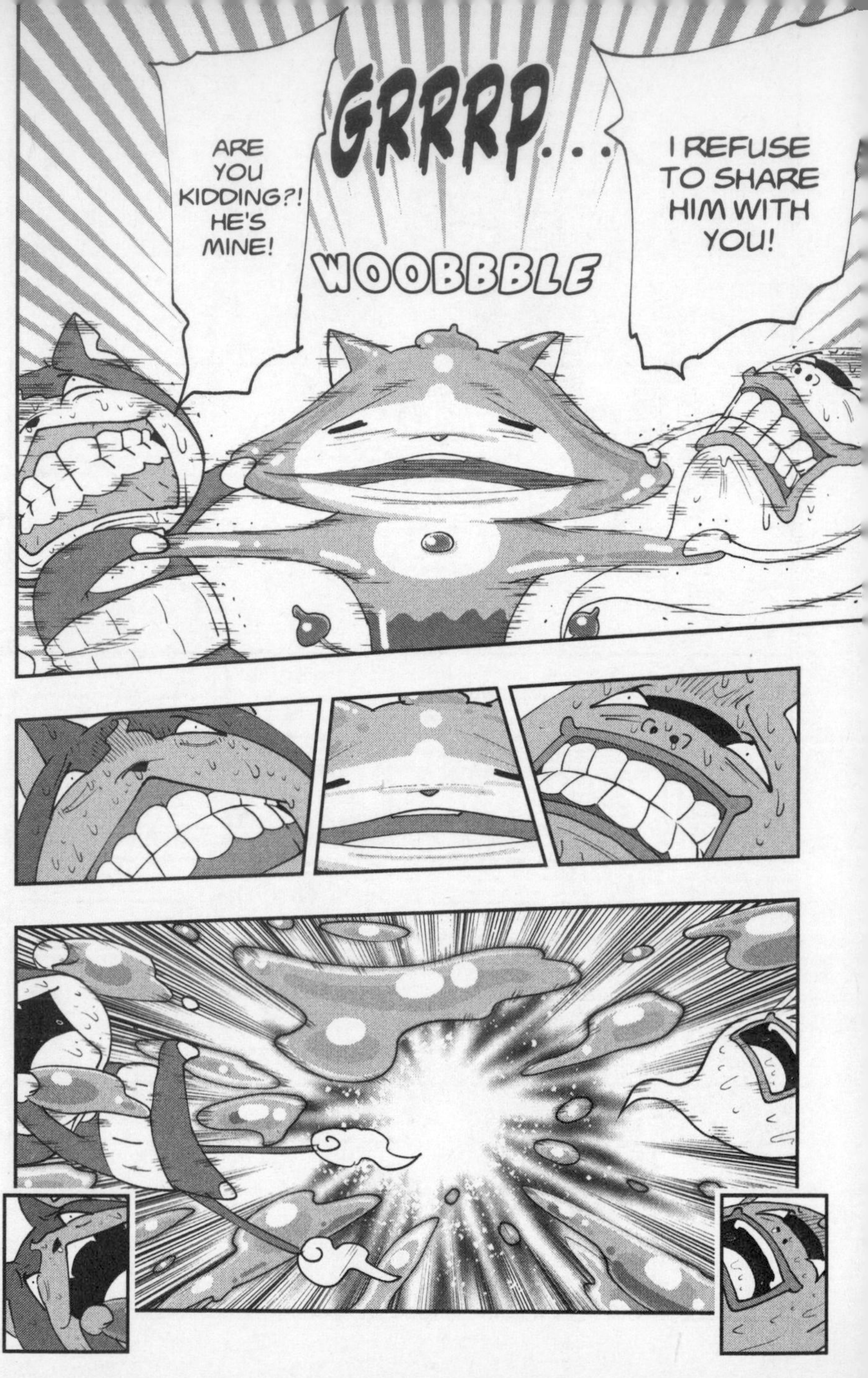
I REFUSE TO SHARE HIM WITH YOU!
GRRRP...
ARE YOU KIDDING?! HE'S MINE!
WOOBBBLE

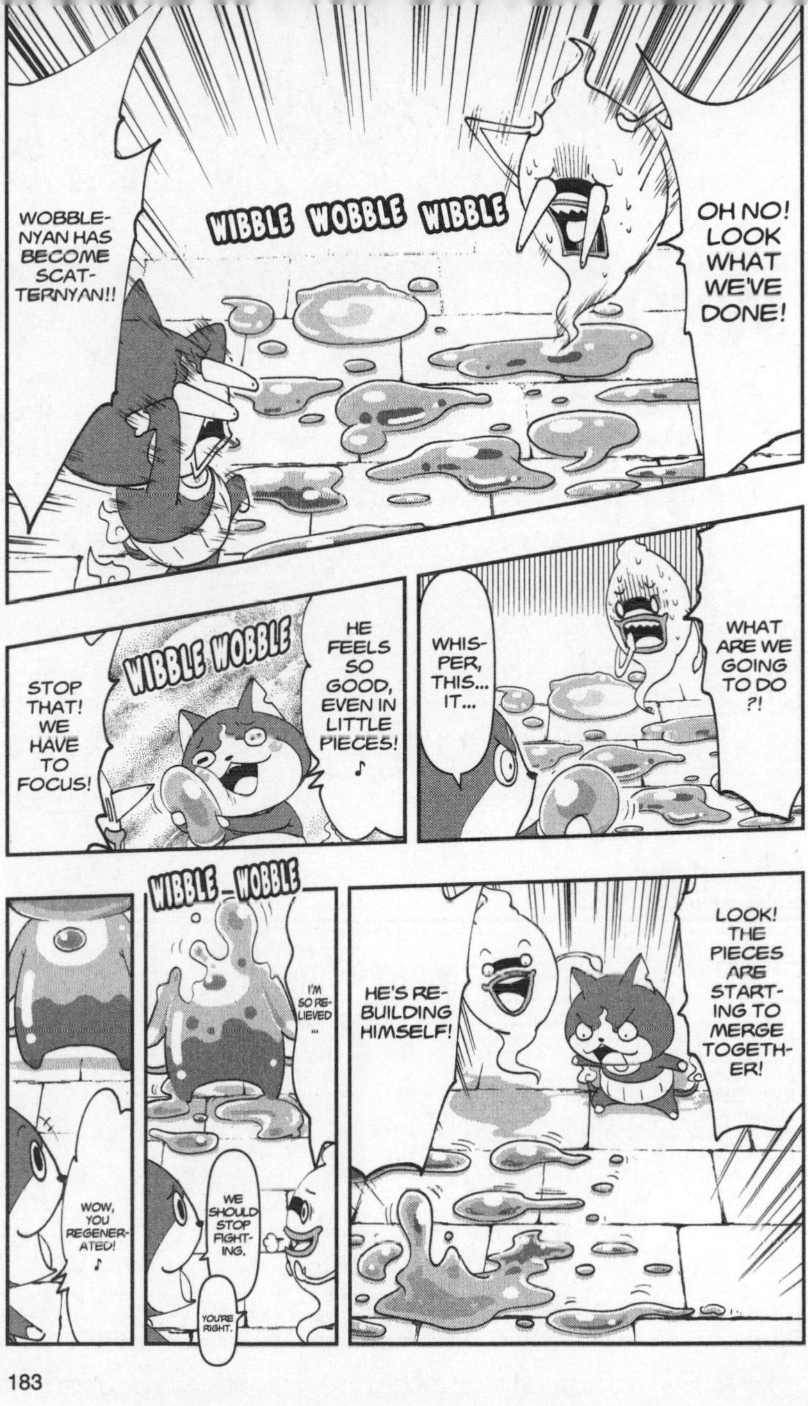
OH NO! LOOK WHAT WE'VE DONE!
WIBBLE WOBBLE WIBBLE
WOBBLE-NYAN HAS BECOME SCATTERNYAN!!
WHAT ARE WE GOING TO DO?!
WHISPER, THIS... IT...
HE FEELS SO GOOD, EVEN IN LITTLE PIECES! ♪
WIBBLE WOBBLE
STOP THAT! WE HAVE TO FOCUS!
LOOK! THE PIECES ARE STARTING TO MERGE TOGETHER!
HE'S REBUILDING HIMSELF!
WIBBLE WOBBLE
I'M SO RELIEVED...
WE SHOULD STOP FIGHTING.
YOU'RE RIGHT.
WOW, YOU REGENERATED! ♪

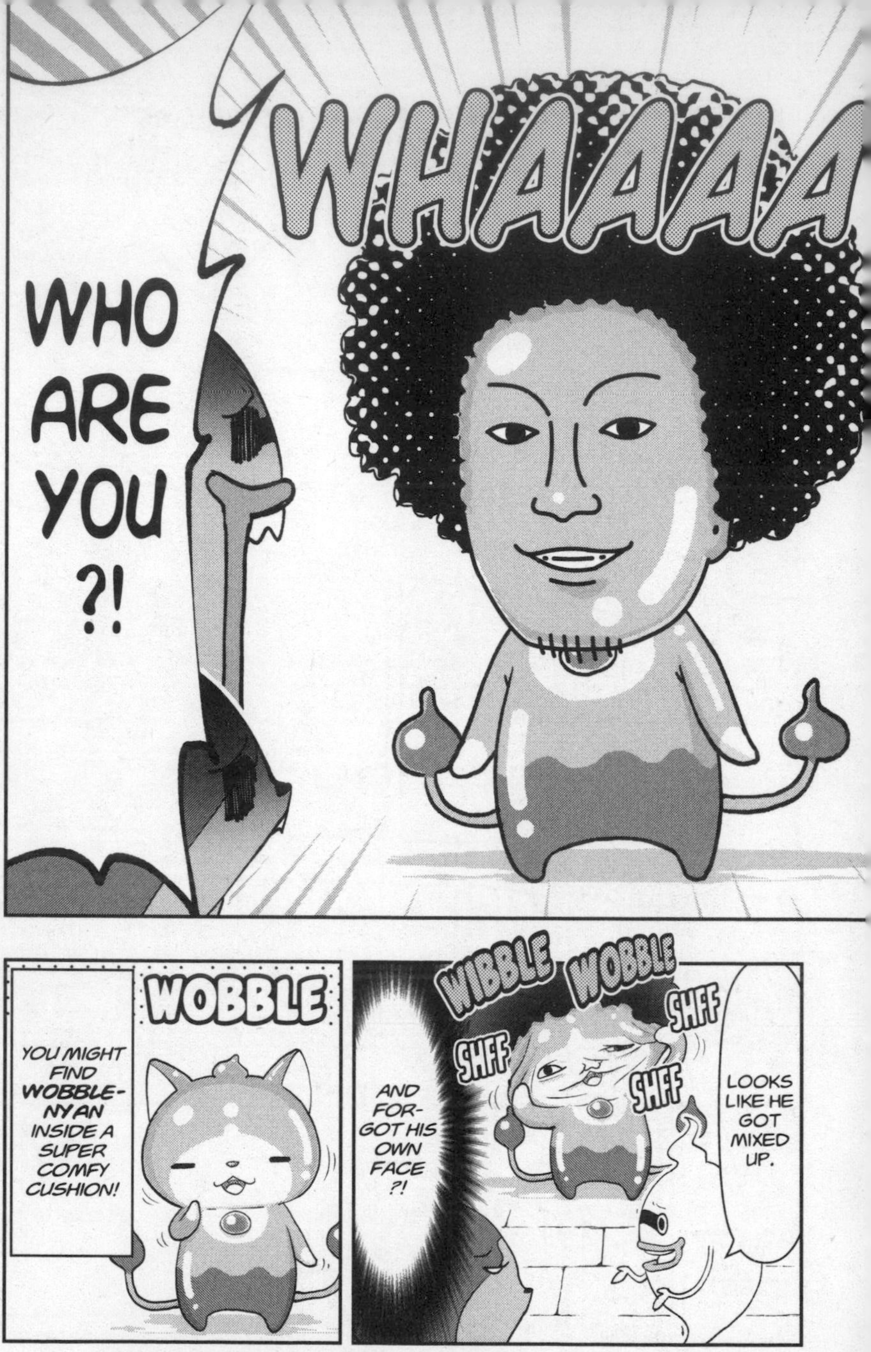
WHAAAA
WHO ARE YOU ?!
LOOKS LIKE HE GOT MIXED UP.
WOBBLE
WIBBLE
SHFF
SHFF
SHFF
AND FOR-GOT HIS OWN FACE ?!
WOBBLE
YOU MIGHT FIND **WOBBLE-NYAN** INSIDE A SUPER COMFY CUSHION!

YO-KAI WATCH VOLUME 20 END! / CONTINUED IN VOLUME 21

HAPPY 20TH VOLUME!

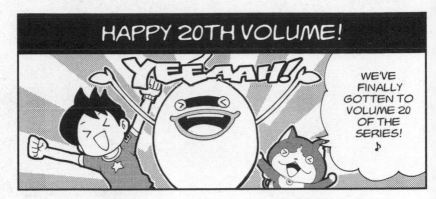

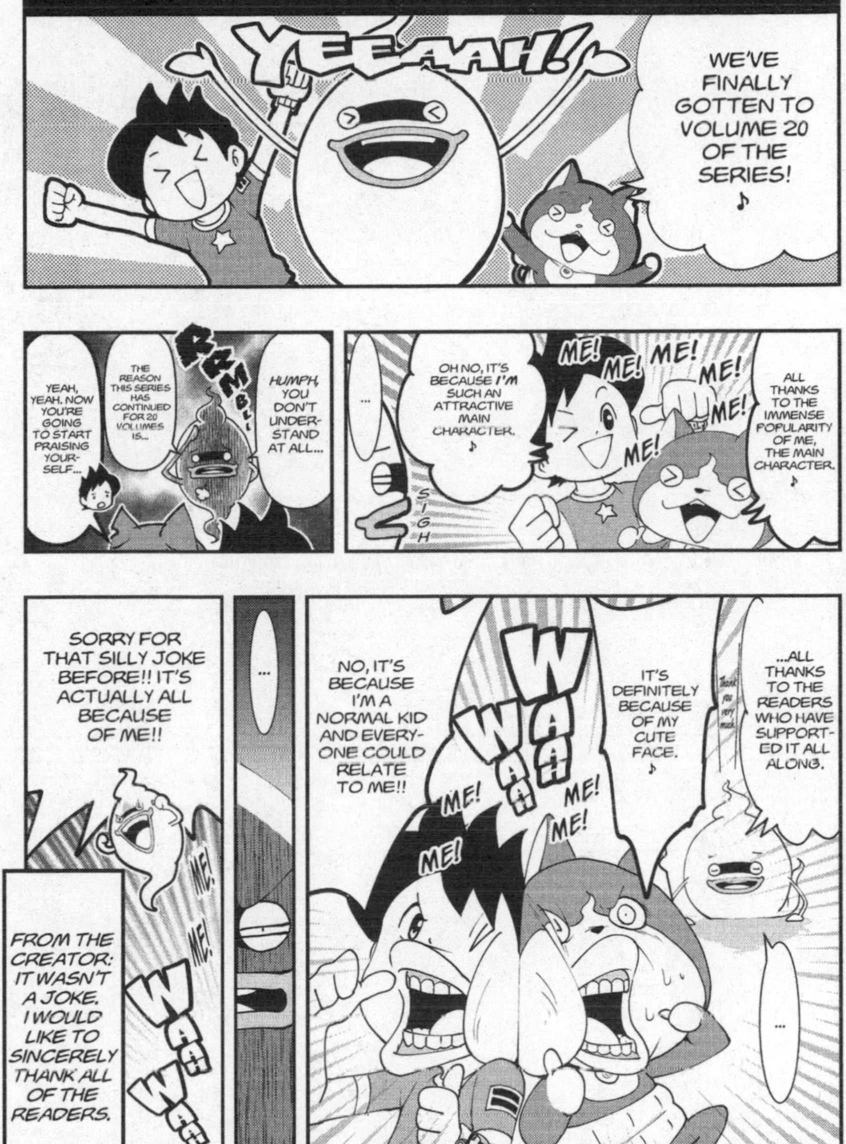
YEEAAH!
WE'VE FINALLY GOTTEN TO VOLUME 20 OF THE SERIES! ♪
ALL THANKS TO THE IMMENSE POPULARITY OF ME, THE MAIN CHARACTER. ♪
ME! ME! ME! ME! ME!
OH NO, IT'S BECAUSE I'M SUCH AN ATTRACTIVE MAIN CHARACTER. ♪
...
SIGH
HUMPH, YOU DON'T UNDER-STAND AT ALL...
THE REASON THIS SERIES HAS CONTINUED FOR 20 VOLUMES IS...
YEAH, YEAH. NOW YOU'RE GOING TO START PRAISING YOUR-SELF...
...ALL THANKS TO THE READERS WHO HAVE SUPPORT-ED IT ALL ALONG.
Thank you very much.
...
IT'S DEFINITELY BECAUSE OF MY CUTE FACE. ♪
WAAAH WAAAH
NO, IT'S BECAUSE I'M A NORMAL KID AND EVERY-ONE COULD RELATE TO ME!!
ME! ME! ME! ME!
...
SORRY FOR THAT SILLY JOKE BEFORE!! IT'S ACTUALLY ALL BECAUSE OF ME!!
ME! ME!
WAAH WAAH
FROM THE CREATOR: IT WASN'T A JOKE. I WOULD LIKE TO SINCERELY THANK ALL OF THE READERS.

AUTHOR BIO

Thanks to the support of all those involved, we've reached volume 20 of this series. If we include the graphic novels of the various movies and spinoffs, over 30 volumes have been published. I am filled with surprise and gratitude for all of you. Thank you very much!

Cover Illustration: Noriyuki Konishi

Noriyuki Konishi hails from Shimabara City in Nagasaki Prefecture, Japan. He debuted with the one-shot *E-CUFF* in *Monthly Shonen Jump Original* in 1997. He is known in Japan for writing manga adaptations of *AM Driver* and *Mushiking: King of the Beetles*, along with *Saiyuki Hiro Go-Kū Den!*, *Chōhenshin Gag Gaiden!! Card Warrior Kamen Riders*, *Go-Go-Go Saiyuki: Shin Gokūden* and more. Konishi was the recipient of the 38th Kodansha manga award in 2014 and the 60th Shogakukan manga award in 2015.

Welcome to the world of Little Battlers eXperience! In the near future, a boy named Van Yamano owns Achilles, a miniaturized robot that battles on command! But Achilles is no ordinary LBX. Hidden inside him is secret data that Van must keep out of the hands of evil at all costs!

All six volumes available now!

DANBALL SENKI
© 2011 Hideaki FUJII / SHOGAKUKAN
©LEVEL-5 Inc.

Little Battlers eXperience

Story and Art by HIDEAKI FUJII

THIS IS THE END OF THIS GRAPHIC NOVEL!

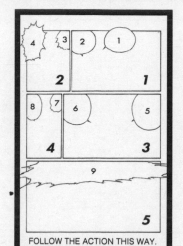

FOLLOW THE ACTION THIS WAY.

To properly enjoy this graphic novel, please turn it around and begin reading from right to left.